"Cat Rambo's writing is everything you could hope for—lyrical, emotional, funny, by turns or all at once. The Beasts of Tabat *gives us a unique, unforgettable world full of wonderfully memorable characters."*

Django Wexler, author of *The Thousand Names*

Beasts of Tabat

A NOVEL

Beasts of Tabat

A NOVEL

Cat Rambo

WordFire Press
Colorado Springs, Colorado

BEASTS OF TABAT
Copyright © 2015 Catherine Rambo

ISBN: 978-1-61475-297-4

Cover design by Janet McDonald

Art Director Kevin J. Anderson

Cover artwork images by Dollar Photo Club

Book Design by RuneWright, LLC
www.RuneWright.com

Published by
WordFire Press, an imprint of
WordFire, Inc.
PO Box 1840
Monument, CO 80132

Kevin J. Anderson & Rebecca Moesta Publishers

WordFire Press Trade Paperback Edition March 2015
Printed in the USA
wordfirepress.com

Chapter One

Introducing Teo, a Boy

Perhaps Teo couldn't change his shape in real life, but in his mind he certainly could. As he shimmied down the rocky crevice, he was heroic Bella Kanto, Gladiator and Champion of the distant city of Tabat. Frozen stone rasped against the leather and wool clothing he wore, but to him it was Gladiator's armor, clinking as Bella climbed down to unimaginable dangers in order to rescue ...

No, not to rescue—to explore some place no Human, Beast, nor anyone from his village had ever ventured into before, he decided as he emerged into the icicle-choked crevice that opened to the cliff's face. He would be like the hero of his favorite penny-wides, someone who opened new paths.

Those penny-wides were the thing that Teo loved best about shipments from Tabat, so far away on the southern coast. Crates came up the Northstretch River on the steamboats or in wagons pulled by oxen or great goats—crates whose contents were kept in place with crumpled newsprint, discarded penny-wides, smudged columns of black type detailing adventures, scandals, intrigues of the heroes of Tabat, primarily the Gladiators, the heroes whose ritual fights determined the fate of the city while teaching the stories of the Gods.

Gladiators. No other figures so glamorous, so perilous, so ephemeral, so suitable for stories with long narratives that included step-by-step swordplay, rescues, and escapes, and detailed conversations from courtiers and courtesans.

He harvested them whenever the crates were unpacked, pulling wads from between vials of medicines and other glassware; tins of foods that would never be found here in the north, soft-lily root and peppers soaked in vinegar; small round cans of coffee beans and bricks of pungent tea. Glass bottles of amber and black liquor, smaller sizes of perfume in red and blue and cat's-eye emerald. And once a cardboard box filled with the coin-sized mirrors folks used to chase away ghosts, enough to last his village for another generation.

And always two jars, one of high-quality black ink and a smaller one of red for Neorn, who acted as the village scribe, along with paper suitable for witnessed declarations. When the Trader left, he or she would carry with them a sheaf of such documents, copies to be filed with the Ducal offices back in Tabat.

Teo thought that they must have an entire drawer full of his village's papers by now. Which was important. It let them masquerade as Human and kept the Duke from sending up troops to exterminate them for being Shifters. They'd maintained the subterfuge ever since Explorers first came across them, almost a hundred years ago now.

It staggered him to think there might be a drawer for every Human settlement, maybe entire cabinets for larger cities. The world was so much larger than his tiny village, so full of wonderful, exciting things that surely room after room must be employed to track them. And none of those wonderful things could be found here, except in the pages of the penny-wides, which arrived out of order, often with gaps that his imagination was forced to supply. Most of them came from Spinner Press, orange pages edged with blue, and concerned the adventures of Tabat's premier Gladiator, Bella Kanto.

Bella Kanto, who'd visited the Old Continent and killed two sorcerers there; who'd ridden a wild Dragon and brought it to live in the Duke's menagerie; and who'd fought foes ranging from the Fish-folk of the Southern Isles, with their poisonous barbed wrists and elbows, to an entire Centaur Tribe bent on keeping her from approaching their village.

Bella Kanto, whose love life was a constant array of nobility, warriors, and conjurers of either gender, who was forever giving up people for their own good, and leading what seemed to be a star-crossed but thoroughly enjoyable existence.

At fourteen, Teo's knowledge of sex had been well informed by observing animals, but his ideas of how it all worked with people, the flirting and wooing and such, still mystified him.

But not Bella. She was gallant, she was brave, she was dashing. She was everything a hero should be. The smudged pictures, steel-cut and rendered in broad lines, showed a beautiful face as narrow as an axe blade, a smile inevitably twisting one side of her mouth.

Bella Kanto, once a Beast Trainer's apprentice, who'd come to the all-female Gladiatorial School, the Brides of Steel, a year too old to be admitted, but who then had fought so well that the school was forced to take her, who had risen rapidly through their ranks until she was the Foremost Gladiator in Tabat, the one chosen to fight for Winter each year. Winter had been slow to release its grasp on the world for the last nineteen years, and the reason was Bella Kanto, who won the ceremonial battle with Spring each year.

Teo had crept out early this morning, saying he was going to check snares, but the truth was he wanted to daydream, and that was best done in an undisturbed spot. A chance to watch the rising sun, to witness the world go pale grey, then violet, then gold and lavender, sumptuous as silk embroidery, was a bonus.

Teo had found the shelter of the cliff long ago while hunting, trying to escape the pitying eyes of the village. He could never hope to match the hunting prowess of the other early teens, certainly, but he could try, at least. And sometimes that attempt yielded unexpected results, like this hideaway that was, as far as he knew, his and his alone.

To reach this open nook, you wiggled down through a chimney that seemed to go into the very face of the cliff. Depending on the time of year, it was slick with ice or thickly overgrown with brambles. It looked out south, and when all three moons were in the sky—tiny purple Toj, vast red Hijae, and Selene, the white moon—you could watch them and wonder if the Moon Priests were right, that their movements predicted everything that would happen.

And everything that had happened.

Was it the moons' fault he couldn't change his shape, run in animal form, the way the rest of the village could? It wasn't fair that he couldn't change, but he'd come to accept that, to live with it the way old Fyorl lived with his missing foot, which he claimed a bear had bitten off but which was, according to Teo's mother, the consequence of being too drunk to clean flea bites when they festered. She said when it had gotten infected the Moon Priest visiting the village had cut it off.

And now another Moon Priest was here, treating someone else.

Teo's mind skittered away from thoughts of the Priest's presence. The solid rock against his back, he slitted his eyelids and tried to force himself back into his daydream.

The white moon was a thin arc, hollowed out with Winter hunger, thin as his sister's face, which kept replacing the black and white image of Bella Kanto. Elya was sick. Elya, Teo's little sister, alive in a way the sister who had been his Shadow Twin never had been. Elya, with big green eyes and a quick laugh, who loved the little animals he carved for her. Elya, who had never rejected him in the way others had for not being able to shapeshift.

She knew he was special, after all. They all did, even if they didn't always remember it. He'd been born with a Shadow Twin. He was the only person in the whole village who could say that, and he was the only person who'd had a Twin that any of them had ever encountered.

The thought didn't make him any warmer. Watery sunlight sifted down on the rock around him, which opened itself to the air, forming a ledge on which he could crouch. The breakfast he'd brought, two withered apples, sat on the stone beside him. From here the river's loop was visible, and he waited, hoping to catch sight of a puff of smoke that might signal the passage of a trade boat.

When he'd left that morning his mother had barely acknowledged his departure. She crouched by Elya's bed, watching her daughter's face as though willing her to keep breathing.

He wiped tears from his face with the back of a skinny hand, ashamed of them. *The Gods take who they will, when they will.* That was what the Moon Priest had said when he first looked at Elya. Who could resist the Gods? Not Teo, that was for certain.

And then they had chased him from the room in order to confer.

He wished he had magic. What would his life have been like if his Twin had drawn breath after the womb? History said that men and women with living Shadow Twins to assist them went on to do marvelous things. Verranzo and his Shadow Twin had each founded an entire city: Verranzo had created Verranzo's New City, far to the east on the coast, and his Shadow Twin (female, as Teo's had been, for a Shadow Twin always took the opposite gender of its sibling) had gone south with the Duke of Tabat and helped found a city in his name.

Teo's Shadow Twin had died at birth and would not do marvelous things. She would not draw on any of a Twin's reputed powers: to extend life or augment magical abilities. Verranzo's Twin had been able to tame creatures with her voice alone. Teo's was dead, and with her any chance of specialness deriving from her existence was gone.

Far below, snow swans flew across the river in a glitter of wings. He'd snared one last year. His father had beaten him because you never knew when a creature like that, a swan or eagle or wolf, might be a fellow Shifter or Beast, and exempt from being hunted or trapped accordingly.

His swan had not been intelligent, so it had been just an animal, not a Beast. But it had been angry when he'd freed it as Da had ordered. It beat at him with club-like wings as strong as Da's fist, and its head darted at his face and hands like a snake, hissing and clacking its bill.

He cut it loose and it waddled away, then leaped up against the sky, its wings driving it upward, frosted with red moonlight. It honked derisively at Teo, poor bruised Teo, who couldn't shift and therefore couldn't tell what was or wasn't a fellow Beast.

If he'd been Human, he would have been famous, might have been taken to Tabat to serve the latest generation of Dukes. But he was a Shifter, even if a failed one, and Humans hated Shifters, even more than the Beasts they habitually enslaved. So he and the other villagers must keep quiet, passing themselves off as unremarkable in the eyes of Explorers and Priests during their rare visits, here in the frontier territory that belonged to no city.

It was why they clung so close to the Moon Temples, sheltering under a Human religion.

Sunlight glinted on the river's frozen mirror far below, dazzling him. Closer, someone was crossing the meadow: his uncle Pioyrt in his animal form, an immense, slope-shouldered cougar, two grouse gripped tightly in his jaws, his whiskers drawn back to avoid their feathers. This time of year hunting was bad, and they'd eaten porridge and baked roots too often lately. At least one bird would be reserved for the Priest, but the rest might be fried with roots for something more appetizing than usual, crisp bits of meat and perhaps even a trip into the spice sack for a couple of peppercorns to grind or a pinch of dried orange peel. His mouth watered.

That was good, to have a reason to celebrate. And the Priest would heal Elya, surely. That was all good, so why did the Priest's presence bother him so? Something about the way the man looked at him. A considering look.

He raised his knees, wedging them against the rock's cold, slick bite to lift himself upwards, snow crunching under his gloves and boots as he scrambled onto the top of the cliff.

He paused to look once more out over the world. Clouds shawled the mountain that rose on the valley's opposite side, its flanks white with snow, slicks of purple and cobalt streaking their sides. The river was a gray and blue snakeskin, laced over with the black skeletons of trees.

Teo sighed and turned his face homeward.

○ ○ ○

No one would meet his eyes.

That was the truth of it, and not paranoia on his part. No matter where he went in the village, no matter who Teo talked to, whether it was Lidiya or his father's hunting partner Dayo, no one would meet his eyes. They'd look past his ear or pretend interest in something at their feet.

What did it mean?

Unease ate at him as he made his way past the hunters' sweat bath and into the village's center. He stopped in to see Lidiya the *alta*, the village herbwoman who had been unable to help his sister. He found the Priest with her and started to move away, but she beckoned to him.

Teo came closer, eying the Priest uneasily. The man was stout but muscular, with the light hair and skin that proclaimed he had as much Northern blood as Teo. He wore red robes, showing that he followed Hijae, the red moon, rather than the white or purple moons.

Lidiya patted Teo's shoulder and said something in her garbled voice that was hard to make out. She'd been taken by hunters in animal form, hunters who had tried to cut her throat and in the process damaged the vocal cords of her Human shape.

But the Priest seemed to understand her. "You're Teo?" he asked.

It was a little alarming to be recognized by an adult outsider. Teo nodded reluctantly.

"Your sister is the child that is ill." The Priest said this not as question, but fact. Teo found the intensity with which the man was studying him even more alarming.

Lidiya said something and the Priest nodded. "He seems well enough favored."

Teo wanted to ask about Elya, and whether the Priest could cure her, but he feared the answer. Priests wielded magic, but would it be sufficient to heal Elya?

As though in answer to his unspoken question, the Priest said, "Your sister will be fine." He waved Teo off. "Go and play, boy. We'll speak soon enough."

Speak about what? But Teo was ready enough to leave. He didn't understand that look in Lidiya's eye, the trace of pity and envy.

He would go home and see how Elya was, he decided. Rounding a corner, he found himself in the midst of a clot of children planning some hunt. They had cleared the ground in a smooth patch. Nika, the oldest, was sketching out a plan on it with a twig. She glanced up, saw it was Teo, and went back to her drawing, but Biort, who loved bullying Teo, couldn't resist a taunt as Teo pushed past.

"Look, it's the Lord of No Shape!"

"Better no shape than a shape like you," Teo snapped and regretted it immediately. Biort's form was that of a musk-ox, which some said was a sign of slow-mindedness. Biort was quick enough to take offense though, rising from where he knelt beside Nika.

Teo raised his fists, resigning himself to the fight. He knew the older, bigger boy would beat the snot out of him, but at least he might be able to land a blow or two of his own. His heart hammered in his chest.

A hand landed on his shoulder from behind, even as he saw the older boy's face fall.

His mother.

She was the first to meet his eyes, but the expression there did not reassure him. Love was there, yes, but a regret that he couldn't understand.

"Come home, Teo," she said. "We need to talk to you."

With a last scowl in Biort's direction, he followed in her wake. His heart still hammered as nervously as it had for the fight, as though sensing that what was to come would be no better.

It wasn't.

o   o   o

"Why would you do this to me?" Teo demanded. He hunched on the opposite side of the table from his parents. His mother sat, palms flat on the wooden surface, brows furrowed, while his father stood behind her, his hands on her shoulders. Teo wondered that they felt comfortable leaving Elya's sickbed long enough to break this news to him. The air smelled of broth and burned roots. The Priest was staying elsewhere and they hadn't even gotten a whiff of grouse.

"You've promised me into slavery! I'll belong to the Temples for life!"

"It's not like that," his father said. "It's a profession, and you can progress in it while always having food and clothing and shelter and a direction in life."

"They'll realize I'm a Shifter and burn me alive!"

His mother shook her head. Her eyes were red from crying, but her face was calm. "The alta says that since you have never changed, you never will. She swore it to me, beyond any question. You will be perfectly able to pass as Human."

"So you are sacrificing me so the village can continue to pretend we are all Human?"

"I know you do not want to go, Teo, but this will be a better life for you than here."

"Better how?" he demanded.

"You will find more reading material in Tabat, for one," she said with a chuckle. She leaned forward. "Think of all that Tabat will offer you! You love reading the penny-wides, now you'll be where their heroes walk and talk. What's the name of that Gladiator you like so much?"

"Bella Kanto," he said, swallowing tears. He stared at his father. "Do you really think I'll do so badly in life that you had to lock me into something like this?"

"Oh, son." His father looked pained. "It's not like that at all. The more one sacrifices, the greater the gift. And we were at our wits' end; we didn't think Elya would recover any other way. So we swore that if the fever broke we would send you to the Temple."

The hurt remained, a pain that centered in his chest like the bruise after a powerful blow. "You chose her over me."

"Perhaps she would have recovered anyway and we made a choice we shouldn't have," his mother said. "Perhaps we made a mistake. Is that what you wanted to hear, that we are fallible? You are still promised to the Temples, due to be taken to Tabat by the Priest, no matter what, no matter how fallible we are. Your name is recorded in his rolls."

He'd seen her like this before. Sorrow made her angry, made her ready to lash out. He stared at his fists. "Like a slave," he said again.

"Not so," said his mother. "Like someone whose family has pledged him; like someone who understands his duty." She looked at him.

Anger wouldn't let him stop. "The real reason is because you think I'll be better off than in a village where I'm a failure."

"No one thinks you're a failure, Teo," she said. "There have been those who could not shift before."

"None alive except me," he said.

His father left her and came around the table to ruffle his hair. Teo held very still under the gesture. He was still sorting out his feelings, but anger weighted the mix.

"Is it because I can't Shift?" he asked.

His father touched his hair again. "Some think it unlucky."

"A few? Or many?"

"Most." His father sighed and returned to his mother's side. Elya's broth bubbled on the fire, setting the pot lid clinking as wafts of steam escaped.

"I will pack food and a change of clothing for you," Teo's mother said. "The Priest will stay a few days yet, but then you must be ready to go."

○ ○ ○

Springtime would come soon, but not yet. Ice shielded the stream, and the thin branches of the scrub trees along its bank drooped with snow.

Teo had come to the riverbank to think. Settled on a boulder, its cold weight beneath him, he could barely hear the rush of the water beneath the ice, only the faintest whisper. He imagined it talking to him, giving him advice, telling him to give in to his parents' plans.

But he didn't want to be a Moon Priest. Giving his life over to serve the three moons. Giving up everything, including his name.

He had to flee.

But to where? Northward the land was more perilous, and westward, even wilder. South was the direction he wanted to avoid as well, for at the end of that road lay Tabat. No, he would have to strike eastward, make for the coast and Verranzo's New City, where all were free. Rumors said that Beasts walked with Humans there and even held land and other properties. Like anywhere else, they didn't tolerate Shifters, but Teo was no Shifter, was he? He'd have no worries there. The alta had told his mother he'd never shift. He must put that dream away.

Drops of water rolled down a tree branch, falling on the snow. Two squirrels chased each other, chuckling or scolding, he couldn't tell which, through the branches overhead.

Leaving had to come soon, before the Priest decided to start off. How long did Teo have? Two days, perhaps. At most.

He needed to consider his course carefully. The Priest would make for Marten's Ferry next. And everyone would hunt for Teo, and all of them were skilled hunters. But if he went along the creek, eventually he would find the road, and there his tracks would simply mingle with all the others.

He reached out and scooped up snow in his mittened hands, packing it into a ball. He threw it across the stream at the largest tree, and hit it squarely, with a satisfying *thunk* and a shower of dislodged snow.

He was young and strong and smart. He'd have no trouble finding work in Verranzo's New City. Think of all the things he could do!

He might become a Merchant or a sailor or even a man of great learning. He knew how to read and write when many in the village didn't. He had taught himself in order to decipher the penny-wides and other newspapers that traders used to wrap their goods. No, he would be fine, once he got there.

He couldn't wait. He glanced up at the sky, clear of clouds and blue as the little flowers, primaflora, that would cover the riverbank, come full spring.

There was no time like the present. Tomorrow. He would leave tomorrow.

O   O   O

That night while they ate, Teo tried to provoke his father and mother to conversation. He wanted to hear them laugh and tell stories, things that he could remember later.

But his mother was sullen with lack of sleep from nursing Elya, and after a long day of fruitless hunting, his father was not inclined to light talk either.

Finally Teo stared into his bowl. He thought that he should eat all he could, for surely meals would be scarcer on the road. There wouldn't be good hot lentils cooked the way his mother always did, with garlic and onions and a shake from the spice bag she kept near the stove, savory and redolent. The smell always reminded him of his mother, for she swore by her spice mix, said it made the food more digestible.

Maybe he'd take a pinch or two with him. He could hunt rabbits and roast them in a fire, and a little spice would not go amiss there. He forced down a few more bites and drained his cup of water.

After dinner, he sat by the fireside and carved. He wanted to leave a last gift for Elya. He chose a Shifter's form, that of a great cat of the sort his father could become, and imagined it was his own. When he finished it, he showed it to his mother.

She turned it over in her hand and a rare smile crept over her face.

"It has your look," she said.

"What do you mean?"

She studied it. "I can't tell where it comes from—perhaps the way you've shaped the eyes or the set of the ears, but it has the same look that you do when you're asking questions."

"Then perhaps it will help Elya remember me." The words came out with an anger that surprised him.

She set the statue on the mantle and reached to touch his cheek. He pulled away just as her fingers were about to graze his skin. Her face fell.

"Perhaps with time, you'll understand," she said.

He looked her full in the eyes. "Perhaps."

The anger lingered with him when he went to bed. Once everyone else was asleep, he slipped to the cupboard and filled a leather bag—a round of bread and curls of dried meat filched from the back of the food cupboard, and three dried plums, as hard as rocks, that had fallen behind another bag and would not be missed.

His mother was not a particularly diligent housewife of the sort given to counting her inventory, but by this time of year most of the food was gone already, so Teo didn't dare make the inroads he wanted to.

How long would it take his mother to realize he was gone? In the morning all she would do was dip oats out to cook and think that he'd gone out hunting or scouting. Perhaps at lunch, she'd think him still afield. But by dinner, she would know. Would they send someone after him then or wait till morning? Morning, he thought, because then his tracks would be easier to see.

Once he was on the main road, though, his hunters wouldn't know which way he'd gone. They'd think north or south, not realizing he intended to cut across it there and continue on through the pine barrens, despite their perils.

No, if she didn't realize till dinner, that was best.

He went to the cupboard where their most precious things were stored. Sorting through it, he found what he sought towards the back: a wooden box, barely palm-sized. He took it out and opened it.

Twin to the pierced coin around his own neck. Both bore the smallest moon, Toj, now in quarter-moon on one side, the full trio of moons on the other. The coins given by the Priest when registering a birth for the Temple rolls. While the villages were converts within the last two generations, they had embraced the faith, which kept the occasional Moon Priest from suspecting they were Shifters, as well as letting them trade with Human settlements.

Teo removed his own coin from the leather thong and exchanged it for his Shadow Twin's. They were identical, after all. No one would know he'd made the swap. And this way he would have something to remember his sister by. Supposedly the coin held his luck. Well, it'd be safer here than out in the world.

And his luck had been bad enough so far. He had no objection to leaving it behind.

His father snored and muttered something in his sleep. Teo took a last look around at his home of the last fourteen years, squared his shoulders, and moved to the door.

In the moonlight, the trees looked still and motionless, as though carved of white and black stone. He went along the river, knowing that it would lead him to the road eventually.

When morning came, he kept walking. He would not sleep till he crossed the road, not until he was safe. The footing was bad and treacherous, slick with ice. Cold crept up his legs and bit at his ears, while his nose began to run.

He could have cried for joy when he finally saw the road, a glimmer through the trees. When he got to it, it was rough and full of frozen mud. Now his new life would begin.

Then he spotted the Priest and froze.

Chapter Two

Introducing Bella, a Gladiator

The blade slices so close to my eyeball that my upper eyelashes brush against it. I pull back from that silver line hanging sideways in the air, roll on my heels on the gritty tiles.

The crowd is silent, watching from the vast stands. Not a full crowd, for a practice match, particularly one no one thinks Crysa can win. But the fact that the Duke is here, watching, brings a fair sized audience. Marta's there, no doubt. Which of us is she hoping will win?

No time for that. Snap my left fist forward. Almost catch her. Almost drive the side of the little round shield into her ribs as I push towards her, but she goes left, dodges with an exhalation that hangs in the frosty air between us.

The bitch is as quick and as fast as that Champion in the Southern Isles.

Built like her too.

Not as experienced, though. She's young. Fresh. If she wins, she wins the right to dress in Spring's armor in a month and try to defeat Winter. Or rather defeat me, dressed in Winter's armor.

She's off balance from the step. Weight on that heel.

Make as though to kick forward into the other heel, sweep a foot backward, into her calf, make her falter.

When you've fought someone in practice hundreds of times, you know them inside out, more intimately than any lover. You know the sinews and lumps of their character, how they respond to taunt or stroke, how they move when pressed to their utmost effort, how they take losing.

So it is with this one, Crysa. I've fought her that often.

This isn't a teaching match, though. She's trying to shortcut the usual climb, challenging me directly. If she wins, she'll be Spring's Champion in another month.

That's where the good ones end up. Fighting me there.

She falls back with a scrape of armored heels on the tiles, never loses balance throughout the move.

She's in peak shape. I warmed up for this bout by fighting a Beast, a Minotaur who'd tried to kill his Master. He didn't score a hit, and now I'm warm and limber, if breathing harder. She came into the fight fresh, so she's holding her own.

She's not bad, not bad at all. She shouldn't be. I trained her myself.

This is her moment, or so she thinks.

They all do, just before I pluck it from them.

My sword comes up.

Skirl and screech, blade sliding against blade, the noises only the closest onlookers can hear, though they can see the sparks catch her in the face. I taste blood.

Touch. Wheel.

Another clash of blades.

The crowd's impatience swells. Idlers and others with time to spare. When the actual ceremonial match comes, the seats will be packed with onlookers.

She angles sideways, trying to keep out of the reflected sun glitter on my shield.

I do the same. Bright sparkles cross her visor, light dances against her eyes.

She blinks.

Time to feint and kick, catching her calf.

She staggers.

It's actually disappointing when they don't last longer than this.

The crowd noise swells. They're disappointed too. But it's not her lack of stamina that makes them mutter.

They want to find someone who will defeat me in the ceremony and win them six extra weeks of spring.

Let them groan and whine.

If they want to change things, they can find another Champion. I'm Winter's, as I have been for almost two decades now. As I will be again this year.

Champion of Tabat. And this year that ritual's even more important, with all the political changes taking place. There'll be more stress to throw the match than ever before.

But I don't throw matches.

She's done. I can see it in her eyes.

She must learn all the steps, even though she's not experiencing them from the side she wanted. I step forward to put my sword to her throat. She droops in surrender; hands up her sword.

I hold it up to the crowd, into the oncoming snowflakes, thickening now.

They cheer despite the oncoming weather, swept up in the fervor.

They are Tabat.

They are mine.

In his box, Alberic, the current and last Duke of Tabat, stands. He waves his hand above his head to signal silence, and the crowd obeys.

He speaks. The Mage beside him amplifies the speech with a device that he holds near the Duke's face, a mesh and gears cylinder.

"Citizenry of Tabat! Crysa Silverskiff has failed her challenge. She will not face Winter's Champion."

Downright boos this time, even though I can see the Duke's Enforcers patrolling the packed stands. Events like this make them ineffectual. Before they can get to a booer, he or she has slipped away through the crowds, which are melting away themselves, the impatient heading out before the final words or the exhortations to pay their upcoming taxes.

It's not as though Winter will continue forever. Only that I've stretched it out a red moon's length. After all this time, you'd think they'd be used to the long Winters, to a delayed arrival of Spring.

17

They'll appreciate it more because of that. And the Gods have given us this ritual, to tell us what the weather will be.

Alberic begins talking about the history of Tabat's sacred Games and I stop listening. Twenty years of this now. I've heard every permutation of pontification Alberic can provide.

I pat the shoulder of the girl by my side.

She thought she was skilled or lucky enough to beat me. And she *was* lucky. Sometimes they don't survive.

"There will be other fights."

Her downcast eyes regard the blue tiles worked with golden chains, endless lines leading the gaze towards the Duke's box. I helped Alberic select those a few years ago. "Not like this one."

I'd shrug, but I don't want the crowd seeing that.

"This is how Life works. Take it on the chin, or stand aside for those who want to."

Now she glares up at me. "You can afford to talk."

I don't want the crowd to see me laughing either. But it's startled out of me. "Child, do you think this is where I've been all my life?"

"You've been there all of mine."

I help her to her feet. She scowls at me still. This time I do allow the shrug.

"Can I change it now? Should I have cheated to let you win, student? Is that the victory you desire?"

She stalks off in silence towards the exit archway.

I roll my eyes as I sweep off my helm. Raising it, I wave once before heading toward the snowflake-carved opposite arch. Alberic's still going on, but he'll have to forgive me. I provide the main entertainment for the event, after all.

Snow is hurling itself down now, heavy white flakes filling the world to mark my victory. Lucya stands out of the wind, just inside the arena hallway as I enter. Although she's my partner in owning the Brides of Steel, the premier Gladiatorial school in Tabat, she is here for Crysa's sake rather than mine. That pains me. Lucya and I have known each other for so long, ever since I first came to the school as a student.

She addresses me.

"You've won again, Bella Kanto," she says.

I shrug. Did she think, like Crysa, that I'd step aside? The Gods guide me. I fight for them and the City.

Tears blotch Crysa's face. Lucya lays her hand on the girl's shoulder, but keeps staring at me.

"How long will it continue, Bella?" she asks.

A breeze sweeps along the hallway, making Crysa shiver. This building is thick stone; Winter's chill seems to linger here even at summer's height.

"It will continue till I lose," I say, my voice as cold as the air, and don't look back as I continue on.

We've had this argument before. We will again.

○ ○ ○

Every battle in the arena is watched over by the Duke's box. Alberic's not always there, of course. There are battles and practices every week, and he has no interest in attending them all. But even when he's not there, the box remains a presence, jutting out from the side of the arena, overlooking the tiled floor with its baleful stare.

Two guards flank the entrance, but nod and step aside as I approach. I am one of the few who always has access to Alberic, sometimes treated as an advisor, at other times more like a concubine.

He's in the mood for the latter when I enter, his eyes sparking as he sees me. He likes it when I'm still sweaty with battle, knows that I'm always ready after one. He's speaking to his Mistress of the Hunt but breaks off to nod at me, waves a hand, flapping her away. She glances at me, bobs her head once, and leaves.

He gestures at another advisor, and they scuttle out as well, leaving only the two of us there, aside from the ever-present guards and servants. But Alberic pays them no mind. To the rich, those folk are invisible, part of the furniture.

He beckons me closer and I approach.

He gestures and I begin to strip off my armor.

"Slower," he says, his voice a growl.

I oblige, pausing as I unbuckle things, glancing up to meet his eyes as I slide leather and steel aside to reveal my flesh. A brazier in the corner keeps the box warm against Winter's chill, too warm for me.

He says, "You left early. No one is supposed to leave until I am done addressing the crowd. Do you want me to punish you?"

"I want you to fuck me," I say. It's the truth. There's something about conquering another being in the arena that leaves me hotter than any pretend play.

I take off my armor, revealing silver scars but skin still smooth, still fine, over long taut muscles, breasts ready to swing loose from the armor's binding. I've begun peeling away the lower fauld, showing the first hint of the wrappings underneath, when it's too much for him.

He pulls me to him, forces my face up and takes a long, deep kiss. His hands are busy removing the rest of the armor. I let him. He's a man who likes to do things for himself.

With another lover, I would take the lead. I have never been one to be passive in my fucking. But never so with Alberic.

He strips away the rest of my clothes, pulls me towards the velvet surface of the couch set to one side, moves me to the position he wants, plunges himself deep within me, not worrying about whether I'm ready or not.

Such is the Ducal prerogative.

He says, as his face lowers near mine, "You've won again. I knew you would."

He fucks me slowly, methodically, as though each stroke were a pen slash affirming his name, signing treaties, claiming new lands. He's done this almost every battle since my first victory, back when we were still new to each other. Over the years we've been on again, off again, but we still come together after I've fought.

As if my thoughts prompt him, he says, "I can feel the Gods' magic around you at these times. Do you ever wonder how you've done it, winning for two decades?"

"Virtuous living," I say.

A smile tugs at his mouth, but he goes on. "You've become so tangled in the magic, in the yearly battle to determine Tabat's luck in weather that you've become something the magic sustains. That's how you manage, despite your age. You've done this twenty years now. It's unnatural. It must be created by some twist of magic.

No one wins more than once or twice. When you did it a third time—and I will admit you did that through talent not anything else—you changed the equation."

So like an aristocrat, to try to attribute another's achievements to an accident. We've discussed this before. He thinks the magic keeps me going. I say it's more than that.

Still, sometimes I can feel it racing in me, making me more than Human. Like now. My blood feels alive, singing inside me, and my muscles are coiled as a cat's. I am ready to fuck, but if that won't do, I'll fight.

I say, "I remain Champion of Tabat."

"And you are mine."

I don't stiffen at the words, although I want to. Yet what I say next has a hostile edge. "And you are Duke still. For now."

He doesn't conceal his reaction. He hates the thought that this time next year he'll be worrying about who will supplant him. Centuries ago when Tabat was founded, his ancestors agreed to this bargain, that on a certain day the city would begin elections, allowing the people to choose who would rule them. Both of us know that they will not choose him, even if he doesn't want to admit that.

I'm not sure how it matters. He'll keep his holdings, his possessions, will still live in the castle far above the city. But his word will no longer be law. And that's what matters to him. Alberic likes to be in control.

I push even though his face has darkened. I say, "Who do you think will win those elections?"

At which he pulls away, as though his cock has softened at the thought. He growls, "What does it matter? It could be those upstarts at the Moon Temples, for all I know or care."

This is dubious. Few people in the city follow the Moon Temples, even if their worship is spread much farther outside, in the frontiers and small villages. There is no official religion of Tabat, but the Moon Temples would like there to be. They are intolerant of other worships, in a way the rest of us are not.

Most of Tabat is easy-going. We like our Gods vague and uninvolved. Even the Merchants, with their endless pantheon of the forces watching over commerce.

I suspect it will be a Merchant house that seizes rule of the city, but I don't tell him that.

He says, "Next year many things will be different. Perhaps there will even be a new Champion. The city will be changing. Perhaps you'll no longer be what it wants to represent it. If our leadership structure is changing, surely our rituals will not be far behind."

He's trying to score points of his own, but I only smile at him.

I am Bella Kanto. I am Champion of the city and will continue to be.

O O O

Of course Marta is lingering for me in the hallway outside the box. I push my way through well-wishers and those waiting to see the Duke towards her. Her face is dark with anger and impatience. She doesn't understand that I need to keep Alberic happy. She's distantly related to him; you'd think she'd know his ways.

More importantly, she doesn't understand that she is only my latest lover, one in a string of so many. They all begin to think they have some claim on me. That is when it is time to break things off. It is well past overdue with Marta, but I didn't want to do it before I won, didn't want the drama at a time when I wanted to focus.

Of course, now I'm regretting putting it off.

Maybe she knows what's going on. Maybe she's sensed me cooling over the last few weeks, pulling away as she grew as clingy as a vine in one of the greenhouses her father, Milosh Dellarose, owns. Despite the trace of Northern blood lending her its fair skin and reddish hair, she is a child of wealth, so many of them are. She's never known hunger or cold or fear of death. Her family has a fortune based on growing plants. Her father knows as many secrets about that as my Aunt Jolietta ever knew about training Beasts.

I suspect his methods are far less stringent.

Marta says as I approach, "I've been waiting for almost an hour now, standing while the snow grows thicker outside. I hate the snow."

She shivers dramatically. Everything about Marta is dramatic.

As though she had to walk in the open. A warm carriage, pulled by horses or some more expensive Beast, will take her home.

"You know that after a bout I must go and report to the Duke."

She sneers at that. "Yes, reporting, is that what you call it?"

"This jealousy does not become you."

I can feel curious eyes upon us. I don't like to conduct personal business in public. I prefer someplace quieter, calmer. Sometimes they cry. Sometimes they make a fuss. It is better to be discreet about these things.

She must know what is going on, for I can only interpret her next speech as a preemptive move.

She says, "I can't deal with this. I can't deal with sharing you with other people."

"I never promised you anything about exclusivity."

Her eyes harden.

"No, and that is something you will never promise anyone. It is too seductive, to be Bella Kanto, with half the city chasing after you, eager to get you into bed. And yet the honor seems cheap when so many have shared it."

There is no putting this off.

I say, "Then let us be done with one another."

"Very well," she snaps. "Far be it from me to try and cage such a wonder." Her voice is bitter as day-old tea mixed with vinegar.

She turns away. Some fool applauds. Others give me sour looks and mutter about Spring.

Marta doesn't look back as she makes her way through the crowd watching the encounter.

Not how I would've chosen to stage this ending, but sometimes people make their own choices. And at least this saves me the trouble of figuring out how to do it later on. Still, it eats a little at my vanity not to have her more upset. She'll regret it later. They always do. She'll send notes, or gifts, or someone to speak on her behalf.

Outside the arena, crowds jostle around food carts, buying twists of spiced bread, nuts glazed with honey, paper cups of soup ranging from salty *chal* to mixtures more dumpling than liquid. I try to slip through the crowd unnoticed, but that never happens.

Many folks want to congratulate me. I shake hands, pat the heads of children, utter words of encouragement to the students who have come to watch. A group of Gladiators wants me to go with them to Berto's, but I am not in the mood for bantering. I manage to slip away without offending anyone and go out into the street where the snow is still falling, flakes whirling in the cold wind.

There's more riding on this match than in the past. Everything is unsettled by the upcoming elections. I've never had so much pressure to throw the match before.

Marta's carriage rattles past and I catch a glimpse of her face through the window, looking out.

I raise a hand as though to hail her, then let it fall.

Sometimes I wish they would stay angry. It would be much easier. Perhaps Marta will.

Chapter Three

Teo on the Road

Teo knew from a distance by the long robes it was the Priest, although the man had belted them up to keep the hem from dragging in the road's slush and mud.

He wanted to run, to flee into the underbrush, to make his way east as he had planned. But the Priest had already spotted him and was fingering a charm around his neck. Teo tried to back away, but his feet wouldn't move, no matter how he strove.

He had never been caught by magic before. It was unfair that the Priest could use such means. His heart pounded. With every step the Priest took towards him, the pressure increased until he could not move at all. Even breathing was hard.

"And we meet again, young Teo," the Priest said. His eyes were shrewd. "I am called Grave. It was good of you to start early. That's wise. It means less delay saying goodbye and gets us along farther."

He said nothing of the village or what they might have said about Teo's absence. Had they realized he'd left and sent the Priest after him? Another betrayal.

Teo bowed his head, feeling the weight of the world slump on his shoulders. After making up his own mind, that decision had been snatched away from him. He had no choice now but to go to Tabat.

O O O

They camped along the road, not on it, but close enough to see it the first night, in a stand of elderly oaks.

Teo had never seen such trees before. It startled him to think that they were only a day away from the village, yet here was something he'd never seen before, something entirely new to him. Bit by bit, he thought, what he was used to would absent itself from the scene, slip away without him noticing, until finally everything would be different, everything new, an alien landscape surrounding him.

The Priest tried to strike up conversation, but Teo was sullen. Why bother making friends with his captor? It would only make it more difficult to make his escape when the opportunity presented itself. So instead he grunted monosyllabic answers, sometimes pretending not to hear the question at all, rather than to talk fully about what he liked, or hoped, or dreamed.

Because that was how the questions went. They weren't about his family, or his village, or anything like that. Instead they were about *him*, interest of a sort no one had ever shown before. What did he like for dinner, what did he usually dream, and did he think he'd miss his little sister much?

The thought crossed his mind that perhaps this was part of the Priest's duties, to deliver not just Teo but also the key to him, the ways the Temple would be able to force him to obey, and how to train him, like a dog that would do anything for a bite of meat.

Wary of this notion, he became even more silent and sullen, dragging in firewood with head drooped, avoiding the Priest's eyes.

Finally Grave lay down the flint and tinder that he'd been assembling.

"Teo," he said. "Look at me."

Teo did. The eyes were sympathetic, but there was firmness in their look as well.

"Do you think you are the only acolyte ever come to the Temple against his or her will? It wasn't a fate I relished either. But it's not a bad life, Teo, and better than the one you would have faced in your village, a more exciting one. You'll see things that they'll never see. Perhaps you'll become one of the Temple emissaries and travel the world." He grinned. "Perhaps you'll find yourself, like me, journeying to collect those who have been dedicated to the Temples."

If so, Teo thought, he would let them go. But instead he nodded and went back to gathering firewood, aware of the Priest's gaze on him.

"We have a thousand words for the kinds of shadows the Moons cast. Those are the names we choose to use. For the first few years you will have no name. Then a Priest will give you one based on their assessment of your nature. That's why I ask questions, to put in my report to them."

"What does your name mean?"

"I was not quick to learn, so I am Grave, the color of shadow on bare earth around a stone. It means more than that, much more, but I chose to take it as reproach and worked harder, till I advanced and became a Traveling Priest."

"What name do you think I would get?" Teo asked, staring into the fire.

Grave looked at him consideringly for a long time, so long that Teo grew uneasy under that stare. It seemed to reach into his soul, uncover all his plans for escape, and expose them for the small, ineffectual machinations and fantasies that they were.

"Gloisten, for the shadow behind cart wheels in the rain, perhaps." Grave said. "You are quick of mind, I have seen that. You know the names for things; every tree and flower and bird I have pointed out. How did you come by that knowledge?"

"Lidiya, our herb alta, let me follow her," Teo said.

"Few villages have an alta. Not many are sensitive and willing enough to take on the plant's life and change themselves with the seasons as the altas do.

Teo shrugged. "She's always been there."

"What do you know of Tabat?"

Spurred by the earlier praise of his intellect, eagerness carried him away into boasting. "Lots and lots. I read all the penny-wides."

Grave snorted. "The penny-wides do not tell you much of the city or its workings. They're only about the Gladiators and the Duke's Court, nothing but gossip writ large."

Teo's heart fell.

Grave poked at the fire and took a metal bowl from his pack, mixing in grain and water and setting it in the ashes to cook. "They live and eat simply in the Moon Temples," the Priest said. "It's more reason to become a traveling Priest. The food is better. But there is always plenty of it—mashed roots and cooked grain, fish every fifteenth day, and at year's turning for all five feast days."

"That's all?" Teo said. He thought wistfully of village food: the dimpled nut rolls his mother made, the goat cheeses rolled in cracked pepper and ash.

"Some come to the Temples never having known what it is to have a full belly. The Temples take in many orphans and those left destitute by one calamity or another."

"The Temples must be crowded."

Grave nodded. "It makes it difficult to ascend in the ranks, it is true. But if you are smart and work hard, eventually you will rise. I came to the Temples a little younger than the age you are now, to wear the same acolyte robes you will don."

Teo plucked the last bits of meat from the rabbit's bones. He might as well savor such dishes while he could. "Are there no cooks that work for the upper Priests?"

"We all eat from the same platter," the Priest said severely.

Teo flinched and fell silent.

"I am not a bad man, Teo," the Priest said. "There are some of my order who are worse shepherds, who take advantage of those they're sent to collect. I'm not one of those, at least."

Teo wasn't sure exactly what he meant, but he didn't want to ask, either. He supposed it meant the Priest didn't intend to fuck him, which was a relief after some of the stories he'd been told. But again he nodded.

"How long were you an acolyte? Before you became a traveling Priest?" he asked.

"Ten years as an acolyte, then another eight before I was set to the road, first to travel with another, then by myself."

"Oh," Teo said. Ten years?!? He licked the bones and threw them into the fire, where they popped and sent up black smoke. The Priest said nothing more, simply sat watching him until Teo curled up in his blanket and went to sleep near the fire.

o o o

It happened when they were crossing the low line of hills that marked the first sight of the river. They'd stopped at the top to admire the view: a vista of dark green pines along grey rocks, unremarkable except for the length of silver shining in the sun behind them, the Northstretch River.

"Once we hit the river, we'll head upstream," Grave told Teo.

"Upstream?" Teo said, surprised. "But Tabat is far downstream."

"Sometimes to take a step forward, you must take one back first." The Priest made his way down a slope of rock scree and ice, testing each foothold beforehand with his walking stick. "Upstream is Marten's Ferry, and we should be able to catch a trade steamer from there."

Teo stopped. "We're going by boat?"

He didn't know why it hadn't occurred to him before. Of course they were going by ship. They would get to Tabat far sooner than he had reckoned. There would be no time to gain Grave's trust, to talk him into letting Teo go.

Sand and rock slipped beneath his feet until he hardly knew which way was up. No matter how hard he tried, he was doomed for the Temples, he thought, as he followed in the Priest's wake.

Grave glanced back. "You must keep up, boy," he said, his voice impatient. The sentence broke off before he could add anything more, for a flat of shale had given way, and he was sliding, tumbling, limbs flailing among the tangle of his robes.

He landed at the bottom with a thump and lay dreadfully still.

Teo's heart leaped. This was his chance. He paused. But he couldn't leave Grave lying there hurt. He had to check and make sure he wasn't dead. He made his way down the slope as quickly as he could. A crow squawked in the tree, summoning its fellows to a fine dinner of dead flesh?

But as he neared the limp form, he saw the rise and fall of fabric and heard the Priest's labored breathing. He went to his knees beside the mass of huddled fabric, the cold ground biting at his knees with sharp, stone teeth.

"Sir?" he said. He stretched out his hand but hesitated, not daring to touch the Priest. Who knew what magics were laid on him to prevent attack?

A groan answered him. Grave stirred and tried to sit up, gasping with pain.

"Leg's broken," he said brusquely.

Teo knew that already. He was trying to avoid looking at the sharp edge of bone protruding through the skin.

"Pull my pack over to me," Grave directed.

The pack had broken loose and tumbled further, but seemed intact. Teo dragged it over and the Priest searched through it with faltering hands, hands that shook as though with fever. His features were white as new stone and drawn. Teo could see the lines of pain pulling at his lips.

"Go and find firewood, make a fire here," the Priest said. Fumbling a tiny bottle out of a pack pocket, he raised it to his lips and drained it. Some color returned to his cheeks as he set it down. "Lucky enough that it's flattish here. We'll make camp and see how I feel in the morning. Go find firewood, and while you're looking, find three or four sturdy poles."

"Are we making a tent?" Teo said.

The look was scornful. "No. Stay here and we'll end up eaten by Beasts or bandits. You're making a pull trailer, so you can take me upstream."

Teo nodded and took the hatchet, going in search of firewood and poles. Again the possibility of escape danced through his mind. But the Priest had spoken truly: abandon him here and he would indeed fall prey to some menace. There was a reason few people lived in these hills.

When he came back to the Priest, he stopped short of the flat spot. A cloud of light surrounded the Priest, a mass of scintillations. It took Teo a moment to realize it was Fairies, a swarm covering the body entirely.

"No," he shouted, dropping the wood and rushing forward, waving his arms. The host fluttered away, rising like a single mass. It hovered in the air a few feet away, and he saw the swirl of coin-sized, feral faces watching him. He stooped and grabbed a rock, but by the time he rose again, the Fairies were gone.

Grave was an unconscious mass of tiny ragged bites. That was a mercy perhaps, Teo thought. Fairy bites brought unconsciousness in order to paralyze their prey. Despite any possible blasphemy, he pushed the Priest's robes aside, searching for any sign that they had done something more than bite.

On the broken knee, a few inches above the kneecap, he found a round hole of the type a Fairy sting would leave. Had there been time enough for the creature to lay its egg within? He thought not—surely it took a while and was not instantaneous. By the look of the bites, they had only just begun to feed on the Priest.

He considered the wound. He should cauterize it, he knew, in order to make sure, but Grave had already been through so much that Teo was afraid the shock of such an operation might kill him. Reluctantly, he bandaged the worst of the bites, fetching water from the stream (although watching the Priest every step of the short journey lest the Fairies return), in order to lave them.

He built the fire high. It would betray them to anyone watching from afar, but it would also keep creatures like the Fairies away. He kept dragging more wood to the heap that would feed it until it grew too dark to see. Then he sat cross-legged by the blaze and fed it knots of wood while he watched the sleeping Priest.

He could leave, he kept thinking. Did he owe this man anything? He was almost a slaver, after all, bringing the indentured to be enslaved to his Temple in Tabat. But Teo knew that Grave didn't think of it that way. He'd spoken of all the advantages that the city would hold for Teo, had talked as though it was no question that serving in Tabat was infinitely better than a free life in the wilderness.

And would it be? Teo had to admit he was looking forward to seeing the site where so many of the adventures he'd read took place. He might even encounter Bella Kanto herself. He glanced over at the Priest. Grave had said he'd come to the Temples himself as a Promised One. It must not have been too bad for him if he was willing to bring others to the same existence.

The stars overhead were a swathe of glitter against the blackness. Sparks flew up from the fire as though trying to join them and become stars themselves, and the pine wood, rich with resin, popped and snapped, each new burst sending up a fresh handful of sparks. The smoke moved with the erratic wind, sometimes enveloping Teo and his companion, other times as docilely ascending as though guided by an invisible chimney.

Teo ate the last of the bread, reluctant to rummage through Grave's pack in search of the grain that they had dined on the previous night.

Grave had taken his moon coin, saying he would give it back when they reached the Temples. It rested, hostage, in the Priest's pocket. He thought about reaching for it. But Grave might wake.

The food tasted of smoke and home. He tasted his mother's spice mix now in the meat. When this was gone, there would be no way for him to remember other than memory, and that would slip away, bit by bit. Would he lose that flavor entirely? What would things taste like in Tabat, where the great ships laden with goods from the Southern Isles, like cinnamon and hot peppers and other spices, sailed into harbor to distribute their wares?

Far in the distance, wolves howled. He presumed wolves, not dogs, but who knew out here? There used to be no wild dogs at all, his father had told him once, but expeditions from Tabat had always had such creatures with them, and sometimes they stayed behind, for one reason or another, a gift or an escape. Now they saw packs sometimes. His village refused to kill them, saying that they looked too much like the Shifters that took on wolfish form.

But they were only animals, and if they thought that they could get a meal from him and this fat Priest, they would be on their heels. Only the fire would be able to drive them back. He shivered, not entirely from the cold. The howling went on, taken up from one distant spot, then another, then another, like a chorus tossing a melody back and forth among its members.

He did not mean to sleep, but in the end, he did, curled near the heap that represented Grave, which breathed in ragged pants, a sound that followed him into his dreams, becoming dogs at his heels, dogs chasing him down.

The song continued, even though he was no longer listening, deep into the night.

In the morning, things were worse.

Chapter Four

Bella in Daily Life

The Centaur is just a boy, a beautiful one.

The air smells of leather, horse shit, straw, and fresh pine from the lumber pile stacked head-high in the north corner. Lucya knows I don't like working with Beasts. That she's been willing to bring me here means she's all but given up on the boy.

His glossy pelt shines on his spindle-thin legs, his eyes are like tumbling chestnuts. He tries to struggle to his feet at my approach before he gives up and lies on his side, coltish legs protruding and his thin torso twisted at an odd angle. His stringy, matted hair falls to tangle with the straw on the planking. His eyes roll and stare off into space, their intelligence given way to vacancy.

From a few feet away, I study him. "Bite?"

"It doesn't react much at all," Lucya says. She leans down to touch his shoulder. The head swivels in ragged jerks to regard her.

I palm his face and tilt the heavy skull to catch the late morning light available through the wide stable doors.

This close I can see them, twin punch marks, as big as a freckle, set where eye meets nose. They're raw still, weeping clear fluid. "Bring me a wet cloth?"

Lucya steps to a bucket near the stack of pine. I wait, releasing the boy's head. It nods back to stare at me. Little intelligence is left in those eyes; perhaps a dog's or one of the smallest ape's.

I use the damp cloth to blot away crusts of blood.

"Are you building something?" I nod over at the lumber before I hold the boy's face to the light, examining it.

"We're enacting a battle in support of the New Year's political rally next month. A small group of students, lots of flash and pageantry. You'd know about it if you were here more."

It's not the first time Lucya has needled me like this. It's why I'm not here more, actually, or at least that's what I've told her, too much responsibility here. At the time I helped stake the expansion of the Brides of Steel, I told her that I didn't want to be an owner anywhere, I just wanted to be behind the stage.

But I like working with the students here. What would I do without that to occupy me but wander about and grow fat eating pastries? I shrug.

"And if you appeared at more of the school events, more nobility and wealthy folk would take us up. They may think my Northern blood uncouth, but they'd be more than willing to overlook it for the chance to rub elbows with the famous Bella Kanto."

"Mmm." The Centaur boy tenses as I finish wiping his eyes, even though I try to be as tender as I can. His long legs and knobby hooves *thunk* across the floor as he tries to gather them. I hiss under my breath, letting the air susurrate while I rub his shoulder. He relaxes and sinks back to the floor.

"He's been dulled." I rise. "Recently, too. Maybe a purple moon at most."

"Dulled?"

"It's a procedure a few Beast Trainers use." I wipe my hands against each other to remove the feel of his slack-weight skull. "They insert the end of a duller—that's a long piece of wire with a handle—there where the eye meets the nose alongside the eyeball. Then they push and punch it back into the skull. Twirl the wire a few times and you have a dulled Beast. Usually they lose the ability to speak, sometimes not, but either way their faculties are much diminished. The procedure's saved for unruly or dangerous Beasts, and it's not always reliable. Most Trainers don't know the knack of it. Can't say much for your stabler if he's never heard of it."

Lucya makes a face of wry distaste. "So it'll stay like this?"

"Yes."

She sighs. "Not much use in the arena. Well, I'm sure I can find some carnival or brothel that will take it."

"You might try the Duke's Menagerie for him."

Lucya shakes her head. "It's been neutered. The Duke prefers breeding stock."

"Still, they might have some use for him. It's worth a try."

But I know she won't. It bothers me, but I have no establishment where I can take him. Perhaps I'll speak to Alberic, but Lucya is right, he wants perfect specimens.

Only the best for Alberic.

Like me.

○ ○ ○

I came to the Brides of Steel when I was fifteen, three days after Jolietta's death. It'd taken a while to sort things out, days that seemed interminable to me then.

Nowadays I'm surprised they were settled that quickly.

Jolietta had named me her heir, the new owner of Piper Hill and all the lands surrounding it. Though even there she carped on how disappointing I had proved in an unnecessary series of paragraphs that the lawyer read aloud in an embarrassed voice as I and the others named in the will listened.

I did not weep at all. I waited for the lawyer to explain out all the hems and haws of Jolietta's estate and all the ways she'd tried to tie me into her life as a Beast Trainer.

Afterward he apologized to me for doing that, said it'd been necessitated by law.

I didn't care. With Jolietta's death, a great weight had risen from my shoulders, leaving joy mingled with disbelief. I kept expecting her sly face to peek around the corner and say it had been only another of her tests and that I'd failed once again.

I gave it all into the lawyer's hands, said to sell the house and the land. I did my best by the Beasts she had kept. I saw the Oracular Pig settled with the family that would keep her well and would not sell her flesh. I gave most of the Beasts to owners who would take care of them, although I will confess that the three who had made my life the most miserable, the cook and Jolietta's two Minotaur bodyguards, were sent to auction.

I sent for Phillip, but I could not find to whom Jolietta had sold him.

I went through her books and papers trying to find the bill of sale, but it was not there.

The chamber was closed, the curtains drawn. A Unicorn's hide covered nearly one wall, and she'd fixed the horn above the doorway like a spear awaiting an unwary guest. I flipped back through a year's worth of pages. Nothing. Had she thought I might hunt for it when she wasn't around?

I looked up from the ledger propped across my lap and saw a dish of candies beside her bed. I could smell her everywhere; that musky scent she wore mixed with the smell of leather. It made bile rise in my throat.

I couldn't stay there.

After signing the necessary papers, I packed my things and went to enroll for training as a Gladiator without looking back.

It took me less than a day to get to Tabat. It was Autumn shading into Winter, and the skies were gray. I refused to take that as an omen. I caught a ride with a farmer who was going into market, sat in the back of his cart amid the turnips, and wondered how I would be greeted at the Brides of Steel. I'd heard of them, that they'd take on older students rather than requiring they enter at the early age most schools demanded. I knew that was where I wanted to be, I knew that was how I could become a Gladiator. They weren't the best school then. I made them that.

What drew me to the Gladiators was a feeling that there I would find direction, that there I would find out how to be strong and how never to be pushed around again. Jolietta had come close to breaking me, but she didn't succeed.

Tabat was how I remembered it. The fish-scaled green tiles of the rooftops glimmered greasily in the late afternoon sun. The last of the late-blooming sea roses filled the gardens and frothed down the terraces of the Stairway Park. Gulls hung overhead, riding the wind and watching a baker's cart as though afraid it might escape.

I hadn't been in the city for over five years. Jolietta never let us outside Piper Hill, even when she went traveling herself. It felt like home immediately. It felt like the place I distantly remembered from childhood. I should have sought out Leonoa's family, which would have been the proper thing to do. Instead, I went straight to the Brides of Steel.

It disappointed me from the outside, although I don't know what I expected. It seemed a little run down, even. Everything I knew about it I had gleaned from the penny-wides, and it was stories of the Brides of Steel that had made me pick that school rather than any of the others. It was the only one that took only females, but it was also the one that had produced the most Champions of Tabat.

The gate was made of iron. The pattern of crossed swords cheered me a little because that was more of the sort of thing I was expecting.

When I rang the bell, it took a while for someone to come to greet me. A woman answered, with her hands stained from digging in the garden, so I presumed her a servant. Back then, Lucya was still supplementing the budding school's income by selling the simples and ointments she made in spare moments.

I said, "I want to see the head of the school." I was very worried they wouldn't take me seriously, so my tone was that of Jolietta's dealing with a lesser creature.

It was not the best first impression I'd ever made. The woman straightened, wiped her hands on her apron, and gave me a look, eyes sharp and green. I'd come to know that look much later on, a look that was stern, a look that demanded the best of you, but somehow more subtly than Jolietta's rigor ever had been.

"I'm Lucya," she said. "I'm the head of this school."

I blushed. I stammered out something about what had brought me there, my ambitions to become a Gladiator.

Her reply crushed me.

"You're too old."

"I will work harder than any student you have ever had," I said. She shook her head.

I put my hand up to the gate, feeling the cold iron bite at my fingers. I said, "Please. Please just give me a chance to show you what I can do."

What I said after that may have been the thing that changed her mind, rather than my earnest face and my pleading tone. "I can pay. I can pay well."

She said, "I can bring you in and let them test you. But I tell you again, you are too old. You have learned bad habits. Our students come when they are scarce a decade. They work for years honing their skills. You are close to the age of graduation, how do you think you will learn what you need in time to graduate?"

I said, "I have been Jolietta Kanto's apprentice. You cannot work me harder than she did."

The gate screeched protest as she swung it open and gestured me inside.

They did work me hard. They put me in match after match with scarce a break between them. I knew I was fighting badly, that I lacked the skills that my opponents possessed, but I was determined. Time after time, I lost and said, "I will try again."

Later, Lucya told me she had never seen a student so determined.

And when they finally agreed that I could study there, on probation for the first year, I knew that they would not regret that decision.

I am Bella Kanto, and I never give up.

o o o

Usually I like working here. It's the only all-female Gladiatorial school. The students vie for my attention. They defer, they dance attendance, they're eager to catch my every word.

But today the unease the Centaur boy has stirred in me makes everything into aggravation and nuisance to the point where I wish I'd simply stayed at home.

Though I agreed to be a silent partner in the school years ago, I pretend I'm just an instructor. That way no one makes me wade through tedious decisions. Lucya's competent to handle it all. But being an instructor obliges me to put in an appearance at least once a week, to justify the handsome wage they pay me.

And the girls enjoy the glamour of my lessons. Hero worship makes them try harder. It's good for the soul. I had my own heroes when I was a pupil here. Striving to outdo them made me what I am. If the students knew how much hard work had gone into becoming Bella Kanto, they'd falter, stop wanting to be the same glamorous figure.

I make it all look effortless. That's the problem. But that's the point of being Bella Kanto, to making the difficult look as though it takes no more thought than breathing.

After the session, the school kitchen is out of hot soup and able to offer only broth and an apology.

I nurse my *chal* at the instructors' table and try to turn my thoughts to more pleasant things. Conversation swirls around me. The Duke has cancelled payment for the Harvest Festival, saying its cost should by rights fall to whoever became Mayor, which puts the Festival overall, usually a moneymaker for the school, in jeopardy. I put all my loose coins into the basket brought round to fund the Festival. It's a petty act on his part. Then again, Alberic has always been one to pinch a coin until it screamed.

Lucya grows increasingly insistent that I must shoulder more work with the school. She thinks I need to lay down the groundwork for work I can do after I retire from public fighting.

That's not anytime soon, but she'll remind me again that I'm Tabat's oldest practicing Gladiator by a good five years. I don't need reminding of such things, not on an already dismal day.

To top it off, I find my favorite student has left.

"Got called back to manage the estate," Lucya says with a twist of a smile. She doesn't like the way I "play pets," as she calls it. It's true, I do favor some over others. That's how it works, how it always has. That's how you encourage them to work harder, and make them earn your praise.

It's a long trip down to the Southern Isles—a few weeks. I hope Naresh keeps up daily practice, that she'll get there and find some able relative to take over her parents' plantation, and come back swiftly, or at least in time to fight me in the next Winter Battle. I'll have to find another to take her place. Jenka? Djana?

"We need to talk," Lucya says. I sheathe these thoughts and focus on her sharp-witted face. She's readying herself to speak, I can tell from the way the lines around her eyes tauten.

"A fine new flight of students are readying themselves to enter the arena in a few months, Bella," she says. "And I just took on three of Dina's."

Dina's school may be the Brides of Steel's only rival. They suffered a fire last month. I cannot say Lucya was saddened by the news that they've had to close down for a year while making repairs.

I squint sideways at her. "Any of them good?"

"Two are well-pocketed," she says slyly.

"And the third?"

"I'll be curious to see what you think of her."

We stand together at the gate watching the young women of the school make their way across the courtyard in the evening snow. A cluster of older buildings makes up the school, once a Merchant's estate but now housing the Gladiators-in-training and the school's staff. The courtyard was once a garden. Now those trees and flowers are gone, replaced with flagstones and a sawdust circle. Rubble and icy sand fills the fountain.

Piper Hill had a melancholy air, as though thinking about what it once was. But the school feels livelier, as though the buildings here welcomed their transfiguration, their annual crop of new occupants.

Lucya points to a head, dark-haired, indistinguishable from the rest of the group. "The third new one. Skye Doria. Merchant-bred."

I snort. "Soft then."

"You were raised Merchant as a child, and see how far you have come? Which returns me to my point: new students entering."

I look sideways at her frown. "Yes, that usually happens each year."

"You know what I'm getting at."

This argument again. "You think it's time for me to step aside and let some younger blade, Djana for instance, replace me. But you forget—isn't the tradition that we are driven from the ring in ignominious defeat, with crowds behind us, pelting the victor with cherry blossoms?"

"You *know* what I'm getting at. Give us an early Spring for once. Winter has left Tabat late for the past nineteen years because you always play her in the Spring Games. Look at the flowers around us. The city *wants* Spring."

"I worked hard to get where I am." I fix my attention on the students. Snow whirls, obscuring their heron-thin forms. "Did Donati step aside for me? No, my place was bought with blood and sweat and skill. Let them come and defeat me, if they can."

"You are like flint." Lucya's scowl deepens.

"I have found that I am my own best advocate."

Her eyes are shrewd and green as emeralds still. "If need be, I will dismiss you as an instructor. It's not as though you are much of a presence here."

That strikes a pang. It's one thing if I myself were contemplating severing the tie, but it's another thing to have it done for me. Teaching the young women here, seeing myself reflected in their eyes is sweet, seeing younger versions of myself who haven't been forced to waste years with Jolietta, who haven't been forced to wait till the last possible year before enrolling in the Brides of Steel. "You can't." The words seem less sure than they should.

I try again. "Beyond the question of my financial share, it adds to the school's prestige to have me here teaching, even if you don't pay me half what I'm worth."

"And what good does it do the students if they can never advance because you will not step aside?"

I shrug and pull my cloak around myself. The wind will be cold outside these walls. "I'll think about it." I don't meet her eyes. Life has enough petty irritations as it is. Maybe I'll cut my ties with the school.

There's Skye crossing the courtyard. Great clumps of snow tangle in her dark curls. She throws back her head, laughing at something the girl next to her says. Does she see me watching? Is she perhaps preening just a trifle for me?

Not yet. I won't cut ties with the school quite yet.

Chapter Five

Marten's Ferry

Teo didn't like the Priest's look. His hands were clammy but his face was red as though with blushes. His forehead under Teo's hand was scorching hot. After a few minutes of hesitation, Teo examined the spot he had thought might be a Fairy sting.

The lump that lay under the skin confirmed his suspicions. He'd seen Lidiya treat such bites. That would be best, if she did it, but he didn't think there was time enough for that. The parasite would grow and begin to control its host's nervous system, making it little more than an empty shell moving about to suit the host's needs until the Fairy was finally born.

It would not emerge from the wound that shifted under Teo's fingers. No, it would burrow deeply, then upward, till it found itself in its host's brain, which it would devour until sated. Once it was ready, it would eat its way out through his eyes or the soft tissues of his mouth.

It would have to be removed now, before it burrowed any deeper.

He built the fire as high as it would go and put the wineskin from the Priest's pack to the side near it where the wine could warm without its container burning. He took the metal bowl and filled it with water before sifting in the mixture of dried fish and tea that was the last of the Priest's store; this far on the journey, he'd nearly run out, and he'd confided in Teo that he was saving it for some special occasion, but it was the most sustaining and easily fed-to-a-patient substance that Teo could find in the pack. After a little thought, he added his store of dried meat as well. For what he had in mind the Priest would definitely require sustaining.

He had not seen it done, but he had listened to stories. Lidiya had taught him the signs of a Fairy sting and what to do if caught away from the village with one.

He prayed the Priest would stay asleep during the operation. That would make things easier. But as his knife poised above the mark, Grave's eyes opened.

"I have to do this," Teo said to him, afraid that the Priest would take this as some attempt to escape. "You have a Fairy egg in you. I need to take it out before it hatches and starts eating inward."

Grave's lids fluttered, but he said nothing. His forehead was red with fever. Teo wondered if the man even saw him. How would he react when he felt the cut of the knife? Would he thrash around, or think himself attacked and attack Teo in turn? He hesitated, not sure what he should do.

The words were barely audible, a breath escaping the Priest's dry lips. "Give me something to bite on first," he whispered. "I do not wish to crack a tooth as well."

Teo took the leather bag that had held his meat and rolled it into a tight cigar, putting it sideways between the Priest's lips.

"This will hurt," he warned. He felt the words' foolishness as soon as they left his mouth. Of course the Priest knew that this would hurt. Otherwise he would not have asked for something to bite down on during the operation. Teo took his own deep breath, steeling himself, and set the knife's tip above the wound.

It was not a simple job. Blood welled up in the cut, obscuring the flesh. Teo had to keep pouring water over it to clear it, eliciting a hiss of pain from the Priest each time. Otherwise he remained silent, jaws clenched around the piece of leather.

Teo sluiced the wound again as he peered into it. There. As gently as he could, he eased the knife's tip into the dark spot he could see. The flesh resisted for a moment—he should have sharpened the knife even more beforehand—before giving way with a tiny, delicate pop. The Priest inhaled raggedly.

That would kill the egg, perhaps, but it was not enough. Left inside, the creature would rot and the flesh around it would follow its example until the Priest would have to face the same choice Fyorl once had: cut away the limb or die.

Carefully, carefully, he used the thin tip to open the egg further. Clear fluid drained out. Then there was something struggling at the end of the knife blade, bumble-bee big and fighting to preserve itself and burrow further.

He jammed the tip into it. Muscles spasmed in the Priest's face but he remained rigidly still.

Teo hooked the loathsome thing out and took no time to contemplate it as it hung mewling and wailing on the end. He flung it into the fire as quick as thought. With a last whimper, it curled into ash.

He washed the wound once more with water, checking to make sure there were no more traces of the creature. Then, taking the wineskin from where it lay near the fire, he directed the hot wine across the flesh to keep it from putrefaction. Tendons of agony twisted in Grave's face.

He took needle and thread from the Priest's kit and took four careful stitches in the skin, tying it back together to close that painful looking mouth of flesh. All the time the Priest was silent and still. When Teo took the leather from between his lips, he saw that it had been bitten almost entirely through.

When he had finished, Teo brought the Priest a mug of soupy tea and broth. Grave leaned back against the makeshift chair Teo had made of mounded snow and his bedroll and sipped it. His face looked as wan as the pale moon, just rising and silvering the snow.

"Thank you," the Priest said.

Teo shrugged, uncomfortable and unsure what to say. "You're welcome."

"This changes nothing, unfortunately," Grave said. "I know you don't want to go to the Temples but I must take you there."

Teo met his eyes. *Why not*, he wanted to ask. *I saved your life. Can't you let me have mine?* Teo had dared to hope it, though he'd never said it out loud. Surely Grave would free him.

But if the thought crossed the Priest's mind as well, he gave no sign of it. He closed and buckled his pack. "I understand why you had to go through my pack," he said to Teo. "But be aware that according to Temple law, I could have you flogged for it. There are some in the Temple that take advantage of such things. You would do well to remember it in the future."

"But if I hadn't gone through it, I would not have been able to wash the wound," Teo protested. "Wounds go bad readily in these parts, particularly Fairy bites. I had to make sure all traces of it were gone."

The Priest regarded him, knife-eyed gaze intent. "Some might not trust in your knowledge of these things. Others might have something in their belongings that they cannot afford to have word spoken of. And others might simply take a dislike to you."

"To me?"

Teo felt oddly wounded. He thought he was a likable enough fellow. It heartened him, actually, anticipation of Tabat where there would be no expectations that he would shift into another form and he could be whoever he pleased.

Thinking about it, though, Likable Teo had to admit that the Sullen Teo Grave had traveled with so far might not have been quite as pleasant.

"I am glad to be alive. I would have hated to have never seen the Temple Garden again or smell the flowers there when the purple moon is full," Grave said. "But I will need time to recover. When we get to Marten's Ferry, there should be a boat there, the *Water Lily*, about to head down to Tabat. I'm going to put you in the Pilot's charge. His name is Eloquence, and I'm told he's a good, devout man. He'll get you there safely."

He clearly meant the words to be reassuring. They only sunk Teo further into gloom, as though each syllable was another stone, weighing him down, making him sink down to his inevitable fate of servitude in the Temples.

In the end he nodded and went to get more firewood.

○ ○ ○

The rest of the trip was the worst thing Teo had ever endured.

He dragged the travois holding Grave over hills and more rocky slopes. He managed to wrestle the Priest across a stream. All the while, Grave, wrapped in ever-increasing fever from the wound, muttered and threatened him, although the threats seemed not so much directed at Teo as at phantoms. The Priest called him mother at times, uncle at others, and a scattering of other names to boot.

When the main road finally glimmered through the dark line of the trees, he could have sobbed with relief. Even then, he pulled the Priest another mile before a cart overtook him. An elderly driver taking two cows to Marten's Ferry allowed him to pile Grave in the back. Teo was so tired he wasn't sure he could pull himself up onto the cart, but he managed to climb up beside the Priest.

He crouched beside Grave, clutching at the cart's side for balance as the vehicle bounced along from icy rut to icy rut. Grave muttered and turned his fever-flushed face from side to side as though seeking something.

In his weary haze, Teo barely noticed when they finally entered the town. When they pulled up before the Marten's Ferry inn, the driver helped him half assist, half carry the Priest inside.

Grave's flesh was hot as fire, even through the cloth of his robes in Teo's grip. What if someone thought he'd done this to the Priest deliberately? Had he? Had he been careful enough cleaning the wound or had some sleeping part of his mind woken, glimpsed a chance at escape, and made his hand falter?

He found himself thrust aside as the innkeeper, a tall woman whose brassy hair piled atop her head made her seem even taller, became involved. Hands on her hips, she dispatched a maid for boiled water and clean towels, set another to building a fire in a ground floor guest chamber, and sent a runner to summon the town's apothecary.

Teo hovered near the door of the chamber wondering what to do. He glanced out across the main room's expanse towards the front door. If he made his way out, what then? Surely Grave was in no shape to identify him. He could claim some other destination, find another cart willing to carry him. Hope stirred in his heart. He could make the best of this.

Behind him, there was a harsh whisper.

A hand pulled at his shoulder.

"He wants to speak to you, boy," the innkeeper snapped.

He moved to the bed where Grave lay tangled in blankets. The innkeeper fanned the new fire on the hearth, making it crackle and hiss.

"Boy ..." Grave beckoned Teo closer.

Teo stepped nearer, trapped between the warmth emanating from the Priest and the fire's matching heat. Despite his fever, Grave seemed alarmingly coherent.

A step in the doorway. Teo turned to see a new man there, a tousle-headed blonde wearing finer clothing than Teo had ever seen. Grave's hand lifted and fell, summoning the new arrival as well.

"Eloquence Seaborn," the man said, moving near.

"A good ... Temple worshipper name," Grave said, eyes moving between Teo and the man. "You are the Pilot of the ... *Water Lily?*"

The man nodded. Teo's heart sank.

"Take this boy ... to the Temples."

Teo looked to the door, but the man's hand settled onto his shoulder, companionable but firm.

Grave fumbled in his robes and drew out Teo's coin.

"Teo." Grave's eyes glittered with fever. "I will be along when I am fit to travel." He handed the coin to Eloquence and sank back onto the pillow, eyes closed, as the apothecary entered.

Teo's coin slipped into Eloquence's pocket, along with all his hopes.

Chapter Six

Bella's Cousin

The warehouse overlooks Loom Way, but here on the tiny street a door leads into the stairwell to Leonoa's studio. I ring the hand-bell beside the door, shivering. The rain clouds have lifted but have left ice on the streets in their wake, gleaming in mingled moonlight.

A window slides up; Leonoa stares down.

"It's me," I shout towards the sky.

"I'll be right there." Leonoa's head withdraws. My cousin's labored steps come down the stairway. The wooden bar slides back and the door creaks open.

As it opens, a wash of white moonlight enters to silhouette my diminutive relative. Leonoa Kanto stands with her habitual hunch, one shoulder drawn up half again as high as the other, a foot twisted sideways on the stairs.

"I suppose you're planning on sleeping here tonight," Leonoa says. Irritation and affection mingle in her tone. She beckons. "Well, come up."

I trail behind my cousin on the splintery stairs, matching my pace to Leonoa's. I wish I'd thought to bring something. Leonoa likes it when I pass along some of the dainties that admirers shower on me, particularly after a match. But this morning, I hadn't thought I'd need the dose of comfort that contact with my cousin usually brings.

"I have a friend already here, so be warned," Leonoa tosses back over her shoulder.

"Really? Who?" Leonoa rarely has visitors this late.

"A friend." Leonoa seems about to say more but then bites back the words as we reach the doorway. "You'll see."

Inside, the painter's studio is warm and redolent of linseed oil and turpentine and freshly ground minerals with an edge of rotten egg. The space would feel ample were it not for the stacks of canvases, the shelves of paints and pigments, the paint-stained rags on the floor. Leonoa uses her sitting room more for painting than just entertaining.

I pause inside the door, taking off my cloak, then curiously scanning the room.

My first impression of the friend is gold—golden hair, a Northerner? Then my jaw slackens in amazement, bemusement as I realize the golden glow isn't hair. What is Leonoa thinking? What will her mother say? For that matter, what am I, Bella, going to say? Because surely I have to take a stand right now, here and now, or else forever keep my peace about this misalliance.

I look at Leonoa, see the tension around my cousin's eyes, the set to her jaw, and think, *She believes I'm about to make her choose, and she knows which way she'll go already.*

So instead I smile and set my discomfort aside as I turn to the woman with golden wings where her arms would have been, covered with great rose-gold feathers like a metal swan's.

As she moves forward in turn, I note additional details: the odd device that cinches her waist and chest, a chain and leather harness holding two metal and gear-work extensions—mechanical hands, five brass rods set like fingers in each one, agile enough for all but the finest work. A series of straps fit the harness to her form around her chest and belly, fine metal tendrils on each leading to the energy globe, caught in a netting of brass wire, that powers and controls the arms.

Who could be her owner? I wonder. Magic is pricey, and the arms would fetch gold, not silver, from any pawnshop, particularly if fully charged. She is an expensive ornament.

"Pleased to meet you," I say with pleasant, practiced ease learned from years of public appearances. "I'm Leonoa's cousin, Bella Kanto."

I don't stretch out my hand, a calculation made in the instant I turned. It seems to have been the right one. The other woman's Old Continent blood seems as apparent as Leonoa's or mine in her dark hair, visible against the shimmer of gold feathers and her dusky skin. Perhaps she is some impossible hybrid? I've never seen anything like her before. She inclines her head in turn.

"I'm Glyndia," she says.

Leonoa pushes past to fuss with the iron kettle nestled in the coals.

"I'll make mulled wine," she says.

"I can. You sit and visit with your cousin," Glyndia says.

The smile she gives the artist is full of affection. Tension loosens in my shoulders, although I still eye the visitor with a touch of question. Is Leonoa actually playing at friends with a Beast? A dangerous game for either of them to take up. A dangerous game just to be associated with.

I say nothing of this but sit on the couch, drink wine, and chat. Outside the wind quickens, rattling the windows impatiently before rebuking them with renewed rain. Two whale-oil lamps flicker on the mantel over the smoldering hearth, flanking an elaborate porcelain and aluminum clock.

The clock chimes as I turn. Two figurines emerge to dance around each other, just as a third thimble-sized automaton appears and circles them in turn, knife in hand rising and falling. The gruesome clock marks each hour with a different crime. Alberic bought it to amuse me, but Leonoa fell in love with it the first time she saw it chime out this murderous hour, eight o'clock. I yielded it up without protest. I found it more unsettling than amusing.

"Have you heard from your mother, Leonoa?"

"No, she's still on her trip to the Southern Isles, though I think she's back any day. That's how I met Glyndia, actually. She accompanied a friend who'd agreed to come and model for me."

"That's an interesting change for you, isn't it?"

Leonoa, ever restless, is cleaning brushes in the corner of the room. She's on her second mug of hot red wine and she moves methodically. She dips a brush into a glass then wipes it clean with a rag, leaving red streaks on the cloth. "What do you mean?" Her tone is as sharp as the turpentine's tang.

The shrug I give is as deliberate with ennui as any performance I've used to mock an opponent in the ring. "You've been painting Gladiators for the past few years. As far as I know, Glyndia moves in no Gladiator circles."

I turn towards the other women, feigning amused curiosity. "Unless you're from some new school that I haven't become acquainted with?"

Glyndia's smile is equally mask-like. "Shall we continue circling this topic or cut right to it?"

"What do you mean?" I ask, even as Leonoa says, "No, Glyn, you don't owe her any explanation." I feel a pang at the anger in my cousin's tone, but it only strengthens my sense of self-justification.

"You are thinking," Glyndia says with chilly precision, "that your cousin, whom you love and want no harm to befall, has taken up with a Beast."

"And why shouldn't I think that?"

"I am not a Beast. I'm a Human under a spell, as well-blooded as either of you."

We stare at each other.

"I see," I say. I sip my wine, which is warm and smells of cinnamon. The silence stretches out until the clock strikes the quarter hour with a chime and a twitch of the miniature knife, a blood pool irising open.

"I'd hoped to sleep here tonight rather than walk home in the rain," I say into the silence. "Is that all right, Leonoa?"

"Of course," Leonoa says. "If you don't mind me keeping you up a while. I'm finishing a couple of canvases yet for my show. You're coming, aren't you?"

"Aye, probably Adelina and I are coming together."

Leonoa sets the turpentine aside and moves a canvas onto its easel. As is her habit, she keeps the picture turned away from us. She is intensely private about her paintings up until their first exhibition.

"Shall we play cards?" Glyndia asks. I nod, pulling a small table over between us. I watch the brass hands shuffle the parchment deck and deal out the hands with deft movements. I wonder again who funded the expensive work of creating her mechanism. Surely not Leonoa?

"When are you going to let go of Adelina?" Leonoa asks. She picks up a brush, considering the picture before her, then sets it down again. From my vantage point, all I can see is the mug of wine, disappearing and reappearing.

"What do you mean?"

"Is she still in love with you? You've been keeping her dangling a very long time, Bel."

I throw down the Hanged and Shrouded Moon to take a trick. "Isn't that something best kept between Adelina and me?" I don't care to have my business discussed in front of a stranger, not that I can think of any circumstances where I would have *liked* to have my cousin pass judgment on my life.

"You're not being fair to her. You let her buy you presents—"

"No, no presents."

"Dinners, then. And tickets to plays and pedal-carts home."

Glyndia plays the Cask and takes a trick in turn. She is politely silent as though not listening to the conversation, eyes fixed on the cards.

"Adelina has plenty of money. She likes to spend it."

"And you betray that generosity, for you will never give her anything back."

The assertion rubs me even rawer. I am no betrayer. Adelina has said outright that she enjoys spending time with me. Is friendship with a Gladiator—a celebrity of Tabat after all!—worth so little?"

"I go about with her, do I not?" I say. "Adelina is pleasant company. Is one's time not the greatest gift you can give to anyone?"

"Is that what she gets from you, time? Or just odd moments left over from more significant occasions? Time you would have spent running errands, or playing court to the nobility so they'll sponsor your precious school?"

"I will not argue about this." I snap a card down. Glyndia plays a False Prophet.

Leonoa rises and pours herself more wine. On the way back, she leans on the couch's back, looking over Glyndia's shoulder. She brushes her cheek along the feathers, which gleam like yellow silk in the lantern light.

"Are you almost ready for bed then?" Glyndia says. Her wing flexes, unflexes, shifts along Leonoa's face in a caress.

"Let me put my paints away and I am."

o o o

When the other two have withdrawn to the bedchamber, I shape myself to the narrow sofa, draw the knitted blanket about my shoulders, and watch the last coals gutter.

On the mantel, two automatons set fire to a tiny hut. Red glass flames slide out from behind the clockwork arsonists. A pea-sized face, arms upraised in appeal, peeps from an upstairs window.

I cannot help but worry. Whether Glyndia is indeed Human or whether she is some sort of Beast playing a trick on the painter, either way, it is unseemly looking for someone of Leonoa's stature to take up with what is very close to a Beast in appearance, even if not in mind, which has yet to be proved.

I usually let people do as they will. It is one of my points of pride, in fact, my easygoing nature. But if there was anyone in the world I feel protective of, it is my little cousin.

I've never minded scandal. Once I wore Tabat's armor, I might even have courted it. It amuses me to be thought outrageous.

But Leonoa has suffered so many slights over the years and gone on to make art that seizes the heart and refuses to let go. She must be kept safe.

I hear a murmur—who?—sweet and drowsy, with a smiling undertone that tugs at my heart. I remember Leonoa confiding in me that as a child, she'd lie awake all night. Some frailty of her eyes made darkness impenetrable to her. So she had lain there each night in a lather of imagination, hearing a *tap-tap-tap*, the scrape and slither of the window opening, a floorboard's slow groan, a rustle of leafy robes.

My cousin's nightmares were rooted in reality. When Leonoa was very little, visiting her grandparent's summer home in their estate outside Tabat, a Mandrake broke into the nursery one night. Only a footman's vigilance, noticing the open window as he emptied slops outside, saved her.

I turn over, thumping the pillow to soften its adamant outlines. After the attack, Leonoa lay in a stupor for four and a half days, waking for an evening before lapsing into bone-stretch fever for another three.

The disease's delirious contortions permanently thwarted her spine, shortening one arm and leg, and throwing the plates of her skull awry, gnarling her like a knotgrass doll. Even after she recovered, even after the family had returned to Tabat, she lay awake, an insomniac each night, or plunged, despite her best efforts, into nightmares, shrieking the rest of the household awake.

Her parents, Leonoa told me, tried many remedies. Before he died, Coro Kanto sought apparati that applied magnetic or electrical energy, setting each muscle into feverish twitches, while Galia Kanto designed diets rich in milk or green leaves or fish or other ingredients that gave Leonoa the runs or made her stomach twist to the point of revolt. They tried poultices smelling of verdigris and brine; hot, cold, salt, and mud baths; an exorcism of the nursery; corsets of iron, leather, whalebone; chicken bone and feather charms; soporific candles; a harpist to play her to sleep each night.

But it was only when I, newly orphaned, arrived for a few days' visit while my fate was being determined that the nightmares vanished, driven away by my presence.

The household slept at night, and the visit stretched to a year, then three, four, five, and more. But at thirteen, I was confronted with my Aunt Jolietta, a frightening, gravel-voiced apparition that arrived to claim me as an apprentice, despite the recently widowed Galia's protests.

I roll onto my back and stare up at the ceiling. Dark times came after that, but I endured through the worst of them.

The clock strikes two, a *bing* and then a *bong*. I'm not sure what the figurines are doing at this time of night. Sleety rain sizzles on the wide gutter and against the windowpanes, lulling me to sleep.

o o o

In the morning, I'm dimly conscious of someone stirring, lowered voices, the noisiness of people trying their best to be stealthy. I burrow down under the knitted blanket, seeking its latticed warmth. Finally, long after one presence has left, the door slamming behind it, long after I've heard Leonoa's halting steps preparing the morning fish tea and slicing bread to toast over the freshly-kindled fire, I roll over and blink at the sunlight coming in through the window.

To my dazzled eyes, the air seems full of golden light and floating dust motes illuminated by its glare. For a moment constellations hang around me, vast sweeps of stars. Then I blink and see Leonoa grimacing at me fondly, bread knife in her hand.

"I know you prefer honey, but all I have is jam and fish-paste for the bread," Leonoa says without apology.

"What sort of jam?"

"Apple butter."

"Pah, not even truly jam. But I'll take it over fish paste."

I nurse the mug of salty tea that Leonoa hands me and stretch my shoulders. "Your friend gone already?" I ask.

"She works for a minor Merchant house," Leonoa says.

"Interesting. What does she do there?"

"She is a Clerk."

"An odd sort of Clerk. Can she fly with those wings?"

"I believe," Leonoa says dryly, "she can flutter."

A spark of humor leaps between us, but I keep my face straight. "So she could break her fall when plummeting long distances. Not a highly marketable skill."

"You never know," Leonoa says. "The Duke has commissioned a grand zeppelin, of the sort they are making up in Verranzo's New City. I am hoping to paint a mural in one of the sitting rooms."

It seems more than plausible. It's exactly the sort of thing Alberic would do. I snort.

"I am looking forward to it, actually," Leonoa says. "Imagine what it will be like to see the world from such a vista, to be able to study it!" Her eyes gleam.

"I am usually too busy keeping my food down when flying on a Beast," I admit. "Too worried that a wing might slip and that they might lose their grip on the air."

Leonoa gives me an amused glance. "The great Bella Kanto admits a weakness! I will sell it to your enemies and make hundreds!"

"Hundreds?" I protest. "Thousands, at least."

This time it is Leonoa's turn to snort. "You have always thought very highly of yourself, Bella Kanto."

"If I do not do it, who will?" I look at my cousin.

Jolietta always referred to Leonoa derisively as "the dwarf." I bit back a retort each time. My aunt was quick to discipline Beasts or apprentices who displeased her. I learned early never to contradict Jolietta. Although the lessons were easy for neither of us, Jolietta had decades of encrusted cynicism and shaping of others to her will on her side. Many of her training secrets went to her grave with her, for I won't record them, no matter how much gold or favors the Duke's chief Beast Trainers promise.

The years with Jolietta shaped me in spite of my best efforts to reject them. I would never have said it out loud, but sometimes I find myself looking at Leonoa as Jolietta would have, seeing the twisted frame and recognizing the constant, dire pain that shapes Leonoa's waking existence.

If Leonoa had been a Beast in Jolietta's care, she would have put her down without a second thought.

Chapter Seven

On the Water Lily

Teo and Ridley, who was working his way as a cabin boy, shouted in unison as they pulled in the line. With a last pull, a vast catfish landed on the deck, its gills shuttering and opening as it lay gasping on the blood-slicked wood.

Others companoned it on the deck's planking. The boys had set out lines baited with lumps of biscuit dough and caught almost two dozen of the bottom-feeders overnight.

The cook fried the slices in a pan, breaded in a way Teo had never seen before.

He asked the cook, who grunted and showed him a queasy bowl of yellow. "Eggs." He pointed at the chicken coop that rode the boat's port flank, opposite the side where the Dryads were kept.

He'd eaten birds' eggs at home, but that was a rare springtime treat. Imagine keeping birds so they would lay eggs for you! Already he was learning new things.

After breakfast, they sluiced the slimy, bloody deck with buckets of river water, and the Dryads made fussing noises as the water edged towards the railing where they were chained. There were a half-dozen of them, captured to be taken to the Duke.

Tending them was only part of Teo's duties. Life aboard the *Water Lily* held more work than he'd expected, but Eloquence, even when finding tasks for Teo to perform, made sure he was well-fed and even supplied gossip and news of Tabat. Eloquence was tall and lanky and stern but soft-spoken, where Captain Urdo was short, barrel-shaped, and full of shouts. Ridley, who had joined the ship only a week before Teo, had also become his guide and ally in this new life.

After breakfast, he scrubbed decking. The *Water Lily* had a great deal of decking and it required scrubbing with a harsh-bristled brush, river water, and soap, which left a trail of iridescent bubbles bobbing amid the icy fragments and water in the boat's wake. Eloquence sat on a stack of crates with a few feet of discarded rope, unbraiding and rebraiding it, shaping it into bracelets for a wrist smaller than his own.

"Who are those for?" Teo asked. "Do you plan on selling them?"

Many of the crew engaged in small side ventures, like buying eagle feathers or some other easily portable commodity, to be sold when they returned to the city. He and Ridley spent their own free time staring at the shore, hoping to spot a Dryad grove for the substantial Duke's bounty it would bring.

Eloquence's stare was severe. "They're for my little sisters. Blanca has some saffron and scarlet dye. I'll color them before we reach home."

"How many sisters do you have?"

"Nine," Eloquence said. "All younger. Obedience, Compassion, Silence, Absolution, Grace, Mercy, Wisdom, Honesty, and Perseverance."

"Why aren't those like the Moon Priests' names?" Teo said.

"Those not bound to the Temple are encouraged to take names of the qualities they teach us to strive for."

"That's a lot of sisters." Teo had found two—one living and one dead—more than sufficient. He wondered what it would be like to be the eldest of a pack of siblings. It might be a lot of fun to boss that many around. "Do you always bring them presents?"

"Aye," Eloquence said, twisting a braid under itself to form a neat little loop through which a matching knot could be slipped. "And half my wages for my mother, so she can pay for things like their clothing and schooling. You were asking earlier what the

Temples were like. They're like that, like having a family you're responsible to."

Teo felt dubious. What sort of family fed you mashed roots and stewed grains and never let you outside?

"There's a hierarchy and a way of doing things," Eloquence said. "You always know what you should be doing, and there's never any questions of how you should act. The Moons know, and they tell you through the Priests."

"What does your mother do?" Teo asked.

"She mourns my father." Eloquence's tone was clipped. Teo thought he might be offended, but he wasn't sure what he might have said that would prove unwelcome to the Pilot.

Eloquence tucked the bracelets away in a deep, saggy-lipped pocket of his worn blue coat, time-polished but warmer than the shawlcoat Teo wore. "The Temples are a very structured life. You'll always know what to expect and what's expected of you. I envy you that."

"I would trade with you if I could," Teo said. Perhaps Eloquence might be persuaded to look the other way, let Teo slip away into the city and circumvent his arrival at the Temples. But the Pilot only smiled.

"You'll become used to it with time," he said. "I've spoken to Priests and thought about it myself, but I have family to support. Those who live by the Temples' way come to embrace it, and gladly so."

Teo wasn't so sure of that. Still, the Pilot's conviction shook him. Maybe it wouldn't be all that bad. Maybe it could even prove a good way to acclimate to the unfamiliar life in the city. Eventually, though, he knew he'd want out of the Temples and into an existence in the city itself.

Definitely not a life within the confines of the Temples. There were so many things he could become in Tabat. His mother had been right. He loved the penny-wides and all the roles they offered up for his imagination to take on. He was still young enough to train as a Gladiator, for example. Or he might apprentice to a wealthy Merchant or Cook or Sea Captain.

"How did you become a Pilot?" he asked.

Eloquence said, "The Duke advertised for likely men and women and promised good pay, just for doing the training. He pushes at the frontiers, that one, and plenty of steamboats are an important part of that effort."

"Oh," Teo said. "It wasn't that you'd always wanted to be one?"

"I read the same accounts that you did, I expect," Eloquence said. "The early expeditions, the *Mercy* and the *Tenacity*. Flying islands and talking cactuses. Rivers of golden feathers and lakes of fire."

"Yes!" Teo exclaimed. That was exactly the sort of thing he dreamed of.

Eloquence laughed at him, but not in a mean way. "Well, there's still some to explore, to be sure, but the great wild places have all been discovered and mapped, son, with the Duke's council already planning how to divide up anything of value."

"The westernmost lands are still a mystery," Teo protested.

Eloquence waved an impatient hand. "Grass and Centaurs. No rivers, so no trade except along the coast."

"And the Northern reaches."

"Forest, forest, and more forest. A few tribes of Shifters and Beasts, but no Human wants those lands except for what they yield in trade."

Discouragement slumped Teo's shoulders. "You're saying I might as well give up these dreams and resign myself to the Temples?"

"I am saying there are worse things than letting the moons determine your life." He clapped Teo on the shoulder with a companionable hand. "Now come and get some chal. You can't enter the city until you have acquired the taste."

Teo didn't think that would happen anytime soon. The cook kept a pot of chal, Tabatian fish tea, boiling night and day and all the crew drank mug after mug of it.

Teo wasn't sure he liked the taste of fish in the first place. He knew he didn't like it mixed with black tea and bitter greens. He choked down half a mug for the sake of its warmth and went back to scrubbing.

He'd rather be sitting watching the water, but all in all, the labor wasn't too bad. It kept him warm and he could look at the landscape.

Even though the day was chilly, it blazed with sunlight, which cascaded down on snow-laden banks and trees until everything dripped, and black tree limbs glittered with water, sending it everywhere in rainbow dance. The Dryads murmured together, braiding each others' weedy hair where it grew like ivy, along the railing.

The current pulled them on, aided by the throb and splash of the boat's engine and wheel. Eloquence had gone back to the Pilot's seat and was watching the river, but it was wide and deep and not dangerous here, particularly with the ice melting away from the edges of the channel broken by boat travel. The *Lily* had been kept north too long by the ice, Ridley had confided, and most of the crew, Tabatians, were ready to be home after five months of travel, ready to spend the money from their shares in the cargo, mainly furs and northern plants.

The boat couldn't travel fast enough for them. But Teo wasn't ready for it to arrive.

o o o

Ridley woke Teo late that night. "Come on," he said. "Eloquence is sitting watch by himself. He'll tell us ghost stories if we sit with him."

When they appeared in the Pilot's house doorway, Eloquence nodded, solemn as an owl. He poured amber liquid, three shot glasses half-full, and set them on a shelf to one side. The liquid roiled sap-thick in the glass, trembling as the boat shifted.

Ridley took a glass, passed Teo his. He licked at a smear on the rim: sweet, blindingly sweet. Eloquence watched him with an amused smile.

"I suppose you have Fairy honey all the time. The pleasures of the bucolic life," he said. Teo wasn't sure what he meant, but he did know what Fairy honey was. Back home, a hive of it would be drained if found, half to be saved for the Duke's share and the other half for consumption or trade, depending on the village's finances that year.

Ridley sipped, smacked his lips, and rolled his eyes in pleasure. "Fine as I remember it."

It smelled like flowery beeswax. Its perfume cloyed in his nostrils, but he drank. Fire and sweetness filled his mouth, and seconds later he felt an odd sensation, as though his spirit had been removed from his body and placed a foot away in misalignment. Odd and disquieting, the warmth in his stomach spread like sunshine, making him calm. He took another sip.

"Carefully, carefully," Eloquence said. "That's your allotment for the night. It comes out of my share, and I've nine siblings at home with unlined pockets."

"I'm sorry," Teo said. "I could carve something for your sisters if you like. As payment."

Eloquence looked even more amused. "Perhaps it will come to such barter, now that I know you can carve," he said. "But for now we will leave it to my standing you a glass. And you telling me a ghost story I have never heard."

"No, tell us a story," Teo said, emboldened by honey glow. "Can you tell us one of the Bella Kanto tales?"

"No," Eloquence said, reaching towards a shelf. "But I will read you something else. Let us go outside where the air is sweeter, while Septa spells me a little while."

The *Water Lily's* wheel was silent. They had tied up just off an islet, anchored in a nook that sheltered them from the icy current's drag. Stars gleamed in the sky overhead, so thick they reminded Teo of the Fairy lights surrounding Grave. He wondered if the Priest was recovered yet.

Eloquence set the lantern on a crate near the Dryads and settled himself onto the planking. He opened the book, large and leather-bound, and tilted it to catch the lantern's buttery light. The boys sat down nearby.

Curiosity sparked in Teo. "That's not a penny-wide," he said, leaning forward to get a better look. The book was handwritten, with jagged and spidery script.

Eloquence looked flummoxed for the first time since Teo had first met him, but Ridley filled the gap. "Eloquence writes his own," he declared with pride.

"Really?" It had never occurred to Teo to think that a person lay behind the tales of Bella.

"Aye," Eloquence said. His cheeks were red.

"He's going to write for the penny-wides!" Ridley elaborated.

Eloquence waved a hand as though shooing the words away. "I have a meeting, once we're back in Tabat, to speak with Spinner Press."

"That's the one that prints all the Bella Kanto adventures!" Ridley leaned forward to supply more, but Eloquence gestured him to silence. "If we're going to get started, then let's do so."

Ridley settled back.

"Tales of a River Pilot," he read from the water-damp page.

Near them, a Dryad said something to another one, her tone low and bitter.

Eloquence's nose pointed through the darkness at her. "I don't have to read it here."

The Dryad kept silent.

The page rustled with a bat wing sound as Eloquence turned it. "When we begin, the boat has left Tabat and travelled three days north."

Eloquence read with a finger passing below the words, but he read as well as anyone Teo had ever heard back in the village, including Neorn. Eloquence's voice dipped and slowed, just enough that you knew this was a performance, something special, that every word was weighted.

He just wished Eloquence had been reading a Bella Kanto story rather than this one, which was slow going. It was not until river pirates entered the scene that the story got interesting.

A shiver of fear worked its way down Teo's spine, but it was delicious fear, quivering along the edges while he held the scene in his mind and while Eloquence's grave voice supplied the details, one by one, to be savored. Everything around them was silent except for the splash-song of the river and the plangent cry of an owl overhead. The Dryads were quiet, clustered near the railing, their hair grown together in a great green and brown clump, strewn with tiny amber and yellow flowers, shining in the lamplight as though determined to create the spring they would never know.

Eloquence's voice graveled with the arrival of the sorcerer in dreadful league with the pirates. Teo shivered. Sorcerers and Sorceresses might do anything. They had surrendered themselves to magic, so their slightest whims and impulses might become real.

That was only one of the things that made them so dangerous. All of the magic of the Colleges of Mages in Tabat and Verranzo's New City were devoted to discovering Sorcerers (and Shifters) and keeping them from taking over the New Continent, lest they destroy it as they had the Old Continent, which was nothing now but fiefdoms of ash and magic detritus.

But in the end both sorcerer and pirates were eluded. Teo thought it would have been more interesting if there had actually been some fighting, rather than just sailing.

Eloquence turned to the next story.

"No, no," Ridley said. "Tell us about Tabat."

"Ah, Tabat," Eloquence said. "What should I tell you? It's a wonderful city. It sits on the southern coast, fifteen terraces leading down to the water where the harbor lies. The rocks to the west form a range that twists around to protect the harbor, and you can see the Duke's castle at the highest point, with flags flying blue and gold."

"Fifteen terraces? How do people get up and down them?" Teo asked.

"Stairways, and plenty of them, and the water lifts. Or if you don't mind paying, the tram line. There's three ..."

"What's a tram?" Teo interrupted. "It sounds like a kind of basket."

"And in a way it is, for great metal baskets full of people slide up and down the wires. It costs a copper skiff. I'll give you each a coin to ride the center one, the Great Tram, which runs along the Heart Garden."

He paused and glanced out the window.

"What are you looking for?"

"River pirates, like in the story," Ridley answered before Eloquence could. "They lurk in the bends, though, and we're in a straight stretch right now. Isn't that so, Eloquence?"

"Aye, but it never hurts to be careful," the Pilot said. "What I heard, though, was the Captain's door. You boys best skedaddle before he comes patrolling." He closed his book and rose.

Urdo's footsteps came up the stairs as Teo and Ridley ducked behind the crate. The footsteps paused, presumably to survey the silent Dryads, then continued on to the Pilot's house, where Eloquence already sat.

That night dreams of the river pirates haunted Teo. He woke, imagining every shudder of the boat was a pirate climbing aboard, knife clenched between his or her teeth.

Gradually his heart stilled. He lay back to dream of Tabat, and watching Bella Kanto fight.

Chapter Eight

Judgments

Sheets woven of silk from the Rose Kingdom cover Alberic's bed, but my bed at home is the most wonderful place to be.

Ice glazes my window, takes the sunlight pouring through it and makes it into glowing lace, while the shadow of a Fairy outside flits past. I wake fast—I always do. But then I linger.

The sheets, thinly-woven cotton from the Southern Isles, cover a thick swan-down mattress, and are matched by an equally feathery comforter. The chimney leading up from the kitchen fire, lit earliest of any household fire, puts off a wash of drowsy heat from where it runs behind the bed. The air practically undulates with the heady smell put forth from the bouquet set on the low table near the window: Winter roses and hothouse-forced jonquils and tuberose.

Marta had placed a standing order. It amuses me to see how long it will take the Merchant to remember she's done so. I suspect she has those bills sent quarterly, for she's had plenty of time to cancel it.

A tap on the door. "Be wanting your breakfast, Miss Bella?"

"Aye," I call. I slide from between the sheets and go to the door.

It opens to reveal a laden tray in the hands of the landlady. Abernia Freeholder runs one of the most select boarding houses in the city, but few of her customers can boast that she personally brings them breakfast in the morning. Abernia's happy, not just for the steady flow of coin to her pocket, but to have associated glamour for the house in the form of a famous Gladiator as tenant.

Abernia sets the tray down and moves back to the door. "Your cousin sent a messenger, saying as you might want to join her for lunch."

"Excellent, lunch." Will there be another lecture about Adelina? It's getting tiresome. Perhaps my taking a new lover will dissuade Leonoa. I certainly can't go back to Marta. I burned that bridge far too thoroughly. I'll have to find some new ardor.

The set of crystal and silver armor sitting against the wall regards me as I dress after eating. It's waiting for the fight. Then it will be time to put it away for another year.

I splash my face with water and slip two good luck charms around my neck. This close to the Games, I can't be too careful.

My home does not smell of linseed oil and turpentine, but rather of domestic comfort: linens and lemon oil and the candles Abernia burns to keep down the smell of Scholar Reinart's dog Cavall, which she used to burn up here, when Gelerta was still alive.

I picked this house for its quiet. I could afford a household of my own, but that is tedious, all that arranging of things, so why bother? Abernia sees all my needs are met and houses me well in her third floor rooms with their wide windows overlooking her high-walled little garden letting out onto the Canal.

Here on the Fourth Terrace of the city, we are far from the factory noise of the Slumpers and close to shops and the largest of the tram lines, the first one built: the Great Tram itself. The shadows of its lines cut across the garden's snow in blue slashes.

The garden keeps me entertained, though Abernia doesn't approve. Two years ago, I kept her from calling a Pestcatcher when the Fairies first nested in the evergreen outside my window. I knew they were lesser Fairies that wouldn't group more than half a dozen, and no danger to anyone. Not like their feral kindred in the wilderness who produce great stinging hives that kill unwary travelers or those who come in search of Fairy honey.

I've trained these with sugar lumps and bits of table meat. When I lean out into the cold morning air outside the window, they fly around me, darting in to take candies from my fingertips. They chatter like parrots, too high-pitched for most to pick out words.

Where another might have named them, I've listened long enough to know the names they have for themselves: Dust and Yellowhair, and their offspring, Finch and Flutter and Wall. They shelter in the evergreen and build nests of scraps of paper and rags. In this cold, they wrap bits of cloth around themselves in mimicry of clothing.

They like candy the best, but meat second to that, the fresher and bloodier the better. They scorn vegetables or breads, though they will take fruit when it is at its ripest, just before it spoils.

They trust me.

Yellowhair lights on my fingertip, and I can see her body, the wings like bits of glass or candyfloss, the limbs so fine and spindly. So perfect. Her wings flicker, keeping her balanced, moving so fast that you can't see them, only their shadow in the air.

She eyes the line of mirrors lining the sill, set vertically along it to repel ghosts. Fairies have a love-hate relationship with mirrors. I've seen them scold them and try to feed them more than once.

Abernia hates the Fairies, but I pay her enough to overlook my eccentricities and to ignore the demands of the estate a few houses down, whose garden the Fairies raid each summer.

I've assured her I won't let them in the room. I've only broken that promise once or twice, when it was truly cold.

The Fairy clings to my hand, watching me.

What do they think of me? I have tamed them as surely as Jolietta ever tamed any Beast, but I used different methods, bribes and caresses. I turned on her in the end; would these Fairies turn on me if they thought it would gain them more candies?

I would like to think not, but Beasts are ever true to their natures. Humans too, perhaps.

o o o

Lucya tells me the new student, Skye, was the best in her class, that Dina was grooming her to face me eventually. But she hasn't had the advantage of my training. Over half of those who've faced me in the arena have been to this school and were trained to my standards. Sometimes the other schools do produce prodigies, but I suspect it's natural talent shining through, not any of their teaching. That's the only time I've faced men standing for Spring, when another school has produced such a contender, and Lucya counts each time a loss for the Brides of Steel.

I test the new students one by one. The first two, the ones Lucya has taken because they'll swell her money chest, are unremarkable. Like most new students, meeting me leaves them nearly speechless, staring down at their hands as though afraid my gaze will turn them to stone.

Not so Skye. She's dark-skinned, old Continent blood, and holds herself with the arrogance of the well-to-do. Her eyes are jet-black, set round with lashes so thick they'd make a poet weep. She's tall, with the angularity of her age, slightly taller than me, but I'm used to that. She meets my gaze with a hint of challenge, a hint of something else too, and steps into the ring with training sword up, ready to meet me.

I test her methodically. She's fast and strong, but she doesn't know many of the counters for my moves.

She's pretty as she dodges. Graceful.

I ignore that, leave her a few bruises as I feint, and easily avoid her counters. She's breathing hard by the time we're done. That's not good. She'll have to work to build up endurance, do the exercises I lead the best students in, build her reserves of strength if she thinks (as all of them do) that she'll meet me in reality one day.

I smile as I step out of the ring. A mistake. She grins at me as though we were equals, puffs up her chest, knowing that she's done better than the other two.

I make my tone severe as I say, "Adequate." That takes the wind out of her sails, and lets her know she's been presumptuous. I see her droop and an unexpected pang touches me. Still, I keep my face stern. It does no good to coddle them.

Later she catches up with me in a corridor, comes running up fast and desperate enough that she almost bumps into me. She skids to a halt as I pause, looking at her.

The words rush out of her. "I just want you to know it means a lot to me that you're my instructor. I've read all the penny-wides about you. You're why I wanted to become a Gladiator."

I nod. She waits as though expecting me to say something back to her, but adulation bores me. I've seen this look in the eyes of students before, many times.

She says, "I will work very hard in order to catch up. I've studied hard, but I know that the students at the Brides of Steel are the best. That's why I wanted to come here."

I nod again.

Color rises to her cheeks as she stands looking at me.

I say, "I will come by at dawn. You'll go with the group I am training."

Now that is what she was waiting for. Her eyes sparkle, her lips purse in delight, and she throws her shoulders back, standing a little taller, a little straighter.

I nod again and go about my way without saying anything more.

I don't tell her that she's the best I've ever seen. I don't tell her what enormous potential I glimpse within her. Such talk only makes them overconfident.

I wander the school, pretending to myself that I am noting items that need taking care of, but truth be told, Lucya is far more efficient than I.

Even in her hobbies. She grows a few plants to supplement the kitchen as well; starts them indoors each year and brings them outside only when it's warm enough. While they are growing, she sweeps her hand back and forth among them, bending the stems but not breaking them. This makes them tougher, makes them used to the blows that they'll experience later from wind and rain.

That's my philosophy with students as well. Bend them, but do not break them.

Sometimes you need to find out how far they can bend first.

o o o

I never know what mood Alberic will be in. Sometimes he's imperious, sometimes wanting to be dictated to.

Today he receives me in the menagerie, where he's examining new acquisitions, a medley of Dryads. He's been trying to breed them lately.

He's explained it to me. A forward-looking man, he knows someday the forests will stop yielding the Dryad logs that fuel the city. Even now they're scarcer by far than a few decades ago when the College of Mages first learned the secret of using them to fuel the Great Tram and the engines here beneath Alberic's castle.

A sullen and unpromising lot, these five Dryads. Hair gone straw brittle with travel's rigors, their skin stretched over their bones till you can see the shape beneath it.

Chained while in his presence, the custom ever since one tried to strangle the Duke three years back. They're stronger than they look.

He sits on a carved wooden chair looking them over. Sometimes he chooses a Beast for his bedchamber, but he won't pick one of these. They're too miserable looking, lacking the spark of defiance he likes. He beckons me over. I disengage from the cluster of servants and advisors and go to his side.

"You have a good eye for these things, my dear. Which shall I take?"

I don't want to play this game. Offer them a slow fatal existence in the menagerie or a quick death that at least doesn't force them to endure his experiments?

I shrug and smile. He's not a kind man, he never has been. He flicks his hand, irritated by my refusal, and I come closer to pronounce my judgment.

He gestures. A Dryad is dragged to kneel at his feet so he can look her over. He leans down to run his hand along her shoulder, testing the texture of her skin.

I'd thought he'd wanted some bed-play from me, but it seems that today is just about making me dance to his tune. He's been doing that increasingly this year, and I know why. The elections are still coming, much as he would like to pretend that they're not. He's caught by the decision his ancestors made when Tabat was first founded. Easy enough for them to promise a descendent would step down when the time came. Now he's living with that promise, and it eats at him more and more every day.

He's always been a pretty man, but anger's eroding that from the inside.

I don't like standing here. It's too much like being back under Jolietta's tutelage, under her rule, being forced to help her train her Beasts. I entertain myself with thoughts of Skye, of how she danced sideways when we sparred. A good move, and one I might have used myself, that crab-step and feint combined. I told Lucya I'd take Skye as one of the special students. She was unsurprised. She likes to think she can predict what I will do.

No sign of this as I examine the Dryads. If I don't approve them, though, Alberic will send them to the furnaces and use the magic of their burning flesh and wood to fuel the city. This is part of the magic that keeps Tabat alive. For the last twenty years, ever since the College of Mages discovered the process that releases Dryad magic, Alberic has sent expeditions out to harvest them. He keeps a few in his menagerie, for entertainment and for the sake of his collection's completion, and if—or rather when—they dissatisfy him, to the furnaces they go. I hold their lives in my hands.

It's not a feeling I like.

"Which?" he says again. I point at random.

"That one." I don't look at her or at any of them. I feel as miserable as I did with Jolietta when she winnowed her stables.

Alberic points at her as well. She goes in one direction; her fellows are dragged in another. I don't think about their fates. I don't want to know.

I don't even know if I've done her a favor.

"Come and see the menagerie. The Dragon gets cranky when you do not come speak to it often enough. And I have some new Beasts, kinds you may never have seen before."

I doubt that somewhat. During my time with Jolietta, Beasts flowed through the estate. Some she nursed, others she trained, and others she bought to study. I say, "I need to get back to the school. I have students there waiting to be trained."

Alberic laughs. "You don't fool me," he says. "I have never known anyone who liked Beasts as little as you do. You never want to come and see the menagerie."

I don't explain to him that I actually like Beasts, that they prove better company, sometimes, than Humans. But I do not like the menagerie, do not like seeing the Beasts in their cages, their enclosures. They should be free, I think, even though such thoughts mark me as an abolitionist. But I can't preach sedition, for I'm a public figure and have responsibilities.

I remember a Beast, a Unicorn. Jolietta used me to catch it. I remember the weight of its head in my lap, the coarse shine of its mane, the way its flower-pupilled eyes looked at me, and the smell of lilies and vanilla that seeped from its fur. They are rare, Unicorns. Jolietta knew she could get a pretty price for this one.

They caught it with ropes and nets. I scrambled away trying to avoid its thrashing. They dragged it into the stable and locked it in a stall.

The next morning, I went down to see it even though Jolietta had forbidden me to do so; she had said I would disturb its training. I opened the stall door, thinking that I would give it a handful of sugar that I had filched from the kitchen.

Everything smelled of blood and shit. It had battered itself to death against the stable wall trying to break out of its prison. It lay on the floor amid the dirty straw, and its white fur, that had shone in the sunshine the day before, was matted and discolored with its drying blood.

"They don't take well to captivity," Jolietta said. And then she beat one of the Minotaurs, blaming it for what had happened, saying that it should have secured the Unicorn better. It was an unfair accusation, as most of her accusations were, but I did not speak in the Minotaur's defense. I didn't want to draw her ire upon myself, for she was in a fine fury that day knowing that she'd lost a good sum.

She ordered it butchered and made the most of it, selling the hooves and certain internal organs to the College of Mages. She had it skinned and hung the shining hide and horn on her bedroom wall.

These are the thoughts that haunt me whenever Alberic forces me to walk within his menagerie. I can never tell him so, for he does not take being thwarted well. He would take criticism of the menagerie as a personal offense. Every Duke leaves their own mark on the city, like the 99 statues along Salt Way, commissioned by another Duke long ago. The menagerie is Alberic's.

A petty legacy for a last Duke.

"I don't like the menagerie," I say. "It makes me sneeze almost as much as spring."

Alberic looks amused. "Say that too loudly and they will begin making up tales that Tabat has languished in the grip of Winter all this time to ward off your hay fever."

"Hardly that."

"Why then? Why do you love playing Winter so?"

Why indeed? I keep silent, thinking. Is it the chill and silence of Winter, the touch of ice preserving whatever it grasped, perfect and unchanging?

Or something else?

Years and years before the death of the Unicorn, while still at Leonoa's parents' house, Winter came back unexpectedly—a sudden storm late in the Spring, as though to make one last threat, pitch one last tantrum. I rose in the morning to find the world sugar-glazed, painfully brilliant in the early morning sunlight.

At that age, I was always hungry, but it had been before the days with Jolietta. Hunger was still a half-stranger, a tease, a flirtation, not a weapon that could be used against me with measuring-spoon precision, not a cudgel that could be used to drive anyone, anything to their knees. So I hadn't worried about breakfast that day and had gone out in robe and slippers to walk in the rose garden that had been Coro Canto's pride and joy.

All of the roses were encased in ice, better preserved than in any museum case. On the outskirts of the garden's circle were great crimson roses like wounds in the air, further in were white roses like chalk and ivory and eggshells, and in the heart of the little garden were the sunshine and citrus colors that Coro's son, long-dead Cosmo, had loved, roses shaded candy yellow and orange, bright as toys.

The ice cased up each rose's fragrance, bottled it in crystal, hid it away with jealous closeness.

Yesterday when I had walked through the garden, the sweet perfume of each rose had bludgeoned me in turn, cloying as old sorrow, sweet as muscavado sugar from the Southern Isles.

Now, without the fragrances to distract me, I looked more closely at the flowers. A poet would have come up with a thousand ways to describe them, the tousle-headed blooms saved from their downward swoon, and upright, chaste buds who would never open their cores to the sunlight and now stood undrooping, filled with virtue and wasted potential.

Standing in the midst of the ice and silence, I tried to free a great red rose, shagged with petals like a lion's mane, big as both of my fists laid together. I wrestled with its thick stalk, bending the stem back and forth, abrading it until it could be pulled apart. A thorn ran into my thumb, leaving a dark splinter in the soft pad. I swore—a schoolgirl's oath that twitches me into a smile now—and picked it out.

I felt for a moment as though I was in a fairy tale. As though everything around me had come into focus, sharpened, become more significant. I held my breath. What was about to burst upon me? What figure would appear, the sky splintering around it? What would the Gods manifest in order to guide me all my days?

I waited, but nothing happened.

A bird fluttered in the tree dislodging clumps of snow. Scuffs of horsetail clouds marked the high blue sky. The shadows of trees laddered the gravel paths. Frozen dew had made glittering lace of the spider webs stretching between bushes.

I wanted something to speak to, wanted—well, I've never found it, not then and not later as a Gladiator. I was told, before I ever set foot on the arena's tiles, that I would be taken over, would become the very presence of some God or Goddess on earth. My actions would show what was happening in the Spiritual Realm.

The wonder of it all was that such flabberjabber still worked, even when I don't believe a word of it. For a long time, Winter seemed more sacred still to me, and somehow retained a vestige of that sensation, no matter how desperate the disappointment that had followed.

I had thought, in the cold, with the taste of my blood on my lips, *I am the instrument. Play me, play ME!* I flung my spirit out into the aether in acquiescence to the universe's wishes, seeking, grasping, falling.

And I found nothing waiting there to catch me.

And now? Winter reflects the emptiness of things, I think, and that is why I like it. Winter makes no empty promises of pleasant existence. It is bare, cold life with no other claims. It is the Gods' reminder to us that life is hard, that it can always be harder.

But I do not say this in answer, but instead shrug and let Alberic take my arm and tuck it through his own, taking me to the menagerie as though he hasn't heard my protest.

○ ○ ○

When I can, I slip away from Alberic and make my way out through the kitchens.

There are those who refuse to eat the flesh of any creature that displays the power of speech. They will not share a household feast of the kind that occurs whenever an Oracular Pig dies, for example, refusing to partake of the meat that most folks believe will give them luck.

This is not a common attitude in Tabat, though. There are those who make their living off the flesh of Beasts, even a few slaughterhouses devoted to the techniques needed for a creature well aware of the impending fate when going to the butcher.

At Piper Hill, no body ever went to waste. No body. Nobody.

But even with those memories, I have never abstained from such flesh. It is the way of the world, to feed on or to be fed upon. Even so, venturing into the kitchens that serve the Castle and Alberic's court, I feel a twinge when I see the great standing roast that once was a Dragon's rib cage and the flesh clothing it.

I tell myself it's because it's such a waste. Dragons are rare and are harder to capture than almost any other Beast I know. They do not live well in captivity. That glistening meat covered with a slick red sauce redolent of garlic and honey and turmeric cost more than the entire year's tuition for a student at the Brides of Steel, and the school is not known for its cheapness.

I do not believe, as some do, that eating a Beast's flesh bestows its powers on the consumers. Pig flesh does not make one's luck wax, no matter whether it comes from a speaking swine or its more silent kindred. Dragon's flesh possesses no innate virtue, and it is tough as a leather strap and gamey to boot. Only its rarity and price give it savor.

The kitchens bustle around me as I pass through. One assistant cook crouches over a tray of tarts, frosting them with blue and yellow icing, her fellow beside her peeling potatoes, the long brown curls falling into a basket that I know is destined for the Duke's menagerie. Like Jolietta, Alberic is ever one to save coin where he can. I rarely used to visit this place, but more recently I've found it a useful way to escape the castle without being intercepted by any servant Alberic might have dispatched to fetch me back to whatever conversation I have fled. Now I am avoiding speaking to him further of the Dryads. I have no way to save them, but increasingly I am loath to stand by and watch.

The servants here are too busy to pay me much mind other than an eye roll as I pass, a murmur or a whisper. That's nothing new, that's something I encounter every day on the streets of Tabat. More recently, the whispers have been hostile at times, so I almost expect it here in the kitchens, but they are more civilized, perhaps. Or at least more aware that I could have them turned out for some insult.

No one dares say anything when I slip a napkin-wrapped tart into my pocket or take one of the golden fruits sitting on the table waiting to be peeled as well. These plump orbs, furry-skinned and sweet, are called sun fruit in the Southern Isles, which is the only place that they will grow. They come to Tabat on the ships that go back and forth to serve the Duke's pleasure, the fleet of fat-bellied trade galleons that supply those here with spices and sugar and, sometimes, Oracular Turtles.

Why only Turtles and Pigs might be capable of glimpsing the future, I do not know. A Mage lover tried to explain it to me once, but the conversation got lost in talk of the stars, tiny animals, and waves of energy until I stopped him with kisses because he was boring me. I make no claim to understand anything of these matters.

The only things that really concern me are those that concern the safety of the city—the city I protect and guard. Some people claim this makes me shallow. I prefer to think it rather that I have a narrow focus.

Chapter Nine

Teo Escapes

Fireworks slapped bright fingers across the night sky above the *Water Lily* as it arrived at the city's northern river docks. Three quick booms startled Teo. Each time he flinched, a whistling scream and explosion of brilliant color followed: silver, red, purple. *Was this what life in a city was like?* he wondered. *Fireworks every night?* He'd read descriptions of them in the penny-wides but these were bigger, brighter, and better than anything he'd imagined.

Sparks glittered down across the water in which the terraces of Tabat were mirrored. The reflections wavered, jagged stairs leading away from the belt where the two worlds, real and reflected, collided.

Teo stepped back from the steamboat's railing, dazzled by the noisy splashes of light, then recovered himself. Overhead, sparkles continued to sink from the sky, leaving chrysanthemumed smoke trails lit by each new splash of light.

He looked around, embarrassed by his reaction, but the others on the boat also gawped upwards. They had more important, more interesting things to watch than his awkward moments. He felt more insignificant than ever. It was more likely that city life would be like *that*, the depressing knowledge of his insignificance. He felt small and lonely.

But it was hard to feel miserable with fireworks lighting the sky. Another distant boom shook the deck underneath his feet. Teo leaned over the railing, feeling its cold line against his belly. Slowly happiness overtook him and he grinned until his jaws ached, shivering. A new world was opening up, bigger than anything he'd ever have seen back home. Though he shouldn't think of it as home anymore—just the place he'd left behind. He was as unmarked as fresh ice now, historyless. Unfailed. He *would* be happy here, he'd make it so.

Despite the wind's bite and a shout from Ridley reminding him that there was still luggage to unload, he stood there, watching the dusk-shrouded shore approach. He had arrived—what could he expect next?

The day had been a weary blur for Teo. Captain Urdo had pushed the *Lily's* crew hard in order to arrive by nightfall. Teo's wrists and arms and the long muscles on the back of his legs ached from rearranging cargo, carrying luggage, clearing the back deck and the litter accumulated there. Fresh sunburn rode the back of his neck. Unlike the early, leisurely days of travels, there had been no time to sit and rest in the shade.

Upriver, they had passed through sharply crevassed valleys. The wrinkled mountain folds filled with pines and cedars that reminded Teo of the land surrounding Marten's Ferry. Snow draped the branches and sheets of ice edged the banks where the water was stiller.

The river's zigzag course had brought the steamboat through the mountains, then between white cliffs pocked with the mouths of mines. Teo remembered thinking that they would never arrive, only to hear a shout go up from the front of the boat as, between the shout's beginning and end, they shuddered free of the rock's embrace and glided onto a flat, broad stretch of river surrounded by snowy plains that sloped down towards the dim line of the rocky tumble marking the city.

Ridley shouted at him again. He scurried to stack suitcases for a passenger: the Advocate, who had boarded at the last stop and said he had to get to the Ducal Offices as soon as possible once the steamboat had landed. Teo ran back and forth, gathering up the Advocate's belongings.

As he stacked them beside the railing, Teo let out a sigh. He had not minded life on the boat at all, but always at the back of his mind this had worried at him, an insistent tug like testing the edges of a scab: What would happen next? He had tried to avoid looking at it. He jittered where he stood, knowing he should fetch the next brass-bound trunk, but he was consumed by his own worries, approaching as insistently as the shore.

He certainly knew what was expected of him. To let Eloquence hurry to the Temples of the Moons and turn him over as a new acolyte. He didn't want to go to the Temples. He didn't want a life of piety and drudgework, no matter what promises his parents had made on his behalf.

The *Lily* rode low in the icy river, its hold stuffed with furs and salted fish, northern goods brought from small hamlets in the wilds, like Teo himself. He could see workers on the dock and wagons awaiting their cargo. Everyone was busy, everyone was bustling about, even Captain Urdo, who was hurrying up from below decks with a sheaf of papers, the quartermaster in tow behind him.

Finally the Advocate was readied and the other luggage had been stacked near the gangway. Teo returned to the boat's side to watch the fireworks. He rubbed his palms over the railing's cool brass, so recently polished, oblivious to the smears he left.

The white moon, Selene, had gleamed full and fish-belly white on the icy banks when he'd first stepped on board the steamboat. Now it sailed above him while the rockets reached ineffectually for it. Toj, the tiny purple moon that changed full to thin and back again every few days, trailed in its wake like a bull-pup chasing its mother. Hijae was a thin, blood-colored crescent.

By the time the *Water Lily* approached the pier, Captain Urdo watching as the Pilot maneuvered the ship into its berth, the sun had vanished below the horizon. Clouds hid Selene and Toj. The solitary red moon left bloody snakes in the dark water, as though the boat had been wounded, its life seeping outward to be swallowed by the river's darkness.

The ship jolted into place. The railing trembled beneath his fingers. Teo gripped the brass, more to feel its solidity, so unlike his stomach's lurch, than for balance's sake. The *Lily* was one of the last few boats still alight, not dark and sleeping. Here and there on the land, though, he could see people moving along the muddy, half-frozen street. The river looped here, avoiding the walled city and splitting into waterfalls that set the city's northern boundary.

Cannons boomed in the distance as Urdo stepped up beside him. Teo braced himself, ready to be scolded back to work, but the Captain seemed willing to overlook his idleness now that they had arrived. Maybe the fireworks marked some event that had pardoned Teo of responsibility.

"Is it a celebration?" he asked.

Urdo snorted. "The Duke wouldn't waste the money. Politics, boy." He'd trimmed his hair and beard sometime that day, Teo noted. Pink skin shone next to the weathered, tanned spots that had been exposed to the river wind and weather.

"Politics?"

Teo hadn't dared speak to the Captain since being placed in the boat's charge. He was too aware of the Captain's grandeur and his own skinniness, his ears that protruded like jug handles waiting to be grabbed, the intimation of fuzz on his face. His blonde hair bristled wildly, no matter how much he tried to slick it down with water or oil.

Now, though, excited curiosity filled him, squirted out of him in the single word.

"Tabat's rounding up on its three hundredth year," Urdo said. A pair of rockets spoke and flashed again, setting his hawk-nosed features in relief. He was Old Continent blood, his skin darker than Teo's even at the end of a long, bright summer. "One of the Duke's ancestors promised it would become a democracy before that happened. And so it is, and all the city's alight with fireworks and frenzies and candidates juggling for their positions in the race. You've arrived just in time, boy, to find a city full of changes."

"I don't want it to change," Teo said. "I just got here!" The vehemence in his tone surprised him. Exactly when along the long trip had his excitement built to this point, taken fire without him noticing?

Three rockets arched in parallel over the ocean before bursting into showers of indigo and gold sparks.

Urdo laughed. "You've arrived well," he said. "All three moons in the sky." He pointed eastward, where the triumvirate gleamed above a bank of clouds. "They say finishing a journey under three moons is good luck, and under one is sorrow."

"What about two?"

"Then your luck is nothing out of the ordinary."

Teo's hand strayed to the coinless thong around his neck. Eloquence held his coin, entrusted to him by Grave. He'd refused to let Teo have it. If he went to the Temples, they'd give it back to him.

What if they blamed Grave's accident and absence on him? He couldn't be blamed for the Fairy bite, though. He'd done his best and saved the Priest's life.

He licked wind-bitten lips, feeling a chill run its fingers along his spine. Time was running out. He had to get away before the Temples swallowed him.

"What moon are you?" Urdo asked.

"Toj."

"Toj the Trickster." Urdo nodded, but said nothing more. He turned as Ridley approached. "Did you rouse the Dock Keeper?"

"Aye," Ridley said. "He's bringing his crew round."

"Very well."

Ridley squeezed in beside Teo and the angle where the railing shaped itself to the boat's contours. He half hung over the rail, his eyes excitement-wide.

"I never seen buildings like that before," he said, staring at the street. "Look how high they are! That one's got three stories! Must be building with bricks. And smell that, do you? Eloquence says it's from the factories on the northern side of the city, the Slumpers, where they make all the tiles."

"Why do they call them the Slumpers?" Teo asked.

"Dunno. Townfolk, go figure. Look, there they are." Ridley pointed towards the street as a bulky form obscured a distant window's light. "Bet you didn't see Beasts like that back home, Teo."

Teo squinted through the darkness. "What are those?"

"Minotaurs," Urdo said. "Dock labor needs heavy lifting, and those Beasts have stronger backs than most. You'll find Tabat full of Beasts, Teo. Minotaurs, Mermaids, Piskies—anything you can imagine. But you'll need to remember that here the divisions are stricter. It's not like your village, where Beasts might get treated as though they were regular people. Country ways are looser. Here, people won't think much of you if you act as though Beasts and Humans are the same."

Ridley said, "There's Abolitionists in Tabat, aren't there?"

"Abolitionists?" Teo asked even as Urdo said, "It doesn't do to get mixed in with that sort. Claiming that Beasts should be on the same standing as Humans. Fools and criminals, that's all they are. I pity the man or Beast who gets tangled in their foolishness and lies. Stay away from such folk."

He gave Teo a warning look. Teo blushed, staring down at his toes before glancing towards the dock.

Three great Minotaurs paced in the wake of their Keeper, pulling an empty wagon. When they stopped they unbuckled their harnesses in a laborious, thick-fingered process.

The impatient Dock Keeper prodded them into place, and the Beasts, several heads higher than any of the sailors around them, began passing the crates and barrels to the pier and onto a waiting wagon.

Teo watched, fascinated. They were as ponderous as ancient oaks. Ripples of muscle moved as they shifted the cargo, crawled beneath their skin like furrows of earth following a plow's line.

As the darkness thickened, two streetlights sprang to life beside the dock. The brilliant white light made Teo gasp as it showed the network of scars across the nearest Minotaur's back, silvery weals and keloids that gave the dark skin an irregular, almost corrugated appearance. Past the lights Teo glimpsed a lean, middle-aged man in a bright blue coat leading a cart with what Teo thought must be a Gryphon harnessed to it.

Urdo laughed as Teo jumped. "Welcome to civilization, boy! The Duke developed those lights with the College of Mages. By the end of the year, they'll be throughout the major parts of the city."

"How are they fueled?"

The Gryphon was bigger than any ox back home. Its beak, as large as his head, reminded him suddenly of the eagles that nested at home in the tall pines, but he put the thought away. He was here in Tabat now, in a new place, one that would be different from his village. A place where he could be more than he could ever hope to be back home.

Urdo tapped his nose. "Magic." He returned the Gryphon driver's wave before turning to Teo. "Anyhow, you can't stay here tonight, boy. Go find Eloquence. He'll see you're taken to your Temple."

"What?" Teo said with a rush of panic. "Why can't I just sleep in my berth again? I thought he'd take me to them in the morning, so I'd have time to explore the city."

Urdo shrugged. "He said to tell you to come find him."

Ridley touched his shoulder as the Captain headed towards the gangplank to speak to the Dock Keeper. Teo stared at the water under the pier, where spangles of light danced like false coins. His spirits felt sodden and sorrowful. "I thought I'd have more time."

"You still do," Ridley said. "You have to—remember, Eloquence gave you a skiff to ride the Tram!"

"How can I do that? Once I enter Toj's Temple, they won't let me out till I'm done with my acolyte period!"

"Look," said Ridley. "Maybe he'll let you meet him in the morning. You can rough it on the streets for a night. You deserve a chance to see things before you go into the Temples, eh? Not like you were the one who promised yourself."

Teo nodded uncertainly. Grave had healed Elya in exchange for the promise of Teo. If he reneged, would his sister relapse? Or was it all just an excuse to remove his failure from the village? Doubt crawled in his heart.

But he didn't need to go to the Temples right away, did he? The moons wouldn't betray him if he played truant just long enough to learn the city and see its sights.

Eloquence hustled him down the gangplank. Teo found himself on Tabat's river dock with the other passengers taken on over the course of the journey—two Merchants who dealt in pine gum and fine papers, the traveling Advocate and her clerk, an elderly man who wore a grimy top hat and refused to speak his business to anyone, and the sailors, along with the cook. The Advocate, trailed by her clerk, left quickly as soon as they stepped on land. The rest of them milled around, collecting luggage, saying goodbyes, and settling up accounts. Teo wavered, unsure which way to go, then fell into the majority's wake.

The dock shook as they passed along it, onto the street and under the two great aetheric lights, suspended seven feet in the air atop iron poles. Others joined the throng as they moved along. Eloquence took hold of his arm in a firm, but not unkind, grip. "I'm going to see if the Mage will take you to the Temples."

"The Mage?" Teo said, panicked. He'd never seen a Mage before.

"Don't be a fool, boy, he won't turn you into a marsh-fly."

As they approached the wagon, his eyes met the gaze of one of the Dryads. She was a captive like himself, just as miserable, just as trapped. All through the long journey, the Dryads had been chained to the railing, their long hair growing down along it. Teo and Ridley had cleared it more than once, harvesting the lengths and stuffing them in burlap bags, to be sold in Tabat as well.

She was as thin as a sapling, and her skin was patchy where the sun had beleaguered it. But her face, narrow as a rock cleft, still held defiance.

They locked stares. Both of them trapped, both of them far from home.

Something sparked in her eyes. As Eloquence released Teo's arm and stepped forward to speak to the Mage, she launched herself at the man from behind, locking her wiry legs around his throat while she clawed at his face with twiggy hands, raising runnels bright with blood. She rode his shoulders like a bucking horse and the Gryphon pulling the cart shrieked, a piercing note of protest, and raised an immense claw as though to pluck her away.

The man screamed as the Dryad looked at Teo one last time.

Run, her look said.

Teo ran.

○ ○ ○

Despite the shouts behind him, no one chased him down the alley. For a second he thought it dead-ended, and then he caught a glimmer of light from a side passage. He dashed through a warren of alleys behind the large buildings, finally emerging in another square. He was still in the city's outer confines.

Caught in the middle of the press, Teo stared down at the confusion of shadows underfoot. Where should he go now? How quickly would the Priests learn that he'd arrived? How would they track him down in such a vast, well-populated place?

He could go anywhere from there, he thought. He could go anywhere in the city. The thought seized him. He could go anywhere. Become anything. All he had to do was learn to fit in.

His heart stuttered in the hollow of his throat. Bodies jostled him this way and that. He moved with the crowd. Most travelers here were on foot, but a flock of pedal-cabs raced past, each triangular vehicle holding the driver and a passenger or two. It took nimbleness and agility to stay out of their way.

Steam-wagons clanked by as well, boxy metal constructions with wheels as high as he was tall. Jets of harshly scented hot mist shot out around the massive metal wheels. Familiar looking fur bales rolled by: pine marten furs striped black and white stacked beside silky beaver pelts—the cargo from the *Water Lily*.

He needed to get further away, away from any place he might encounter the others from the ship. A wash of fear struck him. He'd angered a Mage. Who knew what the man would do in pursuit of him?

Up ahead, guards were stopping travelers and checking them. As he approached, he expected to be grabbed and inspected. The guards had more important fish to fry than a skinny northern boy, though. Three had surrounded a pair of travelers coming out of Tabat pulling a handcart.

"No contraband, no escapees?" a guard said, nodding at the cart.

The woman drew herself up. She was dark-haired, dark-skinned, pure Old Continent descent. She wore a bright blue entertainer's cloak with "The Amazing Rappinos" embroidered in florid cursive across the back. Teo wondered what had brought her to an entertainer's role. "Do we look like Sorcerers or Abolitionists?"

"Yes," the guard said. "Search the cart."

Another guard gestured Teo in, watching the drama. As Teo moved past, he saw their goods unpacked and flung on the ground. A pottery vessel shattered on the stones. He heard a guard say "Aha," and glanced back to see the red-bound book the other man held up. But before he could hear or see more, the crowd pushed him on and before he knew it, he was inside Tabat's Hillside Gate.

Despite the jostling, he fought his way to the crowd's edge. Inside the gate, limestone buildings lined a plaza. Signs hung over double wooden doors indicating they were Government offices in charge of assessing goods and taxes. Ice-capped gargoyles guarded the corners of the nearest, newest buildings, and a pair of the brilliant, sorcerous lights marked each entrance.

Bewildered and alone, Teo made for the harbor, moving downward along icy stairs and sodden streets. Papers fluttering on an ice-slicked wall, shag-faced with orange handbills and broadsides, caught his attention and he moved over to inspect them. Here was news of a political rally on the Rights of the Worker, and another on the Formation of a True Democracy, and another titled the Burgeoning Upsong of Our Most Democratic Future. Here was a sale of Beasts next Auction-Day, listing each creature to be sold: "One Buck Unicorn, seven hands high, Halter-broke. A proven Breeding Pair of Sturdy Minotaurs. One Mermaid from the Southern Waters, trained in Felicitous Singing."

He studied the signs, sounding out the syllables. There were news accounts and public announcements as well. He read of a suspected Sorcerer taken to be drowned in the Harbor, with "no less than a hundred-weight of chains upon his feet." And next to that another illustration, a Shifter family burned at the stake, parents and children alike. His stomach turned at the engraving illustrating the last. He turned to survey the square. If anyone realized he was a Shifter, he would be burned alive, too.

He stood there while the wind rustled the papers behind him, watching the crowd and trying to determine his path. He rocked back and forth on his heels, contemplating this new world. No one in the entire city knew him, he thought. No one at all. No one expected anything of him or expected him to do anything. To be anything.

At home, wondering what it would be like to be in Tabat, he had never anticipated the loneliness that swept through him now as he stood there in the midst of the crowd.

Nor the anger. He let himself pick at that wound. They'd promised his life so his little sister could live and hadn't consulted him in the matter. He wasn't even sure that the Moons had cured her. Who cared about him? Not them, certainly. Shipped off to be a servant to Toj's Temple. They had ways of making sure he'd never leave that service.

Well, he'd decided differently, and that would be the end of that. He would make his own choices from here on in.

The streets splayed in a handful of directions around him. The fireworks spoke again, and he chose the path they marked, which led down a set of terraced steps towards the sea itself. He knew he was moving away from the Temple to which he had been promised, but he didn't care.

Staircases laddered the sloped terraces of the city and he made his way down them, lower and lower. Snow drowsed in planters along the upper streets but gave way to stacks of garbage and indrawn bushes cloaked in the falling snow, the light from the fireworks coloring them purple, then red.

He passed open tea shops and closed stores neighboring them, iron-barred store windows filled with spices followed by displays of alchemical ingredients, then leather goods, then chinaware.

He was cautious but walked along like any of the other late night pedestrians around him. It wasn't so bad, this city. He could get the hang of it. The exhilarating thing was that no one seemed to pay him much mind. It was as though he were invisible, as though there were no expectations of him.

Would life be like this in the Temples? He doubted it, somehow, and the thought pushed a quicker rhythm to his step. He wanted to get down to the harbor before the fireworks were over, to have his first close look at the sea marked by their graceful arcs of sparks, as though this were something momentous. He thought, "I'll remember it all my life, the first time I see the ocean."

But it was farther away than it looked. A half hour later he was making his way through rows of warehouses shouldered side by side, close enough to the water that he could smell the salt in the air. He rounded a corner and caught sight of water sparkle, but the fireworks had died away and not spoken for several blocks. He felt disappointed, deflated.

Before he could go another pace, two men caught up with him and fell into step on either hand.

"New to town, sonny?" the left-hand man said. He had steel-gray hair, cut short, and an aggressive jut to his beard. He was dressed in serviceable, unremarkable, but well-kempt, clothing. On his breast, as well as that of the other man, blue and red feather cockades bristled. Teo had seen other people wearing these ornaments in a variety of colors, but their meaning escaped him.

Teo nodded, wary. Was this the sort of trouble Captain Urdo had warned him of? He had only two avenues of escape—back down the alleyway, or further on into darkness.

The man said with an approving nod, "Good lad. You're right to be careful of strangers, ain't he, Legio?"

The other man grinned agreeably. "Indeed he do be right for such. Good lad indeed!"

Despite himself, the praise warmed Teo. He allowed himself to relax. They seemed good enough souls. And they were Northerners like himself, that was sure enough, he figured. Northerners had to stick together or the Old Continent bloods would high-nose them to death.

"We was wondering with such a fine young lad, if he be interested in picking up some coin. In order to have a little to spend on the splendors of this here our fair city."

"I might," he admitted. He wasn't sure yet. Could he trust this unshaven pair? A scar scrawled across Legio's face, a single knife mark splitting his cheek.

"Indeed! Indeed, he do be interested, you hear that, Legio?"

Legio beamed his delight at learning the news. Surely this was just good luck, Teo thought—Toj looking out for his new arrival.

"That's right, lad. The city's a plum just waiting for a smart boy of the right sort to reach out and pluck it. All you needs be doing to earn three copper skiffs is to be fleet of foot, ain't that so, Legio? Get this to Granny Beeswax in Stumble Lane, boy, and there's that many coins in it. More if you're as fast as you look. And maybe just as many again for bringing something back this way."

"What do you want me to take to her?" he asked.

His new friend pressed a grubby envelope on him. "Take it, quick as you can, and tell her Canumbra sent ya."

"How do I get there?"

"Head up this street, Eelsy, then take the stair down where the street ends. Come to the bottom, go right, and go three doors down and into the alley—towards the back be a little door, painted green with a candle in the window, you'll see it, sure as salmon spawning. Now off with ye!"

Relief spurred his heels—see, the city wasn't so frightening after all, and here he was making his way in it already, about to earn more money than he'd ever held. He rattled down a stairway and along a smaller street.

Canumbra's instructions had been clear enough, although as Teo progressed downward, he wished the aetheric lights spread this far down to light his path. Instead, guttering torches hung outside a few buildings, half-heartedly illuminating the icy cobblestones.

A white door, and then an unpainted one, then faded blue. An alleyway formed by overlapping eaves. More like an extended arch that led into a chilly maze, walls barely visible in the darkness. A squat red candle flickered in the window. He knocked twice and stood back.

The effort of the run had finally caught up with him. For a few minutes his heartbeat thundered inside his head while he fought to regain control of his breath. The cold wind here swept along the alley's curve with the impact of a punch against his run-fevered skin. He wondered if anyone was awake inside. Had he perhaps been sent too late? But no, the candle signaled *someone* was not asleep.

Inside, a shuffle and a mumble. A slant of light from Hijae from over his shoulder played across the door's surface with a bloody luster as it creaked open. The face that peered out through the narrow darkness was an unfriendly, wrinkled apple until he said, "Are you Granny Beeswax? I have a message for you from Canumbra."

"Canumbra!" she said. "He sends me all the fine young bucks. Are ye interested in a sailsome life then, me boy?"

She stepped back. The door swung open with a protesting creak, a syllable of complaint that the wind snatched away, shrilling and hissing as though reluctant to see him venture inside.

She ushered him into the reek of smoke and rancid fish oil. A tiny coal stove crouched in the corner topped with a kettle, its chimney pipe slanting towards the ceiling. A rocking chair teetered beside it, and a basket of grubby tatting partnered with a china mug was laid near one of the bowed runners.

The furnishings were sparse: The stove, the chair, a coffin-shaped cupboard, a wicker basket full of coals. The candle glowed in a saucer on the windowsill, swallowing the moonlight and lighting the ragged quilts tacked onto the wall, billowing where the wind puffed through the cracks behind them. Despite the wind's howl, it was much warmer in here, too warm. He tugged open his cloak, baring his throat.

She took the slip of paper he pressed on her and shuffled to the windowsill. But instead of reading it, she laid it there and turned back to him, still smiling. Darkness and candlelight played across the landscape of her face.

"You'd be new to town, lad?"

"How do you know?"

"Oh, a little of this and a little of that, by way of a clue," she said, studying him. "Yer accent, for one. That fur and fustian shawlcoat yer wearing for another. Here, let me hang it up for ye, lad. Put your pack right here. I'll make you some tea to drink while I'm reading Mr. Canumbra's letter and writing down a reply."

She pulled the garment off his shoulders. He tried to protest. Its pockets held his money, and the pack the rest of his worldly goods, other than what he wore. But she pushed him down into the chair and turned to open the stove and stir its embers before adding more coals.

"Please, I can't take your only chair," he said, trying to stand. The rocking chair was small and low to the ground, contending with his legs' lanky length to keep him from rising.

She shook her head. "I'll fetch us both a mug." She turned away to pull crockery down from the cupboard.

He coughed, trying to clear his throat. He pushed half-heartedly at the floor with his heels, but truth be told, it was pleasant to be sitting after the long walk and run from the upper river docks. It was nice to be fussed over.

As he looked around, he saw a fat black rat warming itself in the shadows of the stove. It sat upright on its hind legs and regarded him.

When the old woman approached again, the rat slid back into darkness. Even so, she cursed and handed Teo the mug. Stooping, she grabbed a coal from the basket and threw it with surprising force and decisiveness into the shadows. It hit with a clatter that said its target had eluded it. Granny Beeswax muttered something.

"Drink up, drink up," she said, giving him a motherly pat on the shoulder. He gave her a grateful smile in turn.

She stared expectantly at him.

He raised the mug to his lips, but its bitter, unpalatable smell reminded him of spring nettles. He lowered it again to his knee.

"What's wrong with it?" she demanded.

"There's nothing wrong with it," he faltered. He took a tiny sip and smiled broadly.

"A boy likes some sugar, I reckon," she said, leering at him. She fetched a bulgy-sided pot from the cupboard and used a spoon to tap a few white grains into the mug. Two delicate clinks sounded against the rim as the sugar sifted in. "There. Try it now."

He took another sip and set it down. "Did you have a message to be sent back to Mr. Canumbra, ma'am?" He wondered how impolite it would be to broach the subject of the payment Canumbra had promised.

She sighed in exasperation and reached out, whispering something rapid under her breath. Her fingers grasped his sleeve.

His senses swam, strings plucked by each syllable that passed her lips. The walls pressed in, then away, then inwards again as though breathing in time with him. It had gotten very hot again—he wasn't sure when that had happened.

"What?" he gasped. He tried to gather his feet beneath him but his muscles were weak and watery. Granny Beeswax's hand pressed down on his shoulder with the strength of a steel-jawed trap.

"Drink your tea, boy, it'll make you feel better. You must be wracked from the trip. It'll settle your stomach and set things straight for ye. Drink up, drink up."

Teo let the mug fall from his fingers, despite Granny Beeswax's words and the waves of weariness spreading outward from her touch. How could she have drugged him without him drinking any? Was this magic? Was she casting on him? He lurched, falling forward and away, landing on the floor on his hands and knees and scrabbling away on all fours from her outstretched hand.

"Settle down, boy! I mean you no harm!" But she kept reaching for him as he kept scrambling forward, managing to gain his feet and grab for the door's latch, fumbling with it.

"Sit down!" she snapped. For a second it felt as though his muscles were not his own, as though he were a puppet, strings twitching to turn him. He shrugged it off, his fingers seeking the latch again.

"Still standing," the old woman rasped. "What are ye then?"

The china knob rattled as the door swung open.

"None of that!" she said, yanking at his sleeve again, pulling the breath from him. He managed to stagger his way out the door's slippery outline and into the alleyway. He flopped and lurched along, his limbs still reluctant, managing to stay ahead of the crone's frenetic hobble. Cold washed through him as his senses returned.

Gaining the safety of the larger street didn't seem to matter though, and he heard her still coming up behind him. She shouted, "Stop! Thief!" and the sound of doors opening spurred him on.

With every step more of his strength ebbed back. He hobbled, sobbing for breath, up a staircase, and into an almost-deserted avenue lined with aetheric lights.

The city streets seemed much less friendly now. He heard more shouting as he ascended a staircase. He hesitated, but this was in front of him, not at his heels. He pressed on, wondering what was happening.

He saw the answer spelled out in the first frozen moment after he came around the corner from Eelsy to Whiteroofs. Blood on the cobblestones, clockwork skeletons crouched above them. Were they leopards, tigers, chimeras of gears and pointed steel? Whatever they were, the ducal insignia blazed on their sides in blue metal, glittering in the sunlight that had toyed with the city all afternoon, appearing and disappearing.

"Peace Keepers!" someone shouted. The acrid smell of lightning and sulfur in the air hurt his nose. Teo shrank back into the shadows as the crowd dispersed, chased by the machines.

When they were gone, he gawped at the bloodstains on the cobblestones, the scarlet film that glistened on the stone, transforming it into something new, a mineral he'd only rarely glimpsed in the wilds of the North.

In the very oldest days, Da had once said, every building had a spirit built into it, a sacrifice that might be animal or Human or something else, depending on what was at hand and how important the building was. He wondered, *What are they building on these streets that must come out of blood drenching the stone?* He imagined golems rising up out of the cobblestones and shuddered.

He kept walking, his legs moving like a mechanical's, numb and unfeeling, until finally he ducked into a little park, and sat on a bench, shivering, his arms clutched around his knees, trying, unsuccessfully, to stop the shaking.

He wasn't sure he had a handle on the city after all.

Chapter Ten

Bella Eats at Various Establishments

I hate the Duke's Teahouse, the fusty old place, but Leonoa loves it.

Buying her lunch there I say, "You can't expect me to believe you're penniless, you know. There are limits to even my gullibility."

"I like to make sure I have enough laid aside," Leonoa insists.

"People always buy your paintings! Where does all your money go?"

"This and that and the other thing." Leonoa shrugs.

I sigh and watch the plaza. Here towards the front of the teahouse, tall, narrow windows, barely more than slats of glass, are fixed into the front wall. Pedestrian shadows pass by in rapid succession, like the blades of a fan.

"Have you ever listened to the political speakers out there, Bel?" Leonoa asks, tilting her head towards the plaza.

"Not a one," I say promptly, pouring myself more tea. "Why stuff other people's ideas into your head? Don't you have enough of your own?"

"Do you ever think we need to hear other ideas?"

"Sometimes they're just a needless distraction."

"Not so with art." Leonoa's face, pinched as a two-skiff needle, eases as she elaborates on her words. "Art needs new things, all the time in order to keep getting better. Maybe people are the same way."

"I don't think so. Where would we be if we were changing the Gladiatorial ceremonies all the time? Centuries of tradition discarded for the sake of some new trapping."

Leonoa breathes out dissatisfaction, blowing on the surface of her tea to cool it.

"I get new ideas," I say, trying to placate her. "I try new techniques all the time. Like you, trying new painting materials."

This distracts her in the way I thought it might. She says, "I'm looking for silver talc right now. A painter from the Southern Isles spoke of it the other day."

"Ah? I can keep an eye out for such, and talk to some folks heading that way." I glance at the light coming in through the front. "I'd been planning on going down to see if the *Bloom* has come in yet—"

"It hadn't as of yesterday," Leonoa supplies.

"—and then if it has arrived today, I will be first to greet your mother."

Galia Kanto has been gone for several months now, on a Ducal expedition to the Southern Isles, but Leonoa seems unimpressed at the prospect of her mother's imminent return. Since her illness, her parents treat her as though she were a prodigy, a circus freak who should not even really be alive, let alone painting.

"I have a present for you," she says.

I perk up at this. "Oh?"

She slides a package wrapped in brown paper across the table. "A new book that claims to be written by a Beast trained by Jolietta Kanto. I thought it might interest you."

Not touching or acknowledging it, I lay coins down on the table. "Shall I come around and see you in a few days?"

"Glyndia will be there," Leonoa says. Challenge rings silvery in her tone, echoing the coins.

"I have no quarrel with her," I say.

"No? She said you made her uncomfortable...."

I bark out a laugh. "Ah, wouldn't want the newcomer uncomfortable."

"She's the best thing that has ever happened to me."

"She's the newest thing that has happened to you. You know how you are, Leonoa. Fickle as the wind."

"Don't take me for yourself. Irresponsibility in love is not some familial trait, just something you've perfected." She leans forward. "Irresponsibility in everything."

"What do you mean?"

"Have you never thought that there is something wrong in you holding the office that you have for so long? Something *unnatural?* Look at yourself, you barely age—in fact, you seem to improve as the years pass. You cannot fool the eye of someone who's painted you. How are you still Champion if something other than yourself is not meddling with you?"

"You envy my health," I say with chill courtesy. "Quite understandable, given your condition."

It is an unspeakably foul blow but I cannot take it back. We leave, silent with anger and not looking at each other.

The book stays behind on the table. Let the waiter find it and be educated.

I know enough about Jolietta and her methods.

O   O   O

When I met Adelina first, I didn't know she had hidden depths. She was a pretty thing, dark-haired, dark-eyed, tall and slim as a willow. It wasn't until we had our first fight that I found out her secret.

Perhaps she knew my patterns—knowing Adelina, she would have researched them before we ever went to bed. Or else she guessed that was how I usually begin pushing lovers away when they pull closer, by picking fights over petty things, and becoming unreasonable.

Either way, it worked. She confessed her secret, and it was so intriguing that it renewed my interest. I thought I knew all the rooms of her soul. Then she opened the door, and I realized I'd only been wandering in an entryway furnished to deceive casual visitors.

That's a strained metaphor, as I understand them. Adelina is the one gifted with words, able to spin them into nets of story.

She told me her tale, how in school she began writing penny-wides in secret, keeping the money hidden. And when she had enough coin, she bought a printing press and pretended to her mother that they hired her, all so she could have her secret still.

Her mother Emiliana would be furious. She barely let her daughter escape the ties of the family business to become a Scholar. She pretended to be appalled by the choice, but I've seen the gleam in her eyes when she speaks of the honors Adelina's scholarly histories have garnered. She's never dreamed her daughter might be concealing a merchantly soul the equal of any in Tabat, pricing paper and ink, driving bargains with provisioners, calculating the mysteries of supply and public demand as accurately as her mother on any day.

But I will take some credit for the success of the press. It was not until Adelina and I came up with the idea of telling my stories that she truly became successful. My adventures, some actual, others entirely fictional, fund every other book that Spinner Press produces.

Someday her secret *must* come out. That's the nature of secrets. You cannot count on them unless you keep them entirely to yourself. The moment you tell another person, that secret begins to make its way out into the world, because that person will tell another person, swearing them to secrecy of course, an oath they will evoke from another in turn as they continue to spread the story.

Today I am, as always, not telling secrets. Instead we are coming up with lies, not even based in truth this time, in order to create the next penny-wide. We'll plot it out, and then Adelina will take the scraps of conversation, the handful of ideas, and somehow turn them into something that will enchant and delight. I don't know how she does it. I think I am good at telling a joke or two, but I cannot hope to enrapture people the way that Adelina does when she begins. They listen to her when she speaks.

Sometimes I envy that a little because the only way that I can speak is by *being*. Being Bella Kanto. Being the person who lifts sword in Tabat's service. All these decades now.

Adelina says, "I was thinking of sending you back to the Rose Kingdom."

I object, "People know I have not been there in a decade."

"Yes." Adelina paces the room, tapping the end of her quill on her face, eyes narrowed and intent on some internal vista. "But we could always say this is an adventure from that previous visit, one that was never set down on paper before. After all, only two penny-wides came out of that trip."

"That's because, all in all, it was a very boring trip. The Rose Kingdom is much safer than anyone gives it credit for. The Hedge keeps it so."

"Which gives us plenty of room to create new and exciting tales."

"At least," I tease her, "I know that you will never add your voice to those who urge me to step down. What would Spinner Press do without Bella Kanto as the Champion of Tabat?"

Annoyance narrows her eyes. "I think it could hold its own," she retorts. "I've just taken on a writer who is devoting his stories to tales of the Explorers, and the exploration of the continent beyond and up to the north. People like to read such stories. And his have the advantage of being entirely true."

I haven't heard that tone in her voice for a long time. It's one that used to be reserved for me.

"Who is this fellow?"

"His name is Eloquence Seaborn. A river Pilot."

I shrug. "What sort of stories does he spin? We sailed a day, then anchored. Sailed another day and anchored. Came to a town and bought furs. Then back to Tabat."

Adelina snorts. "You'd be surprised. River pirates and mountain lions. Not every danger occurs in the arena, Bella. You don't have a patent on heroic actions."

"I never said that," I protest. But she has turned away already, avoiding this discussion, and is fishing through the stacked papers on her desk.

She turns back, a packet in her hand. "I need for you to go over these proofs, see if there are any mistakes or inaccuracies that need to be fixed."

I roll my eyes. "You always ask that, but there are never any problems that I find."

She shrugs. "I call it due diligence. This way you can never claim that I put something in that shouldn't have been included."

The thought amuses me. "Did you think I would hire a Lawyer and haul you away to court if you violate some guideline? It's not as though we have some sort of contract."

"Actually we do," Adelina says. "You signed it long ago. Perhaps you don't remember."

It's hazy but I do recall her giving me some papers when we first started this storytelling.

"Is that really necessary, Adelina? We are friends after all."

"And I intend for us to remain friends," she says. "It's for your protection as well as mine."

"Very Merchantly of you," I say. I don't realize it's a dig until it leaves my mouth and her lips thin in response. She holds the package out to me without another word and I take it, searching for something to say. What is it recently that causes me to put off the ones I love? At this rate, I will have no friends left unless I learn to watch my words.

Still, I find it nettlesome, this lack of trust. I take the packet from her and bow formally, meaning that gesture as a reproach, but it is one that seems to glide off her, for she only bows in return.

○ ○ ○

At Berto's, the cages full of little birds house quarrels and squawks. One lets out indignant chirps beside my ear. Outside, the day is still blindingly bright, sending shards of headache up from every puddle's reflection.

My mid-afternoon chal cup holds three squares of seaweed surrounded by clusters of oil circles besieging them. They float in a green triangle, Gladiators surrounded by foes in the cup's arena. Back-to-back, compensating for left or right-handedness. Which is only a matter of training, for I've found myself ambidextrous within the last decade. I don't remember exactly when I realized it.

Leonoa's voice in my mind says *unnatural*. I ignore it, studying the battle. Training and thought can win out against hordes, but there is always a point where there are simply too many opponents.

In which case you consider other options.

Someone settles into the opposite chair. I abandon the tactical analysis of my tea to greet them.

It's my former student, Danokin Smallnets, a one-time foe, fallen as Spring—how long ago now? Over a decade, surely. Well-favored enough, though I've never been attracted. But as oily as my tea. Still, I salute him, open-palmed, one Gladiator to another.

He returns the gesture, studying me.

"You're looking well," he says in his usual truculent tone. It's habit with him, not active intent, and I ignore it.

"Doing well enough. And yourself?"

"Retiring."

"What?" The startled twitch of my hand sends ripples across the tea. One square floats apart from its fellows. Oil blobs surround it, ready to drag it down.

"My knee's never been the same since that Enfield tore into it three years back. I've been offered a good position, steady and plenty, for overseeing the security at Bernarda's gallery."

"May the Trade Gods favor you in that," I say sincerely enough, but he grimaces at me.

"We can't all be Bella Kanto and fight forever," he says.

"I hear this chorus enough without you singing it," I snap back. I'm prepared to say more, but just then three cages come to life, their occupants deciding to engage in the battle they've been sidling toward. Feathers fly and the birds scream as Berto flings black cloths over the cages to calm them.

"What's wrong with them?" I ask as Berto muffles the cage near my elbow.

"Some have readied to breed too early and attack the others."

"Nature is upset by all these late springs," Danokin says. "Even small things suffer for your arrogance."

I ignore him as I count coins onto the table. The last time I fought here in Berto's, he threatened to ban me on the next occasion. Danokin sits. I can feel him, arms crossed, leaning back in his chair, studying me. Resentment roils from every inch of him.

Will Skye come to resent me like that?

Or is she the student I will be ready to step aside for?

I leave.

I have enough opponents that I don't need to number Leonoa among them. My cousin will listen to my apology, will forgive me.

On my abandoned table, the seaweed floats as the oil pulls inexorably at its edges until, cooling, it sinks and drowns.

o o o

I will go back and apologize to Leonoa.

I will explain that I'm cranky, that since rising I've felt a tension around me, a vibration beneath my boot soles. Someone, somewhere, is working spells against me.

I know the sensation well. Each year it starts a few weeks before I'm due to fight Spring. Trip-you-can cantrips, barbed hexes, and encompassing ill-wishes smudging everything around me.

Leonoa would not work magic against me, but I will keep her sweet-tempered for her own sake. Ill-wishes should not worry me. I pay a hex-wife well to keep me warded, after all, and toss a coin in every fountain I encounter.

I do that now as I pass along Salt Way. Part of a previous century's civic beautification efforts, fountains are spaced at each crossroads along the broad street. A stone effigy of one of Tabat's long past notables watches over each of them. I pass the noseless effigy of Sparkfinger Jack. Someone's chosen to use him for politicking, which strikes me as ill-omened. Still, there in the statue's hands is a placard advertising a Jateigarkist rally next purple moon.

I'll be glad when the elections are over and their silliness no longer crowds the streets.

By the time I step off Salt to find the top landing of the Tumbril Stair I've flipped ten coins into fountain basins. I hurry down the steps. Closer to the harbor, the damp air smells of tar smoke and salt. Seagulls arc like inverse pendulums above me. An air Sylph rides the winds among them, wings gleaming like mica. The city attracts vermin and scavengers of all sorts.

That is what I want to talk to Leonoa about.

But Glyndia opens the warehouse door.

"She's gone to buy brushes," she says without preamble. Then, like an afterthought, "You can come up and wait for her if you wish."

Stairs creak beneath us as we ascend. From behind, all that is visible of Glyndia is the satin fall of her wings, her dark hair a shadowy wick to the burning gold.

Sunlight fills the studio, the curtains thrown wide. The light is why Leonoa rents this place. Its brilliance mutes the metallic splendor of Glyndia's wings. She wears a blue silk dress with intricate ruching across her chest, expensively tailored.

"I do not drink chal, but I can offer you barley tea," she says.

I shake my head. "When do you think she will return? How long ago did she leave?"

"Just moments." Glyndia stands at the fireside, refilling her mug from the steaming kettle. Despite the seeming frailty of her mechanical limbs, they are strong. The swan-woman might prove a formidable opponent in the ring.

Then I realize what Glyndia has said. She didn't mention that I might have been able to catch up with the slower-walking Leonoa. She deliberately waited until it was far too late.

My jaw tightens. Is this the way of it then?

"I've changed my mind, I needn't wait," I say. "Tell Leonoa I called."

Glyndia shrugs. "Suit yourself."

She doesn't bother to see me down the stairs.

O O O

That evening, I build the fire high in my room to keep out the chill that creeps in through the window glass. The wood snaps and pops, sending up sparks, and the smell of burning sap makes me think of summer. For a moment, I think it would be nice to be warm.

I crawl into my bed, burrow down under mounds of feather comforters, feel their soft embrace like an undemanding lover's. I take the package that Adelina has given me and set it on my lap as I prop myself back against the clean white pillow, smelling the scent that Abernia sprinkles on linen before she sets an iron to it.

I don't like to read much, as a rule. It isn't a particularly useful skill. There are too many things you can't learn from a book, from how to birth a basilisk whose eggs are stopped (one of the most delicate arts Jolietta taught me) to how to deflect a dagger blow. And things in books aren't true sometimes, something which I know better than most.

I don't usually read what she's written about me, actually. I just give them back and say I've no complaints. But lately there's been so many people urging me to step down, so many people who feel I should not be Champion of Tabat, that I start to wonder where they are getting the idea. Surely not from the penny-wides that Adelina has written?

When I open the bundle that contains the proof, I find not one but two books there. The second is bound in cheap red cardboard. There's a note inside it from Adelina that reads only, *I thought this would interest you.*

It's the same book Leonoa tried to press on me. I can understand why my cousin and friend think this would interest me, that I might find something of myself in its pages, but I don't want to read about Jolietta. I need no reminder to help me summon up her face in my mind, the wrinkle that sat between her eyes, the narrow nose, the scar on her temple that I never asked about.

I feel no need to return to Piper Hill, even in memory. My life didn't truly begin until I reached the Brides of Steel.

I put the red bound book beside me. It can go on a shelf, and if Adelina asks after it I will tell her that I haven't had the time and imply that it is there to be read, even though I have no intention of ever opening its pages.

It does cross my mind to wonder which of Jolietta's creatures has put these words down. Perhaps one of the Minotaurs, in which case I *know* I do not wish to read it; I do not want to see my aunt through their loving, loyal eyes, which never marked her cruelty because it never fell on them. But satisfying that itch is not sufficient to prod me into what I know I will not like, what I fear will bring me nightmares.

Is this cowardly of me? But I am Bella Kanto. I am no coward. I simply do not have the time nor the inclination. Instead I pick up the proof and flip through it, not reading carefully and finding mistakes in the way that Adelina would wish, but simply letting the words flow over me, comforting in the picture they paint of me, my daring, my boldness, my heroism.

Chapter Eleven

Candy

The Fairies are quarrelsome today. I've seen them do this in preparation for driving out one of their members, but I can't tell which of them in all the buzz and swoop of their wings. I'd planned on letting them take shelter in my room tonight, for I can tell it will be bitter cold, but not in this mood. They'll make noise, create disturbance, and Abernia will be angry for days.

I put the handful of candies, plucked from a bowl at the castle, out on the ledge, lining them up one by one. The Fairies watch but make no move to come get them. That makes me uneasy. Tamed creatures don't lose their training unless someone is doing something to them.

Yellow-hair hangs in the air watching me, but it's not till I step back from the sill that she advances, dives to seize a candy, a ball of amber sugar as big as her head. As though she's emboldened them, the rest come in turn. I try to see which of them might be looking more bedraggled than the others, but I can see little difference.

Jolietta kept chickens. There you'd see it. One more miserable than the rest, pecked and sat upon, with ragged bald patches. Animals have no patience for the weak, nor do Beasts. Is one of the Fairies ailing, perhaps? It seems to me there are fewer than usual.

When they've taken their candies, I go back to the window, lean out despite the cold wind, and peer into the boughs. There, that little shape, is that a huddled Fairy? Snowflakes whirl, obscuring the sight.

What can I do? I cannot catch it. No one ever caught a Fairy except with lure or net. I don't have the latter and I don't want to alarm the rest of them. Baffled, I pull my head back in.

It's only a Fairy, even if I've come to think of it as *my* Fairy. Only a creature. There are others. There are always others.

That's how Jolietta taught me to think of them.

O O O

"It is necessary," Jolietta said. Even as she lectured me, Jolietta kept at her work, checking and trimming a heavy hoof. "There are many practicalities in life that we would prefer not to exist. I am not fond of defecation, for example, and yet I do so on a daily basis."

I tried to wrench my mind away from a vision of Jolietta's sturdy body on a water pot. "It's not the same," I said. "You won't die if you refrain from doing it."

"Some might if I don't. A gentled Beast is less likely to lash out at its trainers, or worse, at an audience member. I work with dangerous creatures, Bella—have you seen the Undine's teeth? The Gryphon's beak?" She slapped the heavy flank, investigating the musculature, which twitched as the goat tail twitched.

"They talk. Surely that means they have souls."

"So do parrots. Should all bird cages be emptied for their sake?"

"Yes!"

My aunt snorted, a choked out laugh that never failed to leave me feeling small and embarrassed. "Childish, romantic notions!" She ran a callused hand through the Satyr's hair, pulling his face down and back to check his teeth with the other hand. "This fellow, now, knows what biting would bring, don't you, my boy?"

The Satyr nodded. Sweat beaded the thin features drawn in terror and starvation.

And even with the quickness of that nod, with the docile stance as Jolietta examined and discussed him in intimate detail before her apprentice, an hour later Jolietta drugged and castrated him while I stared down from the sliver of a window of the attic into which I'd been locked, kicking and screaming.

Phillip, the only Centaur Jolietta kept rather than trading, opened the door finally. I tried to push past him, tried to get to the boy, but his hand closed on my shoulder, inexorable in its strength. Like the boy outside, he was half horse, half man, but unlike the boy, he was rippled with muscle, his handsome face placid and unperturbed.

"She doesn't have the right!" I said.

"The Duke's Chorus wants a strong young soprano," he said. "They paid for his siring, his bearing—everything has led him to that path." He studied me. "Why are you so upset? You've seen geldings before."

I turned away from his look, went back to the window. Outside a trio of crows circled past the window, shrieking protest while the rain sluiced down. There was blood on the cobblestones, and Jolietta was using a hot iron to staunch the bleeding.

The boy's scream pulled a sound from my throat.

Phillip's hand closed on my shoulder. "You didn't do anything with him, did you?"

"Do anything?" I said. Phillip's fingers bit into my shoulder. There were old bruises there—Jolietta had shaken me for stubbornness only a few days ago. I knew without looking that they were re-purpling. "What do you mean?"

"You know very well what I mean, Bella Kanto! Did you kiss him, touch him? Your aunt would have more than his balls in such a case, and you know that!"

"She doesn't know anything!" I pulled away, or tried to at any rate. "Phillip, you won't tell her, and neither will I, so what's the harm?"

He gestured outside where Brutus and Caesar were pulling the Satyr to his feet. "He could tell her. Or any Beast with an inkling of suspicion wanting to curry favor or harm you." He groaned. "Why would you do such a thing?"

"I didn't!" I protested. "Or, just a little, anyhow." I remembered the feel of his eager fingers on my breast, the graze of his palm across the nipple, soft and sensitive as a new deer's horns, like an opening of the floodgates of my body. Even remembering I felt that thrill deep inside.

Phillip shook me once, hard, then shoved me away. "This is not the place or time!"

I crouched, weeping, on the floor where I had fallen.

"Go tend the dragons and wash your face," Phillip said. "Don't let anyone see you mourning him—don't go to him. No." He forestalled my protest with an upraised hand. "You can't afford to be seen talking to him. The Duke will be collecting him tomorrow at dawn, anyhow."

I still tried to see him that night, but Phillip anticipated me and was waiting in the hallway.

"I have to say goodbye!" I hissed.

"It will do you no good. Jolietta has dosed him to unconsciousness. Go back to bed and dream your farewells, it will do just as much good." His eyes were hard. "I don't know why I bother protecting you from yourself, stupid girl."

And why had he bothered? Did he think that in the end? I don't know.

O O O

Far down past the florist on Greenslope Way is Ellora's Daughter's Candy Shop. That close to the College of Mages, plenty of shops and stores supply magical wares to the elite. Or things whose production is assisted or enhanced with magic; trinkets for the rich, like Glyndia's arms or Leonoa's clock.

Magic-animated, a swarm of candy soldiers jockey for possession of a marzipan chessboard in the shop window. Imagine what my Fairies would do to these tiny Gladiators. A crowd of street children watches wide-eyed, huddled with each other against the cold.

The candy-maker, Ilyia, is another dropout from the College, like the florist. These living confections are her specialty: butterflies with sugar-pane wings or elbow-long dragons that roar and breathe flame before falling apart into cake with green and scarlet frosting.

There's always a mage or two in the shop, it seems, sneering at Iliya and her three busy apprentices while trying to hide unease at her success. The College likes to pretend that it doesn't depend on money like the rest of us, that it only deals with higher things.

I've never liked the College, and they've never liked me that much either. You would think we would be bound by magic, but theirs is a different kind, a thing of calculations and ingredients. Mine is action, calling the Gods to me.

They take forever to pay their bills, Adelina tells me.

I step into the shop and an assault made of brewed burnt sugar, a thousand pleasant spices, fruit boiled in sticky syrup, and even scarce and precious chocolate.

I should like it, but it makes my heart race, my spine stiffen. I buy my bag of hard candies quickly and exit fast, despite the Human clerk's attempt at flirtation.

Jolietta used hunger as a training tool. We'd supplement it however we could, knowing that if we were discovered eating illicit food we'd be punished for it and severely. Still, I'd go through the orchard picking up the windfalls. We were supposed to keep them for making cider, but a half-rotten apple was too much of a treat to resist sometimes.

On the rarest of occasions, when she needed to assail the particularly strong-willed, she assailed our resistance to tattling on each other with sugar. She kept trying to harden me towards the Beasts, to the things she said were necessary to train them. And each time she rewarded me with candy.

There's a point when you're growing so fast that you'd kill for something fat and rich. When your bones hurt because you're growing, pulling on your internal reserves. I remember licking a finger dragged through the butter or across a pan's bottom, rich with congealed fat and bits of browned meat.

She got her chocolate from someone down in the Southern Isles, a mage she'd known as a girl, who oversaw plantations of chocolate and sugar now. We'd know when a ship had come in: a crate would arrive, holding bottles of vanilla and thick bars of bittersweet chocolate, golden cones of muscavado sugar, and jugs of sticky, blaze-tongued rum.

I still can't stand the taste of rum or the smell of it on some-one's breath.

I see the Sphinx from the College of Mages coming down the street. She nods to me as we pass one another. She spent some time herself at Jolietta's, a half year while her temper was sweetened for the College. She and Phillip were good friends, but I never spoke to her. Something about her frightened me then.

Not so now, when I'm not afraid of anything. But she makes me uneasy still.

We've never spoken of Jolietta. Or what happened to Phillip.

○ ○ ○

Abernia knows not to bring me breakfast every fifth day. Lucya likes the instructors to eat with the students every once in a while, and today I'll be doing that. Still, I pause in the kitchen to grab something from her tray, one of the pastries they call eyes, a hard-boiled egg wrapped in spiced dough. I eat it, scattering crumbs for the sparrows, as I jog down the Tumbril Stair towards the school.

The room where the students eat was once a ballroom: high ceilings and ornate frescoes on the wall, now faded with age, peeling and chipped, marked where students have decided their legacy should be preserved. The room somehow manages to retain its graceful proportions, built by Serafina Silvercloth, who Adelina tells me was an important historical figure. She's admitted I'm one too. She wants to write a proper biography, something serious rather than all the lurid stories she and I (mostly she) have concocted.

I don't want that. It would mean going back. Reliving moments I don't want to relive. I won't return to Jolietta, even in memory. She's dead and gone, despite the handful who still mourn or worship her—or rather, her training secrets.

Ten long wooden tables, each packed with students. I sit where I always sit, amid a flight of giggling girls excited by my presence. All twelve girls are exemplary students, chosen to sit here as prize for something or another. Skye is among them. She's too inexperienced to recognize how quickly she's risen in the fighting ranks here. Agile in mind and body. Possessed of a determination that might match my own.

"The cook skimps on spices here," the girl, the little Khentor, beside me complains. Like most of the girls here, she craves spicy, or overly sweet, or salty. Preferably a combination of all three.

I don't reply, but beside her another chimes in, "We eat terribly! My mother says with this exorbitant tuition, the table should be better than the Pot King sets."

Skye catches my eye before looking down at the grainy lumps on her plate and grimacing. She looks up again, thinking to make me laugh.

Displeasure stiffens my spine. What is it about this girl that eats at me so, lets her get under my skin like a burrowing insect?

And what does she know about hunger?

Skye is spoiled. The child of a minor Merchant house, she's never known want. Never known hunger. Never known the sort of appetite that could make any breakfast palatable. And it's not as though the Brides of Steel sets a bad plate, although the food is plain.

She's upset by my reaction, I can tell. She doesn't understand it. I find myself softening, shrugging at her. She's not entirely satisfied, but ducks her head back towards her plate and begins to eat. She doesn't complain about it anymore.

The windows here, multipaned, are not clean. I'd take a complaint about that more seriously than the cuisine. It's just food, Jolietta used to tell us, and that woman could pinch a copper skiff until it shat gold.

I remember early mornings at Piper Hill. Jolietta ate fresh-baked bread, and sausages, and dragon eggs boiled in the shell, their pale pink yolks glistening on her plate. We had bowls of cooked oats with nothing to make it more palatable, unless you'd managed to snitch a lump of the sugar she kept for training.

If you worked outside, you could glean a little: wayside berries or a carrot stolen from the bunches you gathered. That was when I learned to chew anise seed, filling my mouth with flavor if nothing else.

Even now, when there's plenty, when I know I'll never starve again, I still fall into the habits of those old, bad days: I break a pastry in half to tuck part away in my pocket against later hunger, and measure my plate against others to make sure I'm getting my share. To eat to repletion remains my favorite luxury, and stinting myself for training fills me with resentment, even with no target for that emotion other than myself.

Adelina figured that out early. Rather than woo me with jewels or flowers, as so many had, she brought me edibles: a steaming pastry from the cart she'd passed on the way or a handful of spiced nuts from the seller down by the docks who makes the best in the city, crunchy and hot, with a bite of spice and sugar mingled. No other lover really figured that out, and I miss it still, moments of bed-play where I licked syrup from her breasts, sating one appetite while bringing another to full boil.

Skye steals a look at me as she takes another bite. Seeking my approval, her pretty face is uncertain. She wants to please me.

Impatience clutches me. Spoiled children who have never seen deprivation or painful longing. Or at least, I think, looking at Skye's expression, they have not known the former.

I must learn to be patient with them, Lucya always tells me.

But why? No one was patient with me in those early days. They expected me to fail, too old to learn what they had to teach. Life is full of unfairness and tribulation. Look at the Beasts, born to serve us with no choice in the matter, their position only an accident of birth.

Skye has a crush. I've seen them before, although I've never been on her side of the matter. Leonoa said one time she thought me incapable of love. That stung. I've saved my love, not spent it on a mere person, a fragile body prone to breakage and age.

Instead, I've given it to this city, promised to serve it as a Gladiator, and it's rewarded me for that act, made me its Champion. I owe everything I am to this city and no one else.

Lucya passes, dispensing chal. Guilt twinges. I do owe something to the Brides of Steel, but even there, there are hindrances and jealousies, petty feuds and politicking. And people agreeing to do each other favors. I reminded Lucya that no one stepped aside for me, and that made it all the sweeter, the day I dressed in Spring's armor and struck Donati down, and thus began my career, for each Spring becomes Winter in turn.

I would not be here if the city—not just its populace, but the city itself—did not love me. Cities are not fickle in the ways that Humans are.

When I push myself away from the table, Skye's gaze follows me. The girl beside her giggles and whispers something, but Skye says nothing.

I leave them to their breakfast. I've stayed long enough to inspire them. That's all that's needed, and worth much more to the school than my skills as an instructor.

Lucya watches me too, her mouth a thin line of disapproval. She wants to talk to me again and no doubt has prepared arguments for the occasion. I won't linger and give her the chance to trot these things out.

I pause in the stable on my way out. The Centaur boy is there no longer, and no one can say where he is gone. Lucya will know, they say. Instead I go out onto the street where the air is cold, but I can breathe despite the snow being swept along by the wind.

Chapter Twelve

Teo's Life in Tabat

Teo stood at the Moon Temple Gate.

Along the tile-paved Moonway leading past the Moon Temples, the path underfoot shifted in accordance to the foremost moon's state of wax and wane, changing shade from dark to light. A subtle magic, but one he loved. Frail apricot trees lined the path. A few days earlier, they must have succumbed to a sense of spring's imminent warmth, putting forth a flurry of flowers now frilled with dribbles of icy sap.

Sticky drops fell on Teo where he stood watching the gate, mixing with the icy rain dampening the cloak he'd improvised from a piece of stiff sail canvas. It kept out the wind, at least.

Three times now in the last two days, Teo had gotten as far as this gate. It was the one most pilgrims passed through to reach the Temples of the Moons, the second busiest a garden gate a few blocks away. The high archway, a lizard's ruff of gray and sand colored stone, was carved right to left with triads of moons, ice-inset crescents, then halves, then full rounds.

If he passed beneath those markings, he would not come out again for years and then, only at the Temples' whim, never his own.

Directly under the archway, dressed in robes dyed with Hijae's ruddy hue to match her wind-chapped lips and cheeks, a matronly

Priest smiled and nodded to each pilgrim as they entered. Most were fair-haired Northerners, travel's rigors apparent in their dusty cloaks and unwashed hair, as though they had come straight from stepping off a steamboat. Once Canumbra and Legio had walked by, carrying long wooden staves, and he'd slid back into the shadows. That wasn't the first time he'd seen them, either, but so far he'd managed to escape their notice. They hadn't gone in the Temples, though, just past them.

A squat wicker basket sat beside the Priest, and passing pilgrims dropped coins in it. Teo thought the basket must be filling at a startling rate.

The Priest nodded another perfunctory thanks and turned to glance at the street. Was she looking at Teo? He ducked his head and felt another cough coming on. He'd had it for three days now. It wracked him for a few shuddering moments before he regained his breath.

The Temples reeked from the rotting lichen covering the lower portions of the walls, a latrine-like stench as though this wall served as piss-pourer for the entire neighborhood. A Winter's worth of raindrops had left mottled stalactites of color under the eaves.

There were no animals or plants beyond the omnipresent lichen here. Even the little sparrows were shooed away by an apprentice rasping a twig broom over the flagstones inside the gateway, wider than Teo was tall, and no pigeons cooed or spooned on the moon-scalloped eaves.

As clean on the inside as it was dirty on the outside, yes. As clean and sterile as a moon's face, sad and droopy-eyed with home-sickness.

The inner courtyard was full of people who wanted to be there, unlike him. People who had been sorted into their places, people who knew where they wanted to be, and knew furthermore that their desire coincided with where they were supposed to be. He shrank back into a corner between buildings. He hadn't been warm for a long time and he wanted to gather what he could of the sunlight's warmth—but not under the greeter's eye.

His stomach threatened to crawl up inside his ribs and go hunting for itself. That's how hungry he was, and from time to time, fever grabbed him, shook him, made him doubt his sanity. He was surviving by running errands and finding scut work. It wasn't enough. He'd hadn't had the same spot to sleep two nights running. Someone always drove him off.

There was food for him inside those walls. And warmth and shelter and an escape from Canumbra and Legio.

Still, he couldn't bring himself to enter the Temples and leave this new world he'd discovered. He pushed himself away from the crevice, still avoiding the Priest's eyes. As he wandered down the street, he felt her watching him, but he did not dare look back to see if it were true.

What would Bella Kanto do?

A thought struck him. He was in her city. He could find her.

He went down two staircases and stood on an upper landing watching the people getting on and off the tram. When he'd arrived, he thought he'd never seen anything so splendid.

Since then the city and its wonders had lost its glow, tarnished by the passing days. He had eaten stale bread doled out at the back of bakeries, an eel coaxed from under a pier to be roasted at an edge-town communal fire, where the very poorest rubbed back to belly, trying to get by.

The Moon Priests seemed to be everywhere. He'd learned to pick out the color of their robes, red or white or purple, depending on which moon they served. They seemed to be in charge of many of the city's small doings: they drove night soil carts and collected refuse from the streets.

Several times he'd had sausages and beer from a political rally. By now he'd learned the magic of the feather cockades—they signaled what political party you had signed with, and as long as you were willing to pin one on for a bit, the rally would feed you.

Bella Kanto lived on Greenslope. He knew that. But heading up that road, he saw the Mage, the one from the docks. He ducked into the mouth of an alleyway, stiff with terror, but the man strode past him, turning into a florist's.

He wondered if the Mage or Eloquence had reported him to the Temples. Or when Grave would return and reveal his absence. He was long overdue. How much time did he have before the Temples dragged him in, whether he liked it or not?

○ ○ ○

The third day, he saw a Shifter burned.

He had been hovering on the edges of a Jateigarkist rally, where they were passing out sausages and the purple and green cockades promising allegiance to the party sponsored by the College of Mages, promising new wonders for the city if they were elected, better than the sewer system created long ago by Ellora Twosails, better than the Great Tram, or the Duke's waterfall or any of the other amazing things the College had produced.

The gates of the College, great spiky iron constructions, were now swung open and adorned with flutters of amethyst and emerald bunting, so the populace could crowd onto the courtyard before the College's main building, its stone towers thrusting upward impatiently in the indifferent cold blue sky.

Teo was fifteenth in line. He'd been counting. He was waiting for one of the sausages steaming in the great iron pot. He jiggled in place a little to keep warm, but the bulk of people around him kept out the wind's worst gusts.

He tried to see through the crowd when he heard the shouting. Purple robes could be glimpsed through the figures, hustling someone along. The Temples enforced many of the laws here, he knew. The Duke's forces were called out for civil unrest of the sort that often seem to accompany the political rallies, but for day-to-day matters, it was the Moon Priests who sought out those who had worked magic unlawfully—or whose very existence was unlawful.

The crowd surged in that direction. Teo tried to keep his place in line but was carried along by the people pushing and shoving.

"Got some Shifter," he heard, and his attention wavered. He hadn't eaten yet that day, though, and the sausages smelled amazing.

"Going to burn 'em," he heard another person say. He cast another look at the sausage pot. Sometimes they ran out. But the fellow was covering the pot, clearly thinking the event's draw over.

Teo managed to make his way to the back of the crowd and followed in its footsteps. They headed to the Duke's Plaza, the waterfall's roar battling the muttering of the onlookers.

The three Moon Priests hauled their captive to a central pole. It was fixed in the stones directly below the space where the water would have poured, if it had not vanished into the great round of silver hanging in the air above them. This close, Teo could look up into the onrushing waters as they poured themselves into nothingness. He shuddered, imagining the weight of the falling liquid.

The Priest chained the man—Teo could see him better now—to the pole. He was an ordinary enough looking man.

"Don't look like nothing," the man next to Teo said to the woman beside him.

"That's what makes them scary," she said. "Could be anywhere. Anyone." Teo's empty stomach roiled as she rolled an eye over him. He tried not to look furtive or guilty.

Two Priests took what looked like water skins from their belts. Each had several tied to their waist. They poured the contents over the man, taking care to distribute it evenly. He shook his head wildly, pleading with them, it looked like.

Terror froze Teo to the spot. He watched as a Priest took out something and sparked it to light. The man's head shook even more wildly, but the Priest tossed the flame onto him without hesitation.

The mass of his oil-soaked body burst into fire. Thick black smoke surged up and roiled from his struggling form to the crowd.

That was all right until the thought came to Teo, *It smells like sausages,* and that was too much for him. He stumbled away to the outskirts of the Plaza to the shelter of a statue, and kneeling, poured out what little was in his stomach upon its stony feet.

o o o

He hadn't meant to intrude on a street corner claimed by someone else. He'd thought the other boy not there that day, and so he'd taken up early morning post outside the Manycloaks dock offices, which frequently needed runners, and waited.

When he saw the gang of street children approaching, he knew they wouldn't listen, but he tried, holding up his hands. But as the kicks and blows continued, he curled into himself until they tired of the sport. The cold street cobbles bit against his skin. For a moment he wondered if they would kill him in their anger.

When they finally let Teo go, he fled the area, dazed, reeking, and bruised. His sides ached and whenever he took too deep a breath, he could feel a stab of pain. A broken rib, he suspected.

He cleaned himself as best he could in a rain gutter's icy drip, shuddering at the cold. Afterwards he felt cleaner, but the damp clothes clung to him like snares for the wind's chill.

He went north where, after a brief up and down of a rocky spur, the city gave way to a long, sandy beach cluttered with driftwood and weathered logs. Drying kelp fluttered like rags on the rocks at the shore's edge among chiming shards of ice. The water was intervaled in dark and pale blue. In the sunlight, the kelp leaves had a dusky, autumn-colored translucence.

A line of smoke split the sky up ahead. Smoke meant fire. And fire meant warmth and possibly food. Shivering, he pressed on, stumbling in the soft sand.

From afar, he could see the group clustered around the pile of burning driftwood, but it was only when he got nearer that he realized it was a group of Beasts. They stirred at the sight of him, but did not flee. He suspected he might be the least threatening figure possible—bedraggled and blue with cold. He paid them little mind. The bonfire was his main objective.

But as he moved to the fire, a figure interposed itself.

He stared. Where the Minotaurs at the dock had been bulky, imposing walls of muscle, this one had been stooped by age. His brown eyes were clouded, one completely misted by cataract. His gnarled horns spiraled inwards.

"What do you want, boy?" the old bull-man said.

"Please, may I stand by your fire?" Teo blurted. His stomach growled as the wind teased him with a whiff of soup. A kettle nestled to one side of the fire.

"Go away, little Human. This be a fire for Beasts."

"I'm not Human!" he said.

Every head turned to him, every gaze focused like a steel spear.

"Indeed," the leader said. His tone was almost conversational, but there was menace in his posture. "You look Human enough to me."

"I'm a Shifter," he said. Relief washed over him. The Beasts would accept him, save him. Would protect him from Canumbra and Legio, and the beggar boys, and all the other perils of the city. They would take care of him.

"Prove it," hissed a figure, its snake tongue flickering out.

He tried. If he tried hard enough, surely. Surely.

He closed his eyes, strained imaginary muscles, willing the change. Nothing happened. He squeezed his eyes tighter shut and took a deep breath, ignoring his rib's twinge. He pushed and squeezed internally, tried to pull himself into another form.

Nothing.

He opened his eyes to their hostile faces. "My parents are Shifters," he said. "In the north. They sent me to the city."

"It's a stupid ploy, child," the old Minotaur said. "Men hate Shifters for being able to pass as Human, and Beasts hate them for the same reason." He took a step towards Teo. "You're the most incompetent spy the Duke's sent yet. Go back and tell your Master we're no threat to him."

As Teo opened his mouth to reply, a blow from a massive fist knocked him to the sand. His rib blasted pain and he yelped.

"A ten count and I will let them kill you," the Minotaur said, gesturing at the others. "One."

Teo did not wait for two, but scrambled to his feet and ran southward. There would be no rescue from that quarter. His feet thudded dully in the sand, and the laughter of the Beasts pursued him as he fled.

O O O

Sides aching, led by a distant roar, he clambered up stairways and arrived in the Duke's Plaza. In the center, the waterfall thundered down from the cliff's face, falling into the immense silver hoop suspended in nothingness. As the water poured into the glimmering circle, the gilded lip of a vast, invisible goblet made of a ribbon of yard-wide gold, it vanished.

As before, below it in the plaza no water touched the people walking about in the shadow of the ring except for a coiling mist, damp, tendrilled, but almost imperceptible.

At the opposite edge of the Plaza, beneath a pair of green-leaved rhododendrons, their ice-stunted blossoms like wads of sodden paper, a young woman dressed in severe black had set up shop. At the foot of her cloth-draped apparatus was a decrepit Gryphon on a chain.

"Souvenirs!" she called to the passing crowds. "Have your portrait taken with a minor Gryphon, patron animal of Tabat!"

She paused in her speech as another woman pushed forward through the onlookers, trailing a pair of twins, six or seven years old. They were dressed alike in blue and umber uniforms.

The photographer arranged them on either side of the moth-eaten Gryphon. "Mind your fingers!" she admonished. The children stood trustingly, hands tangled in the desiccated, dry-weed mane while the animal clacked its beak irritably. The photographer disappeared beneath the tent of draped black gauze.

Soon afterwards, a puff of acrid smoke set everyone in the vicinity to coughing and made the Gryphon clack its beak even harder.

The photographer gave her customer a card—"Ready by tomorrow, noon, at that location!" she said as she removed the twins from the Gryphon's striking range.

"Who's next then?" she said to the crowd. "You?" She beckoned to Teo. "You?"

He backed away, holding up his empty hands. "No money, ma'am."

"Sit down," she ordered. "I'll do it for free, and add you to the gallery. You have good bones."

He tried to step away, but she pounced on him. He found himself perched on the stool, waiting for the puff of smoke, being snapped at not to move. The Gryphon rested its heavy head on his knee and contemplated him. He sat there for an eternity before the smoke puffed and the coughing began anew.

"Here's my card. Come by the shop tomorrow, and I'll show you what you look like," she said when the process was done. It read "Jilla Clearsight, Photographer." The Gryphon clacked its beak in reprimand at him as he stepped away.

He paused. "Say, ma'am," he said. Her face seemed as though it might be kind now that she was no longer scolding him for not sitting still.

"Yes?"

"You don't know anywhere a fellow could swap chores for a place to stay, do you?"

Her gaze was as piercing as the Gryphon's. "What sort of chores?"

"Well, I can chop wood, for one," he said. "And clear a trap line, but I don't suppose you have much call for that sort of thing. I can cook stew though—peel potatoes and make flatbread, too."

"Come back in an hour and help me pack up," she said.

He wanted to grin, to stammer out thanks, to dance in celebration, but he coolly nodded and went wandering across the plaza. Easy enough to kill an hour and then return and help. He wondered if she needed an assistant, some sort of permanent arrangement. Perhaps she'd take him in. If he had a place to live, he could claim he had always been here, that he had no connection with any northern boy, that he had never been promised to the Temples.

Circling the plaza like a curved comb set on its spine were the tall iron poles of the aetheric lights, each plastered with a new orange bill advertising a rally for the Friends of the Beasts Party. To the southwest stretched pines and summits of the buildings of the College of Mages, covered with complex contraptions: many-limbed lightning rods and contradictory weather vanes against a spider web of silver wires securing a tethered zeppelin.

Past that, the Duke's Road climbed its way towards that distant, pine-edged point. The sun was high overhead, and the light hit the waterfall full on, rendering it into an immense, sparkling construction.

Directly underneath the waterfall, the roar of the water was thunderous. He stood with head tilted back. The water ended with a knife's cleanness. The writhing spray formed odd lines and curves.

"Can you see them, then?" A voice beside his elbow.

He turned, startled. A stooped figure, all wide skirts. It straightened, and he took in the kerchiefed head, the hedgehog bristles barely betrayed at its edges, her blackened snout. A Beast of a kind he'd never seen. Tabat was full of them.

"Can you see them?" the old woman repeated. Her voice had a peculiar whiney, snuffling sound to it. "See their faces?"

He squinted upward. "It sort of looks like faces, yes."

"That's how they get their power." She pointed her non-existent chin towards the College. "Here. Tiggy will keep you safe from their notice." She fumbled in the basket that she carried, a profusion of paper flowers, and took out a purple and white blossom. She reached up to pin it to his collar with stubby fingers.

"I be a political speaker here most days," she said. "You come and listen, boy, maybe you'll learn something."

She smelled like home, somehow, with her sharp animal scent.

She chuckled, and his embarrassment burned. Could she *smell* his thoughts, like an animal? He backed away hurriedly and went to sit on a bench at the edge of the plaza.

"You come listen sometime!" she yelled after him. "You're always welcome, boy!"

o o o

"Where did you get that?" Jilla said, pointing at the flower pinned to Teo's collar.

"Some old woman," he said.

"You want to be careful which political party you ally yourself with." She gestured at him to pack the equipment crates. Together they folded the black cloth as darkness sliced across the plaza.

The Gryphon hobbling at their heels, they stepped off the plaza just as the aetheric lights began to blaze behind them, illuminating the waterfall.

"Where is everyone?" Night fell early this time of year, but the streets seemed empty.

"The riots," Jilla said. "There's still plenty of unrest." She made a sour sound. "But I don't know why they bother. Kanto wins, Winter continues. That's how it's been as long as I can remember. It's a waste of money."

"Oh." He followed her along the icy street. He couldn't imagine sounding that blasé about the Battle. The penny-wides made it sound as though it was the event that kept Tabat running. Was this what city life did to you, jaded you to this point? He wondered if he'd ever be this calm about it all.

Her house was nearby. As he followed her into the hallway, he saw paintings filled it, placed everywhere there was wall space.

Paintings of ships, ranging from large ones bristling with masts to smaller clipper ships, all depicted in painstaking detail, down to the names on the prows and the faces of the figureheads.

"Are these yours?" he asked.

"My father's."

"Does he live here too?"

"He died a year ago."

He murmured something abashed but she didn't say anything more. She fixed him dinner, an omelet made from strong cheese and leathery little eggs from a reed basket sitting beside the sink, and a mug of cider, sweet and hard enough to make his nostrils twitch.

Hunched over the table, Teo ate as though it was his sole occupation, a job he'd been bred for. He made a determined, steady progression through the omelet, three slices of heavily buttered bread, another half omelet, and then more bread, this time with citron marmalade as well as butter. He ate himself into a happy, gluttonous daze, sitting in the small kitchen with paintings on every side. He could hear the distant roar of the waterfall and the occasional cart clatter outside the curtained windows.

"So all of these are by your father?" He gestured at the nearest trio of paintings, each showing a different ship at anchor, labeled *Primrose*, *Cowslip*, and *Peaseblossom*.

Beside the door a tin tray sat on the floor, laden with a tiny empty cup and saucer, no bigger than his thumbnail. The boxy wooden cupboard beside the sink turned out to house a block of shiny ice. Jilla took out the pitcher on the shelf beneath it and poured a drop of cream into the saucer, not looking at him. "They're all by my father, aye. He was a Recorder for the Duke's Navy."

"What's that?" He pointed at the saucer.

"Sssh," she said. "I'll tell you another time."

He shrugged and crammed the last of the bread in his mouth. He peered sadly into his empty mug until she laughed and poured him more. Under the influence of the food, the hot liquid, the fever faded away and he felt steadier, the coughs and ache seeping away. He settled back in a happy stupor. Maybe the city had sent him a savior.

"There's a cot in the studio," she said. "I'll make sure there's linens for you."

○ ○ ○

Despite the scratchy wool blanket Jilla fetched, it was chilly in the studio. He had taken off his cloak, but now he draped it over himself, trying to maximize his warmth.

It was quiet, an almost ghostly silence. Purple and silver moonlight struggled for supremacy, washing in through the bull's-eye window glass to be reflected in ghostly rounds by the camera lenses on every side. On the table was a stack of red-bound books, their spines in precise alignment, and the moonlight battled over the embossed letters, *Narrative of a Beast's Life, by the Centaur Phillip.*

He lay on his back on the cot and tried to get comfortable. Every time he shifted his weight, the legs beneath his head gave out a ghastly creak. If he tugged the blanket up around his neck, it left his toes cold, and vice versa. He sighed as the cot creaked again.

The wind was so loud now. He'd never heard it howl so loud at home. He tried to relax. This was much better than sleeping outdoors, but he still twitched awake at any sound that might signal someone creeping up on him.

Over the wind's moan, he heard a man talking in the kitchen where Jilla was washing up. He hadn't heard the outer door open.

Blanket shrugged around his shoulders, he crept towards the door. It was glass-paned and securely closed. He set his hand on the chill metal of the handle and tested it. Unlocked.

The man said, "Three moons, red and white and purple, that's how many will shine."

"Hush," Jilla said in a gentle voice accompanied by the watery clatter of dishes.

"When we think we can let the moons control us, that's where we go wrong."

Teo tried to ease forward, and the door let out a shrill squeak. There was silence from the kitchen before Jilla said, "Go to sleep, Teo."

His cheeks burned, but he pushed forward. Jilla was alone in the kitchen, standing at the sink. The Gryphon was curled around her feet. Teo's gaze swept the small space. Could the voice have come from the icebox? That blue jar set on a high shelf? The covered basket beside the hearth? He frowned and shifted from foot to foot. His toes were cold on the cracked white tiles underfoot.

"Who's here?" he asked.

"No one. You must have been dreaming."

"In the morning, can I help you with the studio? Or I could set up the booth."

"Tomorrow I'll be sorting and developing pictures. It's easy enough. I can train you to do it quickly."

The assurance in the words warmed him. Finally someone had a place for him. A place in Tabat.

He returned to his cot and curled up. It seemed warmer now, even with the wind shrieking outside the windows. He thought about the future.

He would become Jilla's assistant, and eventually—though quickly—work his way up to partial ownership of the shop. They'd replace the Gryphon with more splendid, picturesque Beasts—a little Dragon, perhaps, or a four-armed bear, or a beautiful Mermaid. Nobility would come and be photographed there.

He'd pay off the Temple for his apprenticeship. Surely he wouldn't be the first to do such a thing. It would be a simple transaction. How could it be difficult? Jilla would help him.

He let the thoughts of her become erotic and drifted to sleep, cushioned by hope.

Chapter Thirteen

Bella's Test

I gauge Skye's guard. The wooden practice blade *clacks* quick, and again, down at the hip then up across the chest, deflected each time.

"Good," I say. "You've been practicing."

"Enough to make you break a sweat?" the girl challenges.

I mime disdain, dance back, sword raised between us. I bend right and left in parody of the training exercise every student learns their first day. "Hardly that."

Skye snorts and presses forward, boot soles sliding for purchase on the well-worn planking of the training chamber. A great mirror against the western wall reflects the last of the day's dim sunlight across the room. Aetheric lights, newly installed and still shiny and unscathed, blaze from either side of the entrance on the same wall to overpower the sunlight. They cast an unforgiving light across the neat racks of wooden weapons on the northern end and the three-row set of stands facing it on the south.

I prance sideways. I like to irritate my students. Moons know they'll face enough of it in the arena. That might make a fine pamphlet for Adelina. Advice on irritating opponents, with illustrative anecdotes. I've been running out of adventures, and Adelina is too fond of making up wild stuff to fill in the gaps.

Skye isn't paying enough attention to my expression. I sweep in, catch her across the left calf, deliberately angling to catch the soft flesh rather than the shinbone. Some would say I coddle them. Lucya would. But Skye will have a nasty enough bruise as is.

"Come on," I taunt. I flip hair out of my face and grin at Skye. "Make me sweat."

Narrowly avoiding a swipe, I pull back and wait, watching Skye's face.

At these moments, I both love and hate my students.

Love, for how can you not love someone you've taught to move, to strike? Someone who you give, freely, everything ever given you and some things that you've had to acquire on your own?

It doesn't happen with every student, certainly. But the ones with the spark, the ones whom you glimpse yourself in, the self that was once all angles and insecurity and terror that someone would expose them.

A mask of challenge over an uncertain core.

The ones that have the same potential that you once had. The potential you lived up to, now skills engrained in muscle memory, now realized.

And that is why you hate them too. You are only sharpening the dagger that will depose you. You look at all of them, wondering which would be the one.

Decades now, student after student has thought her- or himself ready, has met me in the ring, only to be thrown down, securing Winter's grip on Tabat.

Is that actually what the Gods intended? Have they chosen me for such a purpose? I would like to think so.

Otherwise things seem far too random.

○ ○ ○

After I've put her to the test and delivered a precise chain of bruises along her forearm, while we sit in the hot baths beneath the school, Skye says, "Some girls say you live on the Fourth Terrace, near Eidolon Canal, because a lover of yours died there years ago, a suicide."

"Who says that?" I ask. It always amazes me what a hearty interest the girls take in my life.

"Jenna. And the little Khentor girl."

The little Khentor girl has at least two hands in height on Skye. But she says it in the same tone I would, and she's started affecting several of my mannerisms, like chewing anise seeds to sweeten the breath and whiten the teeth.

I use a pumice stone on my feet, sanding down rough skin, steam-hazed into a fleshy outline. "Don't be ridiculous," I say between strokes. "Given what you know of me, why would I choose the Fourth Terrace?"

"Not because it is convenient to a tram or canal boat."

"One cannot set oneself enough such challenges in a day. If the breath I earn taking the Twelve Stairs will win me an advantage in a fight, it is effort well spent. You cannot rest on what circumstances you have—you must always be looking for chances to develop your edge."

I've delivered this lecture before.

Skye says, "But such inconvenience might be true of many neighborhoods. So convenience or its lack is not a criteria."

I splash my feet through the water trough that runs between the benches before toweling them and beginning to rub in peppermint and beeswax salve. Lucya makes it in great batches each spring when the mint fields on the northern bounds of the city yield up their first crop, but this time of year, it's starting to run out. I smear the last fingerful from the jar onto my sole.

Watching me, Skye says, "It's because of the bakeries near the grain market."

I tap my nose with a fragrant finger. "And the cheese shops only a level down. Remember there's food booths all along the Twelve Stairs."

"And Eidolon Canal? There's nothing particular about it?"

I consider how much to say. "I like the trees along it. They remind me of my parents' summer house."

Skye's sudden interest is like a sponge, sopping up all enthusiasm. It surprises and repels, this attention. I wonder what forms my life takes, told and retold by (generations of them now!) students. Who is encouraged by the story of a girl a year too old to be admitted at fifteen, insisting on fighting teacher after teacher until Lucya finally agreed to admit her provisionally?

Do they mention that I didn't win any of those matches, that it was perseverance, not talent, that won Lucya over? Judging from the hero worship I see so often in student eyes, that part of the story has escaped history.

I tell Skye, "You shouldn't believe everything you hear. People like to talk, to pretend they know secrets, so they can trade them for attention."

Skye shrugs, an impatient twist of her shoulders. "I know that." She rises, shaking off sweat and moisture, and goes to the rack mounded with towels. "You don't need to tell me anything you don't want to."

Sometimes she acts like a girl wanting me to court her. She wouldn't be the first, and usually I'm not tempted. But Skye is alluring, with her firm young length, her slender calves and forearms, lean and muscular.

I sigh. "There are willows along Eidolon Canal," I tell the steam hanging in the air. I can feel the girl listening. "I can see them from my window. When I was little, we used to go out to the country, where there was a pond and willows and ducks. My parents died a year later, and that's my strongest memory of them."

The girl considers what to say. "I'm sorry."

"It's not anything you or I can help."

Skye hovers on a foot, awkward as a colt, eyes a green that belies her name. She is the best of her year; the best of the last decade. I won't tell her that, lest it go to her head. I grunt and hoist myself off the stone bench, taking the towel that Skye hands me. She turns away to go into the cooler, clearer air of the changing room.

My mother died when I had barely reached the age of eight.

I do remember her somewhat. But I am unconvinced that the figure of my memory, smelling of fresh towels and peppermint, is not actually a confusion with my favorite nurse, an efficient woman whose efficiency did not allowed her to escape the fate of my parents: dead in a carriage accident on the road north of Tabat.

I imagined my mother's presence for a long time after the deaths, hearing her voice in conscience's scoldings, or comforting, cajoling. When Jolietta took me as an apprentice, though, that voice faded to a whisper, then just a hum, a thought, and finally silence. I did my best to re-summon that maternal presence, but with Jolietta around, there was no pretending that my mother still watched over me.

But it's there that I learned the determination, the force of will that brought me here. The will that carries me through, with or without working at the school.

○ ○ ○

Snow softens the rigid outlines of the clock tower near the Brides of Steel. In the summer, ivy shrouds its walls; now only the skeletons of the vines and gnarled clumps of leftover leaves are there, holding the snow in what deceptively resembles a handhold but is quick to give way under a climber's grasp.

This tower was built by Alberic's grandfather. Tabat is full of such buildings, commissioned by Dukes and Duchesses. What will the city be like when decisions are made differently? Even now it's changed, filled with an angry bustle of a sort I've never seen before.

I keep a sharp eye on the students gathered with me at its foot. This exercise gives rise to a broken limb or two as often or not.

The intricate brickwork on the northern side is a web of holds. Skye goes up as nimbly as a squirrel. The rope around her waist, reaching over the roof, shifts a slab of snow sideways; it slides off the tiled roof, revealing a gleaming expanse of mottled green and purple, like a turtle's shell emerging from cloudy water. She glances back over her shoulder, seeking me. I try not to smile.

Lucha dances sideways, head cocked back to watch above herself. She's a small, compact girl. Like all of the students here, she's one my considering eye has chosen, marked for extra lessons and advice that will ensure that she, like the favorites before them, emerges as a prime Gladiator, bound for splendor in the ring.

"Up, Valia," I say. Valia freezes like a rabbit who's spotted an eagle on the horizon.

"What is it?" I'm cold and want chal. It's not as though I'm doing this for my own good.

"It's so high," Valia says. She fell from a lesser height three months ago and snapped a rib. Ever since then, she's balked.

I consider her. Pale and straw-haired, a charity case, lucky to escape the warrens near the Slumpers.

This weakness can't be tolerated. Enough is enough.

"Well," I say, "I suppose you can always find work as a kitchen maid."

Valia blinks. Snow drifts down and tangles like woolly burrs in her hair. Like all of them, she wears no coat, only a thick doublet. I keep them active enough on these sessions that I'm not worried about losing anyone to cold.

Someday at least a few of these will face me.

Perhaps not Valia.

"Think on it," I say. "But not for long. Then go up or find some employment other than Gladiator."

"You don't have the authority to remove me from the school!" she protests.

"'Deed, I might not. But I will give you lessons no longer, and how well will you do without them, girl? You'll never gain the ring—you'll become someone's bravo or bodyguard, wielding your sword for coin rather than glory, an adjunct to some burly Beast, like a Cyclops or Minotaur."

Beside her, Lucha makes a tiny sound, a gasp. Valia's face goes white as the snow sweeping between us. Her hands seek the rope around her waist as though searching for a lifeline. Tears and snowflakes mingle in her eyelashes, the hairs so fine and blonde they're barely visible.

Pathetic. No wonder I've stood undefeated so long. None of them have the backbone I had, the iron determination that carried me to my current position, foremost Gladiator of Tabat. I travelled across the world to test my blade against the Gladiators of other cities, other continents. I am the foremost of my generation.

Perhaps even of all time, I sometimes think.

Valia begins climbing.

On my third victory, I commissioned my own set of Winter's armor, dedicating the whole of the purse to it. Lucya called me vainglorious for it. But I lived up to that splendid set of crystal and silver, so heavily ornamented that it sparkles like a snowflake in the sun. Now I can do no wrong.

Except win. There's more and more pressure for Winter to lose, for the seasons to return to their sometimes-yes, sometimes-no, cycle. But throwing a fight goes against everything I believe in.

Valia is high above, parallel with Skye. Both rest against the wall, their lines momentarily slack.

"You may begin."

As Skye feints and Valia recoils, scrambling sideways, snow bounces off my upturned face, soft animal kisses, unquestioning, unjudging, uncaring of the weather. Lucya wants me to help the Brides of Steel's Beast Trainer, merely to save a few coins. It's what I dislike most about the woman who was once my teacher and now is my business partner.

Skye misjudges, scrabbles for a new hold, regains herself just as Valia makes her move in turn and bounces off Skye's upraised forearm. More snow slides from the roof above, falling mainly on Lucha, though none of us escape it entirely.

Perhaps I'll find some student with an interest in Beasts, train them up, rather than hire someone. It'll seem enough to Lucya like I'm doing it myself that she won't protest.

Not Skye, though. I have better things in mind for Skye than cleaning stalls and tending inflamed frogs.

Valia slips, falls perhaps ten feet before the rope brings her up short. She's breathing oddly. I signal to her to descend. She does so in jerks, rappelling off the glassy bricks.

When she lands with a thump, I demand, "What's wrong? Are you hurt?"

Tears glaze Valia's face as she lifts it to my gaze.

"Please don't stop teaching me, Gladiator Kanto!" The words are almost lost between sobs.

I'm at a loss. I reach out my gloved hand and pat Valia's elbow. She keeps sniffling, a warbling snort that reminds me of a Clovian rabbit's wail.

The lugubrious sound reminds me, that to others, the Brides of Steel may be as important as it was for me. It was arrogant to assume Valia ready to reconcile herself to anything other than the path her teacher has forged.

I have no words for it so I wave the next pair of students to go up, but keep my hand on Valia's arm as the snow swirls around us and the other students battle in the sky.

○ ○ ○

Skye manages to disarm me in practice, and I have promised a trip for chal with any student who manages that. The girl opts for Berto's, the same choice any student in the school would make.

She sits across the round table in the watery, green-tinted light, licking seaweed and broth from her upper lip. I feel warmth that has nothing to do with the heat of the spices Berto's uses, and force myself to look away.

This time of day the late morning sunlight pours in through the eastern windows to splash against the wall of plants, red-flowering sage and lucky ivy, its heart-shaped leaves filling the tun-sized planters, glazed red in Hijae's honor. The air is full of the smell of sage and tea and the noise of the singing birds swinging in cages above the plants. They were quarreling last time I was here, but now all seems harmonious.

Skye reaches across the table and touches cool fingertips to the back of my hand. "I need to tell you something."

Alarm bells sound in my head. I straighten, withdrawing my hand. I've heard too many confessions of crushes from hapless students before. "Indeed? But we do need to head back to the school."

Skye persists. "No, it's important."

There will be no avoiding it without injuring the girl's feelings. I give that a fifty-fifty chance once we hit the moment of rejection.

Skye surprises me. "I wanted to tell you how much your example means, to all of us, not just me."

Pleasure and embarrassment squirm together. I take a sip of tea and watch my cup's rim as I set it down.

"Thank you." I strive for a formal tone. "It is good to hear, and I urge you to say it to all of your teachers who merit it."

"It's not that," Skye says. "I mean, you're a good teacher, of course."

"Of course," I echo.

I reach for my tea again, and check the other tables to make sure no one is close enough to hear. The Gladiators have a rich tradition of mockery, and this sort of thing, no matter how touching it might be, will only fuel that. Can Danokin over there hear what Skye is saying? He catches my eye and raises his mug in salute; I rather suspect he can.

Skye continues. "It's because you've achieved so much, so many things that inspire us to reach for the same heights." Her cheeks are red with strong emotion.

"Skye," I say. "I know what you mean. I appreciate that." My gaze flicks towards the watching Danokin. "Come, I will walk you back to the school."

Birds chitter at the blast of cold air as the door swings out to admit us to the outside world. The sunlight is gone, lost in clumps of wet snow, falling from the sky as though trying to strike the world, find revenge for some petty slight, hard ice needles on any and all exposed skin.

Skye is silent all the way back. Embarrassed, perhaps.

After I leave her at the school, I don't head homeward.

Down along Stumble Lane, which leads away from Pin and Needle, winding into darkness. The Duke's new lights are still reserved for the larger public areas, for the richer neighborhoods that can afford to subsidize their installation.

How many Dryads fuel those lights?

What will Alberic set to burning when there are no Dryads left?

A running boy stumbles past, heading up the Tumbril Stair. I pause, staring after him, but only see his heels flickering along the steps.

I wait, itching for a fight, but no one pursues him. The snow has become cold rain, which gusts and ebbs, carrying on a conversation of its own with the rooftiles. The omnipresent steam wagons trundle on a few streets over. I turn and go on.

Chapter Fourteen

Teo's Continued Adventures

In the middle of the night, the Gryphon roused him, nosing at his pillow as though trying to slip underneath it. He presumed it wanted outside, and so he stumbled to the door and let it out. He waited a little while to see if it would come back in, but it didn't. So he wandered, half-dreaming, back to the warmth of his cot.

In the morning he heard Jilla stirring in the kitchen. And then he heard her voice, high and shrill with alarm and anger. Throwing on his clothes, he scrambled into the kitchen.

The old Gryphon lay shivering on the tiled floor. She stooped and wrapped a blanket around it, gathering it up into her arms. She picked it up with difficulty, and the movement sent it into a coughing fit.

"Should I not have let it out?" he asked her back.

She said nothing, just kept holding the shivering Gryphon. She held it closely, carefully.

"Jilla," it said, its voice clear. It raised a trembling claw as though to touch her tear-marked face. "Jilla."

Teo recognized the voice he had heard before. "It can talk!"

"It was my father's," she said. She dipped her forehead to touch it to the Gryphon's beak. "It speaks with his voice."

But the Gryphon was silent now, and would not speak again with any sort of voice. She wrapped the blanket around it, totally obscuring its form, and laid it down on the table.

"I'm ... I'm sorry," Teo said.

She rounded on him in a blaze of fury. "As you should be! You let him out into the garden to die of the cold! You killed him with your carelessness!" The muscles of her throat stretched taut as windblown rigging as she shouted at him. "What were you thinking?"

"I don't know," he stammered. "I was dreaming, maybe."

"Dreaming?" Her voice rose in pitch.

He grabbed his clothing and scrambled for the door, unable to bear the anger, the disappointment, the grief, the fear in her face. His heart was shattering with disappointment. He'd botched things. He'd wrecked the painting of a perfect world that had almost—so close!—been bestowed on him. He stumbled away down the street, not looking behind himself.

All the world had been held out to him and then snatched away so fast that the image of it lingered like a phantom, lovely and un-achievable.

If only he'd thought about it, he would have realized that he shouldn't let the old Gryphon out into the cold. How stupid was he not to have grasped that? He felt heavy with disappointment, as though made of lead or stone.

He'd heard a story that when the ninety-nine statues lining Salt Way were commissioned, there were only ninety-eight. A clever artist had brought in a Medusa, used it to slay a rival, then slipped him in among the other statues. What would that feel like, to be turned to stone? Maybe it would be a relief not to have to feel all the emotion that haunted daily life, all the sorrow and anger.

And disappointment.

Perhaps he should leave the city, head up along the coast to Verranzo's New City. The Moon Temples didn't rule up there. People said things were different in that city, that Beasts and Humans lived together, that some Beasts were even accounted citizens there, with rights and no fear of being captured and forced into servitude.

But even there, Shifters were not welcome.

And Verranzo's New City would not have Bella Kanto.

He sorted through possibilities. He had come to Tabat in part because of Bella Kanto. Therefore, he would find her, and he would lay his problems at her feet, though perhaps not *all* of them.

But she would know what to do. If only he could find her, speak to her. Surely many must seek her counsel, but perhaps—just perhaps (and here a surge of hope ignited in him like a flame, despite his best efforts to douse it)—she'd speak to him.

He'd go to Spinner Press. She must come there sometimes.

But lurking outside the building, he was alarmed to see Eloquence exiting. Was the man looking for him? How had he known to come there? But no, he'd spoken of writing for Spinner Press. It must all be coincidence.

The city was Bella's. He'd wander it, and perhaps somewhere, somehow, he'd find her.

Shivering and sneezing, he moved onward and downward, onto Twicetold Street, where the morning presses hammered like the hearts of leviathans in the great warehouses, slamming out sheet after sheet of gray and tangerine-colored broadsides. You could feel their shudder underfoot as you walked, a sideways feeling that reminded Teo of his days on the *Water Lily*.

A belt-shaped park, filled with icicles and yellow forsythia, separated the presses from a quiet neighborhood. When he heard the blast of music it spun him around where he stood to see a tiny parade making its way along the edge of the park.

A calliope rumbled along, singing its tune with blasts of steam. It was painted red and gold and white, and a window in its side showed the brass workings. It hooted and wheedled, whistled and warbled, a song that kept falling down and picking itself up with the cheerful imperturbability of a drunken Piskie. An elephant pulled it, ignoring the blast of noise occurring behind it, as though disdainful of its indignity.

Heading to the park's verge, Teo hurried along in the calliope's wake, hunched against the cold. This time of day the ovens on Bakery Row would have been roaring for a while and one could lean against the stone brick walls to soak up heat, and maybe beg some burned rolls from someone taking out the trash.

The procession led him into an older neighborhood, its buildings completely assembled and now occupied. Curtains twitched, and children's faces peered out from the lower halves, a jostled jumble of expressions, gapes, and gawps before a parent called from the warm kitchen, teakettle hot, buns and bacon on the breakfast table. The curtains fell back into place, and Teo felt sad to see the other faces go. He missed being part of the pack of village children.

He walked along slowly, keeping the calliope in sight, thinking of home. They had pitied him at home. But at least he could live in Tabat unmolested, while they could not. It was a mercy, really, that he was *not* a Shifter.

How could he find Bella Kanto? He could wait for an occasion to see her in the arena, but that would give no chance to speak with her.

The calliope's disgruntled song sang up and down, wavered and wandered, as lost as he was. The brassy notes led his feet in an illusion of purpose.

The elephant pulling the calliope cocked its tail and shat, a liquid spattering on the cobblestones as it loped along, a string of curses coming from the driver in the guttural, half-choked language of the Southern Isles. A gray and white cat sat licking its paws in one doorway, eying the elephant.

The wheels, trundling through the long puddle, left a slimy green line in their path for a few yards. The small porches, each two or three chairs wide, held snow-capped flowerpots.

A passerby jostled Teo and he blinked, realizing that he'd been standing still, daydreaming. He watched the other wagons in the caravan trundle by.

A wagon passed, its doll-sized dimensions emblazoned with flowers and fruit, sinuous wyrms crawling among the ripening colors. The Ape driver cracked his whip, hurrying the Manticore hitched to its wagon while beside the harnessed Beast, the Sphinx from the College of Mages walked, unhurried, speaking in a low rumble of thoughts.

Teo shivered, not entirely due to the cold wind. He'd heard of the Sphinx's reputation. No one of the street crowd he'd met, beggars and con-artists and whores, would have dared to try to sneak onto the grounds of the College of Mages.

A troupe of black-scarved jugglers moved along, juggling anything and everything that came to hand. A baby was snatched up and whirled through the air before being restored to its startled mother's arms. Three old men found their canes partners in a quick, airborne jig. The jugglers juggled coins into a fruit vendor's hands, and he tossed them smooth- and hairy-skinned fruit, and fruit-like smiles and winks or round "Ohs" of surprise and approval.

Teo moved on.

He had to find Bella Kanto.

Chapter Fifteen

Bella and Adelina

Leonoa's recent question nags at me no matter how I try to cheer my morose mood with thoughts of Skye or the Brides of Steel. Is Adelina Nettlepurse still in love with me?

It would make sense, after all. Adelina would hardly be the first to fall. My conquests range from the Heliotrope Sorceress to the upper echelons of Tabatian society, even the Duke himself. Everyone loves Gladiators, a fact I've been happy enough to take advantage of over the past two decades.

It's a question of fairness, though. Am I really betraying her, capitalizing on Adelina's fondness for me? Do I provide nothing in exchange? A troubling thought, even for someone who doesn't follow the Trade Gods, who doesn't reckon life as a series of exchanges.

I walk along the edge of the high limestone wall that edges the Nettlepurse estate and its great gardens, balancing with practiced ease. All three moons are in the sky. Their light glints like signal fires on the shards of dragon-glass inlaid along the wall's top, spelled to bite deep into an intruder's hand. Red, white, white, purple. Purple, white, red, white, white, white, white.

What is it about Adelina that keeps me from pushing her away, long after our romantic entanglement? She was an ardent lover—I wasn't her first, but she admitted, I was the strongest, the deepest, the most passionate. But does that account for the friendship?

Not in my experience. I'm not known for leaving lovers happy. A choir of disgruntled Merchants' and Nobles' daughters and sons lies in my wake.

I blame some of that on myself. When I'm in full charm mode, no one can resist me. Including a Scholar Merchant who's been called the smartest woman in Tabat.

Before I reach the gate, inset with two shouting homunculi, I somersault into a willow tree that seems too far to reach. I hang there, watching the gardens for any sign of movement.

For what it's worth, Adelina lasted longer than most of my lovers. Not the longest, certainly—but it was a good six months before I found myself avoiding her. Finally she tracked me down, confronted me, and said bluntly that if we couldn't be lovers—and that was fine with her—then we'd be friends, at least.

And to my amazement, Adelina has managed it, for close to twelve years now.

I shimmy down along the trunk.

A barbed trap crouches in one fork. I step around it and continue downward.

It's true, I think, moving past its fellow, placed where my foot would have naturally fallen in by avoiding the first, that Adelina tends to see the most of me when I'm between lovers. Even so, we spend time together at least once a moon, even if sometimes it's only a hurried break for chal.

At the tree's foot, I wipe my hands off on my trousers and slip between low-set bushes and mesh-covered beds, green sprouts barely visible beneath the burlap.

Evening shadows embrace me and the dark purple cloak I wear. Underneath a smaller willow tree, half concealed in the downward-dangling wands, I take three bits of gravel from the pathway and flick them in rapid succession up towards Adelina's lit window where it hangs in the darkness.

I wait. Soon enough the window's latticed panes open outward like wings above the tangle of false balcony, and Adelina's head appears silhouetted in the trapezoid of light.

She's still not fully dressed, I note with a twitch of irritation. Adelina's lateness is notorious among her friends. The most infamous incident was her showing up two days late to a country party four years ago.

It's not so much the tardiness as her lack of acknowledgement of it. She goes about as though it were as normal as the city clocks chiming in the night.

"A quarter hour, and I'll be down and meet you in the front hall," Adelina says.

"We're late as it is! Although missing the initial speeches and the Presentation to the Duke—that I'm willing to forgive you."

"Go round. I don't know why you insist on testing the gardeners by sneaking in. I told them you'd be coming and to let you be."

I grimace but make my path through the bare bushes that line the southern wall of the Nettlepurse mansion. I glance in the windows as I pass. Each displays a well-lit vignette of wealthy Merchant life.

First the parlor, creamy wallpaper flocked with dark-blue ships, lustrous cobalt and burgundy rug underfoot. Above the fireplace, a portrait of one of Adelina's ancestors. I never remember exactly who, but "uncle" figures in somewhere among all the "greats"— the ancestor who accompanied the original founder of Tabat, Giuseppe Verranzo's Shadow Twin, and served as quartermaster on his ship, the *Loonblossom*.

Like deferential servitors, golden candlesticks hold candles atop their poised fingers, filling the room with light. Adelina's family is, if not the wealthiest in Tabat, at least one of the top three contenders, along with the owners of the Moon Bank, the Silvercloths, and the House of Two Sails, with its fleet of Merchant ships.

Persistent ivy tugs at my heels as I move along. The next window shows the Nettlepurse ballroom: elaborate parquet floor and siding, double chandeliers of crystal, luminous witch-lights swarming like a cloud of fireflies around the Wood Sprite servant who is cleaning the tear-drop shaped crystals.

He swats irritably at the lights with his duster as I watch. They scatter before settling along his hands and face, gleaming on his vulpine muzzle.

They're feeding on the salts and oils on the boy's skin. As a child, I possessed a glass tank of witch-lights. I loved putting my hand in among them and watching them paint my skin with brightness before I withdrew it, and they remained, tethered by their lodestone, a dull grey rock in the middle of the tank.

Framed by different windows, the servant appears and disappears. I take care to stay out of the light, but his attention is turned entirely to his duties. I round the corner. Here the bushes are evergreens, trimmed into waist-high ovoids, precisely measured in their configuration. Dry grass crackles underfoot as I pass into the pool of illumination cast by the witch-lights and trot up the flagstone steps.

The majordomo ushers me with cordial grace into the sitting room. I gave him a glove for his daughter—ten at the time and among my many fans—a few years ago. Ever since, he's favored me, despite the coolness the house's mistress, Adelina's mother, maintains towards me.

The sitting room holds both sofas and a handful of chairs, all invitingly deep and plushy. I choose to ignore them. Instead I stretch my legs, pacing back and forth in front of more portraits: Nettlepurses bearded and balding, wigged and wattled. One maiden, who had died young, stands out among the others, her face pale and drawn with consumption, her arms thin as matchsticks in their heavily embroidered sleeves.

The door opens behind me and I turn to see Emiliana Nettlepurse. Adelina's mother stands in the doorway looking at me.

I've never been able to read her. Emiliana is head of the Merchant's Guild, a practiced negotiator whose wardrobe of expressions consists, as far as I can tell, solely of studied blandness or mild irritation. A small, heavy-set woman, she wears rich clothes, skirts stiff with the embroidered emblems of her house, ships, and telescopes. My practiced eye can place the tailor, Three Coins, the one I myself patronize, and the most fashionable in Tabat.

I incline my head. "Good evening, Master Merchant."

Emiliana nods to me. Despite the difference in our statures, she inevitably makes me feel as small as a mouse contemplating a tomcat. "And here you are again in our house, Bella Kanto."

An icy edge to her tone warns me of storms ahead.

"We have a few moments before Adelina will be ready, and I wish to speak to you."

I wait.

"I intend to arrange a match for Adelina, and I'll thank you not to interfere in any of the matter," she says frankly.

I arch an eyebrow. "I don't know why you think I would do such a thing...." I begin, but Emiliana continues.

"She thinks the world of you and you have the power to influence her opinions. If the matter of marrying should come up, I'd prefer you exercise no sway. Let her choose by herself."

"Why do you think I'd interfere?" I say, indignant.

"You take a great deal of advantage of Adelina, in my opinion."

"She is my friend if that is what you mean to imply."

"She acts as your patron, with few of the benefits the official position would accord her." Emiliana's smile is Winter cold. "Believe me, it's nothing personal. I've profited from you over the years by betting that supplies would be dear by the beginning of Spring."

"Perhaps you'd prefer that I leave right now." I bounce on my heels, holding myself stiff with irritation.

"Don't do that. Don't pretend to be able to manipulate me as you do my daughter. I could make things uncomfortable for you, Gladiator. If you interfere with her happiness, I will."

We stare at each other in mutual dislike until the door clicks open again.

"Ah, there you are, Adelina. Are you ready to go?" I say in relief. I glance towards Emiliana. Will the woman go so far as to forbid her daughter to accompany me? But Emiliana says nothing.

"Petra's fetching my cloak," Adelina says, even as the servant appears at the door with the fur-lined blue length. Like the servant who had been cleaning the chandelier crystals, Petra is fox-nosed, but her pelt holds a caramel color, shading to chocolate at the ears. The Nettlepurses use only Fae in their household—slaves— although I know they are well-treated. I help Adelina into the cloak.

"You look lovely," I say to her. "Is that spider-lace?"

"A friend bought too many and sold them to me," she says lightly. Her eyes flicker in warning towards Emiliana. She still hides her ownership of Spinner Press from her mother, but sooner or later her expensive tastes will give her away. Emiliana knows she can't afford Altosian silk on her allowance from the House.

"Will you be late?" Emiliana asks Adelina, ignoring me.

Adelina glances between us.

"Not too late," she says. "We will hear the Duke's dedication—"

"Not unless we leave soon," I interject.

Adelina ignores me as well. "And then we will eat. I hear Bernarda has commissioned a marvelous new caterer, lots of Southern dishes. We'll look at the pictures, see and be seen, perhaps go out for chal afterwards."

Emiliana inclines her head. Adelina turns to me. "Shall we?"

As we exit, Emiliana says under her breath, pitched for my ears alone, "Remember what I said."

O O O

"Let's take Spray Road," Adelina says as we make our way out the front entrance of the estate, past a gardener who salutes stiffly as we pass.

"Feh, too many people."

"I like to look at the shops," Adelina says. She flutters her eyelashes mockingly at me.

I eye her warily, remembering Leonoa's words.

Adelina pushes the vamp farther, saying in sugary tones, "Indulge me."

I snort. She's not flirting with me but mocking Marta, who still hasn't taken very well to my break with her. Her distant relationship to the Duke makes it hard to ignore her. If I were forced to admit it, I'm taking Adelina in order to keep Marta at bay, and Adelina is as aware of that as I am.

We walk along the quiet promenade, passing below the ancient oaks there to make our way down a side stair and emerge onto Salt Road.

It's busier here. Vendors call to the hurrying pedestrians, offering fried fish and spun candy, bread knots and salted nuts. A hurdy-gurdy blares, reeling listeners in while two little girls crank the machine. The song is "Waltzing Josephine."

I could have brought Skye, but she is already preening herself a little and thinking herself overly important to my existence because I haven't discouraged her chasing after me. She's already setting up house with me in her head, and that only leads to heartbreak and uncomfortableness.

That is why you shouldn't kiss students, no matter how pretty they are. It's a complication I've avoided before today, and one I will keep avoiding.

But stern thoughts do not belong in this pretty evening, with the city lights jewelling its terraces. I spin to take Adelina's hands and dance her through the crowd, maneuvering her for a giddy moment, people parting with indulgent expressions while the sky gleams overhead with evening's promise. I smile, imagining the picture we make.

Two small wagons, their bodies nothing but cage, the fronts set with high driver's perches, pass. One is pulled by striped black and white horses and is full of chattering monkeys. Shaggy humanoids, towering over the crowd, tow the other which houses a fat Satyr clenching a wine-jug and shaking his cock at the onlookers. The city is so full of circuses and other election entertainments lately, how could anyone be unhappy with it?

The drivers speak back and forth as they go by at a leisurely pace.

"Heard your outfit got caught passing the pox on to the populace at large, Amos."

"Yeah? I heard they caught you feeding glamour dust to yours and trading them off as Unicorns."

"How's your mother been? I ain't seen her in a while."

"She's coming up from Caloosa. She's been running a hootch and pony show. I'll give her your love."

"You do that, aye, see that you do."

I laugh and draw Adelina's arm through mine. I smile at the passing people and they smile back, recognizing their Champion.

It is a fine evening. I deserve a fine evening, in the city I love most, with my friend.

Everything will be fine.

But the charms around my neck warm at moments, deflecting spells. There are still those out there who wish me harm.

Let them try. I am the undefeatable Bella Kanto.

○ ○ ○

Shouting Tabatian citizens swarm the plaza outside the gallery. The crowd, perhaps forty or fifty all told, are a scrabbly lot, dressed in sail-cloaks and cloth lashed boots. Many hold signs, neatly lettered. *You'd think a professional had done them,* I think. The signs read things like: "Beast and Man—Separation is Order!"; "Beastly MANners to Mix!" and "Art For the Social Good!"

Across the way on Printers Row, workers line the windows, watching the tumult, while on Spray a steam-wagon has flattened a pedal-cab. The drivers stand shouting at each other, a secondary crowd gathered around them.

Two Gladiators, one of them Danokin, stand outside, their cross-armed presence the crowd's only deterrent. The protestors press forward in waves triggered by each surge in shouting, but the Gladiators form islands of stillness defined by the reach of their brawny arms.

I give the fighters a flat-palmed salute. Both return the gesture as I shove my way through the crowd. Most of the protestors recognize me and fall back, but one man, all beard and bristle, returns a shove and finds himself flat on his back. The printers observe the action from their windows, shouting down insults and catcalls at the crowd, agitating it.

"Danokin, Reticence," I say, approaching with Adelina in my wake. "What's going on?"

"Bella Kanto, an example to us all. Mostly shouting from this lot and more from inside," Danokin answers.

A black, pearl-studded anchor and moon medallion glitters at his neck. "Nice trinket," I say. Around us the crowd jostles and mutters, but all three of us keep an almost exaggeratedly calm manner. I know how to maintain a blank, bored face as well as how it can be used to goad opponents.

"Times are good," Danokin drawls. "And yerself? When not inspiring future generations, that is."

"Can't complain." I glance over my shoulder at the crowd and drop my voice, words coming more quickly. "Look, let us in, all right? That's my cousin in there. Did the Duke leave already?"

"Aye, he was here snap at the hour. Marched off already, him and his dandy band." Danokin spits, eying a burly man in a dockworker's cap who's come too close. He steps aside from the door. "Head on in."

We push our way past a flurry of slogans through the doors and foyer.

I pause at the entrance, taking in the scene. A lifeboat-sized table is overturned in the middle of the immense room, appetizers strewn across the floor, almost to the polished edges parquetted in darker knotwork. Pink liquid puddles on the floor beside an overturned punch bowl. Shattered cups school around it.

As Adelina makes her way towards Leonoa, I meet the eyes of a woman near the overturned table: White-haired, dark-skinned, younger than me by perhaps a decade. Dressed in rich, strange fabrics, their cut formal and out of date. Drawn like a blade of sky-iron to its fellow-forged, I drift towards her. The woman wears no House chain. Perhaps she isn't from Tabat, but from some other continent, the Eastern Desert Lands, or the Protected Empire.

The sweep of my bow is graceful, evocative, and languid as a post-coital yawn. I've practiced that bow before my mirror on more than one occasion and use it to deadly effect.

"A rose amidst the chaos," I murmur, letting my lashes hood my eyes.

Is she amused or charmed? I can't quite tell. This surprises me. I'm used to knowing the psychology of any opponent, either in the ring or in the bedroom.

"Selene," the white-haired woman says, and lets me take her fingers to press a kiss on the tips. Her accent is pure as a tutor's but tinged with a breathiness that makes my pulse race.

"Named for the moon, how pretty. Quite a bit of excitement, eh?" I venture. Adelina gestures at me from across the room, beside Leonoa. "Perhaps I'll see you again tonight." With a wink, I make my way towards my cousin, resisting the urge to glance back.

Leonoa stands on the other side of the table, fists planted on her hips, confronting Bernarda.

Canvases lie crumpled like fallen moths on the ground, their colors dun and fur and flesh, edged with splintered lines of gilt.

Angry scuffmarks set parallel on the white walls show where the paintings have been dragged down. Two men have other canvases rolled and bent like boomerangs in their hands while a plump and earnest young woman flutters around the fallen paintings, trying to stack them without looking at their surfaces.

I see Marta across the room. Her reddish hair is ribboned with pearly curves gleaming against its midnight fall. There is an unpleasant sneer on her face, as usual—but still—I take a moment, just a moment, to admire the curve of her cleavage before I feel Adelina's elbow in my ribs.

"Eyes front!" Adelina hisses in my ear, even as Marta notices the stare.

Much to my surprise, the Merchant's daughter doesn't reciprocate with the lingering, come-hither look I expect. Rather, her sneer deepens as she regards Leonoa.

"Bitch," Adelina mutters, loudly enough for Marta to hear her. Eyebrows that I called wings of victory and desire, which I'd dedicated last year's late Winter to, rise.

Here she comes. Marta pushes past fellow Merchants, her usually graceful gait stiff and angry. I appreciatively note her translucent skin and the angry glitter to her eyes.

"What did you call me?" she demands of Adelina.

Adelina draws herself up to her full height in a stance that echoes her mother to a degree that would horrify the Scholar Merchant if she realized it.

Before she can speak, angry tones pull our attention elsewhere.

"I did not pay you for pornography!" Bernarda shrieks at Leonoa.

"I delivered what you requested. Forward thinking art, art which pushes the boundaries!" Leonoa shouts back.

"No one wants to buy such things!"

"You lie. Letha Silvercloth has already told me she's buying three! You can't rip down my paintings and then refuse my fee!"

"I can, and the law is with me. You are disturbing the City Peace and provoking a riot! You will be fined for this behavior, and I'll see that you never show another painting on this continent!"

Leonoa's body vibrates with fury like a demented top.

"You are a provincial, profit-blinded tart!" she spits out. Seeing us, she beckons me over with a hand quivering with anger despite her white-lipped efforts to control it.

The room blazes with unfortunate light, and the lanterns, augmented with sprays of witch-light, display the broken-winged, crumpled canvases in pitiless detail. I stoop to turn the closest over, Adelina peering over my shoulder.

The deep impressions of Leonoa's brushwork give the picture a vivid presence. Fierce, clear light streaming through a many-paned window shows a Centaur, side-slouched on a sturdy couch. His pose should look awkward but doesn't. The sunlight finds its answer in his heavy, well-kept mane, the orange foxfire of his eyes. His lips are full, pouting like summer-kissed grapes. His eyes are deep, bruised wells.

Regarding it, my senses kindle with a fire's warmth. Old, guilty thoughts stir as I look away.

But the Centaur's clothing chills me: the uniform of a Summer Guard, as though Beast and Human have been blended. The appalling, heretical juxtaposition hits me with a blow's force. Beside me, Adelina recoils, her shocked breath audible.

I keep my face expressionless as I replace the picture and pick up the next. It shows a Dog-Woman dressed in Spring's armor, gilt flowers mixed with real ones. A shiver continues down my spine, at odds with the room's hot press.

"Leonoa, what's going on?"

"This ... trull says that she is closing the exhibition and will pay no monies for the paintings she has ripped down and destroyed!"

"These abominations do not deserve the name of paintings! They are no more than Abolitionist propaganda, showing Beasts as though they were Human!" Bernarda retorts, face purpling to match the velvet she wore.

"If you do not wish them here, I will take them, but you *will* pay me for the goods that you have destroyed—months of work, expensive paints, and not to mention model fees. And you will pay the sum listed on my invoice!"

"These are worthless trash!"

"To you, perhaps, but to me they are quite valuable. And from the look of Scholar Reinart, he thinks so as well." Leonoa points at someone stooped in the act of tucking a painting torn from its frame inside his vest. It's the fellow who lives downstairs from me, the one with the dog.

He blinks at Leonoa. "Trying to preserve it?" he ventures.

They say nothing. He sighs and hands it over to the plump young woman, who unrolls it away from herself, like someone battling the light and heat of too fierce a flame, and adds it to her stack.

Outside the crowd shouts and a stone crashes through the window beside my elbow. Danokin pokes his head in the front doorway.

"I wouldn't stick around much longer," he says.

The gallery lights are merciless as a theater's light bridge, showing the lines of pain etched on Leonoa's face and the crows-feet around Adelina's eyes. Has it really been that long, I wonder, for them to have aged so?

Adelina looks at me with her customary reserve, but she senses the battle itch building inside me, the tremble so particular to the pre-battle moment. Leonoa and Bernarda continue to face off in silent fury.

Outside the gallery shouts are loud and angry. A tension fills the air that hasn't been there before, mingled with the smell of spilled punch and sweat. Outside the nearest high window, slogans sway dizzily as though drunk on the prospect of violence.

I assess the exits. Fight strategies are second nature. I've been in crowds before when things have gone bad. The fact is, I've been in fights in nearly every bar in the city, not to mention the occasional Gladiatorial match where the crowd disagreed with the outcome—most recently, Merchants tired of Spring's lateness.

The shouts outside grow louder and angrier. Another rock smashes through a window, sending a shower of glass across the floor, a crash followed by the tinkle of landing shards. Bernarda screams, holding her long-nailed hands up as though to frame her face.

"Torch the place!" someone shouts outside.

"You would think the Duke's police would be here already," I observe to Adelina.

"You would think so. What shall we do?"

Adelina's calm confidence that I know what to do is reassuring, if irritating. Just once, I'd like to see a Merchant less assured that the world is run to suit them, that everything will be taken care of by someone else.

"There's a door to the back there." I nod at an archway half-hidden by striped damask curtains. "That should lead to the kitchen, then to the alleyway that heads out towards the street on either side. I would take the branch that leads away from the crowd. Unless they are more organized than most mobs, they won't have watchers out there."

"All right," Adelina says. She turns to head over toward Leonoa but I catch at her sleeve.

"Wait."

"What?"

"If we all leave that way, we'll drag the crowd after us. I'd rather you and Leonoa slip out first. I'll follow later."

"You're staying here? But what if they attack you?"

I grin cockily at her. What indeed?

She wavers.

Taking my friend's elbow, I steer her through the room's confusion. Bernarda is fluttering around near the window. Perhaps the next thrown stone will strike her, I hope uncharitably, or strike Marta, who is being dragged away by the man who brought her. Others cluster against the walls, unsure of anything except that they do not want to face the angry mob.

"But what about my fee!" Leonoa says when we explain the plan to her. "I know how this works, Bel. Let them get away with it once, and my prices start dropping, and then no one values my work anymore. I can't afford not to sell these paintings."

"Then I will buy the lot of them! Have Bernarda send me the bill. But let us get you out of here safely, so you can go paint more paintings and charge even more exorbitant fees for them."

"I'll stay with you," the young man beside Leonoa says. He has hair of an unremarkable shade, pulled back and clasped with a black pearl and opal bauble. His face is bean-shaped, oddly askew, but appealing. He is clean-shaven and has little hair on his arms, which are exposed by the gauziness of his sleeves. Over the filmy shirt, a laced leather vest matches his boots.

I glance between the two of them. There's something about him.

Or maybe it's just the incipient fight. As I've noted before, fighting sets other juices stirring.

"This is Miche. He came to talk about buying one of the paintings," Leonoa says.

Miche bows. I smile at him. Leonoa and Adelina exchange glances.

"Go," I say, turning back to Adelina. "Triple moons, Addie! For once in your life don't argue with me."

"Unfair," Adelina says. "That's so unfair."

I kiss her hand, conscious of Miche observing the gesture. "Yes, unfair. I'm sorry. Sweetheart, take Leonoa and get out of here. I cannot fight unless I know that both of you are safe. I will meet you at the tea shop on the Duke's Plaza."

"Very well," Adelina says.

It's not until they vanish through the doorway that I relax.

I can handle myself in any fight. But I've always hated the arena matches that require keeping some target safe from attack. Particularly when it's a living target. Living targets are prone to panic, to running in the wrong direction only to spit themselves on a sword. It tries my patience to deal with such things.

There's a reason why I've never had children. The teenaged students of the Brides of Steel mature enough to be interesting in time, but young children are annoying blanks, packages of squawks and yells serving no purpose but to give their parents something to worry about; just more targets to be protected.

Not that I mean to compare either Adelina or Leonoa to children, I think, checking my sword as I make my way towards the other Gladiators.

But still.

"Crowd's grown," Danokin says as I join him.

"How many?"

He shrugs. "Under a hundred."

"Ah, and three of us. Sad to see them so outnumbered."

We all grin. I feel a touch of pride. Gladiators, tough and bold, something out of legend. Heroes of Tabat. I can tell the others are feeling the same. Behind them, I see the white-haired woman—

Selene?—and inwardly preen, forgetting Miche. Fighting is an aphrodisiac, for both combatant and bystander. Selene will be around afterward, surely.

Selene's hair glimmers like white moonlight. She is the opposite of Skye's innocence; there is a *knowingness* about her. Her lips are parted and her eyes seek mine. Deep inside, I feel a touch like a ship's anchor colliding with some vast Serpent, setting the proud masts a-twang like a harp, forcing a gasp from me.

Miche steps up beside us and I lose sight of Selene as I wave him back.

"Jump in if you see the chance, if you're so inclined," I tell him. "But we're used to brawling, and you're not. Stand back and keep the onlookers out of the way."

As we open the door, the crowd's roar modulates into a disappointed mutter as it realizes its members face three Gladiators rather than the crippled artist for whose blood it's been calling.

"Time for you to disperse, good citizens!" I call. I allow a small you're-not-worthy-of-being-taken-seriously smile to cross my lips. It'd be a shame not to provoke at least one or two into action.

Few seemed nettled enough by my tone to step forward. The wind has shifted and sleety rain drizzles down. Random gusts twitch the curtains of water this way and that. The streetlights shine, supplementing the failure of the obscured moons overhead.

"We don't want any bloodshed," Reticence says.

Speak for yourself, I think, *I could use a good fight to help get my mind off Skye.*

My smile deepens. The crowd surges forward and everything is lost in the fight.

O O O

There are some things worth doing well, for they are beautiful when done so.

Shoulder to shoulder, Reticence, Danokin, and I bob and weave, duck, swing roundhouses, kick, and dance. Fighting in pairs is common enough in the arena, and a trio isn't unheard of, so we know how to move in unison, how to keep an inner beat that lets us know when and where to be.

A blue-hatted man draws a knife. Reticence and I exchange feral smirks as our own blades come to our hands. A delicate, dangerous dance.

There is nothing like this in the world.

The crowd is a hostile haze of movement. My blade swings in arcs to match those of Reticence and Danokin. I'm disappointed when I hear the shrill whistles of the Peacekeepers, the sound of the Duke's officers' boots rushing along the cobblestones of the street. By then, two of the crowd lie unconscious, and another has reeled away to rest against the closest wall, a hand over the ribs where I stabbed him through. Blood seeps between his fingers.

I recognize the two Peacekeepers and they me. The blue and buff uniformed officers drop respectful nods as they gather up those of the crowd who have not realized what was going on or were too slow or injured to flee.

I deliberately control my breathing. I can hear the rumors in my mind—"Faced off a crowd and wasn't even winded!" before I incline my head in return.

One of the mechanical, wheeled men trundles in their wake, weapon barrels bristling like a spiky sea anemone. I hate the blankness of their stare. Something unnatural—not Beast or Human or even animal. Something other, something outside the natural order of things. With their mechanical soldiers, the College of Mages has finally gone too far in serving the Duke's whim.

I say nothing of this. I don't even let my expression change. The Human Peacekeepers chain their prisoners to the mechanical men, silver lengths stretched taut as an angry sentence's arc. What does it say about their future? Impossible for anyone, or anything, to tell.

I stand watching the convoy move off along the street, dispirited shuffles turning into a more energetic trot as the prisoners realize the unforgiving nature of their captor.

"Time for a drink?" Danokin says.

I scan the crowd, searching for dark skin, a fall of moonlight hair.

"Who are you looking for?" he asks.

"Girl I was talking to. Did you see her?"

He shrugs. "All cats are gray in the dark."

I laugh and nod but look again before shrugging.

Selene is gone, dispersed. I frown, then shrug and nod towards Danokin. Miche is still inside. I'll dazzle him a little with his luck and take him home with me to scratch my itch. I'll send a message to let Adelina and Leonoa know I won't be coming.

They'll understand. They always do.

Chapter Sixteen

Together

Teo worried because his birth coin was gone, even if it was back home safe.

He worried because the coin he'd taken was gone as well. Had the Moon Temple discovered his ruse? Or did they think he had forfeited his soul with the coin? He wasn't entirely clear on what would happen if the Temples—and by extension the Moons themselves—were displeased with him. Were the Moons like people? Would one stop by a Temple and, while sipping chal with a Priest, say, "By the way, that boy Teo is down on Salt Way right now. You can find him if you send a messenger."

No. If the Moons acted like that, people would be more scared of them. It seemed more like they talked about the Moons a lot but never really acted as though the Moons were watching.

What if the coin had no power over him, no matter what?

And what did it mean, that they had his Shadow Twin's coin? She was dead, to be sure, but a Shadow Twin was as close to a ghost as it was. Could a ghost be harmed?

Wandering underneath the docks, he picked up a purplish red stone, fat and smooth, from where it lay on the icy sand and flicked it into the water. There were dead fish here, which were not good, but the little crabs that picked at the corpses provided a mouthful or two, particularly if you could get a fish cart to cook them by giving them an iron nought or by looking sad enough. Or you might chance on a canal eel by fishing with a thread and a pin, if you were lucky enough to have such things, and that was good for a fine dinner when cooked and half the meat given to the cart owner in payment.

Some places were good for scavenging, others were not. Any-place there were food carts, there was promising detritus, but you fought for it with the gulls and the other street dwellers. Still, several times before he'd gathered a meal of bread ends and pastry fragments in the Waterfall plaza or near a tram platform. He could do that again.

The best was to find one of the political rallies, where they passed out food to draw people, but if you were under voting age, they would turn you away. Teo couldn't pass for a full grown man, no matter how tall he stood.

He knew that many in his situation gave up to go work for the Moon Temples, but just as many preferred not to commit their lives for bread in their stomachs. Some adults joined and left, joined and left, a beggar confided to Teo, but after a while the Priests would turn them away.

They wouldn't turn Teo away. He was promised to them. The thought still came to him: Wouldn't that be easiest?

They would take him and keep him, and he would not see the outside of the Temple for years.

That was not an option.

Teo had been in very few of Tabat's buildings so far, aside from stables, Figgis Bakery, and various sheds. Bella's house—the one he'd been told she rented, at any rate—was not what he expected of a hero, but it looked comfortable. At least as comfortable as Jilla's, perhaps even more so.

It was on Greenslope Way, one of a series of neat, three-story brick buildings, the tiles of their rooftops gleaming in the bare spots around their chimneys as they shouldered side-by-side. Slate paving led up to wooden stairs and then to an ample porch. It had the usual fan of colored tiles lining the doorway, and he recognized the one that stood for Bella.

He peered through the thick oval of glass—a glaring eye set on its side. A wide wooden staircase, the carved banister solemnly proceeding upward. A hallway and wide arch, shuttered now with sliding wooden paneling. A rug, moon red, growing darker in the shadows as it led towards a narrower archway.

Footsteps. He fled down to the street and hesitated.

He would go back down a few blocks. Figgis Bakery was there, and its alleyway was sheltered. They rousted people every few hours, but if you got there just after they'd cleared it, you could snatch an hour or two of warm sleep and perhaps even scavenge bread from the burned loaves they threw out.

○ ○ ○

The day's as cold as iron and just as gray. I jam a knitted cap on my head as I leave, irritated by the need for it. I prefer to let my hair stay unfettered. Some admire its sleek dark shine. Miche left in the early hours, or rather I let him know it was time for him to return home. I don't like waking beside a lover. They get ideas then of partnership, clingy and close.

I like waking by myself, knowing I need worry about pleasing no one. Jolietta used to rouse me with pinches or hard pokes. Once, back when I wore my hair long and braided, she grabbed that and jerked my head back from where I'd let it droop onto the table.

I still keep it short, but only because I do not want an opponent to have that advantage.

Not that I fear any opponent. Or even the reaction to my victory. Alberic predicts riots. So let them riot. A few fires will not destroy my city. If the Gods want Spring, I will lose, and that is that.

I stop in Figgis Bakery. I wonder what sort of pastry Skye finds most toothsome but then shove the thought away. A bag of pastries under my arm will put me even further in the students' favor. That's not something to be underestimated, with Lucya so cranky lately. I don't think she'll actually try to oust me from the school. Long before she comes to that decision, she'll reckon the pros and cons with Merchantish accuracy and realize that, despite any perceived flaws, I'm more financial asset than liability.

That thought makes me smug as I survey the bakery's interior: Counters full of pastries and loaves, and clerks in their neat white caps and aprons. The air's unpleasantly warm in here; I snatch the hat off and jam it in a pocket before I run my hand through my hair. I ignore the usual sidelong looks as I wait at a counter, directing the bright-haired clerk's harvest as she fills the bag with jam-stuffed rolls, cream-filled horns, and a dozen hyacinth cookies. I scatter coins on the wood, not bothering to count them, and leave with the bag clamped under my elbow.

I pause in the mouth of the alleyway running beside the bakery to adjust the bag's position. Angry words catch my attention and I look to see another of Figgis' clerks chasing a vagrant teen boy away from the side door. He backs away from the door and the menace of the clerk's broom, almost colliding with me.

"Mind your feet," I say. Startled, he spins, the ice underfoot sending him sprawling in the dirty snow lining the alley. I extend my free hand to help him up.

A northern boy, by the look of him: pale skin and brown-blonde hair. Badly dressed and skinny. The chain of bruises lining the side of his face touches me, makes me recall Jolietta's unpredictable slaps and blows.

He reminds me of *me*, back before I acquired a glaze of confidence.

I pull him up. He's lighter than I would have guessed, even given the gauntness of his face. I release his hand. He retreats a few paces, brushing ice from his clothing's tatters.

Fishing in my pocket, I extract the cap and proffer it. "Here. You look like you'll make better use of it than I."

He says, "Are you Bella Kanto?"

I nod. His eyes widen.

"I've read all of your adventures, all of the ones in the penny-wides."

"Every single one?"

He gulps as though I've caught him in some terrible falsehood. "The ones that made it to my village."

"And your name?"

He sticks out his hand. "I'm Teo."

We shake hands. His fingers are cold as ice.

"It's a chilly day, isn't it?" I say. "Come inside the bakery, and I will buy you an apple dumpling to warm your hands."

He says, "They won't let me in there. They chase me away."

"That is because you are not with Bella Kanto."

He trails at my heels as I reenter the bakery. Sure enough, a clerk steps forward as though to say something. But another clerk puts her hand on his arm and gestures to him to leave off. Teo remains at my heel like a well-trained hound as I go to the counter.

Here in the warm bakery, he manages to look even more bedraggled, colder, skinnier. I signal to the clerk to put three meat rolls and an apple dumpling in a bag and I hand him another of the dumplings. I push coins at her as he takes the bag.

The other patrons give us a wide berth. They're not used to seeing the underside of the city in their warm and cozy shops, in their warm and cozy lives. A wool-skirted Merchant twitches the folds of her clothing aside as though afraid he'll infect her. I quirk an eyebrow at her, smiling, and she turns red.

Teo trails me still as I exit. Outside we stand to watch the bakery carts rumbling in and out of their portal. Each time it opens, a wash of heated air surges out as the driver goes past. Some of them scowl as they see him, others smile and nod to me.

"Where are you living?" I ask.

He says around a mouthful of dumpling, "Here and there." He shrugs over-nonchalantly.

"On the street, you mean."

He shrugs again, then licks his fingers before he goes in for a meat roll. He crams the entire roll into his mouth.

I know that kind of hunger. I've been there far too often. It nipped at me all through the years with Jolietta and still haunts my dreams. It endears the boy to me even more, somehow.

"Come back to my house, Teo," I say. "I'll see you put up for the night. We can probably scare you up some warmer clothes as well. At least there's a meal there for you." I eye him. I'll slip Abernia extra coin in order to fatten the boy up. He looks so miserable.

I feel a little guilt, not for the first time, about Winter and the rigors it poses for those living on the streets. They would have welcomed an earlier spring. How they must've cursed me over the years.

He's ragged and filthy. Abernia will object. I'll see him bathed and clothed before I present him to her.

○ ○ ○

I swing the door open. "Wipe your shoes on the mat or Abernia will fuss."

I can tell the warmth inside is welcome. He shakes snow from his poncho and wipes his shoes clean with scrupulous care. I spark an oil lamp into life with a green tinted match and point up the stairs.

"I'm on the third floor. Door on the right as you hit the landing."

He trots upward and I follow. The house smells of cinnamon and baking and citrus oil, and under that a whiff of dog. A thick runner of cloth, colored like its downstairs counterpart, covers the hall floor leading down the stretch of black-and-white pictures staring at us. He turns and goes up a tight spiral. Up above sunlight gleams feebly through the icy glass skylight, competing with the lamp to illuminate the confines as I come up behind him.

My doorway is painted with the blue and gold Gryphons of Tabat.

He raises an eyebrow.

I shrug. "Abernia makes the most of my presence here. So she plays up the Champion thing." I unlock this door and open it. I step aside, and gesture him in.

Yet another hallway, but this one opens up into a much larger room. The sunlight welcomes us again, this time shining insistently through the glass.

Plushy softness, brilliant blue and gold, swallow our footsteps. Here the atmosphere is lemon oil and paper and penny-wide ink and leather polish with a hint of anise and metal and candies and the ginger and tomato leaf of Lucya's ointment. He advances across the room toward the wide window, framed with stiff blue depths, revealing from outside, snow-laden pine boughs.

Movement in the trees catches his eye. He stiffens.

"There are Fairies out there!"

"Nothing to be frightened of. They're minor city Fairies."

"On the way here they attacked the man I was with."

"Yeah? What did they look like?"

He says, eyes wide at the memory, "They laid an egg in him."

"Ah. Only two kinds do that." Jolietta drilled all of this into my head until I could have recited the names for all the minor species in my sleep.

I've adopted her pedantic tone, I realize. "What happened with the egg?"

"I cut it out of him." His Winter pale face goes paler at the memory.

I pat his shoulder. He wavers like the Centaur boy under my hand.

"They attacked because you disturbed a hive, no doubt. Or one of you seemed easy prey. It's their nature, boy."

The thing that separates Beasts from Humans, Jolietta always said. Humans can overcome their nature, but Beasts cannot. That is why the Gods have set us over them.

"I've got fish biscuits around here somewhere. And those." I point to a bowl of greenhouse fruit that Abernia stocks daily. I go to the tube and ring the buzzer beside it in order to shout down the tube. "Chal for two of us, please!"

I look at Teo, who is eyeing the fruit. I add, "And a round of soup and dumplings, and more biscuits perhaps?"

Teo goes back to staring out the window.

"Tell me your story," I say.

He turns around to face me, his expression earnest and scared. I look back at him.

I've seen the look he carries in his eyes before. It's one more manifestation of the great Beast made up of all my fans. This boy has grown up on stories of me. He has played at being me. The first time that happened, it startled me. But nowadays there are people who've been reading the stories since they were old enough to unfold the pages of the penny-wides. More and more of them each year.

He doesn't see me. He sees a smudgy illustration, something Leonoa drew while I read through the story, both of us laughing till our sides ached at the lies that Adelina had stuffed into each line.

"I was promised to the Moon Temples. But I didn't want to do that. So I ran away," he stammers.

I see. A runaway, and with as valid a reason for most runaways—that it wasn't what we wanted to do. That was why I had left Jolietta and Piper Hill behind and had never looked back, never taken up as a Beast Keeper, nor sold any of Jolietta's secrets to the other trainers or Scholars who come looking to talk to me every few years. She was legendary, Jolietta. She could get Beasts to do things that no one else could, had techniques for training that no one else will ever knew.

The door rattles as Abernia comes in, carrying a tray. She likes to keep an eye on my visitors, to monitor who's coming and going. If I'm lingering too long in the front hall, she'll wander out of the kitchen to keep a careful eye on what could be happening.

Is someone paying her to spy on me? No. That's one reason I pay her so well. She's just nosy when it comes to her most famous boarder.

She stares at Teo as she sets the tray down on the table. He returns her look, his eyes nervous but wanting to trust, like a colt's limpid depths.

She turns to me. "Anything else, Miss Bella?"

"You were complaining yesterday that the scullery boy had quit?"

"Aye. Ran off in the middle of the night. Took an armload of the best silver with him."

I point at Teo. "I found you a new one."

The meaning of it washes over them at the same time. Their mouths gape and they both say, "What?"

"You heard me. He's been living on the streets. I'm sure he'll work hard for his room and board. And for the occasional coin."

Abernia looks at Teo's face, which is radiant with hope.

"It's not fancy quarters, nothing like this room. But it's warm enough, and dark enough for sleeping in, at least. And all the meals that you need."

She eyes him as though estimating how many days it will take to flesh out those emaciated ribs. Abernia is the sort of woman who likes a puppy now and again.

He holds himself straight under our gaze, eyes looking to my face for approval.

How long has he been on the streets?

"When did you arrive in Tabat?"

He cast his eyes up to the ceiling, calculating. "A white moon, give or take a few days."

"How have you been living?"

"Badly," he admits with a wry grimace. Still, it takes resourcefulness or very good luck to live as he has for more than a few days.

Good luck. Perhaps some of it will rub off on me. The fight's not far away, and every magicker in the city must be casting ill luck charms my way.

o o o

"I'll send him down to you when he's ready, Abernia," Bella said. "I'll find him some clothes and get him cleaned up first."

After rummaging through a closet, she gave him an armload of clothes. "These would've gone to the rag picker anyhow. They'll suit you for now."

The trousers were black canvas. He could tell they'd be baggy on him, and luckily she'd included a sky blue sash that would hold them up for now. There were two shirts of worn white cotton, socks of knitted wool and a scuffed pair of low boots, and a fancy wool jacket with bright brass buttons and patterned with sprigs of flowers.

Each garment she handed him roused a fresh surge of happiness. He'd known that if he could just find Bella Kanto, all his problems would be solved. And here he was, like a character in a penny-wide. Perhaps he'd even be in one, maybe save Bella's life, or perform some other service worthy of being chronicled.

"Take a change and go bathe." Bella directed him to a door painted with golden lilies on a cheerful green background. As the door closed behind him and he found himself alone, he gaped at the enormous tub of cast-iron, uncertain.

It was monumental. It crouched on bird's feet, grasping enormous metal balls with ferocious tenacity. Silver pipes and faucets clustered at one end.

He examined it. Turned a tap experimentally, recoiled as water gushed out, turned it back off again. Then on and off again to test the water. It was cold as ice.

So was the water from the other one.

He pondered, then turned both on. He'd swum in mid-Winter rivers, sometimes it was worth it to be clean.

But by the time he pulled off his clothing, the left-hand tap gushed hot water. He happily readjusted the water ratio and got in.

There was soap smelling of minty citrus sweetness, a great yellow sponge three times bigger than his hand, and a scrub brush with a back carved of tortoiseshell. He experimented with all of these, and used the soap to wash his hair. He applied the brush with vigor to his feet, elbows, and hands.

He lay back in the soapy water and sighed happily. His hand gripped his cock and after a glance at the door, he soaped his hand to masturbate, letting the ejaculate float on the water in a cloud.

Emerging, he toweled off. The small table held a basin, more towels, and scissors, comb, and brush, too, all in matching tortoise-shell. The towels were blue, edged with tiny gold Gryphons that looked as though they'd be scratchy but weren't.

He wrapped a towel around himself and looked at the mirror. He used the scissors to cut away much of his hair, careful to catch it in his hand, and put it in the basket for such things in the corner. He trimmed it back and it was better, sure, but still rough and uneven where he hadn't been able to cope with the curls.

Bella rapped on the door. "Everything good in there?"

"Almost done," he called. He shrugged on the shirt, gave his chin a hopeful examination for stubble, but still nothing was there.

He sighed and went out to what he hoped was a new life.

O O O

Abernia's kitchen had brick walls bookending it on two sides, bricks protruding outward to form tiny shelves, on which perched brightly colored dolls, two or three inches tall. An enormous cast iron oven crouched near a back door, as short and round as Abernia, the red glow of its top echoing her gingery hair. A set of narrow stairs snaked around and behind two towering cupboards. The vast double sink sat to another side.

Abernia saw him looking at the dolls.

"The Trade Gods that watch over this house," she said. She pointed a few out: "Hospitality there. Good Value there. Fairness in Dealing. Attention to Detail. They have longer names in the trade tongue. I'll spare you those."

She turned on him, meeting him eye to eye. "You know how lucky you are, don't you, boy?"

He stammered, "I'm very thankful."

"Plucked out of the gutter by the likes of Bella Kanto. Serve her well, boy, and she'll do right by you, set you in some good profession, perhaps."

"Does she follow the Trade Gods?" His eyes returned to them. Fairness in Dealing held a tiny pair of scales; Hospitality a miniature jug and broom. They would've delighted his sister.

"No." Without elaborating, Abernia opened the back door. It led to a room that looked like it might have been an open porch at one point but was walled in now. "It's not the warmest room, but the cot's set near the wall where the stove is so it's always warm at night. There's blankets aplenty there. You can put your things in the chest."

Two windows looked out to the backyard, full of pine trees still green despite the snow that covered them.

"When you're done, come back into the kitchen." Abernia said and vanished back through the door.

He looked around. His good fortune rendered him nearly breathless, let alone capable of speech. A bed! With blankets! He prodded them experimentally and savored the thickness of the wool. The floor was made of unvarnished boards but so straight and true that a machine must have lathed them. He looked under the cot in case the previous occupant might have left something, but he found only a crumpled sock, thrice-darned, with a fresh hole in the toe.

He stroked a hand over his new clothing again, and then went to report to Abernia in the kitchen.

She surveyed him. "My maid is out sick, so you're getting thrown into the middle of it. Go up and knock at each door. If they don't answer, go in; if they do, wait until they call you in to enter. Swap out their towels and take away any food dishes or trays they have lying about. Don't let the bard keep you standing there talking.

In Scholar Reinart's room—you'll know which I mean, it's full of books—remember to check the desk for dishes. Make sure Miss Bella has three washcloths, and if she's out of soap ..." She chuckled as he blushed. "There's plenty in the towel cupboard." She gestured him off.

He tried the downstairs first, but as he paused at the door, Abernia shouted from the kitchen, "The Captain's off to sea; no need to bother with his room."

Upstairs, he knocked on the first door. No one answered.

He tried the door and cautiously opened it. "Hello?" He stepped into the room. It was lined with books.

Tacked above the fireplace was a canvas, as wide as Teo's outstretched arms from fingertip to fingertip. It showed a dog, a mastiff, with two women standing between them as high as their waists, their hands tangled. Something in the women's faces echoed that of the dog, and their brown hair matched its brindled hide. Elsewhere tall bookcases stretched from floor down to ceiling, crammed with books, some set vertically, others stacked and shagged with loose papers. A basket-woven chair, its arms shiny with wear, sagged beside the doorway to the bedroom.

A shape rose to greet him, growling—a dog, identical to the one in the picture, its teeth bared in menace. They were a rarity in the north, and he had never encountered one until he had visited Marten's Ferry. And even there, he'd only seen them from a distance. It was not until he had begun to wander Tabat that he had fully encountered such creatures, and most of the time they seemed to be devoted to either keeping him from entering or chasing him out of a particular place.

But Abernia wouldn't have sent him into danger. He stooped and held out his free hand, the one not gripping towels. "Just here to change at the towels, fella." The dog sniffed his hand and dropped his head, permitting Teo to scratch along his ears.

Teo did so for longer than he thought Abernia might have approved of. The thought made him stand. He went to the bathroom, the dog at his heels, its claws clicking on the tiles.

Towels littered the floor. He gathered them up and put two to replace them on the chair by the door.

Going back into the other room he cast his eye about for dishes. He stepped to the desk. The dog growled again.

Teo said, "Looking for dishes, boy; no need to worry."

He could've sworn the dog dropped a nod, but at any rate it stopped growling at him. He took a small plate, littered with crumbs and a large smear of butter, and three old tea mugs from the desk and went out, closing the door behind him.

In the kitchen he put the mugs in the sink and asked Abernia, "What is the dog's name?"

"Did he leave it there by itself? Not like him to do that to Cavall much. He's a friendly dog, sweet as silk. Take the towels down to the tub in the cellar, that's where the laundry is."

When he tried the next room, he understood what Abernia had meant when she said not to let the Bard keep him talking too long. The man there, who introduced himself as Lyman, kept up a cheerful flow of questions: How long had Teo been in the city, what did he think of it, had he been to any of the theaters, what ambitions did he have in life, and on and on. He ducked his head and said little. The man didn't seem to notice, just kept up the commentary while Teo gathered up wine glasses and bottles and street food wrappers.

Bella wasn't in her room anymore when he went up, though he hadn't heard her go out. He desperately wanted to explore her rooms, but at the same time he thought it wouldn't be nice of him, particularly when she had been so wonderful so far.

He stared out the window at the Fairies again, still feeling a thrill of fear despite Bella's assertions that they were harmless. One buzzed near the window outside and he flinched back, heart hammering.

It hovered there, staring in at him. He couldn't tell what it was thinking. He didn't know whether they really thought anything or not. He went into the bathroom and replaced the soap that he'd used and all of the towels, picked up the few plates that were lying about, and then went back downstairs.

As he clattered down the wooden stairs, a wave of contentment overcame him. He thought, *I'm warm and safe for now. Bella Kanto has overtaken to see to my future. Who knows what sorts of wonderful things will happen now?*

Chapter Seventeen

Bella Dreams

Bella," Alberic, 10th Duke of Tabat, says. We are dozing side by side in the hot springs below the castle. Musicians lilt and strum somewhere behind a screen. Alberic always has musicians near. A harp's strings sound, echoing off the high ceiling and stony walls until I can't tell where they come from. Layers of colored glass mute the aetheric lights till blue and gold stripes, Tabat's colors, lie in stripes across the water slicked surfaces of our naked flesh, his dark skin beside my olive shade.

He strokes the inside of my thigh with a forefinger.

"What?" I know that tone, syrupy with assurance and the ability to back up promises with a thick purse. It means some unreasonable demand is coming: *Be my Champion in the Southern Games, Bella. It'll be two months or so of journey there and back, that's all, and there's a lovely vineyard in the offing to add to your country estate if you do.*

And hadn't that been a nightmare, fighting sharks and Water Human attitudes, all in the name of getting the city better prices on certain spices, and sugar, and Alberic's favorite rum, along with a deal on the whale-bone used for parts of some mechanicals.

Or: *Teach my Guard a few tricks, Bella,* and unbeknownst to any of them, an assassin from the Rose Kingdom was brought in by the Duke so I could "show them what real action was like." I'm still paying guild-duty on that man's death.

"The Merchants are making noises about Winter."

"The Merchants are always making noises about Winter."

"They say there will be riots and burning as a sign of what's to come if Winter wins yet again. Get the rules changed and play Spring."

"Spring must be younger than her opponent, that's always the case."

He abandons his exploration of my skin and reaches for the whisky cup perched on the edge of the bowl we sit in, carved from the rock around the spring's natural base. The aetheric lights give the steam arising around us a peculiar hallucinogenic sheen. I watch a stripe of blue sweep across his face. He is still handsome enough, although giving way to middle age. I look with satisfaction at the taut line of my own leg, laddered in yellow.

"Just think about it," he coaxes.

I shake my head. "I will do you many favors, Alberic, but I won't change what I am for you. As long as I am the foremost Gladiator in Tabat, I will play Winter, and play her to win."

The song ends as I speak. The words hung in the air. Alberic sips his whisky staring at me. He returns to stroking my leg, but it is less a seductive gesture than a possessive one. I like this mood of his least of any of the mercurial changes and tempers which Alberic is prone to.

Years ago, when Alberic sent me one fall to the Southern Isles, I stayed with the Governor and his pretty children on the side of a red-rocked volcano. In the mornings I swam in a lagoon surrounded by frog drum and cricket drone. Sorties of birds had blazoned overhead as I sliced through the clear water.

In the afternoons, I went out fishing, my guide a merfolk of uncertain legal status—technically he was a Beast and could only be owned by someone. The mistress of the local inn owned him in theory, and I paid his day's wages each evening in three-sided copper coins, one reserved for him, to be tucked into his gum with long-knuckled grace.

I became enamored of the colors of the reefs. I learned to see them in the translucent water, to see the wave break, shaped by the thing I could not see but knew was there.

That skill was like dealing with Alberic. You try to steer through the imperceptible collisions of old and sometimes imagined slights, long-buried childhood resentments still adamant beneath the nebulous surface.

How bad could his childhood have been, though? His parents lasted until his late thirties, and while it was sad to have lost them both in the span of the same rainy Winter, I think it more survivable than the tumult of my own early years.

"I am the Duke of this city," he reminds me.

"For another six months, until the elections."

"Fah." The force of his recoil against the edge of the bath sends ripples across it. "Why should I be bound by a promise made 300 years ago?"

"Because your family has always sworn to live by it. You have plenty of holdings outside the city that you will not lose, and your castle remains yours. The people expect it. They have been waiting for it for centuries now. You'd have revolt in the streets."

His eyes icy midnight, he says, "As if there wasn't already plenty brewing in anger at you. Get out. I don't want to think about you and all the trouble you cause."

Throwing me out?! I twist my body and am up and sitting on the edge in an instant. "Very well."

I pause. Alberic is prone to sudden remorse at these moments, but this time he shows none. I breathe out resignation and go to put on my clothes. Fine, slippery silk—I always dress to fit my partner when dining or otherwise engaged.

He refuses to speak as I leave. I bite back the impulse to say, "Don't expect me back" over my shoulder. We've played this scene out before, but it has been more frequent in the last few years. We've never been a partnership, just a coming together from time to time, or a chance for Alberic to preen with me on his arm at some great occasion.

A silent servant escorts me to the gate, where one of the Duke's steam carriages waits. I climb in without a word and sit. The driver will already have been directed where to take me; everything in Alberic's household functions with quiet, perfect efficiency of the sort only money and power can summon. I could manage to fund that sort of thing myself nowadays, but that hasn't always been the case.

I would have liked to have seen Alberic undergo my childhood. Sleeping on straw in the stable because a Beast was about to birth, prodded awake by Jolietta's kick, knowing hours lay before you and then a full day's work expected as well. He would have curled up like a caterpillar, incredulous and incapable. I snort to myself.

The driver says, "Beg pardon?"

"Nothing," I say. "Or something, really. Take me to Berto's."

There is always someone to flirt with at Berto's.

But instead somehow I end up at the Brides of Steel.

o o o

I'd thought Miche a transitory pleasure, but he seems determined to work his way up to the position of lover. He comes by with trinkets—nothing valuable, he's wise enough to know that I have other admirers whose pockets are far deeper—but sometimes little magicky things that will amuse me, like a puppet of a dancing Ape, or some plainer token, the latest penny-wide or a hyacinth cookie.

I meet him on my way out today, the newly appointed Teo trailing me with a basket in hand to catch my purchases as I run my errands.

Miche bows deeply and takes my hand to kiss the knuckles in greeting, in a way calculated to remind me of similar experiences in bed.

"Who's your companion?" he asks.

Teo flinches at the look. He's convinced the Temples are pursuing him. I've told him they've got better things to do than hunt stray boys. Sure, if he walked into the Temple, they'd snag him soon enough, but he's safe with me. Miche's eyes flicker as he notes the movement and he flicks an inquiring look at me. He's too sharp by far, this one.

"This is Teo, who Abernia has hired as houseboy," I say.

"A fine country lad," Miche says. "That hardly seems like a suitable position for a strapping lad. I have a cousin who works with a circus. He's always hiring roustabouts."

"Perhaps once the boy has his bearings, he could see him," I say. "Not today, though."

Something about Teo fascinates Miche. He keeps stealing glances at him. He says, "But the sooner the better, surely!"

I don't like the way he's looking at the boy. The predatory gleam in his eyes sets my teeth on edge. I step between them and say, "We must be going."

"Of course," Miche says through his disappointment. He's as pouty as a teenager. "Perhaps I might come by later?"

I shake my head. That look strengthens my resolve to pry Miche away. I'd thought he might distract me, but it's easy enough to find bedmates.

"I have a book for you," he says. "I think you'll find it interesting. It's about Jolietta Kanto."

The book Leonoa tried to force on me as well. "Written by a Beast once in her care? I've heard of it. I don't care to read it. I know all I need to know of my aunt's training practices."

"It doesn't mention you at all. In case that's what you're worried about."

At first I don't know what he's trying to say. Sly insinuation fills his tone. It comes to me that he thinks me willing in all of Jolietta's practices. As bad as her. Anger rivets me to the spot for a moment. I pry its grip free in order to reply.

"Never speak to me of it again," I say.

The anger that flits across his face is a different kind than I'm used to seeing. What schemes does he think to set in motion that need me? Because that's the look there. But it shutters away as quickly as a slammed window. He doesn't burst into apology, he simply says, "Are you sure, Bella Kanto?"

"I thank you for your kindness," I reply, cool and formal. I don't look behind me as we walk away.

Teo, showing considerable wisdom, says nothing either.

o o o

I pose before my dressing table mirror, glancing past my form to examine the familiar map of my bedchamber, made new territory by the darkness. I like looking at myself in the shadows. They do interesting things to make my nose seem more chiseled, my cheekbones sharp as knives.

When I turn my face to one side I can smell the perfume left behind by the bouquet, but the other way brings the gingery smell of Lucya's ointment. At this time of night, the streets outside the house are quiet. Abernia's snores resound from a floor below, and Miche's quieter breathing echoes from the bed.

I find the sounds comforting. They remind me of the times I've slept in a stable, warm in the straw, knowing other creatures were around. I always sleep better in a group. The presence of slumbering others drives away old nightmares. My retired arena hound Gelerta died when the snows had set in at Winter's beginning two years ago. I haven't had the heart to replace her. The bedchamber and its adjoining sitting room still smell of dog in wet weather—like tonight.

The fire's last embers crackle and pop, sending up sparks like half-hearted fireworks. Another month of Winter, another month of people grousing about the weather and casting dirty looks my way. Everyone finds me predictable. No wonder people think I'm on the edge of failing, about to step aside for someone younger, stronger, more valiant.

I am Bella Kanto. How could they want anyone else?

I go to the window and flatten my forehead against the rain-spotted window glass. The window faces southward, over the garden, across the canal, and down towards the harbor, but I cannot see the water, only rooftops swallowed by rising mist. Bats and fickle ghosts ride the wind outside. I crane to listen to them but hear only the expected night sounds. A steam wagon's whistle and warning hoot lingers in the distance.

In the bed, Miche stirs. After the fight, he proved handy and young and handsome and just as willing as I was. Since then I've fucked him more than once and let him stay until the morning.

Usually I don't go for his sort, but there is a romantic cast to his bony face, his long-lashed black eyes. His pallor with his dark hair make him seem caught between Old Continent and New Continent blood and give his narrow smile an exotic touch. Pretty as a posterboard, a pantomime pirate.

The bedclothes rustle as he slips out of bed. Coming up behind me, his face swimming up in the moonlight, Miche Courdeau ladders his fingers across the flat plane of my naked stomach.

"Do something for me, love?" he whispers into my ear.

I listen to the night for advice but the steam wagon doesn't speak again. I lean back against him, considering.

"Do something?" he repeats. His fingers go on doing interesting things in the neighborhood of my belly, my hips, the crease of my thighs, reckoning the taut muscles, tallying each quiver. I spread my long toes for better purchase on the wooden floor and push myself back into him, testing his strength.

No match for me, really, unless he possesses some unexpected skill or a sorcerous augmentation. No match at all, not like Skye. But like her, young and smooth-skinned, and supple as a Selkie. And possessed of the same arrogance of youth, the presumption that his sinuous grace has enchanted me. I sigh inwardly. Am I getting old, that he thinks to trick me so easily? I've heard that wheedling tone before, from other lovers, and it never means good.

I reach back and feel at his neck, but he does not wear the pierced silver coin that Moon Temple followers carry. "What moon were you born under? Some say that you can tell a person's reliability by the moon that rides them."

"Hijae's red stare," he says.

"Ah, Hijae of blood. Not auspicious."

He drops a kiss on the bump of bone at the top of my spine and lets his tongue slide warmly around it.

"What do you want?" I ask. I'll let him coax this favor from me, but he'll pay for it in many acrobatic ways.

His lips nuzzle the nape of my neck, breathing out the words like afterthoughts, less important than the kisses.

"The boy. What sort of place is that for him, working in the scullery? Let me take him to my cousin at the circus. He'll learn a better trade there than washing pots. I'll make sure he's watched over and you can come and visit him to be sure."

At Teo's age—at any age, really—the choice between housework and circus work is easy. The boy doesn't need to be under my eye all the time. I should do what I do with my students, encourage independence.

Circus life seems chancy, but he'll learn enough there to suit him to some other employment by the time the elections are over and most of the circuses have gone back to traveling back and forth along the coast.

"Let me think on that a little longer," I say. "Ah, do that some more."

He obliges, dragging his mouth along my spine, setting the skin alight with pleasure. He tilts his head to watch my face in the mirror. "Good," he says, licking out the word and sighing coolness across the letters in a way that makes my half-lidded eyes flicker open. "Good."

"Come back to bed," I say and drag him back through the wash of moonlight from the many-paned window, its shadow an inky net on the floor.

O O O

Teo found the book lying beside the pile of boots he was supposed to shine for Bella, thrown there in a pile of other discards, a torn scarf and a glove worn past mending. He picked it up reverently. Books were not something that he had seen much of in his village. They were rare and precious, to be saved for teaching with. And here was one that Bella apparently did not want.

When he opened it and began to read, he realized that it was about the place where Bella had spent her early years, years only mentioned briefly in the penny-wides, sometimes not at all. It was about Jolietta Kanto, the preface said, told by a Centaur that had once belonged to her.

He took the book with him to his room, and that night, by candlelight, began to puzzle it out. It did not begin with Jolietta Kanto, actually. It began with the Centaur in his own land being captured by slavers and the adventures that gradually took him to Piper Hill.

The book made him sad. When he read of the Centaur, packed on a ship with the other slaves, taken forever from his home, he found himself crying. He closed it and wiped his face. What was the good of a book that made you weep? Books should thrill you, should tell you of adventures, not of sorrows.

He was tempted to throw it away, as Bella apparently had. Perhaps it had made her cry as well, although he found it impossible to imagine her in tears. But it was a book, after all, and therefore valuable in and of itself. So he tucked it with the few other belongings he had accumulated: a battered comb, a change of shirts, and a few pretty shells picked up below the docks while scavenging. Elya would have liked them, and he had a notion that sometime he might send them to her.

For now, though, he would give them no way to trace him. Like the Centaur, he would never see his home again.

Chapter Eighteen

Bella in Training

You almost never speak of your life before the Brides of Steel," Skye says. I'm showing her how to throw the sharp little star-knives that fighters from the Rose Kingdom favor.

When I'd entered the lobby, she'd been there, throwing snowballs in the courtyard with some of the other girls. I'd joined in at first, but found her by my side, chattering away as we defended the fountain in the center. Somehow now we're here, by ourselves.

A target flutters on the wall, made of cheap orange-tinted paper, concentric circles drawn with charcoal in its center. I can hear the shouts and smacking snowballs outside still.

I say, "Perhaps I feel that I had no life before I came to the Brides of Steel." My hand flickers, and a knife quivers in the target's innermost ring, trembling with the force of its impact.

"But you had a childhood."

Skye lines herself up and throws, biting her lip in concentration. The knife hits an outer ring.

"Better. Hold your elbow as I showed you."

"Bella!"

"What?"

I collect knives from the target, plucking them out as though selecting flowers for a bouquet.

"You had a childhood. You did not hatch from an egg at age fifteen, there at the gates of the Brides of Steel."

"Yes, I had a childhood. I had toys and holidays. I was raised by parents, and when they died, I was sent to first to live with my cousin's family and later my aunt."

"Jolietta Kanto."

I turn. Skye's face is flushed. She's been talking about me to the others.

"If you know all this, why do you ask me?" I say. "Or better yet, why not go read a penny-wide for clues?"

"Because I want to know," Skye says. "What made you what you are today? Why did you come to the school so late in life? What was it like being raised by a renowned Beast Trainer and why do you refuse to deal with Beasts now?"

"My aunt," I say, clipping each word off with cold, displeased precision, "had many theories on the raising and training of Beasts, which she was delighted to test on a Human child. Do you want more details, Skye? I can assure you that you will not find them palatable. Nor will you wish to replicate my experiences."

Skye takes a step back in the face of that hostility. "I'm sorry," she falters. "I just wanted ..."

"What you want does not concern us here," I say. "What I want to do does, and that is to teach you. Before tomorrow, be able to hit the second ring three times running."

Thrusting the handful of knives on Skye, I make for the door.

"So you'll be back tomorrow," Skye says, so softly that I can pretend not to hear as I leave.

o o o

When I run into Miche in Berto's, I invite him home with me. I try to lose myself in the bed, thrusting thoughts of Skye away while his body clamors against mine. His muscles are lean, sliding under the skin, a slide that reminds me of the feel of a great serpent. He is good, one of the ones that make an art-form of lovemaking.

There's always a certain distance to those, as though they were watching from afar, judging breaths and grimaces and measuring them against previous encounters. It is better than Alberic, who takes without ever questioning his right to do so.

Long afterward, tangled in sleep's petticoats, I dream of a house, the kind I grew up in: several-storied and many-roomed. Passages that go up- and downstairs, staircases hidden behind cupboards and tapestries, cellar tunnels winding torch-lit through the earth, attics full of rats and packing cases.

I know this dream. I'll be inside the walls for a little while—just moved in or investigating the place for a friend or relative. Things will begin to move. Turning to see something settling to a table, I'll know, that seconds before, it was hovering in the air. More and more objects, until finally half the room is floating, lamps and books and knick-knacks and pots of blue flowers.

I stand there, knowing that if only I can say something, I can dismiss this malign entity, this poltergeist. If only I can speak, say something, anything. My jaws work, but no sound comes forth, not even a hiss or whisper.

In the dream kitchen downstairs, a tool lies on the table, glinting in the red moonlight. Am I supposed to dull the ghost? Then I realize it's the other way around. I've already gentled the ghost, long ago.

I wake in a cold sweat.

Moonlight still pours through the window and I see with muzzy surprise—am I dreaming or awake?—Miche near the chest at the bed's foot. Is its lid ajar? If so, only for a moment before he stands, chilly witch light gilding his form.

"What are you doing?" I say.

"I got cold, I was looking for another blanket."

"Moons, it's warm enough in here to stifle an eel!"

He laughs. "I've been down south. You haven't known hot until you've been through summer there."

"There's more blankets in that cupboard, on the top shelf."

"Here?"

"That's not the warmest one, there's a knitted one up on top."

"This will be fine enough."

He drapes it over his side and crawls back into bed, curling up against me. He feels clammy and heavy, but the musk of his hair is pleasant.

After a few moments, I feel myself falling asleep as I watch the moonlight continue to spill through the window, silver strands weaving, embroidering themselves on the air, outlining the white flowers with a poisonous glow, filling up the shadows until the chamber seems bright as day. The red moon has passed, and only the white moon remains.

o o o

Adelina's offices are in the heart of the building. She pretends to be only a clerk here, but in truth it's her printing house, no matter how she lies to her mother. If I were her, I'd flaunt it and let Emiliana see that I'd made something entirely my own, despite all her efforts to steer her daughter's course.

My presence has earned this building the little silver tile set with a white sword that sits to the right of the arch of bricks surrounding the door, amid a rainbow of others. I tap it with my finger as I go past.

Serafina, the clerk who serves Adelina, ushers me into a waiting room. It's not often that Adelina makes me cool my heels, but Serafina is apologetic, deferential, and brings me tea and pastries. I eat half of a fat, sugar-rolled doughnut, wrap the rest in a napkin, and slide it in a pocket for later.

The little room is well-used but comfortable. There's a shelf of the Trade Gods associated with printing: Accuracy and Advertising foremost among the little crowd of figurines. Books are stacked everywhere. An entire shelf holds the purple-bound volumes of my adventures. I pick up the nearest—*Bella and the Sea Pirates*—and settle down to read about myself.

These are the books that built this printing house. Adelina had been having little success with her historical monographs when one drunken night she proposed writing up my adventures and seeing how they sold in a penny-wide, one of the news sheets spewed out daily to amuse the citizenry.

Now we have these little books. This one has been made for the upper crust, bound in expensive Dragon leather. Gilt dusts the edges of the pages.

Everyone in Tabat reads these. The Humans, at least, and I suspect a few of the Beasts who illicitly learn to read as well. *The Tales of Bella Kanto.*

So little of it is true, but they all believe in it so strongly, this borrowed glamour.

Who'd have thought a dry historian could concoct such stories? And racy ones at times, to boot. Her imagination is richer than any life ever could be.

True, she has me as the central point. Surely any tale launched about the Champion of Tabat will sail a worthy course.

But still. No City's Champion has ever reigned so long.

Adelina enters. Her cheeks are flushed. She's been flirting with someone. I know that sparkle, and I feel a twinge of jealousy and put it down as sternly as Leonoa would want.

As though evoked by the thought, Adelina says, "Leonoa was here this morning. The Bank has frozen her money, saying that she preaches sedition."

"Is that legal?" I ask.

Her shoulders move in a shrug, a graceful motion that makes the jealousy prick at my ribs again.

"She said she would appeal to you, but you have been quarreling." Her eyes search mine.

"Those pictures," I say, the words slow and careful. "Adelina, perhaps they *are* sedition. Beasts and Humans, this is the natural order of things."

Adelina settles on the couch to examine the selection of pastries Serafina has brought. She picks a hyacinth cookie and nibbles at its edge as she thinks.

"I'm surprised to hear that," she says. "I always assumed— because of your upbringing—that you sympathized with the Beasts."

We've rarely spoken of my time with Jolietta. I've never told her the entirety, only enough to explain why I rejected my training, why I chose to become a Gladiator rather than follow in Jolietta's footsteps as a Beast Trainer.

"I object to her methods," I say. "They were harsh and unnecessarily cruel. Beasts are like children. They should be guided. To put one on a footing with Humans would be a disservice to both."

Is that true? I think of Phillip. *Was he not as well-spoken and as wise as any Human?*

But there are always exceptions that prove the rule.

"You feel so strongly about this that you'd renounce your cousin?" Shock fills Adelina's tone. To Merchants, family is always first and foremost.

"No, no, of course not," I snap. "But she has been scolding me lately. Forgive me for not leaping to her defense."

"Scolding you about what?"

I hesitate. I don't want to pry open this particular barrel. Too many rotted things could lie inside. "Many things," I finally say, and am relieved that she accepts it.

"Will you help her, Bella? Or shall I?"

The insinuation that I wouldn't nettles me. "I am short at the moment," I drawl. "I am sure the fortunes of Spinner Press can cover this." She can remember whose adventures built those fortunes easily enough; I need not remind her.

Chapter Nineteen

Teo's Life with Bella

Teo liked accompanying Bella on errands. People often came up to greet her and compliment her, which she always took with a gracious smile and a cheerful reply. There were some who muttered and scowled at her, and she smiled just as cheerfully at them. If they said something, her spine would become steel, eyes gone not hard but absent and impersonal, a shield so obdurate no amount of rudeness could ever get through.

This trip was less interesting because it included Miche. Bella didn't talk to Teo as she usually did. Instead he trailed behind the two of them with Abernia's basket as they chattered back and forth, en route to the press that printed the penny-wides about Bella.

The press was near the Slumpers, the factories that tinted the river here a deep orange with their residues. He knew now that this was the reason the cheapest paper in Tabat was pale orange, used for penny-wides and scratch paper and wrappings for meat and bread and cheese, giving it what people called "Tabat savor," a coppery edge that Teo had found most unpalatable at first.

They went along Spring Avenue, then took the Eastern Tram down. Teo clung to the railing, gazing wide-eyed over the city. It was like flying in a dream, slow and even over a changing landscape, the snow covered trees and bushes texturing the garden strip running alongside the Tram, broken on the odd-numbered terraces by wide streets and on the fifth and eleventh terraces by the double-broad Spray and Salt Ways.

The press was a graceful, three-story building of gray-green marble and black iron fretwork. Three cupolas rose on its spiky roof, wide windowed and overlooking the rainbow water of the river.

Adelina awaited them on the steps. She and Bella embraced before Bella swung back to introduce Adelina and Miche so they might exchange cordial nods.

Bella took the armload of books Adelina was holding, checking the spines before she handed them off to Teo. "We are bound for chal at Berto's next, if you're free."

"No—I'm meeting with a new writer."

"What, someone other than me?" Bella teased.

"Indeed! A river Pilot, who makes stories as alive as any I've ever read. I've spoken of him to you before."

"What's his name?"

"Eloquence Clement."

A pang rooted itself in Teo's chest, pinning him in place. His eyes widened. Miche's side glance caught him, the older man's eyes considering, taking in the information like a Merchant sliding a few coins into a purse.

"Is he due here soon? I'd like to meet him."

Teo was made of glass, poised to fall and break. He tried to catch Bella's eye, to shake his head "no," but all of Bella's attention was set on teasing Adelina, who'd gone pink-cheeked.

"You like this fellow! And yet by the name, a Moon follower. You and Leonoa, setting all the rules on their edges."

"You're a fine one to talk about that," Adelina snapped back, quick as a closing trap.

Miche cleared his throat. "Let's be off, Bella," he said. "The boy and I are hungry."

He smiled at Teo, but the expression was cold and unwarming. It was a smile of reckoning, a smile that said, *You owe me now*, with the careful precision of the many versed and numbered Trade Gods' catechism.

O O O

Abernia kept him well-fed. Teo could feel himself filling out and getting stronger. He liked to sit in the kitchen, polishing silver or sharpening knives, while she chattered away to him about city life. She told him stories about the founding of Tabat by Verranzo's Shadow Twin. It made him think of his own Shadow Twin, of her coin. Was he safe here from the Priests? Bella had said they would not search the city for him, that he need not worry that anyone in the house would turn him in, but it was still with some trepidation that he finally confided in Abernia.

"You needn't worry, boy," she said, folding dishtowels. "Sure, if someone went to the Temples and said where you were, they'd come looking for you. And the law would think that right of them, for technically you belong to them. They have the legal right to take you, and certainly they would punish you, to discourage others from following your example. But have you many enemies willing to betray you to them?"

Her eyes twinkled. He was safe.

But it did not content him. It was odd that it wasn't until he was safe in Bella's house that Teo truly felt homesick. All the weeks of scrambling for existence, of trying to find shelter, the days when he counted himself lucky when he found a nook in which he could doze for an hour or two, none of those had been accompanied by this longing.

There was no sense to it. Here he was warm and fed, here he was safe from the Temples. Here he was in the household of his hero, the woman whose adventures he had followed for so long. And yet at night, as he fell asleep, longing crept over him.

Not longing for his village overall but longing for little things, like the taste of his mother's spice rolls and the feel of Elya cuddled up to him beside the fire. The look of Lidiya's hand gesturing out how to harvest a particular plant, or even, most oddly of all, the smell of his father's cloak.

Somehow it showed itself in his face at breakfast. Abernia gazed at him and said, "Homesick, lad?"

He started to shake his head, then nodded.

"It makes no sense to me," he said. "I couldn't go home. I don't want to go home."

"Sometimes, knowing that you can't return makes it all the more precious," she said. She tapped her teeth with a fingernail, considering him, her head tilted to one side as though contemplating a brisket to decide how many hours it would take to roast.

"You need a day to yourself," she said.

It startled him. "What?"

"Oh," she said, "don't think that it will be a day free of work, but I have errands I will send you on, Teo. That will give you a chance to see the city. No wonder you have the megrims, you've been shut up in here."

"Not anywhere near the Temples?"

She said, "I keep telling you, they have no interest in you unless someone brings you to their attention. There is no reason to fear them, Teo." Seeing how unconvinced he looked, she said, "No, I will not send you anywhere near the Temples."

She took down a shopping basket. Turning, she handed him several coins. His eyes widened. Silver skiffs, not copper! She laughed at his wide eyes and said, "I know you won't run off with them. Spend two copper skiffs of the change on yourself. If I write down a list, can you read?"

"Of course I can!" he said indignantly.

She shook her head. "There's no shame in not being able to read. It's not a skill I would have expected in a country boy. How did you learn?"

"The penny-wides," he said. "Sometimes things come packed in them."

Comprehension lit her face. "Of course. That explains so much." There was amusement in her tone. "No wonder you came to Bella Kanto."

o o o

He hardly knew where to put the coins. He was so worried that he might lose them. Not in a pocket, where they might slip out or fall prey to a pickpocket's quick fingers. Not held in his hand, where he might drop them. In the end he adopted a simple trick he'd seen used on the street. He tucked them in his cheek. They seemed safest there.

Tabat's main marketplace straddled a cluster of staircases. A Mermaid sat coiled in an immense bathtub whose clawed feet clutched wooden rollers. A brake lever was fixed in place, keeping the tub from rolling down the decline. Her hair had the same gilt gleam as the hot and cold taps wound round with strings of pea-sized pearls.

A chain soldered to the spigot led to the collar of an anorexic white kitten that wandered near the bathtub's tail end, eying the Mermaid with mingled antipathy and fascination.

Copper and silver coins half-filled a basket fastened to the outside of the tub's rim. The Mermaid sang as she combed her hair. Her gills were feathered ruffs in the hollows of her skeletal throat, veined like internal organs, dark blue arteries and fanned capillaries, anemone and embroidery.

He picked through the stalls following Abernia's scrawled instructions: two loaves of bread, a packet of needles, an orange envelope of nettle tea.

Abernia had told him to buy the fish from a stall near the docks, and so he wandered down through the terraces. From the lowest one, he glimpsed ships being loaded and unloaded: broad-bellied Merchant vessels from the Southern Isles filled with bales of spices and cloth, the narrow schooners used for sorcerer hunting, towering war-ships which patrolled the western coasts.

The stall was next to a small dock where the fishing boats moored. Looking over the edge, he saw chalky white jellyfish floating in the water like deflated lace balloons, swaying back and forth with the waves' movement.

A little street led up the hillside again. Drawn by the smell of cooking meat, Teo rounded a corner, still google-eyed. How did anyone become accustomed to this place? He wondered how far he could walk in a day. He sniffed the air again and saw the booth that was the source of the wonderful, rich smell.

Planking had been nailed together and draped with canvas, purple and blue feathers stuck along the booth's top edge. Two platters of meat pies sat on a blocky shelf, watched over by a small, grubby child.

Buying two, Teo headed home. He bounded up the steps towards Bella's house filled with renewed enthusiasm, Abernia's basket bumping heavily on his hip. This was the best of all possible lives.

O O O

Rallies crowded Eelsy Street, so he took the long way round. Three stairs up, and he'd be on Greenslope.

Someone grabbed and shook him, hard enough to hurt. Coins fell from his mouth to ring on the pavestones.

"Ah, lad," a voice said. He recognized it instantly: Canumbra. Legio was kneeling to collect the scattered coins. His heart sank. "I thought we'd run into you soon enough. Granny Beeswax would like to know more about ye. And so would I."

The voice was closer as Canumbra leaned forward, hissing into Teo's ear. His breath was foul and reeked of whiskey. "Make a sound, boy, and we'll let them know you're some sort of filthy Beast. Think anyone will come to your rescue, knowing that?"

Legio leaned in from the other side. "They'd kill you if they knew, boy."

Heavy hands on his shoulders pushed Teo along. Panicked and stumbling, Teo didn't dare call out—who here would be willing to help him? Visions of the pyre danced in front of him. Canumbra shoved him into the mouth of an alley, and he went sprawling on the icy cobblestones, trying to roll away but only to find himself crawling up the filth of a midden heap.

Legio guffawed. "Look at him now! Not so cocky, eh?"

Canumbra was sorting through the basket, nose wrinkling. "Fish and bread and needles. Scarce enough to buy your freedom."

Teo tried to protest. They were treating him as though he'd wronged them by getting away, but that didn't make sense. Nothing in this city made sense.

Canumbra's boot was on his chest, pinning him. The sky was chilly blue and white behind his head. Grinning, the man leaned down, replacing the boot with a knee. "Think you're smart, boy?"

"No," Teo said honestly. "Please ..."

"Think anyone will miss you?" Canumbra sneered.

"Yes!" Teo gasped. "I've got a job, and they expect me. I could give you money. When I'm paid, I mean."

Interest flickered in Canumbra's eyes. "Where's the job?"

"It's with Bella Kanto."

Legio guffawed.

Canumbra said, "Pull the other one, boy. Tell you what: we'll welcome you to Tabat, take you sight-seeing, visit the Tram." Canumbra smirked down at him. "Come on. Have you ever ridden it?" The man suddenly oozed horrible charm, ominous beyond measure.

He held onto Teo's shoulder as Legio paid for tickets for all three of them. He shoved Teo into the last of the tripartite Tram chambers and glowered at the occupants, a pair of pock-marked youths in ill-fitting suits, until they took the hint and moved along to another chamber.

Canumbra opened the window of the Tram and shoved Teo against it so he leaned out halfway. From here, the rooftops were quilt patches, bits of corduroy and calico. The tree branches were fuzzes of mold where the quilt had softened and gone to rot. The sky was very blue. Everything was very clear.

He could feel Canumbra's erection against his hip, and for some reason he could smell fish. He wondered where they would throw him down off the Tram and how much it would hurt to fall and be broken. He remembered the pain of last Winter's broken arm. He supposed it would be much worse than that. He thought about Canumbra, *What is he going to do, rape me here in front of his friend?* and wanted to giggle and then thought, *but that's possible, of course,* and resolved to hold very still no matter how Canumbra's hard sex radiated heat and need.

They were passing close to a staircase and someone shouted. He jerked his attention away from Canumbra. A well-dressed man stared straight at them.

"What's that?" Legio jostled both of them from behind.

"Some toff interfering," Canumbra snarled. He pushed Teo out a few more inches, his fist knotted in his jacket painfully tight and cutting off all breath. Teo could feel his heart speeding up.

"Do you understand, boy, that I'm not fooling around, that I'll come kill you if you don't come back with something to satisfy me?" Canumbra snarled.

Teo nodded frantically, trying to grab enough lung hold to breathe.

"All right then." But Canumbra did not loosen his grip. "You think you're smart, don't you, boy?" he demanded. "Think you're smarter than me, that's been living in this city for years and years. Think that I can't do nothing to you in public? That's where you're wrong. I could sling you out of this window, easy as eating a pudding."

The Tram ground to a stop at the next platform. Teo could hear people shouting. Legio glanced out the window. "It's the Richie," he said. "Shove the boy out to distract them and let's leg it."

"No!" Teo tried to shout, but he found himself almost entirely outside the window dangling by ankles and wrists as he fought for handhold.

There were shouts—*Hold on!* And *There lad!* Then people were hauling him into the Tram basket, the structure shaking with the abruptness of his arrival. He was on his hands and knees, feeling the corrugated pattern of the metal floor against his palms.

Are you all right? What happened? Who were those men? The questions pressed in on him, but he managed to reel away and out the Tram's entrance onto the landing, past the entranced stares of passersby and to a quiet corner where he sobbed in a solid breath for the first time and then doubled over, spewing out the bilious contents of his stomach.

o o o

Abernia did not scold him when he returned without the basket, but she frowned and looked displeased. Reaching out, she tilted his head to study the bruise. "Been fighting, eh?"

"No," he said. "They came at me, took it, tried to throw me off the Tram."

"The Priests?" Disbelief filled Abernia's tone.

"No, two men. I met them when I first came here. They tried …" He trailed off. They'd tried to send him to Granny Beeswax, and she'd sensed something about him when she'd tried to magic him. Best not to lead anyone down that path. He swallowed hard. "They took the basket and what was in it. I'm sorry, Abernia. I'll save my money and pay you back."

A knock sounded at the door.

"Go answer it, boy," Abernia said. "If it's for Miss Bella, she's gone for the evening, and knowing her, she won't be back till well into the morning. She fights as Winter soon, and she celebrates beforehand, not after."

An auburn-haired young woman stood there. Teo took a dislike to her immediately. Something in the way she stood managed to be accusatory, and her mouth was pinched at the corners. She surveyed him with disdain, and said, "Fetch me Abernia."

Abernia hustled out when Teo told her of the visitor, wiping her hands on her apron nervously. "Come into the parlor, Miss Marta, and we'll talk," she said. She glanced at Teo. "Here now, since you lost the other bread, you'll need to fetch some from Figgis. Can you stay out of trouble there?" When he nodded glumly, her voice softened. "Get yourself a meat roll while you're at it."

He obeyed. Why did Abernia want him out of the house for a bit? All the way to Figgis, he kept a nervous eye out, fearing Canumbra and Legio would spot him again. But the trip was uneventful.

Coming back in, he snuck along the hallway towards the kitchen, but Abernia heard him.

"Is that you, boy?" she called.

"Yes." He popped his head into the parlor doorway, trying to give the impression that he had been coming to see if she needed him.

The visitor was still there, but in the act of standing and pulling on her coat. "She still takes my flowers then?" she said to Abernia.

Abernia's eyes flicked to Teo as though in warning. "'Deed she do, Miss Marta."

The woman nodded and came to the doorway. Teo hastily stepped aside, but she stood, staring at him, lip curling.

Or rather at his chest. He looked down at himself. He wore the jacket Bella had given him, its brass buttons gleaming in the streetlight.

She sneered. "I see Bella's dressing her household in lover's castoffs. Or are you hopping in her bed like all the rest, is that why she's taken you in?"

Indignation pulled him up to match her height. "I beg your pardon?" he said, channeling Bella in the iciness of his tone.

She was unimpressed. Her eyes flicked over his form, looking him up and down. Then she simply smiled and left.

The smile stayed with him. It had been an extremely unpleasant smile, the smile of a predator. It chilled him to the bone, even when he was back sitting in the kitchen, drinking Abernia's steaming chal.

o o o

After Abernia had gone off to bed, he crept upstairs to Bella's rooms. What had the visitor meant about the flowers?

Bella was out still. She often came home in the earliest hours of the morning. The crystal and silver armor watched him as he went to the bouquet on the side table.

They came every three days, these bouquets, full of fragrant, waxy-petaled flowers. Bella looked amused, sometimes, when watching him change a new bouquet for an old one, but she'd never said anything about it. The smell was sweet and reminded him of Fairy honey.

The bouquets always came in their own vases, made of thick green glass, thick with bubbles and occlusions. Carefully he lifted the bouquet from the vase, not even sure what he was looking for.

Tied at the bottom of each stem was a bit of black thread with a silver bead. He tugged one loose and squinted at it. The bead was skull-shaped, intricately detailed.

He heard noise at the door as Bella came in. She looked askance at seeing him.

He held out the flower to her. "I think there are spells on this."

She took it and examined it and made a wry face. "Indeed. Here." She picked up the flowers.

He followed at her heels as she marched it downstairs, then out through the garden. "What are you doing?"

"Running water drowns most magic," she said, holding the back gate open for him. The vase arched out twenty or thirty feet, to splash into the canal's center. They stood together watching the water as though afraid the curse might re-emerge.

"How did you know?" Bella said.

He didn't want to implicate Abernia. Surely she hadn't known what was going on. He shrugged. "They just felt off." It was as valid an excuse as any. Everyone knew some people could sense magic, that powerful spells had their own presence.

Bella's lips pursed but she said nothing. Overhead the purple moon chased the white one across the sky.

o o o

"You carry yourself as though you are afraid," Bella said the next day after breakfast.

"I am afraid," Teo pointed out. There were so many things to worry about in Tabat, even here in this household.

"Everyone is afraid of one thing or another," Bella said. "But if you carry yourself in a way that shows it, new things will spring up."

Teo could see the sense of that. But it was hard not to show what he was feeling.

"Stand up straight," Bella said. She studied him intently. He sucked in his stomach.

"Now imagine what it is like not to be afraid."

He thought about that. What would it feel like not to worry that the Priests of the Moon Temple were about to find him? Or that Canumbra and Legio were not watching for him? He tried to remember what it had been like at home, where none of these worries had ridden him. But even there, there had been fears and anxieties.

When had he ever imagined he was free of worries? It came to him that the reason he had always loved the stories of Bella was that she had never been afraid.

He tried imagining he was her. He closed his eyes and found himself standing a little straighter yet.

"Well," Bella said. "That's a start, at least."

Chapter Twenty

Bella's Life With Teo

Age has made me only better, I think, whistling my way out of the house in the morning. But there is nothing unnatural about that. I have always been quick of mind. Even Jolietta, who had hated so much about the young me, had been forced to admit that I never had to be shown how to do a thing twice, whether it was how to sex a hunting Dragon's egg or how to trim a Centaur's hoof.

That was what moved me so quickly up the Gladiatorial ranks, that and a dogged determination to succeed, a force of will that carried me through life with Jolietta and, once at school, pushed me to train harder, longer, more doggedly, than the other students.

The others hadn't known how lucky they were. No one taught them how difficult and friendless life could be. They hadn't had to fight just to survive, and that made them lacking in the ring.

And I'd had a promise to goad me as well: my promise to Lucya, that if admitted to the Brides of Steel despite my age, I'd prove the equal of any student the school had ever produced.

I lived up to that promise.

Skye's face has been eclipsing my duty, as surely as the sun outshines the moon. I must put a stop to that.

I could have ridden the Great Tram down and found myself there faster, but I like the way the Tumbril Stair makes me breathe hard, especially at a pace fast enough to dance on the edge of recklessness, reveling in my surefootedness. It keeps me from dwelling on my mission as I descend the terraces, ignoring the occasional murmur, acknowledging the equally occasional greeting. But as I turn and my pace slows, the thoughts return.

Skye has been making it plainer and plainer where her intentions lie. By now I'm a touch unnerved, if flattered, by the pursuit. I'm used to being on the other side of such a chase. And the predatory gleam in Skye's eyes, the scent of her when standing near, too near, makes me feel very much the quarry.

It will be better to have it out. To be firm with Skye. Let her know this is an impossibility and that we must return to normal. The tie between us is teacher and student. Nothing else.

Nothing else.

I find Skye alone in the former linen closet Lucya employs as a map room, hunched over a scroll. My step alerts her and she turns, releasing the edges so they roll up with a snap.

I've been rehearsing the words over and over in my head. I begin immediately, without pausing to greet her.

"We must talk, student," I say.

Skye opens her mouth, but I raise a hand to forestall her. "Let me begin. We are teacher and student. There can be nothing else between us. Do you understand?"

Skye blinks. I see, to my horror, tears welling in my student's eyes.

"Don't you like me?" Skye says in a whisper so soft I can barely make it out.

"Ah, Skye," I say, more quietly. "It's not that I don't like you, but that it's inappropriate."

The wrong thing to say, I realize from the way the girl's face brightens.

"Then you do!" she exclaims. She takes a step closer. "I am of age and only a year left to go at the College before I can fight in public. Other instructors have had love affairs with students more than once, you know it's true."

"And I know that it's wrong."

Skye steps closer yet. "Is it true what they say then? That though you'll share a bed, your heart's as cold as Winter and you'll never fall in love?"

It sounds like a quote from a penny-wide and forces a laugh from me.

"You do not hate me then."

Skye stands very close. How has she gotten so close?

"No," I say, feeling helpless.

Skye looks into my face. "You might even like me, under other circumstances," she breathes in a waft of anise.

"Under other circumstances," I say hoarsely, holding very still.

Skye slides her hands up my arms. I quiver but refuse to move.

"Under other circumstances," Skye repeats. "Circumstances where you might not object to this."

Her lips against mine are like electricity, like kissing one of the little mountain Nymphs that haunted the groves near Piper Hill. Though they tasted of zinc and Skye tastes of anise.

For a moment, I waver.

Then I lean in to the kiss, returning it, and think, "What does it matter?"

I am Bella Kanto, after all.

O O O

The problem with staying on good terms with old lovers is that they continue to be interested in your life and consider themselves both entitled to comment on it freely as well as knowledgeable enough about the ins and outs of one's personality to make such commentary bite deep.

Thus with Adelina.

She sits behind her desk piled with manuscripts and blue bound galleys as though it were a fortress. Leaning out from behind some spiritual parapet, a stone-built tower of self-justification based on the knowledge that she has never treated an old lover badly, she observes, "You could be kinder to Marta. It wouldn't take much to assuage her feelings."

No, not much. But I don't like thinking about Marta. It makes me worry that someday I will find myself in that situation, chasing

Skye after she's rejected me. If I think about Marta's feelings I worry in a way that is unfamiliar to me; me, who has slid through life thus far, at least ever since that first win, decades ago when I put on Spring's robes, and won, and became Winter for twenty years.

Past Adelina's shoulder are more blue-bound books. Strange to think that we've put together enough books, she and me talking it out in the evenings, to fill almost an entire wall, even though it is a shorter expanse than the flanking, longer walls would be. I can read the titles: *Bella Kanto in the Southern Isles*, *Bella Kanto and the Sorcerer's Kiss*, *Bella Kanto and the Riddling Manticore*.

I say, "Why waste time thinking about those who seek to drag us down? We should think about those who lift us up instead surely."

"Who is it that lifts you up, Bella?"

Who indeed? I run through figures in my head, old teachers, former opponents, noble historical personalities, even the Trade Gods and the traits each embodies. I always liked Fair Dealing but the truth be told, I don't measure myself up against others the way I might have once, when I was young. I am all too well aware that no one matches me. Matches Bella Kanto.

Instead I've become that for so many, and much of that is due to the penny-wides, the successive chapters that Adelina brings together into these books, collected by a span of time.

I am nothing if not completed, when I want to be. I say, "I hold myself up to the figure you have made of me, Adelina. Tabat's Champion."

"And how do you think the Champion should treat those she leaves behind?"

"I don't know," I snapped. "In all those adventures, you've never shown my thoughts. Anyone could read anything into the paper doll you've made of me."

Her eyes widen, and she takes a deep breath before replying. "I know you're upset, but there is no need to point your rapier wit in my direction."

I pull myself forward in my chair, propping my elbows on my knees, hunched as though to ward off a blow, I realize, consciously relaxing myself before I speak in turn. I should be reasonable.

Adelina means only the best for me. She doesn't nag me except in my best interests, but it's nagging nonetheless. If I stay here we will be at each other's throats, disagreeing and worrying over the point like dogs.

I stand and say, "I am sorry, I will lose my temper soon." I leave it at that. She knows I prefer to sidle out rather than talk it all the way through to death and beyond.

She nods. "Will you call for me tonight?"

I refrain from saying, "Only if you can promise not to talk about all this." Instead I nod and duck out the door.

I cut up along the stair that most call Eely but which I still know by the name it had when it first was built, Alberic's Procession. This time of day, the latest of the lunchers are returning to their work or homes, only a few moving quickly as though they've just realized how late they are, while most amble in the same spirit that led them to linger over their meal.

Yes, Adelina is right, and if I treated Marta better a lot of the enmity would be turned away. But Marta has not acted particularly well. She has irritated me enough that I'm in no hurry to assuage her irritation. I don't mind rubbing her a little raw, the way she's worked at rubbing me.

I thrust it all away in some drawer of my mind. Slide it closed and hope that I'll forget to re-open it, at least until someone else insists on forcing it. Too bad Tabat seems smaller than it should, at least when it comes to things like this. I run into Marta far too often, to the point where I avoid some occasions now. I used to fetch my dinner sometimes from the shop a few blocks away, but no longer after running into her there three times in a white moon.

I'll swing by the school, ignoring Lucya's usual raised eyebrow. She wanted me at the school more often, and now she has me. She has nothing to complain about. I'll drill the girls for a couple of hours, wash and change, and then perhaps take a handful of them with me to raid the shellfish carts down at the docks. She can't object to that as it's a practice I've done often enough in the past. And if Skye should happen to be among them, still, what's the harm?

No harm there at all.

O O O

I go to the flower shop I always go to when wooing someone. It's on Greenslope Way. I knew the owner, Lorelia, back when she was studying at the College of Mages, before she abandoned her studies and decided to use what she'd learned to grow flowers. She's clever, I'll give her that. Now she owns several greenhouses outside the city limits, and her shop holds the most sought after flowers in the city.

They are expensive. This is where Marta's flowers came from.

I like the Oread, Cinnabar, who Lorelia employs to run the till. Her home, a rough tumble of boulders, crowds the tiny garden out back.

I come into the shop's steamy, scented warmth from the cold air outside which makes my garments feel overly warm, clinging to me in a heavy embrace. The Oread is engaged with a customer, a thin woman picking out daffodils and tulips to surround a huge crimson blossom whose petals flutter like butterfly wings as she settles the other flowers around them.

She wraps it all in a cone of heavy brown paper, tucks the edges over, and tells the woman, "You'll want to keep it warm, get it inside as soon as possible. Are you in a carriage?"

The woman nods. The Oread looks reassured and smiles at her as she takes the heavy handful of coins.

As she turns away I advance on the counter. Cinnabar should smile when she sees me, but her expression is odd for just a second before she puts on the expression I'm expecting.

Her fingers flicker in greeting, scout-talk. *How can I help you, Bella? What flavor of lover are you looking for this time?*

What would Skye want? Daughter of Merchants, she'll be used to opulence and expensive trinkets. I could afford such things, but she'll be more charmed, I think, by elegance and simplicity. Flowers that speak of poetry.

I move to the case of simpler, unenchanted flowers, clots of color, tiny white bells sending out a powerful scent, pink roses, and tulips fresh from the greenhouse. I point to the irises, slender reflections of Tabat's blue and gold flag, patriotic and yet graceful.

Cinnabar wraps the hard stems in damp orange newspaper imprinted with an auction listing before she hands me the flowers. She waves away the coins I offer her and says, *Mistress has said never to charge you, Bella. You know that.*

I push the coins toward her on the counter and lift my hand away in order to sign, *Take them then and buy yourself something.*

She smiles and scoops them up. *Very well then.*

She pauses. *You have flowers that come each week to you,* she signs.

Marta's order. Does she know something about the ill-luck spells on them?

But no, Cinnabar signs, *Are they to your liking?*

I nod. *Pretty,* I sign. *Fragrant. But the order is cancelled now.*

She bites her lip, eyes flickering past me to the door as another customer comes in. *We'll speak of it another time,* she signs.

We bow to each other, another of the habits practiced by those that have hunted in the northern woods, an affectation on my part, perhaps, but one she embraces.

She seeks a bond with me, as so many do. It delights her to have something in common with the famous Bella Kanto.

o   o   o

Skye receives the flowers as I knew she would. She holds them reverently in her hands and sniffs at them before raising her eyes to my face. She smiles at me.

This is the moment in a love affair when we first confirm fondness for each other, turn guesses and hopes into realities. I know she's experiencing this giddy rush. Being able to see it in her eyes reawakens memories in me. Not the same as that true first brush, but close enough. It still shines despite the edges that have rubbed away.

"You want to put those in water," I tell her.

She nods and turns. "I'll take them to the kitchen and get a vase."

She takes a step, stops, and looks back over her shoulder. "You'll be here?"

I nod. She vanishes through a doorway.

Someone clears her throat in one of the other doorways. Lucya. She steps out and puts her hands on her hips as she looks at me.

"Come a-wooing, Bello Kanto, have you?"

I blush. I'd been hoping to avoid this moment.

"What are you playing at? I've never known you to do this before. Has being the Champion finally gone and swelled your head so big there's no room for thinking in it?"

I say, "This time it's different. She hasn't been my student for years and years. With one of them it would be inappropriate, but she'll graduate within a year and be old enough then that there would be no questioning such a relationship."

"Fiddle faddle. How long did it take you to think up that whirligig of justification?"

"Do you think I haven't asked myself all of this?"

"You haven't asked hard or long enough, it's apparent." She folds her arms. "These things are forbidden."

"But certainly not unknown. You've looked the other way on more than one occasion."

"Can you imagine how much scandal this would cause?"

"I would think you would welcome this. My changing my habits. Perhaps attaching myself to a student enough to want to step aside as Champion."

"Is that what this is all about? It's still utterly wrong, Bella. They all worship you. Don't destroy their idol. Don't dishearten them."

Before I can reply, Skye returns. Her arms fold in mimicry of Lucya's.

Lucya says, "Skye, this is not permitted."

Skye says, "Why? I'm old enough to take a lover."

"It's not about your age. Teachers should not fuck students. If you cannot stop listening to your quim's demands, go and take a lover from among the other girls. There's plenty enough of that."

Skye goes beet red, but squares her shoulders. She looks to me to defend all this.

"We can wait, Lucya," I say. Skye's mouth thins but she doesn't say anything.

"Very well," Lucya says.

There is silence. It becomes apparent that Lucya has no intention of allowing Skye and I to speak to each other alone. I raise an eyebrow at her.

"It's not as though I won't get to talk to her at some point," I say. "She is my student, after all."

"I will have a promise that no conversations of love will take place," Lucya says. "Else you will be her teacher no longer."

This does rouse a protest from Skye, who steps forward and says, "But my parents are paying to have me study with Bella Kanto. That is why they agreed to enroll me in the school."

Trust Lucya to squeeze a student whose skill should have won her a scholarship.

I glance at her. She understands what I'm thinking and manages to shrug and look a little shamefaced all at the same time.

Skye says, "Please, headmistress. I … we … will do as you say. But I must study with her. I must learn everything that she has to teach me."

She looks back and forth between the two of us. Her eyes are open wide, imploring as though we were considering sentencing her to execution or not. How long has it been since I felt anything that deeply?

Lucya looks to me for confirmation. I nod.

A year is not very long.

○ ○ ○

Lucya stares me down as I leave. Underneath the argument about Skye lies the older one, the one about the Championship. Winter's battle is in a week. She'll try again to make me step down.

She doesn't understand. That's not what the city wants, nor is it what I want—to give way bloodlessly, painlessly. They'll take Winter's crown from me only with a fight.

Too many rules. Too much to think about, too many people trying to make me do what they want.

So that night, I go out. I start in Berto's, where things are civilized, and after that I seek other places. I drink strong ale and stronger wine, and find a group of fellow Gladiators more than willing to accompany me on my rounds.

We end the night in a brothel, where I take a pair of brothers to bed, young and supple as Selkies. But even as they work in tandem, touching, stroking, licking, biting, it's not them I'm thinking of. I'm thinking too hard about things and I can't lose myself in the act. Finally I send them away and gather my clothing.

Home and bed. That is what it is to be Bella Kanto.

o o o

I have promised not to fuck Skye.

I have not promised not to woo her.

Servants and tradesfolk are up at this hour, but no one else. Gray light filters over the trees outside, their bare branches a dark shimmer of ice.

I love this time of day, when the world is chill and still.

Skye is waiting when I arrive outside the school. Her cloak is new and stylish, thick blue wool bordered with gold braid, embroidered with little blue flowers that peek out slyly from amid the profusion of gilt, as sly as her face peeping out of its hood, smiling and greeting me.

"Have you been waiting long?" I say as I approach.

She shakes her head, and I smile.

"No matter," I tease her. "I'll make it worth your while."

We walk towards the tram. Ice glazes the streets and the aetheric lights flicker, readying to go out. Blue shadows jolt along the gutters.

"You must get used to early hours," I say.

"Why?" she says, challenge in her tone.

"A Gladiator must be ready to fight at any hour. You must learn to shake off slumber, not succumb to it and grow fat and lazy."

She rolls her eyes.

Half a block down, we pass Figgis Bakery. Its ovens already send out smoke, and the smell of browning loaves reaches us as we pass and a cart trundles out, readying for deliveries. We both inhale appreciatively, exchange glances, and smile.

"Wait here," I say, and vanish into Figgis for a moment.

When I come back out, she keeps pace with me. I like that. Most folk complain I walk too fast, my stride too long for them. Skye doesn't even seem winded. The advantage of youth: your lungs are new and fresh, ready to give you everything you need.

I say, "You've seen the Winter Garden before, surely?"

She shakes her head. "I've lived here all my life, but I don't know what you mean."

"It's what they call the Sea Garden, but only at certain times of the year."

"Like Winter?" She laughs at the obviousness of the answer and almost gives me a wink before she reconsiders, sobering. She's not sure what to make of things still. She's worried how to woo me, how to chain me to her. I've seen that look a thousand times before. I know how to play that mood, give them an edge of anxiety before reassuring them, make them think that they're making me love them, while all the time they don't know I'm sneaking up on them, making them love me.

I can't help it. I'm Bella Kanto.

We round a corner. The crowd of birds perched on the platform's railing burst upward, fluttering.

The platform holds only a few waiting for the next tram. Before the first morning bell, it runs every twenty glasses, and by the time one is visible creaking its way downward, the platform is almost full. A few of them glance at me and murmur to each other, but no one bothers us. If Skye notices the glances, she says nothing.

We shuffle into the car, holding onto the ironwork sides. The conductor slides the gate shut with a *clang*, and we shudder downward, holding onto the rails to keep ourselves upright. I think of the trams as new, still, though it's been seven or eight years since they first began to build them. Skye looks out over the city where everything is gray and still, snowflakes swirling as though we were caught in a glass globe.

Wires sing overhead, glistening with melted snow.

The tram empties as the car makes its way down terrace by terrace. We step off at the bottommost, making our way through the crowd waiting to ascend. The sleepy city wakens around us as we make our way towards the docks, shops readying themselves to open, the tea shops already beginning to open their doors and entice early morning customers with the salty, fishy smell of chal. I head toward the western walkway, cut into the cliff face itself by Ellora Two Sails' magic long ago, that leads to the Sea Gardens.

Half in and half out of the water, the gardens hold marvels of coral in shallow pools, while salt-tolerant plants, blossoms enhanced by magic, thrive in the shelter offered by the cliff wall. Ice clings along the edges of the open water, but the hot springs that bubble up from below the rock keep steam rising from the surface of the water, muting the colors below to pearl and abalone shades. White winter roses, ranging from tight buds to full-blown flowers, lavish with petals and as big as my fist, droop from their hold in crevices dug out of the rock. Snow dusts the upper outcroppings till the gray stone shimmers.

It's false dawn, the sky beginning to show hints of color. The sound of the waves drown out any sounds from the city behind us. I slip my hand into Skye's, guiding her through the dimness. She pauses to take off her gloves, then returns her hand to mine, fingers warm against my cold skin.

Pathways wind between the pools, each five feet wide in an intricate latticed pattern. She follows as I guide her out to the southernmost edge, where the cliff to our right gives way to an endless vista of the ocean. On the left, fishing boats are setting out, passing under the massive arch of rock that guards the inner harbor. A thin line marks the eastern horizon; the sun is waking with the city.

Her fingers tremble, trapped in mine. Neither of us speaks.

Past the pools, we reach a promontory some forty feet across with an abrupt stretch downward to the rocks where the waves labor in endless agitation. Stone benches are scattered along the flat platform here.

I use my free hand to fumble in my pocket and take out the paper bag from the bakery. The rolls are still hot from the oven; when I break mine open, steam rises from the interior.

I turn, not facing the open sea, but the trembling light on the city's edge signaling the morning, and gesture. "Behold, the sunrise!"

We both hold our breath as the sun ventures over the horizon to fling golden light across the terraces and the harbor's mirror and, not satisfied with the effect, produces a number of flowery pink and purple clouds with which to ornament itself. One of the most beautiful sights I know.

I've never brought another person here, never shown anyone this. It was a private pleasure up till now, something that I hid and treasured. But something about Skye makes me want to share it.

The sunlight illuminates her smile, as beautiful as any cityscape could ever be.

I'd thought I would simply bring her here to show her the garden. Not to kiss her, not to take her in my arms.

I remind myself of my promise to Lucya. It stands between Skye and me; keeps me from reaching out as I would like to. More than would *like*. Is it only my imagination that I can feel the warmth of her?

She stands too near.

I lift a hand to brush a strand of hair from her face, and somehow the gesture turns into a caress. She closes her eyes at my touch, but I feel her shiver to her bones.

Everything is touched with light. The waves whisper encouragement. I haven't felt this alive for so long.

The strength of my desire frightens me. I pull away.

She opens her eyes, searching my face for some clue as to what she should do, but I have no answer to give her.

That frightens me most of all.

o o o

All I can think of is Skye.

When Miche comes to call, I finally send him away. I have no need for him. Life is complicated enough without him in the mix, and Skye has already proven herself a little jealous.

He is unhappy with me, which I expect. But he takes it better than I thought he would.

As he is leaving, he says, "The boy, Teo. Have you thought again about sending him to the circus? It would be a good place for him, and he would learn more there than playing errand boy here."

Perhaps he's right, but I shake my head again.

He seems angrier with that than my dismissal, but he shrugs and says, "Let me know if you reconsider."

o o o

Today Alberic is receiving visitors, and there is no reason for me to be here, other than his desire to show me off, like a dancing doll on a chain, his possession, his thing that will always do as he pleases.

His audience chamber is set with narrow high windows, the glass clear as crystal, free of the bubbles and impurities that those of us not of royal blood must live with. Snow swirls past, so thick that it seems as though it is all the world. It swallows up any other details that might be visible.

Fires roar in two fireplaces, one on either side of the high-backed throne on which he sits. It was created by a Duke three generations back, whose daughter later put it away. What does it say that Alberic found it in the storeroom where it had been set and pulled it out? He is so concerned with the trappings of office. Not for the first time, I wonder what he will do when all of this is no longer his.

He hears a few requests from the Merchants, but they do not truly need his permission to send an expedition past the Southern Isles to the land filled with snow and fire or eastward to the Stonelands. They are merely obeying custom. Even if he wanted to forbid these expeditions, he could not. And why would he want to? This is what has made Tabat so great, its Explorers moving out and bringing back so many things that the city has come to rely on. Like Dryad logs.

After all of this is done, a new group arrives. The Rose Kingdom has sent an envoy to accompany the healer Alberic requested. There is no reason for him to have a skilled healer; he is no more prone to disease than any other man, but he likes to think that he does have something that no one else has, and there are no other such healers in the city.

It must be nice, to have the world dance to your bidding from the day you are born. Perhaps this is why I wonder about Tabat's future so much, because I am looking forward to seeing this change. Will it change enough to satisfy the slight itch of irritation and envy that his presence raises in me? I don't know that it will. I have always been skilled at keeping a grudge alive.

I remember my journey to the Rose Kingdom. We came to its western edge and the port there, bordered on one side by the beginnings of the hedge, the forest of thorns created by magic long ago which surrounds the kingdom on three sides leaving it only approachable by the sea. I had gone to bargain for something Alberic claimed he needed, but which, as always, turned out to be a matter of whim. Still, I spent two months there, learning it and its ways. Adelina has written two accounts, as dry and full of historical fact, as though her scholarly writings were creeping into the penny-wide. Perhaps that is why she wishes to write another one, to see if she can make this one interesting.

I do not know if the healer knows what sort of place he has come to. He kneels at Alberic's feet, and seems too young to have the skill he is said to possess. His head is shaven till you cannot distinguish the color of his hair, other than the fine gilt eyebrows and thin mustache that ornament his face. I do not know that the healer will do well here. The Rose Kingdom is so different and does not have the delineations and compartments of society that fill Tabat. Here he will be an anomaly.

Alberic turns to me. "Bella, you will take him to visit Milosh Della Rose." Turning back to the healer, he says, "The Della Rose family knows more about plants than any other in the city, and their greenhouses are famed across the continent."

I know that last part well, for Marta, Milosh's daughter, told me it more than once.

This is not an oblivious moment on Alberic's part. He is well aware that Marta and I parted badly, and it amuses him. There is a challenge in his eyes, asking if I intend to push back.

But he is the leader of Tabat, and I am sworn to the city. What will it be like, when someone else leads? I let that thought warm a smile for Alberic, and he smiles back, thinking I am acceding.

○ ○ ○

Every city has its own customs, and Tabat is no different. They grow from and are shaped by the circumstances around them, the history and the geography and what is plentiful or scarce, which exert a much greater influence than any individual ever will, even the Duke. One of the things Tabat has much of is clay, mined from the marshes north of us and processed in the Slumpers. That is where the great kilns roar day and night, baking clay into tiles and pottery, glazed green and blue and purple. And a very small portion of that clay is used to make the tiny marking tiles that are set in the doorway of any building that has been distinguished in some way by a particular denizen.

In this way history is kept, tiles whose color tells of famed Scholars or Government Officials or Generals or Explorers or even great Artists. At one point there was a particular tile that marked a Champion of Tabat, but did not distinguish between them. Ten years ago it was decided that I would have a unique tile, one that marked my presence, Bella Kanto's presence and no one else's. An honor given very few indeed. Only the rulers of Tabat have held that in the past. While he has never challenged me on it, I know that it grates on Alberic, and that he thinks it is not truly due me. That it was presumptuous for the tile makers to come up with the idea; that it was even more presumptuous of me to accept.

I have received many honors over the years, but few of them have thrilled me the way that tile does, though. There is something about seeing it set between the other tiles, and knowing that it will still be there for as long as the building stands.

I rarely thwart Alberic. In this, I did.

The Della Rose house's entrance is ringed with tiles, including mine.

I never spent the night with Marta here, though I dined here more than once. Technically, they should not have set my tile in the entrance. It says something of Marta that it appeared after the first meal I shared with her. Perhaps her way of trying to mark me as hers, but that is something I have never allowed any lover.

I am tired of Alberic's games, of dancing to his tune. I find myself almost looking forward to the elections, despite the chaos that I know that they will bring. At least I will be rid of him then.

I was irritated when Alberic directed me here, and I realize now that I have been discourteous to the healer. But when I turn to speak to him, he does not seem to have noticed. He looks around himself with curiosity and the serenity that the citizens of the Rose Kingdom all seem to possess. He is slender and slight of muscle, but moves gracefully. His robe is too thin to truly keep him warm, but he does not shiver. It is made of rough woven green silk, the color of a new leaf unfurling with bands of blue and red flowers along the seams, a style that almost makes me smile, recalling as it does my days there.

I say to him, "Do you know of this family and their work?"

He shakes his head, eyes downcast to the glaze of ice along the cobblestones. His shoes are thin leather, dyed to match his robe.

There is something odd about him. Something that reminds me of something I'd forgotten, but I cannot think what it might be. I shake that thought away, for surely my mind is playing tricks on me.

I say, "Each Merchant house takes its name from the wares that they have built their business on. Their family name is Della Rose, and their ancestors were the first to do business with your kingdom long ago."

His eyebrow rises. "Then I would think I would have heard of them." There is question in his tone.

I shake my head. "Tabat has been in existence for almost three centuries now. There is no wonder that you have not heard of something that happened so long ago. Nowadays all trade with the Rose Kingdom comes through the Merchant's council rather than any individual family."

I raise my hand to the door and knock out a brisk *rat-tat-tat*. Over my shoulder I say, "But they have maintained their interest in plants, although they deal in much more than roses now. Their greenhouses are without equal in this city. That is why the Duke wishes you to consult with them, so you know what plants you may draw upon."

Before he can ask any other questions, the door swings open. I know the servant there, and he knows me, of course, and knows enough to raise his eyebrow in turn, clearly wondering what Marta will think of this and whether he should call her.

I say quickly, before he can ask that question aloud, "We are here to see Master Milosh."

He nods and stands aside. I shake snow off my cloak and ice from my hair, wondering again how it is that the healer does not feel such cold. Perhaps he is a failed Rose Knight and has undergone their training. And even more importantly, undergone the process that they all undertake: the grafting of branches from the hedge into their flesh, until they are as much plant as Human. I have fought Rose Knights. They are among the most dangerous opponents I have ever faced, between the thorns along their arms and the thick armor that clings to their skin.

The healer looks around curiously as the servant departs to fetch the master of the house. The Della Roses are wealthy, and this house's furnishings are the equal of any in the Duke's Castle. The household sigil of flowers and leaves are woven into the carpet underneath my feet, thick and plushy and swallowing every sound. The furniture is ironwood, and smells of beeswax and lemons, as though newly polished.

Perhaps these are even finer than their counterparts in the ducal castle. Merchants are always given to show, for they count it advertisement for their house. I have learned this over years of dealing with them.

Milosh arrives, smiling at me. I find myself smiling back, despite my worries that Marta will appear at any moment. He is a kindly soul.

I introduce him to the healer and explain why I have brought him. Milosh nods and says, "Come, I will show you the green-houses." He looks at me with the same question the servant had in his eyes and I shake my head quickly. He tries not to smile but makes a surreptitious gesture, a flapping of his hand at me, that lets me know I am in the danger, as I suspect, of encountering Marta at any second and that I should flee.

Milosh knows that his daughter is thornier than any blossom in his greenhouses. Perhaps it even amuses him that she is capable of making a Gladiator flee.

And so I do flee, back out into the street and the cold and the ice.

Somehow, it does not surprise me when I find myself, yet again, before the gates of the Brides of Steel.

But it does surprise me to find Skye waiting there. As I approach, she says, "I knew that you were coming."

Does she possess some magic, or have I become predictable?

I suspect it is the latter.

As we spar, I am distracted. Not by outside thoughts, but by Skye herself, the way her body bends and sways, the way I cannot help but imagine it under mine, my lips setting her alight, the way she might cry her pleasure out, or else bite her lip and keep it all inside. Finally, I say enough.

She says, "You're off your game."

I turn, surprised by the impudence. She bites her lip, but meets my eyes and says, "I thought that perhaps the baths might help."

It amuses me to hear this. I've used this ploy myself, in the past. I know what she really wants or at least what I hope she really wants.

The silence as we descend to the baths confirms it. Normally I would see other girls down here, but for some odd reason, a reason that I think has much to do with Skye, no one is about. The baths are deserted, even though fresh flowers have been scattered on the surface of the smallest pool.

I say, "How much did it cost you to have them all clear away?"

She doesn't pretend not to understand but instead says, "I'll be doing other people's chores for a month. And all of my spending money."

I say, "Will it be worth it?"

She says, and this time her eyes meet mine, clear and direct and trusting enough to give me qualms, "I don't know. Will it?"

I turn away and begin to prepare myself for bathing, stripping away the fighting armor, buying myself moments in which to think. This would make Lucya furious. If she finds us I do not know what the consequences will be. Usually I can predict how she might react, but she is angry enough about this, angry enough about all the times I have refused to step down, that I do not know what might happen, although I suspect the worst. I hear Skye behind me, stripping away her own clothes, then a pause. When I do not turn around, I hear the soft splash as she slips into the water.

When I turn, naked, she is watching me, but I cannot meet her eyes.

I am trembling. I do not know that I have ever trembled like this before. It is as though each place her eyes rest on my skin is set afire. No, not afire, that is a different kind of burning. There are no words I know for this.

There are no words I know for what I discover in her arms, there, dipping in and out of the water, where I kiss away the torchlight that adorns every inch of her skin.

○ ○ ○

We are lucky. Lucya does not discover us.

But I know that if this continues, that if we dare to do this again, she will, eventually. Perhaps not the next time, or even the time after that, but it is inevitable.

I do not know what to do about it. How can it be that I, Bella Kanto, the one who always knows the answers, am at such a loss?

○ ○ ○

I walk alone in a daze. I keep feeling the memory of kisses on my skin, a memory like a second touch, one that sends new shivers down my spine. And they are not shivers evoked by the cold wind that sweeps along the streets. I am feverish. I am consumed.

This happy haze sustains me all the way home. It buoys my step as I come in through the door, and lightens my heart, making me smile as I pause in the kitchen to steal a fish biscuit from the platter that Abernia keeps waiting there, exchanging a conspiratorial wink with Teo.

He says, "You have a visitor. Abernia showed her up to your sitting room."

"Oh?" I say. "Who is it?"

He shakes his head. "The woman who sent the flowers, I think," he says. Boyhood still tilts his voice high.

Armored, I go upstairs.

Marta says, "My father said you came to visit." She sits posed in the armchair near the window. I am sure she is aware of the picture she makes. She is dressed well, and blue paint gilds her eyelids, her lips are red as though she has been biting them. I know the scent she wears; it is the one she thinks the most seductive.

I say, cautiously, "The Duke asked me to bring a visitor to see your father." I curse Milosh for telling her, but perhaps that is unkind. Perhaps a servant told her and she simply went to confirm it with him. Either way, he could have lied to her. Although it may be asking too much for him to have any loyalty to me, we have been allies in the past against Marta's temper tantrums.

It is as though she does not hear the words that leave my lips. She gazes at me with a touch of complacency. She doesn't realize I know that the flowers hid a spell. She has deluded herself.

But for the first time, I understand why. How would I react if Skye were to turn me away? I would haunt her doorway. I would follow her. I would make her realize her error. This is what Marta is trying to do, so I only look at her, trying to figure out the words that will discourage her without snapping her heart in half.

But I am no good at this sort of thing. I see her register the expression on my face, see her process it, see the thoughts slide behind her eyes, the realization that everything she has convinced herself of is wrong. Entirely wrong. Then I see her fury rise at that mistake. Not directed at herself, of course, but at me, as though I am responsible for all of this. Somehow, I suppose that I am.

But I cannot let regrets consume me. Even this new perspective on all my old lovers is not something I will allow to sway me. Otherwise I will find myself re-saddled with Marta, and that would not be good for any of us. Not for Marta. Not for me. And even more, not for Skye.

She snaps, "Do not pity me!" I hadn't realized that was what was causing her anger, rather than my rejection. The thought that I might find her pitiful is somehow worse than anything else I could do, but it is a blade that I do not know how to blunt.

I take a step forward as though I will go to her and comfort her, and then realize what a mistake that would be as well, and stop. She rises hastily, glaring at me.

Anger tightens her voice as she says, "I will destroy you, Bella Kanto."

I make another mistake. I laugh.

But I cannot help it. It's like a line from a penny-wide, a line spoken by some story's master villain, drawn much larger than life, a creature of emotions too grand for any Human to stomach. Is that how she sees herself?

She screams imprecations and obscenities at me. She starts to throw the vase that's close at hand, but I have had enough of this and pluck it from her grasp. I propel her towards the door, and say, as calmly as I can, "It is time for you to go now."

She senses something. How does she know to ask, "Who is she?" Am I so changed that it shines out of me without my ever saying a word? That is dangerous. That is very dangerous, that I would betray myself that way, without knowing.

She cannot know anything about Skye. I can defend myself from her malice. I do not think that Skye can, and I cannot protect her without being constantly at her side, another impossibility, even if Lucya would allow it. It crosses my mind momentarily to throw some other victim in her way, make up a name, perhaps? Or even some old lover better suited to keeping themselves from harm, Adelina perhaps, who is well versed in Merchantly feuds. But that would be a bad gift to my friend, to saddle her with this. So I do not answer but only close the door between Marta and myself.

She will drag everyone into this if she can. I will protect Skye. And Teo. I will send him to the circus that Miche has suggested. That will keep him safer and unassociated with me.

She does not go away immediately. I hear her shouting at the door, which is not thick enough to keep out all the ugly words. Abernia's steps come up the stairs, and then her voice speaks, low and reasonable, but firm. Somehow she coaxes Marta away. I begin to sit down in the chair she has left, but her smell still clings to it, and it twists my stomach. The smell seems to fill the room, a too-sweet musk.

I open the window and let snow and wind, crisp and cold, sweep the smell from the room. I look out into the darkness. The lights of the city glimmer and gleam here and there, but the snow obscures so much.

Chapter Twenty-One

Teo Goes to the Circus

The only small flaw in life with Bella was Miche, who seemed so fascinated by Teo. It seemed to Teo the man watched him. He wanted something from Teo. But what? He mulled it over as he fell asleep. The man's face swam in front of him, and a voice began to talk to him.

It was almost familiar—a forgotten friend—talking and telling him its story while hazy visions of its words floated before him. It said:

My father's tower was full of Beasts. They were the only company beside myself that he allowed. He bred them, created new things that the world had never seen, all of us living there together. The tower was immense and ringed with windows, the last remnant of a great castle.

Teo wanted to ask who the voice's father was, but it ignored his silent question and continued.

The Beasts shat in the lowest level, as did we, and in time that grew to such a vile pit that Father had a staircase built out of one of the second floor windows. After that, we used it to go in and out, while downstairs massive heaps of composted shit accumulated, so rich and magic-tainted that it spawned mushrooms—spotted, speckled, and sometimes bearing eyes on tenuous stalks, or unfolding from their caps' flesh and gifted with speech. When anyone went downstairs or tried one of the outer doors, they broke into floods of incomprehensible babbling, and at night we'd hear them singing old folksongs against each other, none singing the same as any of the others, like bizarre, broken rounds.

Far away, Teo could hear the sound of the mushrooms singing, a shrill piping on the edges of his hearing.

When I turned fifteen, my father let me start selling the fungi to traveling peddlers, who fit them into tiny, soundproofed vials with two or three pinches of the tarry basement soil, to take and sell as wonders in the city. Kept damp and sheltered, the mushrooms could keep for weeks, perhaps even months.

Teo could smell the rotting compost and hear the squeaks of the imprisoned mushrooms.

You might think otherwise, but one thing I never did in those days was dabble in my father's magic. He taught me that lesson early.

He had gone out—to bargain with a nearby farmer for beef to feed the Beasts. I went to experiment, having watched him cast a spell to cure my toothache the night before. I did not know he had set a charm on his equipment.

I reached out to touch a beaker that bubbled with lime-green liquid. As soon as my finger came in contact with it, my hand blazed with agony.

I reeled away, clutching my burning hand, blundering against the cabinets and shelves, in crashes of glass and paper and clanging metal. Finally the pain died away, little by little in a teasing way—it kept returning just when I thought I was finally rid of it. I did not clean up any of the damage I had caused—just looking at that table made me break into a cold sweat, made my fingers coil into my palm in remembered torment.

For the first time there was pain in the other's voice. Teo wanted to reach out, to touch his shoulder, but they were suspended in mist and fire and flickering water. The voice steadied and went on.

When he returned, he said nothing about the mess. He whistled a charm and the shattered glass sorted itself into piles of the salvageable and the unsalvageable. All of us went barefoot, including the Beasts, so he whistled away every scrap, every splinter. That night when I went to bed in the pile of blankets I nested in, I found a great long shard, clear as ice, from the largest beaker lying across them. I put it away and did not look at him.

We had many Beasts throughout my childhood. Their lifetimes varied, but most are short. Only the most humanly featured Beasts have long lives—those and the Dragons as they used to be. Not as they are now.

For a while, we had a Catoblepas, its body buffalo-wide and scaled, its shaggy head always pointing downward due to the heavy weight of its tusks. It ate poisonous vegetation harvested from the sward beside the marsh, which I gathered wearing great canvas gloves that extended past my elbows, nearly to my shoulders. And a dwarf Unicorn, whose hooves left shining, icy footprints wherever it walked. Riddling Deer grazed in the forest around the tower, but I never succeeded in catching one to hear it speak.

One by one the creatures waddled or danced or slid by. The Catoblepas had whiskers like a catfish's, and the scales covering its back were green and glossy. The Riddling Deer pranced on delicate feet, their eyes as brown as hidden forest pools.

Later what my father insisted was an Ypotryll—although it seemed much like any Chimera to me, despite its camel's hump, and we had had such—and Gryphons and Hippogriffs—by the scadsfull. Traders knew my father would pay well for Beasts, so they brought any they laid hands on. Beyond that, at least two thirds of the inhabitants of the tower came because my father had acquired a name for succoring Beasts, for not requiring that they enact that same sort of servitude that other sorcerers demanded—even a Dragon once, before Bellanora—after that city's fall, the Kettle King's forces came and took her away—enough soldiers and Beast-hunters that my father did not stand in their way.

As they took her away, in anthracite chains that bit at her ankles and draped over her furled wings, she wept oily, sulfur-tinged tears. The sunlight glittered on her scales as they forced her to climb in minute steps, up a ramp to the bed of an enormous ox cart. She lay down there, still weeping, and the soldiers tossed more chains back and forth, prisoning her to the wood, unsoftened by straw or padding. Other soldiers stood by with hackbuts braced and ready, flared muzzles trained on her like ears listening to her betrayal.

The air smelled of rust and blood and rage.

My father was angry as he stood watching, as angry as I'd ever seen him.

"That man claims to rule the Sorcerers now," he said to me. "But if any of them could ever look past their petty quarrels and learn to work in unison, he could be overthrown."

I was wary. Who knew what sort of listening spells the Pot and Kettle King kept on each of the continent's Sorcerers? Decades—centuries, even—of attrition had reduced their ranks to a few dozen. Few enough that he could watch all of them if he lived up to the legends told of him. And, as though he shared my apprehensions, my father spoke no more on that matter.

That night, I crept out a stone-arched window and, my skinny ass planted on a crenellated ledge, listened past the faint fungal sounds from far below, deeper, into the night's heart. The fields near the tower had been allowed to lie fallow for years, and white owls hunted field mice and insects up and down the ancient ruts of rows. The land pretended to be level, but sometimes swooped up and down, breaking into folds that might hold a stream or grotto.

The mist settled and Teo could see the scene: the lanky, lonely boy, face turned away towards the purple moon.

An Enfield came creeping over the tiles towards me in the feverish double moonlight that gilded its fox's ears and the tufts of its shaggy fur. Its talons clicked on the creaking tiles of the roof, which flared out here over the first floor. Reaching me, it rested its head on my knee and closed its eyes, nudging my wrist with a cold-nosed kiss into action, so I would pet it.

These creatures had a lesser intelligence—a smart dog's, perhaps. What was the purpose of such a thing, the awkward melding of fox head and tail, the wolf's body, the eagle talons? These had been created to ward a specific town— Enfield—by a sorcerer who my father frequently regarded as a rival and sometimes as a friend. How this one had come here, I was not sure—as far as I could tell, it had simply showed up one day.

I thought about my father. He paid me little attention, but at the same time, I was clearly his—like the Beasts—and not to be meddled with. Village children threw stones and dried mud clots at me and found them returned at a red-hot heat. Just as the woman who stole a Unicorn colt that had ventured too far away found herself drawn up in painful, inescapable muscle cramps.

I was with my father, trailing after him to see what he was up to that day, as I often did. He walked into the house and came out with the colt wrapped in a grey blanket, shining against the coarse fabric.

He walked out past the bed where the woman lay. Her back arched like a terrible scream, unable to do anything but a slow and dreadful writhing, her face a rictus as grim as the skull that sat on my father's desk and was never to be touched, lest it bite.

What did it mean that he acted one way towards that woman—or me for that matter, setting my fingers ablaze—and another towards the Kettle King's agents? How free was he? How free was I? I scratched the fur around the Enfield's seamed neck, where fox red met wolfish silver, and watched purple Toj edge along the horizon.

For a moment, Teo roused. All around him the house was still and silent. Even the bard had given over practicing and gone to bed.

Perhaps he was still dreaming, though. Beside him, the voice said, *There is something about you. There's magic in you, waiting to be harvested.*

It paused as though waiting for an answer from Teo, but he said nothing. He knew if he only waited long enough, it would tell him exactly what he needed to know. But before that could happen, there was water between them, washing into the room, washing him into someone else's dreams, someone else's memories, once more.

I sold mushrooms for three years, conducting business while my father stayed in his tower. I'd come in and give him the fruits of my bargaining. I never dared hold a coin back. I knew if I did, he'd leave me writhing, like that woman.

It was the voice again. So familiar. Who was it? He should know this man.

I hated going down in the damp stink to gather mushrooms. For one thing, they'd howl. It'd be all noise and stench and queasy lantern light guttering over the oily, slick piles. I wrapped a scarf soaked in vinegar over my face, used that to filter the fumes, and plucked each noisome morsel up to put in the moss-lined basket hanging from my belt.

It paused, and a turtle swam past, glowing in the darkness. It clacked its beak at him and he thought it would say something but instead the voice continued.

One day I found a new kind of mushroom.

Then Abernia was leaning over him, shaking him. "Time to get up, boy," she said briskly. "Work to do."

O O O

Teo could tell there was something different about the girl Skye, who sometimes accompanied Bella. She was a student, and there were other students with Bella sometimes. She took them on walks, or rather runs, usually, throughout the city, or down to the docks to buy them treats, and any number of other field excursions. She'd told Teo that she did it to reward the ones who tried hard.

But Bella didn't act like Skye was just another student. She listened to her, for one, in a way that Teo, even though he adored Bella, had to admit she extended to no one else. It was one of the things you could count on about Bella, in fact, that she usually wouldn't be listening as hard as she could, and that if you caught her at it, she'd only give you a grin and shrug, as though to say, *that's how I am.*

Bella catered to Skye, allowed her suggestions to shape the route or pick one destination, such as a favored chal shop, over another.

She was pretty enough, but she wasn't all that. Not when you took apart her features. It was simply that they combined in a way that clearly pleased Bella. Maybe she reminded Bella of someone else.

She reminded Teo of Biort back home. She had a way of standing as though she didn't doubt she was the most important one in the room. Bella did that too, of course, but Bella had earned it. She was Bella Kanto, after all. Who was this chit that she should set herself up as Bella's equal, and worse, have Bella act as though the opinion was justified?

He found her irritating enough that he ended up avoiding Bella's company whenever Skye was around, which made it even more irritating when the amount of that time grew and grew.

It was a shame. Bella, when by herself, could be coaxed into telling all sorts of stories or imparting advice, or even, thrillingly, showing them how to attack someone using a candlestick or a kitchen knife. Bella by herself was sister and mother and father and hero and instructor and entertainer, all rolled up into one. She was everything he could have ever imagined her.

Except when she was with Skye. Then she was entirely different.

○ ○ ○

Bella called him in early in the morning, directing Abernia to send him up with more chal.

"Miche has spoken to me again," she said. "He has mentioned his cousin's circus once more. He says it is called *The Autumn Moon*, and they are here in Tabat through the elections." She paused. "I think it best if you go there."

She was sending him away? Had she caught one of his looks at Skye, his disapproval of her? She was choosing between them, and he had lost.

"But …" he said. He trailed off. What could he say to convince her? And a circus. That would not be entirely bad. He could lose himself there as easily as here. If he stayed on its grounds, surely Canumbra and Legio would not find him.

All he could manage was, "Could I come visit you still, though, sometimes? Or perhaps you'd stop by when you come to the circus?"

"Of course, Teo. I won't abandon you."

But she already had, he thought. Still, he squared his shoulders and went downstairs to tell Abernia and gather up his things.

o o o

Miche's cousin sent a messenger for him after dinner, a bored looking Satyr who barely spoke to him along the way.

He wants to be rid of me as soon as possible, he thought, and it saddened him. Was that what circus life would be like? Had he made the wrong choice? "Isn't that the College of Mages?" he asked nervously as they turned on Spray Way. He worried that the Mage might be looking for him too.

He'd read the stories. The exploits of generations of Dukes and Duchesses, the boldness of the Mages, the perfidious attempts and plots of the sorcerers, constantly trying to spread their ancient war from the Old Continent to the New.

He wondered if he would meet any of them.

"The Circus stays on the grounds of the College," the Satyr said. "They subsidize us and we draw attention to their political gatherings."

Teo wasn't sure how to reply to this, but he didn't want him to lapse back into silence. He made a noncommittal sound, but it failed to elicit any more interest.

He worried. Wouldn't he be likely to meet the Mage he'd escaped from on the grounds? But it was a large place and surely a circus would provide plenty of places to hide.

The streets were quiet this time of night, and he could smell the meals from the houses, rich savory soups and charred meat, making his stomach growl. He swallowed.

The Satyr acted as though he hadn't heard, marching along. He was surprised how much ground, how quickly, the goatish stride covered.

To their left a wrought-iron fence, backed by ivy leaves, curved to lead them towards a grand gate surmounted by bas-relief trumpeters and harpists. He could have reached out and touched the fence's chilly bars, but its prickly barbs warned his fingers away.

Beyond the gate, a break in the ivy showed a well-trodden field, filled now with tents and wagons. Everything seemed unexpectedly shiny and new. As they passed under the gate's arch, moonlight broke through the clouds and danced on the calliope's brass. Two workers were moving over it, checking it, wiping away smudges with soft cloths before rolling a tarpaulin over it, presumably to keep it from the night's damp. Were they Humans or long-armed Apes? He couldn't tell through the darkness.

At this time of night, the crowds had dispersed except for a froth of curious idlers who lingered, watching the circus workers pack up for the evening.

Someone led a pair of zebras past and he stared, wide-eyed. He'd seen pictures in his primer (there were few interesting choices for Z, after all) but never such a thing in real life, stripes as crisply edged as though they had just been printed onto each hide. Their muzzles were soft and black, and their manes rose like painted broom bristles.

"What sort of circus is this?" Teo asked.

"The *Moon's* like any other circus," the Satyr said. "One of the many that come to town to entertain the masses. Usually we go up and down the coast, putting on shows from city to city. Most places we'll perform once, twice—only large towns like Tabat have enough people with free coin to keep us busy. Working with the College of Mages, though, lets us pitch here indefinitely."

"And you have work?" he said dubiously. What if they wanted him to perform? Back home he'd heard tales of circuses. They had lions, and women who bit the heads off chickens.

The Satyr let out a long *Baaa* of laughter. "We always need people to run concessions and shovel shit," he said. "Don't worry, we won't disguise you as a homunculus and make you predict the future."

He blushed and, watching the crowds as they moved along, realized it was true. He had always thought of circuses as nothing but performers. But here was a group outnumbering them—the roustabouts and workers whose labor had gone into driving stakes, unrolling canvas, pitching tents. A larger, brawnier, and much more unobtrusive contingent. He would be one of those. No one would ever find him among them.

They came to a group clustered around a tank. In it two Mermaids preened and tried to flirt with the elderly man sweeping up the bits of paper and detritus that littered the dusty earth.

One Mermaid's stringy blue hair was done in elaborate, almost-shellacked curls. The other's greener hair hung straight and fine. They sat posed like a pair of house cats, their backs half-turned to each other, but leaning forward, displaying their bare breasts to the oblivious man. His head down, swaying like a blind bear's, he swept the same patch of ground over and over, at least a dozen passes where one would have done before moving onto the next patch.

"Stop and sing to us, Jonas," the curled Mermaid coaxed, and the other said, "Or we will sing to you. Would you like that?"

Fascinated, Teo saw that a white mouse rode the sweeper's shoulder. Its nose twitched, scenting the air. It squeaked and the man paused, holding the broom still.

Quick as thought, the mouse ran down his body, easily holding onto the fabric of his grey garment, so shapeless that it was unclear how many pieces it was made of, and ran over to an orange paper cone glittering with pink beads of melted sugar. Cone held awkwardly between its teeth, it returned to its perch and ate, nibbling off the sweet bits as the man started to sweep again.

"Come on," the Satyr said, moving through the crowd.

The wealth of colors, scents, and sounds dazzled and dizzied Teo. He walked as though in a swoon. It seemed too marvelous to be true, that his luck had shone so moon-bright, had led him to such a place.

They passed through a corridor made of booths, each one's face a bright smile of twining snakes and fire-breathing mongooses, tattooed clowns, and rainbow-haired magic eaters, just as another worker moved down the corridor behind them, closing each booth to show enigmatic shutters, dull white with age.

Past the busy walkways, they came to a place where people moved more purposefully: The backside of the circus, a medley of open bed and closed wagons that had been repurposed into living quarters. He could not help but admire the cleverness of their construction. A tent roof had been unrolled above a small wagon's flatbed to make it serve as a table, and a smaller tent had married the cook wagon, whose sides had folded down wantonly to unveil a canvas and wood kitchen where a pot of chal boiled, a stack of white mugs beside it.

"What's the owner's name?" he asked the Satyr.

"Murga."

The name was familiar, but he couldn't place it.

Would he like Murga, he wondered, and would Murga like him? If he did, now he would be a workingman, earning his daily wage—something different than the scattered and day-to-day street existence he'd been conducting.

Once again, he felt a future settling on him. Did he dare hope that this time it would take? Surely this was where he was meant to be, he decided. A future was a satisfying thing to have, like owning a house to sleep in, or a good knife, or a pair of waterproof boots. A future full of predictable days and nights, free of the uncertainty that some storm might seize him, carry him away.

He ducked his head to conceal his smile at the thought. The Satyr caught it anyway. He said nothing, just gave him a contemptuous look. Teo shrank under that cold stare. The corners of his mouth drooped, and the Satyr smiled as though the corners of his own mouth were counterweights ascending.

It was an unpleasant smile. He had a panicked, nonsensical thought—*He's brought me here to kill me*—that melted away just as fast as common sense reared its head.

The Satyr paused outside a blocky tent, one a little larger than the other living quarters, and called into it, "Murga? Are you there?"

"Aryk." The flap pushed open and a slender man emerged, bowing his head in greeting.

The Satyr bowed hers in turn before stepping back and pointing at Teo. "This is the boy."

Murga looked Teo over. The circus owner was a slender man, pale as though Northern, although the shape of his features were pure Old Continent. He wore a red coat with elaborations of gold braid at the sleeves and collar over shiny black trousers. The outfit reminded Teo of the calliope.

"Come inside," Murga said, pointing Teo in.

The tent's smell reminded Teo of the cramped sweat lodge on the village's outskirts, where the hunters went and sat in the depths of Winter, sweating before they ran out and rolled in the snow. A ritual that he had managed to escape by leaving—he was glad of that, he was pretty sure. The tent's smell edged up into his nostrils and made him feel uncomfortable, pinned.

Behind him, Murga paused, speaking in an undertone to the Satyr. Teo couldn't catch the words. Then Murga came through the flap as well, to sit down at a rickety desk. The inkwell didn't smell of ink. It was filled with oil and magic. Underneath the desk was a box that reeked of blood-soaked earth. His nose itched and the hair on the back of his neck bristled.

"Miche says you are looking for a job," the man said. "I'm Murga, and I run *The Autumn Moon*."

"It's a lovely circus, sir," he blurted out, terrified that he'd say something dreadful within the first few minutes.

From behind the stained canvas, a scent of cinnabar and sweet amber came out of the darkness. He'd smelled that desert scent more than once here as he'd entered the circus, though he'd never seen the heavy-footed presence that it betrayed.

Murga chuckled. "Nervous, are you?"

"Yes." The admission made him relax a little.

"What can you do?"

"I'm strong, sir, and I learn quickly. I know a little wood and stone working from my parents back home."

"And where is back home?"

"Up the Northstretch River, a village near Marten's Ferry."

"Why did you leave there?" Murga's dispassionate gaze surveyed him like a side of meat.

"My sister was dying of bone-stretch fever. My parents promised me to the Moons if she survived. She did, so I came downriver to join the Temple. But I do not feel suited to them."

"What word have you sent to your parents?"

He looked down at the grass underfoot, yellowing and sere. "I haven't told them anything yet."

"I see. I presume the Temples are similarly in the dark."

He looked up to examine Murga's face in turn. It was a curious, expressionless face that reminded him of one of his sister's least favorite dolls, Katar. Katar had dominated their childhood games as an entity to be placated, and in later years he often thought to himself that they had been so firmly under the doll's sway that if it had ordered someone's eyes torn out, they would have schemed to obey it. He shivered at the thought. His skin crawled at the feel of some heaviness in the air, like standing too close to one of the Duke's aetheric lights.

"You are frightened?" Murga asked.

"I don't know what to say," he said. "Miche said you had work for me. If you don't, I will go back to Bella Kanto." He straightened himself, holding his shoulders back as proudly as a Gladiator.

Murga stared at him expressionlessly, then threw his head back and laughed, a derisive caw that seemed to go on and on. Teo could feel his face burning, but he forced his expression to remain level.

"No, boy," Murga finally gasped out, still laughing. "I will hire you as a roustabout, a jack-of-all-sorts, who helps as needed. You'll answer to Sibella, chief of the roustabouts, and you'll get two silver skiffs a week, same as everyone, with one afternoon off of every twelve."

He held out his hand. "Shake with me, boy, and we'll seal our pact."

They joined hands. There was magic here in Murga's grasp, Teo could feel it reaching inside him. But surely Bella would not have sent him someplace he'd come to harm? Perhaps this was a test of some sort. He forced himself still until Murga released his hand.

The circus owner had a small, satisfied smile. "Head along to the cook tent, and have them tell you where to find Maisie. She'll show you around."

"Yes, sir," he said. "Thank you, sir."

Chapter Twenty-Two

Circus Life for Teo

The girl Teo found sitting in the cook tent was a stoop-shouldered, broad-faced thing, wearing thick black boots and a dress that looked like several performers' discarded outfits sewn together. She was perhaps his age, perhaps a few years older. Tulle rode her hemline, making the fabric look as though it were seen through dirty glass.

"I'm looking for Maisie," he told her.

"I know. You're the greenest," she said with a relish that made Teo realize she'd been the former occupant of that niche. "I'm Maisie, and you're taking over my tasks. So one of the things you'll do is collect chal mugs, bring 'em back here, and make sure they're washed and the rack full."

"All right," he said. "What else?"

She studied him in silence, measuring him inch by inch.

"I'm Teo," he offered up in answer to her wordless regard.

"Of course you are." She seemed to have made up her mind as she drained off half her tea and stood. "Come on, I'll show you my rabbit."

As she turned, something odd caught his eye, twitching at the back of her skirt.

"You have a tail!" he gasped, surprised. She must be a Beast, but she spoke to him as freely as one Human to another.

Her look was amused. "We're all Beasts here."

"Murga owns you?"

"You could say that." She shrugged. "Or not. You'll see."

She took him through a winding aisle of painted canvas and new-smelling tents. In the heart of a small complex of identical tents, she knelt beside a cot and pulled a wooden crate out from underneath it. Inside was a fuzzy blue knitted blanket, smelling of rabbit droppings, and an immense furry rabbit, at least twice the size of any rabbit Teo had ever seen. Its size startled him, and he said so.

"Isn't she?" Maisie said. "She's a Clovian winged rabbit."

"Winged rabbit?" he said dubiously.

She fondly smoothed the mass of black fur from which two beady eyes peered, ran her fingers over the velvety ears. She reached out to take his hand and run his fingers along the rabbit's back through the knots of fur there.

"There, do you feel it?" She smiled at him complicitly, and he was very aware of her nearness, her warmth, the soft heat of the rabbit's fur, its heartbeat as rapid as his own.

"I'm not sure," he said, uncertainly. "What should I feel?"

She frowned at him. "Her wing nubs, of course." She giggled. "Why, what did you think I meant?"

He faltered, wordless, and the frown returned. She put the rabbit back in the box with a last caress. It sat and stared at her, not moving, as she slid it back into the darkness.

"You'd better get to work," she said.

"What am I supposed to do, just collect mugs?"

The thought seemed to scandalize her. "No. Everything and anything. Wander and keep your hands busy. If Murga sees you idle, he'll fire you."

o o o

That night, Teo went to his cot with aching arms and legs. He'd helped with cleaning the elephant stalls and thought he'd never raked up so much shit in all his life.

But his dream didn't comfort him. It dissolved into chaos. In it he ran through streets filled with confusion, with fire and shouting and blood.

The little wood was edged with an iron fence. It was the work of a moment to scale it, to leap over the side and into the midst of a confusion of fat, complacent squirrels that had been sleeping in the midst of a ball of leaves. It was quiet here, despite the distant noises. He rested, licking blood from his jowls.

He jolted awake. Covered with blood and bits and fur, rubbing amorously, embarrassingly against the freezing iron fence. His thighs were sticky. How had he gotten here? What had happened? Was this magic again?

He had changed, he realized. He had turned into a cougar, like his parents and their parents before them. But that was impossible! They had sent him here because he had not inherited that talent, had been unable to Shift, and thus was in no danger of discovery.

Teo's thought was first relief—*That means I'm normal, after all, a Shifter like any of them*—and then, *I wonder if they would have sent me away if they'd known that?*

And on the heels of that petulant thought came another that gathered terror and bile in his throat. They would take him, burn him, kill him! Triumph and terror tore him between them. He was a Shifter, after all, and not a failure. But to be a Shifter, to hover between Beast and Human, is dangerous here in Tabat. If he is recognized for what he is, he would be killed.

And where is he? It took a while, but gradually recognition swam up out of the trees. The Piskie Wood, war memorial of the Moonshine Wars, some forty years ago.

You had to have a license to hunt in the Piskie Wood, and while the College of Mages paid for freshly dead Piskies, some war veterans simply went in to kill Piskies. He'd learned that begging beside its gates sometimes yielded well. But you ran the risk of the fury of the three beggars regularly clustered there, war veterans themselves.

Two rabbit-sized Piskie corpses were impaled on a spike beside the gate. Teo recoiled, seeing the dulled eyes, the torn wings. Thoughts of Sorcerers flung in harbors and the bite of flames at his own heels jerked at him, made his muscles seize and spasm in panic. Gasping for breath, he flung himself back along the ice-slicked curb.

He couldn't think—couldn't think—couldn't think. Details flashed at him: the Piskie's eyes, its wings, rain-smeared engravings on mottled orange paper, the ghostly sway of jellyfish, tendrils of dying mushrooms. He fought down the panic as though wrestling another boy bigger than himself, grappling desperately, flinging elbows and knees.

How had he managed to change? What had brought him to it here and now when it had failed so often in the past? Was it simply time or some other force? Was there some curse lingering on him, summoned by Granny Beeswax?

He remembered Murga's grip. Had Murga done this? But how?

He scrubbed himself clean as best he could with handfuls of dry grass, shivering as the freezing wind picked at his privates.

He was far, far from *The Autumn Moon*. He slunk back through the streets in the hours before dawn, cutting through the Duke's plaza.

The roar of the waterfall filling the plaza's center filled his ears, bore down on his sense, overwhelming him. He felt dizzy and sick and destroyed by the thoughts whirling through his head. He was a Shifter after all, in a city that hated them.

A cluster of people moved along the southern edge, talking and laughing, and two pedal-cabs passed along the curve of road and shops marking the outermost bound, side-by-side as though racing. There was music and more laughter, the sort he associated with alcohol, from a building laden with ornamental ironwork, leaning to overlook the stairs down to the next terrace. And the Duke's aetheric lights gleamed, bright and shiny as hatred, worms of brilliance crawling, writhing on the ice-glazed stones underfoot.

He kept pulling at his clothing, trying to duck back into the shadows and armor himself against the wind's intimate chill. The Moons gleamed overhead on a Plaza busier than he would have expected.

"Stupid boy!" Someone stepped forward in a rustle of skirts just as a cluster of people passed. Two Merchants and their guards, the Merchants chuckling at some joke, the guards grim-faced and wary, as though danger might spring out of the Plaza's stones at any moment. She backed him out of the pool of light. A Beast woman, an Oread, carrying a tray of flowers.

"Can't you see your shadow?" she hissed into his ear in a waft of garlic and hot breath. He looked down at the cobblestones under his toes and saw his shadow wavering across her skirts.

Not a Human boy's shadow at all, not hair and ears and elbows, but rather a cougar's feline shape, tufted ears and sinuous tail. Two shadows really—one from the nearest aetheric light, its radiance a brilliant pellucid blue, the other a normal, boy-shaped outline, twin-lapped from the two torches shining beside the entrance to a nearby tea shop.

His thoughts jumbled: homesickness, heartweariness, thoughts of returning home. And above all, fear—what did it mean to be a Shifter in the middle of this city, where a common streetlight could reveal his secret? His eyes burned with tears. He wiped them away with the backs of his hands—were they grown hairier, shaggier? He thought so.

"Everything's in flux now, though the Duke's Peacekeepers have put things calm for the moment. Get out, boy, and don't risk these lights again. They show your shadow as it should be."

He tried to stammer thanks but she was gone.

He made it back to the circus, still dizzy. What would he do now? What could he do? Perhaps it had been a fluke.

Perhaps it wouldn't happen again.

○ ○ ○

The mugs, Teo found out over the next day, were a never-ending task. He suspected he was being tested and knew it for sure when he found a mug tied to the top of the circus tent.

He stood looking up.

Billows of cloth between lines of ribbing made a sky within the tent, white as a snowy day. Vertical red and white stripes lined the vast walls. The main tent pole that held its peak aloft was solid pine, as thick around as his waist, perhaps a little thinner. Metal staples along it allowed him to climb upward.

He had climbed pine trees at home. Their outward thrusting branches formed natural handholds and this pole was easier, even, in its irregularity. He climbed quickly in his enthusiasm, and it was not until he realized he was at the first trapeze platform's level that he looked down.

From here he could see the trails swept in the sawdust by Jonas's ragged broom, long lines and loops and curlicues like a faltering script forgetting how to form words. The thin edge of the wooden hoops marking the circus rings were almost invisible seen from this angle: arcs of red and green and blue worn to a sawdust shade along the outer sides.

Was this how Bella felt, standing in the arena? Surely she was never this frightened. He swallowed hard and looked up at the mug hooked on the underside of the topmost platform. It seemed no closer now than when he had started climbing.

Was anyone watching him? What would be the point of the prank if not? He supposed that his reaction would establish here and now whether he was a good sport, a likeable fellow, or someone everybody habitually picked on. He sighed and refrained from looking around. Better to simply dive into the deep water and get it over.

He climbed and climbed. He squinted upwards, trying to see if the mug were getting perceptibly larger. Finally it was there, almost in reach.

He realized with horror that to retrieve it, he would have to lean out and grab it. This high up, he could see the canvas's rough weave above him and hear the faint splat of icy raindrops against it. He wondered what would happen if he simply refused to cooperate, kept clinging to the pole all through the day and into the night, letting the acrobats climb over and around him on their way up to the top. He supposed eventually he would grow tired and fall. How long could someone live on the tiny acrobat's platform?

Finally, though, he took a deep breath and uncurled one hand's desperate grip on the ladder. He reached forward, feeling the uncontrollable shaking of his hand and his pulse hammering in his throat. It was so far down. When his fingers touched the cold china surface, he could have wept with joy.

He thrust it in his tunic pocket and began to make his way back down, which was far worse than the upward trip had been. He kept imagining his foot slipping on the staple, imagining that he would slide and fall, end up smashed flat in a puff of sawdust.

By the time he was back entirely on the ground, he was shaking and felt queasy. Still, he faced outward, forcing a smile, and bowed slightly, gravely, not looking to see if anyone was watching. He took pride in not stopping to rest or recover himself, instead immediately taking the mug back to the cook tent.

He thought that probably no one had seen the incident after all. It was stupid, thinking it would make any difference. But then a passing workman clapped him on the shoulder, and Jonas offered him a discarded program that could be used to patch the hole in his shoes. At least one set of eyes had witnessed his ascent and spoken of it to others.

In the cook tent, he let the armful of mugs clatter into the washing bin and drew his own fresh mug, finding a seat to one side. He'd done enough for now. He held the first sip on his tongue, trying to puzzle out the flavors. He wondered if they would taste different if he were in his cougar form.

He had not tested his abilities any further. He wasn't sure how. He'd sat staring at his hand, willing the fingernails to narrow and sharpen into claws, tips deepening into pads, hair like fine gold sprouting—but there was nothing. They said sometimes Humans went mad and imagined themselves Beasts—was he one? But if so, how could he be Human when his parents were not?

Dreams of being caught haunted him. They were what made him waver in thinking himself anything other than Human. They would weight him with chains and throw him in the harbor, or tie him to a pole and light him on fire.

As long as he stayed inside the circus, stayed out of the touch of the aetheric lights, he'd be safe. He wanted to go see Bella, but the route worried him.

People moved in and out of the tent without looking at him. Only Maisie and Jonas talked much to him, and Murga was usually only a glimpse. The other workers were a strange mixture of Beasts, and sometimes he thought they might prove friendlier if only he could adjust to their city ways, to their too-quick words full of slang and unfamiliar phrases.

At the table behind him an argument broke out, only half intelligible. He had absorbed a little of the slang—performers were called Faces, not always in a complimentary way. Faces were difficult, demanding—didn't know how to pitch a tent or splice a rope.

There did not seem to be many friendships across the lines, with the exception of Mad Jonas, who worked constantly picking up bits of paper and other jetsam that had landed on the island of the circus.

He was pleased with the image. It did seem an island to him, self-contained.

What would they have thought of him, back home? He was a Shifter now, a real one. Had something happened in the city to provoke the change, or had it been inevitable? Lidiya had told his mother he would never change, but perhaps that had just been a guess, not certainty.

A thought struck him. He could go home. They'd want him there now.

Murga clapped him on the back. His eyes were amused. "I hear they've been giving you a hard time, but you proved yourself, boy."

Teo ducked his head, feeling his cheeks heat up.

"I get good reports of you."

Teo smiled. "Thank you," he said, feeling a wash of camaraderie and pride. The circus wanted him. He could be a valuable addition to it. And if he stayed with it, and didn't go out into the streets much, surely he would be fine. Then when they traveled up along the coast, he'd accompany them and see the world. Who knew what could happen?

o o o

He had hoped Bella would come to visit, that she'd take time to look after his welfare.

But somehow she never made it. A few times he slipped away to go to her house, but he never managed to encounter her there, though Abernia was always ready to give him chal and to hear his stories about circus life.

He wasn't angry about it, though. Just a little sad.

He'd expected better of Bella Kanto.

Chapter Twenty-Three

Conversations

I say to Skye, "Do you know what city dancing is?"

She does. I can tell it by the way her breath catches and her eyes widen. She says, "But that is something you only teach the best students."

"Are you objecting, then?" I ask, even though I know the answer. I love the way her cheeks flush when I tease her.

She shakes her head so quickly I think it might fly off. Fervent protests tumble from her lips, almost too quick to understand.

I hold out my hand. "Let us go then."

City dancing. It is a sport I invented, first as a training exercise for myself. Later, it became the way I made love to the city. I know every stairway, every monument, every tree branch that might offer a grip, every railing that one might leap. I even know the rooftops, the slippery expanse of tiles and timbers. It is a dance you can engage in only when you know what you are doing. When you know not the map, but every inch it represents.

We begin at the top of the Tumbril Stair. She expects me to direct her, but instead I say, "The winner is whoever reaches the docks first." I take a breath and begin.

The stairs are cluttered with people ascending and descending. I circumvent them by racing along the broad banister that skirts one side.

I don't look back as my steps slide along the stone, but I am sure she is following. I take the lead, I know the territory, while at best, she knows the map. She doesn't have a chance of winning. What I'm curious about is how well she runs this race.

Rather than turn where the stair does, leading along the face of the cliff that divides the first and second terraces, I dive forward and hear Skye's gasp behind me. There is an ancient oak there that the stair loops around, and a broad branch that I've used to vault across to the other side of the stairs more than once. I do it now, and even as I let go I feel the thump of wood that means Skye is trusting my lead, rather than slowing herself by taking the longer, better known route.

I move without pausing to think, letting my body and instinct guide me. I hover for an instant in a handstand atop the railing, swinging forward to hit the ground and roll, making my landing part of the motion forward, never stopping, my pulse thundering in my ears, my breath even but strong, feeling alive in a way that I only feel in one other place: the arena.

Most students cannot keep up with me. Skye manages. I knew that she would. In fact as our chase continues, we begin to engage each other. I cartwheel off her shoulders; she uses my arm to swing herself up atop a wall. I have never done this in tandem, a partnership that makes this truly a dance rather than the contest it has always been.

And so we dance the city.

I show her a rooftop shortcut and she follows on my heels, feet sliding over tiles glassed with ice, avoiding the skylight set in the center as though plucking knowledge of its existence from my mind.

This must be fated. This must be something that the Gods have intended for me. Perhaps this is my reward for my service to the city, all these years of fighting for it. All these years of waiting. Everything else is dross beside this golden moment. I feel as though every time I breathe in, more joy enters my body, filling me up like a balloon until I could float and fly rather than run. If only this could last forever. Surely if the Gods will it, it will be so. Surely this is what they want for me.

○ ○ ○

I know the way home, lucky enough, for my steps are slow and clumsy. Drinking to this point's become harder and harder over the years.

The house is dark, its occupants asleep, although Abernia has left a lantern set in the window. Another will be in the hall to light my way up. She knows my habits well.

A shape is huddled on the steps. As I near, it unfolds itself and stands.

Skye.

Of course. Who else could it be?

"I snuck away," she says defiantly, chin raised. "I won't go back till morning. I'll slip into the morning run as it goes along the docks, and no one will know I wasn't there at the start. You fight as Winter in two days. There's a chance you'll be hurt. Let me stay with you tonight."

I open my mouth. She can take my bed: I will take the couch.

That will keep my promise to Lucya.

But Skye is in my arms, her mouth warm against my Winter-cold lips, making my blood surge, a pleasant ache growing, wanting.

And so I take her hand and lead her upstairs.

This night is mine. I will deal with all the trouble it brings in its wake in the morning.

○ ○ ○

Adelina once accused me of having fucked half of Tabat. It was unfair—as accusations usually are. Unfair but not totally unmerited. There are plenty of folk in Tabat who have never shared my bed, and yet are fully qualified to do so. They simply haven't managed to catch my eye.

Perhaps it makes me sound like something I'm not, someone obsessed by sex. I don't even know that it's the sex I desire so much as their attention. In the arena you can drink it in like a sponge, feel it filling like new. So, too, when you lean over a lover and see them looking back up at you, their eyes only for you.

And now a new obsession, but one I've never experienced before, this worrying that if I look in her eyes I will not see her looking back at me. I worry that she will change her mind. I worry that she will grow tired of me. I worry that I will do something to put her off.

I hope she shares some of these worries, that they're mirrored in her. But I fear that's not how it is. I fear that love is never an even exchange, that it is always pursuer and pursued, always someone who loves the other more, always someone chained while the other is free to walk away.

But what would I do if Skye walked away? I've had lovers leave before, but usually when I'm ready for them to do so. Indeed, I have urged them away through prickly disagreements or picking fights over small things. It's never been a matter of ego, and it's not a matter of ego now. It's a matter of something close to breathing, a feeling that without her all the world would be vapid and hollow and gray.

I do not know how I let her past my defenses, the ones that have kept everyone else away for so long.

I am heartless, some have accused, usually those who had hoped to give me theirs. But this is not true. I have simply kept it guarded. Perhaps I was waiting to find someone worthy of it. And even now, how do I know that Skye is the one that I've been waiting for?

But I do. I know that as surely as I know the blood that beats in my veins. She's like a magnet, pulling my thoughts to her even when walls separate us. I go for a walk, thinking to city dance, thinking to run errands, thinking anything but to go to the school, and yet there I am again at the gate, pulling the wrought iron swords toward me in order to swing the gate open and go to her.

The other girls must know what is going on, but I have caught no sly glances, no secret whispers, at least so far. Can it be that Skye has kept quiet about it? It seems unlikely given the gossipy nature of the young, but then again, Skye is so different than any other girl or woman or man or boy that I have ever known.

And yet I could not tell you how.

○ ○ ○

Lucya says, "You drive me to some rash action."

I fold my arms and square myself off with her. She looks as flushed and hot as though she had just come from tending a furnace, but I curb the unkind words that fit themselves on my tongue, ready to be spit out in anger. Instead, I swallow.

I tell her, "I am trying to accommodate myself to your dictates. But there are limits."

"Accommodate, is that what you call it? It seems rather that circumvention is on your mind. And I warn you now, Bella Kanto, a second time. Be careful what you drive me to."

I cannot help it. Fury sparks a rising ire that heats my words. "Be careful that you do not make threats that you cannot live up to. This school would not survive without me."

"This school did well enough before you came along. It will be here long after you are gone."

There is no point in going round and round about this. I leave with her still hissing words after me, not raising her voice lest students overhear.

○ ○ ○

This is all new to me. This bewildered sensation, this constant yearning. This feeling that my heart will tear itself out of my chest. I walk about dazed, wanting to see her, dreading seeing her.

At first it all seemed so certain. I knew that look in her eye the very first day I met her. Someone who had fallen in love with the idea of Bella Kanto, someone who knew all the legends as closely as though she'd studied them in school. Someone who didn't see me at all, I thought.

And then, somehow, she did. She saw through to the heart of me and fell in love with that, not with the character from the penny-wides. Sure, she still thinks me a hero, perhaps. But she knows the cracks that run through me, the oddness and frailties, the insecurities.

She knows the reason I dread waking in springtime is because that was when my parents died, the first day of spring, a day I'd risen ready to enjoy until slow steps in the hallway came to tell me what had happened, which no one was entirely certain of, except for the fact that my parents were dead. That they were certain of.

I keep thinking she'll change her mind. That she'll think the difference between the hero in her head and the person before her too much, after all. For the first time I worry that I am not the true Bella Kanto.

Chapter Twenty-Four

More Circus for Teo

He almost stumbled into the man and woman as they were coming into the cook tent. They wore bright blue cloaks, the kind most of the performers here wore. As the woman turned away from him, he saw the embroidery on the back of her cloak, "The Amazing Rappinos."

Where did he remember them from? Because he did, he was sure of that. He searched through his Circus memories, then further back, then further back still. Oh! He'd seen them the very first time he had entered Tabat, with the guard surrounding them, taking away something they had been carrying.

They looked little less for the wear—although by his calculation it was at least two white moons later—perhaps a little thin around the edges as though they had been living leaner than usual.

He wondered if, like so many others in the circus, they might actually be Beasts, just a type that could pass for Human when people didn't look at them cautiously, or kind that he had never seen before. They seemed Human enough.

The man turned and caught him looking at them, but he didn't seem to think it unusual, just beckoned Teo over. Up close, the pallor to his cheeks led Teo to think he had been somewhere where there hadn't been much sun. The woman's complexion mirrored it.

The man said, "Boy, do you know where the tents for the performers are? We're acrobats, but we've been delayed and are only now arriving."

"I'll take you there," Teo offered. He was curious about the couple and hoped that perhaps he might find out more in their conversation as they walked along. To his pleasure and surprise, they confided much in him as they did so: Their names, and that they had in fact been in jail, although they did not say for what, and what the jail food had been like and what the jail beds and privies and fellow inhabitants had been like. Teo wanted to know more about why they had gone to jail, but he wasn't sure how to bring it up politely. He wasn't sure it would be polite at all to bring it up, particularly given how awkward it felt to ask.

But the man finally said, "I bet you're wondering what we went in there for, aren't you, boy?"

Teo sort of shrugged and nodded all at once, to convey his nonchalance yet evoke the answer, too.

"You wouldn't be here if you didn't have some sympathy for the cause. We were distributing the story designed to wring the hearts of Humans, to twist their emotions into sympathy for the Beasts that they oppress."

Teo attempted another shrug and nod, although he was not sure this one was quite as successful as the first.

"You're just confusing him, Amos," the woman said. She patted Teo's head and said, "I'm sure you hear this talk a lot. Thank you for helping us find our tent. I'm touched that Murga had it ready and waiting for us." She gave her husband a smile. "He seems the kind to look after his folks, haven't I always said that?"

o o o

But Murga seemed less than pleased to see the acrobats. When Teo led them to his tent, the first thing Murga snapped was, "I told you not to come back here."

"But we had nowhere else to go!"

"You were to go to another circus, begin feeling them out!" Murga's eyes fixed on Teo, hovering by the tent flap. "Why are you loitering? Go find something useful to do."

He did not see them again.

o   o   o

Each morning dray wagons brought the countless crates and baskets of food consumed each day by the circus's inhabitants. They drew their water and watered the horses and other animals at the enormous fountain nearby, an ice-glazed war memorial to those fallen in the Shadow Wars, crowned with a Dragon and a woman grappling.

Teo stared at the stone woman's face as he filled buckets to water the lions. It was resolute. She held the writhing lizard at arm's length, despite the great gouges its claws sought to score in her flesh. She wore a crown of frost-white marble, and water sprayed out from it in a curtain that made it look as though the figures, seen through the curdling foam and mist, truly moved and struggled.

The fountain's basin was a good ten yards across, and the circus workers continuously hauled water for the kitchen, for the animals, for the steam boilers that drove the shining machines, the tiny Ferris wheel and the merry-go-round and the whining, wheedling calliope.

Circus work was hard, but not so hard he couldn't keep up with it. Some of it should have felt exotic, he thought, such as tending the striped zebras or the Mermaids, but it was much like mucking out a stable back home.

Horseshit was horseshit, no matter where you were.

He puffed with pride. Here he was, philosophizing as deeply as any roadside Scholar, and a good deal better, what's more, than some of the political speeches he'd heard over and over again.

He'd seen Tiggy out there in the crowds of speakers in the last few days, although never at a time when he'd had the leisure to go and listen to her words. He liked the speakers who had more elaborate words anyhow. Like listening to poetry, all grand crashing sounds and syllables whose meanings could only be imagined.

If he listened for years, maybe he'd learn enough to follow it all, but even so he thought smugly, he was beginning to savvy enough politico-speak to nod sagely in the borders of conversations.

Most of the Circus cared only about the rights of Beasts, and it was this group that listened the most closely to Mrs. Tiggy. Others paid attention to issues involving property in the Southern Isles, letters of marque, and even how to keep the Shadow Wars from spilling any further on these shores.

Teo stayed on the edge of the endless discussions, knowing they would ignore him if he spoke, but enjoying the feeling of being part of the group. He fantasized conversations in which everyone would pause to listen to his discourse on some matter. Even Murga would look impressed.

But for now, standing beside the fountain, holding a red and white umbrella to protect himself from the morning rain, Murga looked unimpressed, giving him his next instructions: "Scrub the Oracular Turtle's tank. Get Jonas to help you lift it into the canvas cradle. Then scrub it out with soap and water and rinse it well, very well, before you refill it with salt water from the wash wagon—I'll send it down to fetch water while you're scrubbing and it will be back well before you're ready. Then you'll need to ride with it to the river and help flush the salt water out."

It would have been a more pleasant task without the layer of silty turtle feces that had settled at the bottom of the tank. He emptied it out into a bramble-choked ditch and sluiced water at the worst of it, shivering. There was no way to avoid getting wet, and the cold riding the wind took full advantage of his vulnerability. He knew this cloudy water somehow. He swished a hand through it, dream slow.

"I know the sound of the flute," Jonas told the Turtle, squatting beside the canvas sling filled with water from the tank.

The Turtle said in reply, "I know the sound of the flute but not who plays it."

Jonas nodded. "A lantern has no wick, no oil, but its flame burns."

Concentric arcs spread out from where the Turtle nosed at the side of the sling. "A lily floats on the water and does not touch its mud."

"Jonas, I could use some help," Teo said.

He swished the brown sponge through the bucket of strong-scented, soapy water, the smell burning at his nostrils. He wiped along the seams of the tank, streaking the sponge with darker matter, slime or mold, he wasn't sure which, but its sweet-rot smell battled with the harsher ammonia scent.

Jonas said, "It's not that a single flower opens, but that dozens open on the hillside."

"Yes," the Turtle said.

Teo tried a teasing tone. "And flowers will open in the tank, growing there if we don't clean it."

The other two just stared at him in silence. Feeble sunlight battled the icy chill in the air, ineffectual as a sick kitten. The water had been hot when he first started, but now it was cold, and his hands burned when they hit the air.

"A moon bird thinks of nothing but the moon," the Turtle said, its voice haughty.

"Listen," Teo said, but Jonas interrupted him and spoke over what he was about to say as though he had never dreamed of saying it. "When the next rain comes, that is all the rain bird will think of."

Teo wondered if maybe the two were just messing with his head. He looked at Jonas, whose face was innocent. On his shoulder the white mouse stared intently at Teo, as though he had never seen the likes of the boy.

The Turtle's stare was harder to interpret. Its face was a snake's, a parrot's, a lunatic calf's grin. He wondered, not for the first time, at a world where the only creatures that could glimpse the future were pigs and turtles. It said to him, urgently, "Who is it we spend our whole life loving?"

"I don't know," he said angrily, and kicked at the side of the canvas tank, although he was careful not to touch the Turtle. "Murga told us to work, Jonas."

Jonas grunted and took up another sponge. They washed at the great six-sided metal and glass tank, which lay tipped on its side. From inside it, Teo looked out at the world of the circus, distorted and green-cast, smeared with lichen that Jonas had carelessly left in the wake of his sponge. Raindrops dappled the outside glass.

The mouse squeaked as water dripped on it from above, and Teo pointed to the side of the tank. "You need to redo that spot. And there. And there."

He would have expected Jonas to grumble. It was what he would have done himself if he had been in the other man's place.

But the janitor just kept on working. The white mouse ran inside his shirt pocket, sheltering from any further drops of soapy water.

As they tipped the Turtle back into the cleaned, rinsed, and refilled tank, it repeated to him in a gravelly voice: "Who is it that we love? We love those that are like ourselves. Who does Murga love?"

Before he could think of an answer, he glimpsed someone near Murga's tent. The Mage from the docks! Come looking for him? He should have remembered that here on the grounds of the College of Mages, he might meet the man. He hurried away from the turtle's tank to the depths of the area that held the cages, far away from Murga's tent, and cleaned the monkey cages, picking away sticky lumps of dried fruit and shit as he kept a wary eye out.

He gave squirrel monkeys bits of apple. Rain beaded the soft grey fur of their arms. They smelled musty and sweet, picking the fruit from his palms with tickling fingers.

The question returned to him.

Who did he love? His parents would say they loved him, and his sister, and the Moons that ruled them all.

Did he love the Moons? He didn't think he did, but he also wasn't sure what they were. The Merchants, Abernia had explained to him, did not worship the Moons but rather worshiped a thousand Gods handling different aspects of trades and transactions. The degree of influence each and their intricate families held over one's life indicated the best path in life to take. The Moon Temples said something similar, but both faiths were careful to say that they were not predicting the future. No Human could predict the future, and even the oracular animals were uncertain and vague....

He continued about his duties. He gave the Fairies honeycomb and fed oranges to the baby elephant. She crushed each one between her back teeth, juice dribbling along her thick hide.

Who did he love?

Bella Kanto, even though she had deserted him.

o o o

That night he dreamed of the acrobats. He climbed up and up the pole, and when he got to the top, he jumped off and only then realized he had no net or line to catch him.

He fell, but then he was back inside the Turtle tank, but it had been turned over entirely, its bottom now the roof over his head, so although he pushed at the cloudy glass of the sides, inexplicably sticky with dregs, he could not budge it, could not tip it over and free himself.

From inside its depths, he stared outward. He was knee deep in warm, salty water, and orange and crimson jellyfish floated through it, translucent and fine as lace. The sister Mermaids were there, they beckoned to him, they twined around his knees. The Turtle was there, and it said to him, *How lucky you are, how marvelously lucky you are!*

He said it, and the words flew out from his lips in bubbles because the water had risen to fill the tank, his eyes, his ears, his mouth. While he wasn't looking, the words flew out like winged bubbles, rising upward to be caught against the floor of the tank. He said, *What do you mean?*

The Turtle said, *You're going to hear more of the story. Are you going to listen? Are you going to know whose story it is?*

Outside, the people were passing, dressed in summer colors like fabulous birds and butterflies. There was a woman with a thousand tiny braids, and each one was a different color. Even though glass separated them, he knew she smelled of rosemary and wine. Fish swam through the water around him and blocked his sight of the crowds, more and more silvery-sided fish, like cleavers swimming in a curtain of flat metallic sparkles. All he could see now were the fish. Each presented him with a single eye, round as a black marble, expressionless, hundreds of them regarding him in a curtain of appraising eyes.

It was the voice he'd dreamed of before.

One day I found a different kind of mushroom.

It was a shelf fungus whose beige gills were mottled with rune-like markings. I reached out and broke it from its hold on the stone wall and turned it open. Each fold was a page, a page with a story, stories that went on and on and on. I could feel them seeping into my fingers, working their lithe way, swimming along the muscles up my arms, my shoulders, climbing the stair/ladder of my neck, and finally lodging in my brain, story after story, of Beasts and blunders and blood.

The mushroom whispered. It told Teo stories he didn't want to know, stories of his mother meeting men in the woods, of Canumbra's secret desires, of a corpse washed ashore under the docks. He tried to turn away, to close his ears, but he couldn't.

I knew the peddler would pay well for it, and so I tucked it apart from the other mushrooms that I showed my father. I did not know if he noticed anything in my manner. Perhaps he was already suspicious and watching, watching for the act that would confirm his beliefs and lead him to ready a spell.

But he said nothing, betrayed nothing.

That evening old Jules lit the signal fire and I changed out of my shit-raddled clothes, took up my baskets, and went down along the fence of leaning sticks, more sign than fence, to the lantern lit clearing that marked our trading spot.

Jules was a scarf-wrapped old man—he wore at least a dozen of them, wrapped around his face, hands, arms, and neck, and he never let any more of his skin show than he had to. He had the look of a broken-backed yew bush, stooped and close to the ground.

He pawed through the first few baskets, muttering under his breath. I kept the last one back. He straightened.

"Thirty silver and whatever's due for that one you're hiding." He pointed a finger at my feet.

"I don't know what it's worth," I said. I knelt and unfolded the cloth over the shining fungus. He stared.

"Sell that one to your father, is the first thing I'd do," he said slowly.

"How much would you ask him for it?"

"A hundred gold, easily," he said. "Perhaps some magic to boot."

"Give me ten gold, here and now, and it's yours."

"You won't be around to conduct the bargain with your father?"

"It's time for me to move on," I said. He gave me the coins and wished me luck. I didn't turn back to the tower. Instead I set off along the lane without looking back, not caring about anything I left behind.

I never heard from my father again. But when I first was taken aboard the ship, unconscious, they said I burned with blue fire. They threw me overboard, but the flames kept burning until all my clothing was gone and I floated on the waves, a mass of blisters. The ship's physician had me hauled back on board as a curiosity, and by the time I recovered and woke, screaming, the ship was long under way. The next two weeks were fever and ointment.

And somewhere in the midst of all that haze of pain, a thought came to me one night.

It must have been my father's magic preventing me from the realization before. How had I never wondered? Who was my mother? Why had my father never spoken of her?

My father, so clever at breeding Beasts, at creating things that had never existed before.

I was something new, something outside Beast and Human and Shifter. I went to the Isles and learned things about myself. People were new to me at first, but they accepted me as one of them because I looked like one of them.

But my sympathy lay with the Beasts, now that I was something so close to one, their plight concerned me even more. When I heard tales of Tabat, of how it fueled its engines, of the Beasts that had built it and now lived in it as slaves, it inflamed me.

And so I came to Tabat, ready to bring it down.

He recognized the voice now.

Murga.

o o o

Murga called Teo into the tent that served him as office and storehouse late the next evening.

"Something about you keeps drawing my eye to you, boy," Murga said, gesturing at Teo to stand before the desk. His chalklike face angled to inspect Teo. "Sometimes I swear you're creeping into my dreams."

Teo's cheeks heated.

"Not like that," Murga said irritably. He tilted his head, as though sniffing the air. "Must I take you apart to discover what it is? We all have our secrets, boy. I'm going to show you one of mine."

Teo stared at him, feeling his heart race. This felt wrong. Ominous.

Something was happening to Murga's face. It crawled and shifted, reshaping itself. The nose pulled in, the lips became fuller. The eyes shaded from black to grey.

He was Miche Courdeau, too. How could that be? Teo's head swam with dizziness. Was Miche some sort of Shifter? But Shifters had animal and Human forms. What sort of Shifter changed between one Human form and another?

"And now I have shown you a secret, and fireworms will eat your liver if you speak of it, I'll see to that. So, boy, what is yours?"

Teo searched his mind for something that might satisfy Murga but still keep Teo's Shifter nature a secret. "I had a Shadow Twin," he found himself blurting out.

Murga ceased motion so suddenly that it was akin to a flinch. Then he stepped closer.

"Had? As in they perished?"

"She died in the womb," Teo said. "Lidiya said she never drew breath."

"Well, well." Murga went back to the desk and sat down. The chair creaked beneath his weight. The tent canvas sighed as outside winds played over it, rippling the walls and setting the lamp's flame trembling in time with Teo's heartbeat.

Murga's stare was an iron gimlet. "If your twin had lived, you would have access to her powers. But you seem ordinary enough for your … kind."

The way he lingered over the last word made Teo's heart race so fast that he was afraid it might burst. The air inside the tent's confines felt as thunderstorm heavy. *Did Murga know what* he was? Relief at no longer having to hide warred with terror: *What if Murga turned him over to the Duke?*

"Do you know why Humans and Beasts alike hate Shifters?" Murga asked.

Teo shook his head, still mute with shock. *How could Miche and Murga be the same person?*

"Because they can't be spotted by sight, the way a Beast might be. They can walk among Humans and spy on them. Humans fear Beasts will rise up against them someday. How much greater that fear if they think they can be fooled into thinking their foes are their friends? And Beasts, they know that Shifters can pass, can pretend to be Human. No one likes them, boy, no one. And the College of Mages, worse yet. The blood of a Shifter and a Shadow Twin? You could work powerful magic with that, boy. Very powerful. They'd take you apart to use you in their spells. If Bella Kanto knew you were one, she'd see you put to the sword simply to spare you that."

It hurt Teo to think that, but it was true. He knew how much Shifters were despised. He'd seen the announcements of their executions.

Murga's hands gathered on the desk. Fascinated, Teo watched them assemble pen and paper.

"You can read, I trust?"

Teo's nod was infinitesimal. Murga acknowledged it by beginning to scrawl on the paper.

"You are an ordinary boy," Murga said as he wrote. "Nothing special to you, only a lingering aura of what might have been. Isn't that so?"

Teo's heartbeat and the lamp flicker slowed. The walls were still and silent.

"Yes," Teo said. Murga didn't mean to tell his secret, but that didn't make Teo any less frightened. It simply meant the man had some use for him.

"Tomorrow, you will run errands for me in the early morning." Murga indicated a crate beside the tent entrance. "You will take a copy of the book there to each of these addresses. Wrap them beforehand in the paper you see there and tie it with string." He looked back at Teo. "Understand that? Cover them completely. I'd not wish them exposed to the vagaries of weather." He pushed the paper at Teo.

Teo folded it and slipped it in his pocket, standing.

"Is that all?" he asked, and heard desperation in his voice.

Murga reached out to the key at the lamp's base. He turned it with a click, and the flame gasped once, then subsided into darkness.

"Go to bed, ordinary boy," he said.

Chapter Twenty-Five

Winter's Battle

The day has come.

Countless times I've stepped out into the arena to take part in the Gladiatorial ceremonies, part public entertainment, part civic ritual, but always, thoroughly a spectacle that allows me to glimpse Tabat's heart. My breath always catches when I first stand on the tiles, feeling the slight ridges and troughs of their patternings through my boot soles, weapon not yet in hand but ready at my hip. My armor, elaborately chased, is light and latticed, showing flashes of the white linen tunic I wear beneath it. Pretty armor, but not something I would care to wear into real battle.

It isn't the noise of the crowd or the sense of their eyes watching me move forward. It isn't the sound of the opposite door rolling upward, revealing my opponent, distance making her a doll-sized figure facing me, come to challenge me.

It's something else, a sense of magic running through me, Priestess of sword and shield. Not just the crowd but the world watches me, ready to shape itself in accordance to my skill. Is this how Mages feel when magic pours itself through them?

It is why I won't quit until defeat forces me. I crave this rush of righteousness, this sense of being something larger than I really am. These are the moments when I become the Bella Kanto of the penny-wides, moving forward to salute her opponent, knowing the end is already written.

Once little Djana, who'd arrived from the Flower Continent years ago, sullen but showing signs of skill, now all grown up and facing her teacher.

My teeth bared in a grin beneath my visor.

We both walk forward until only a few feet separate us, and I'm able to see the device on the tiny, triangular shield she carries to match mine, the slits in the visor masking her face. We unsheathe our swords. Winter's is hilted in crystal and silver, while Spring's blazes with stones, yellow tourmalines, emeralds, and sapphires, as bright as a cloudless day.

Blade touches blade in ritual salute; once, twice, and again. The crowd roars; Skye must be among them, in the section that Lucya reserves for the students of the Brides of Steel. I wear a charm at my throat that she gave me last week.

We close. I strike lightly, a quick *rat-a-tat* test of Djana's speed and strength.

What I discover astonishes me. Has the girl been holding back in practice all this time? Certainly she is the best of a bad year, but both Lucya and I had debated whether or not to put her in the ring.

Joy, not dismay, flashes through me at the realization. It will be a worthy fight, not just going through the motions. How long has the girl been preparing for this, hoping to overtake me?

I will give her a fight then.

I close and slash. Djana slides the blade away by interposing her shield, struck in turn, a blow that skitters along my side, ineffectually seeking entrance.

Something strange about her.

I sidestep, put myself between Djana and an aetheric light. Let the girl squint a bit.

I dart forward, stooping a touch to let the blaze of light hit her full on as I do so. That often works well.

But I've shown my students that trick. Djana moves and turns, pulling me into a new spot where the light falls across us both, dragging our shadows out along the ripples of blue and gold.

We meet. The crowd roars as she slashes, and I knock her blade aside. We withdraw, meet and withdraw again.

This is not Djana. I know her blade work. This is someone else. And with that thought, I know.

Skye.

I spare a glance up to the box where the students and staff of the Brides of Steel cluster. Lucya stares down at me. Her eyes are flinty.

You drive me to some rash action, I hear her say in my memory.

Skye pushes forward.

We close, grappling this time. I find her blade angled at me and duck away just in time.

Did I see something on the blade?

We close again. I weave a cage of air and steel around my opponent as I try to glimpse what I saw before.

There. A blue shine, so subtle, so easy to miss.

Poison.

No time to call out. And what will happen to the weather if the ritual is interrupted? What will it mean for Tabat if Spring wins with a poisoned blade?

Does Skye know? Does she mean to kill me then? That thought is as painful as any blow.

But surely not. She doesn't fight as an opponent would, knowing the blade poisoned, knowing that a scratch can kill. Someone has put it there, and in her ignorance she has not checked her weapon beforehand as a seasoned Gladiator would.

Should I simply let her win?

She will still love me if she defeats me, surely. Perhaps love me even more, for have given her such a thing.

Skye sees my hesitation. She presses forward, eager to end things quickly. Our blades clash again.

I could throw this and she would know. It would rob her of her victory if she thought I had thrown the fight. She would resent me.

She swings. I parry.

I could try to be subtle about it, pretend to make mistakes. But what will it do to my city? Surely it isn't pride that holds me back. Surely it isn't that I cannot bear to give up being Champion for selfish reasons.

Without recovering her balance fully, she swings again. Too eager.

My blade flicks out, angry but calculated, deflecting Skye's point to exactly where I want it. At the same time, I kick hard and equally precise, at the kneecap, settled behind a circle of metal but still so vulnerable to being struck. Not a crippling blow, but a painful one.

The girl staggers even as the crowd groans. A fair move, but not the flashy blade work they want.

She falls forward, grabbing at me. We roll, grappling.

This will not end till blood is shed.

An opening as we roll, flashes of the crowd on their feet, trying to see what is happening, as my hand drives the blade, trying to knock hers aside. There is a skitter of sparks and I feel all the bad luck spells around me closing in, forcing the blade home.

Skye goes limp beneath me.

My blood thundering in my ears and my harsh breaths are all that I can hear as I pull away. A Physician rushes out from a side door. Gladiatorial fights are rarely fatal, but often medical help is needed.

I try to breathe. I can feel that sense of righteousness, that I have performed my duty, that I have done as I should, but overpowering it is worry.

And then guilt and black sorrow as the Physician rises, shaking his head. The crowd screams outrage.

Dead.

This time I've not defeated Spring, but killed her entirely.

I've killed Skye.

Chapter Twenty-Six

Aftermath

Questioned by the Duke's Peacekeepers, none of Skye's fellow students or teachers can think of any reason why the girl should have had a poisoned blade.

I go to confront Lucya. She has caused all this. She has killed Skye with her spiteful act, setting her in the arena against me.

Lucya, though, has an answer for me.

"I know what caused it and that name is Bella Kanto!" she spits at me. "Dead! All for your vanity!"

I reel back.

Skye is dead. Horribly dead, a gap in the world that I can scarcely comprehend, a hole of the sort I have not felt since my parents' death.

But I am not responsible, no matter what Lucya says.

"You are unjust," I protest. "You put her there."

Lucya shakes her head.

"I had no way of knowing what lengths your enemies would go to. This is about releasing Tabat from Winter. They will kill you next."

There is no reasoning with her. I make a stiff farewell and depart the Brides of Steel.

I do not say when I will come again.

Lucya does not ask.

o o o

Skye is dead.

Unthinkable that such a thing could have happened.

How did it slip away from me, how did she get far enough ahead that I couldn't stop her?

I lie in bed, tangled in blankets and guilt, utterly unwilling to get up. I can hear the distant sounds of the house, but they seem muted, as though I were hearing them through deep water.

And no one will sympathize; no one will know I've lost my love, because it wasn't a love I could admit to. Lucya will know a little of it, but I won't show her how far I've fallen. Leonoa will only think I had it coming, for trying to interfere with her and Glyndia. And Adelina will say something practical and correct and utterly infuriating.

Rolling over, I bury myself further in the warmth of the eiderdown. It's cold outside. It will be cold six more weeks, a cold I brought to the city.

A cold it deserves for killing Skye.

It makes me think of other things I don't want to think about.

Jolietta died. They'd taken Phillip away in chains and harness, his head hanging down, lank-maned. Hoof beats, slow, stumbling hoof beats, echoed in my heart. It tore my heart to hear them but at the same time, joy stitched it together again, repaired each wrenching, scarring, hard-scabbed pain at the thought that Jolietta was gone, gone for good.

But before she'd died, the thing she'd done.

I lie back and let myself remember.

o o o

Phillip was there that first night; when I first arrived at Piper Hill. I was put to bed in a small chamber in a bed that smelled of mildew. I waited until Jolietta was asleep before creeping down-stairs, out the back door, and along the stable passageway.

Moonlight and rain drenched the apple orchard. My cloak wrapped tightly around me, an oilcloth dervish, I crept out among the stunted trees, short that they might be more easily picked. Underfoot the rotting, wet fruit sent up olfactory lamentations of fermentation and vomit and slick mud.

The Centaur stood among the trees, so still that I didn't see him at first. He stamped as I passed, stamped twice in the dazzle of moonlight that fell across his long, tangled hair, his broad chest, the flat face and furry, pointed ears.

"Go back," he said.

I faced him, defiant. "Or what?" Could any punishment be worse than the loss of Leonoa and that safe haven?

His voice was surprisingly deep, surprisingly gentle. I was unprepared for that gentleness. It shook me to the core.

"I am not in charge, here, child. Jolietta will not let you escape, though, and she will make you pay dearly if she has to hunt you."

All through the trip there, my aunt had spoken to me no more than she had the crates in the wagon, or the horses pulling it. But I felt a chill at the thought of crossing her.

"Wait until you know what she is capable of before you test her," he said.

It was wise advice, I knew in my heart. But I walked on, and he didn't try to stop me. I made it several miles before Jolietta caught up with me. She said nothing to me, but under her direction, my foot had been propped on a rock by one Minotaur while another raised his hoof and stamped down....

"That will slow you down next time," Jolietta said coldly to me as I curled in the dirt around the throb of the broken bones in my foot. "I will see you in the morning, and I will start your lessons."

But clinging to the back of the wagon, feeling every painful jolt, I realized that they had already begun.

At Piper Hill, Phillip bandaged my foot and did not comment as he found me crutches. We did not speak of our conversation, but that night I found a tray outside my door, despite Jolietta's words, and knew that he had brought it.

As time had passed, I realized that Jolietta liked to pit the two of us, her new apprentice and her former trainee, against each other. For a long time I'd been wary, but gradually I realized that

Phillip placed himself outside that battle, or even colluded with a sidelong wink, a mere drooping of a lid in which I learned to read amusement.

Phillip. My mind circles like a hawk, hovering over the same point—his long-nosed face, his clever hands, his slow, lilting accent. His vanity about his mane, which was long and copper colored, so it shone in the sun. I remember him galloping to dry it, a long shining plume, and another at his tail.

It was as though I've opened the cupboard where I had stuffed all these memories before. Phillip, smuggling me handfuls of dried apples. Phillip, managing to maneuver Jolietta so she gave the task of Dragon tending to me, thinking it a punishment, when all I wanted most in the world was the solitude it offered.

Phillip, whom I betrayed.

That morning, it was my fifteenth birthday. I roused with sweat crawling down my sides. It was the dead of summer and the coast breezes were drained of movement, unable to travel the few miles inland to cleanse the air at Piper Hill. The sheet underneath me was sodden with sweat, limp folds draping the cot, mirroring the torn rags at the windows.

Phillip's quarters were sparse. A patched jacket hung on a nail on the back of the door. A small chest sat at the cot's foot. A jelly jar held sprays of blue flowers on the windowsill—the light entered the glass and was flung out by the shape, scattered into fragments that danced across the blanket's rough weave, the worn wood underfoot, the ancient gilt clinging to the innermost clefts of the wooded curlicues that adorned the graying walls. The air smelled of the pine tar he chewed—a lump of it sat on the windowsill beside the flowers.

I stood frozen in the doorway. How could Phillip seem so here when I knew he was elsewhere? It was as though I could turn my head and find him standing there, scowling.

A board behind me creaked.

I spun, and there he was. The scowling was even more horrific in person.

"What are you looking for?"

"You?"

"Then why not speak when you saw me a few moments ago, headed towards the stables?"

My mind raced, but my lips flapped uselessly.

"What did you really want?"

I dropped my gaze to the floor. It was most scuffed near the doorway, where his comings and goings had worn away the polish to the yellow grain beneath.

"Bella, what did you really want?"

"I wanted to know what you were writing earlier," I admitted.

It was as though his anger made him a foot taller. He took a step closer to me. "And because you wanted, you felt you had a right?"

I stammered several incoherent things.

"You're as bad as your aunt," he said. "I was writing a letter to a friend. Shall I begin passing them through you, to check them and make sure there are no words of sedition in them? You're at a tender age still to be taking up a career as a Censor."

I blushed angrily. "I just wanted to see them."

He smelled of horse and man-sweat and pine, breathing the last in my face as he pressed forward, menacing me. At the same time, there was a hint of sex in his demeanor that I recognized. I had only recently come to an awareness of my power over some men and a few women, how a bold look or seductive gesture could reduce them to incoherency. Several stable hands had begun to ask for kisses recently, finally daring to look outside my aunt's possible anger. My core burned as though to match the fierce heat coming from his body.

I looked up at him and licked my lips, a deliberate, rehearsed gesture.

He kept staring down at me. I could see the heartbeat fluttering in his throat, could feel his warmth as though it were already laid against my skin. It flashed through my mind, *Oh, how this would anger Jolietta.* The thought made me lick my lips once again, looking into his eyes.

He pushed me, which sent me sprawling. I fetched up against the wall with a painful blow along my ribs that drove the breath out of me.

"Certainly I have no rights here, being a Beast against an exalted Human," he said, stressing the last word with a mocking twist. "But perhaps in the name of friendship, you might do me the courtesy of staying out of my things."

"It's not about you being a Beast!" I said. "I was just curious! It's illegal, Phillip. You could get in trouble."

But he said nothing more, simply stared me out of the room.

How could I have done what came next? I was as petty and as malicious as any teenager I've ever taught—and there is a long list of them.

How could I have gone so far as to ally with Jolietta, to take the side of the person I'd hated so hard and fiercely for so long?

But I did.

There was no sunlight in Jolietta's room, which faced the inner courtyard rather than the outer fences, as Phillip's did. The curtains were made of knotted lace, fine as spider webs, and everything about Jolietta's immaculately clean room spoke of careful, costly elegance.

Jolietta stood in the doorway. The lamp behind her made her look like a spider made of iron, axe-blade harsh and cruel.

"What is it?" she said.

"I've seen Phillip writing letters," I said.

Even now, decades later, shame blazes in me at the memory, at the betrayal. I had known it for one—I just had not anticipated its cost.

Jolietta didn't say, "Are you sure?" Instead, she pushed past me. But she did not go immediately to Phillip's room as I had thought she would, but to the infirmary. I trailed after her.

A shudder went through me, bone deep, when I saw Jolietta take the black-sided case down from the third shelf.

I said in protest: "Surely you're not going to put him down?"

"No," Jolietta said. Relief loosed my neck and shoulders, making me realize all at once how tight they had been. "I'll have him for breeding and simple work stock, if nothing else. It is a shame, though, to lose a skilled physician. I'll have to begin training one or two of the others up."

In the yard, me still trailing her, Jolietta signaled to Brutus and Caesar, who lumbered after her in turn. Jolietta's staccato of heel clicks led the slower, more ponderous tread behind her in turn. She did not knock at Phillip's door, but simply turned the knob and went in, the Minotaurs after her.

Brutus's bare back blocked my view—I saw in sharp detail the scars across his back, the swell of bullish muscle, the blotches of old sun—but I could not see Phillip or Jolietta.

"Hold him," Jolietta said. "Pinch his nose shut."

"Is there no other choice?" Phillip said, his voice high and desperate. "What is it that you think I have done?"

Jolietta did not speak to him.

o o o

The tip of the wire slid in and I saw the light go out of Phillip's eyes. I screamed and struck out, but Caesar held me and would not let me go. Then I tried to look away, but at Jolietta's bidding, he caught my head and held it, forcing me to witness.

I had never seen a Beast dulled before.

Afterwards she gave me chocolate as a reward for betraying him.

Here's the most shameful thing of all: I wept, but I ate it anyway.

Afterward, I tried to press the knife into Phillip's hands, over and over again, but he would not take it. I gripped the steel curve, freshly sharpened that afternoon at the great round of the grindstone. Me pumping its pedal with a steady rock of my foot. Sparks showered away whenever the blade touched the moving stone.

Even now, whenever metal sparks like that, I feel the burn of that afternoon's memory, sitting in the stable sharpening a knife to kill my aunt, the taste of blood in my mouth, the lack of sleep burning in my skull.

And after all of that, I was unsuccessful. I tried, but Jolietta had me beaten and sold Phillip away. She locked me in a room on the second floor. "Until I know what to do with you," she snarled.

I spent an uncomfortable night. While my aunt couldn't dull me in the way she could a Beast, she did have the right to punish a wayward apprentice, depending on how much dirty laundry she wanted to air in public.

And then in the early morning, I lay on the floorboards, wrapped in my cloak and staring at the ceiling, wondering, worrying what Jolietta would do. I heard the dawn stirring, the household servants going about their work, the creak of the cook at the pump, the smell of wood smoke as she got the stove going, followed by the creeping smell of coffee.

I heard what must have been Brutus knocking at his mistress's door, a steady solid sound that had ended with a crash. I wasn't paying attention until that crash, and after it I heard the stentorian wails, the grief. Some of Jolietta's creatures had known only life with her, and Brutus was one. When he appeared in my doorway, he looked oddly withered, like a plant forced into the wrong form and then deprived.

He said, "Mistress Jolietta is dead. She died in her sleep. We have sent for the doctor, but you are the mistress now."

I gaped at him. He hulked there in the doorway, long-lashed cow's eyes downturned.

I said, "Dead?" My mind felt about for strands of logic, like someone in the water looking for debris that might let them rest.

"Dead," he repeated.

And with that, I was free.

Enough.

I am still free.

O O O

I go to the window and look into the whirling snow. There's a limp little form in the corner of the window. Wind and snow greet me when I slide the window up, but I manage to gather the half-frozen little Fairy—Finch.

He's fought with his fellows. They must have tried to drive him away.

Finch stirs and flutters against my hand till I release him.

He moves to perch on a shelf, watching me.

I've heard them chatter in mimicry of Human speech, like parakeets. Or more like mockingbirds. They repeat the sounds of their day: the distant bells of the duels of the Duke's tower, the cries of the food carts. But they speak their own words as well, if you take the time to listen.

His stare is as direct as a cat's.

I open the drawer that holds a bag of jewel-like hard candies, flavored with vanilla and molasses.

I can hear the bard on the flute a floor below, the sound buoyed up through the floorboards by the resonant notes of a blow horn accompanying him.

How can Skye be dead?

Teo comes in without knocking, and I feel a flare of irritation at his presumption. He no longer lives here. He is a visitor, and that is how he should act.

"Miss Bella, I need to talk to you about something that happened to me." The words rush out. He's so preoccupied that he doesn't even notice the Fairy, now watching him intently.

All my enervation is gone now, swept away in a crimson tide of rage. How dare this boy intrude on my sorrow? How dare he think I'm concerned with whatever petty problem has ruffled his existence?

"Get out," I say.

He blinks. "But ..."

"Get out! Out of this house!" I don't know what I'm doing, taking out all my anger on this target that deserves it not a whit, but it eases my soul to let this temper claim me, to do what it will.

I know how to scare him. "I'm sending a messenger to the Moon Temples to come and claim you from the circus today!"

He flees.

O O O

I try to go about business as usual.

"I've taken on a new apprentice," Adelina tells me.

I'm surprised. "What happened to all your vows to never take an apprentice? You said, and I quote, it was a corrupt system."

"Well, it was when I was one," Adelina says. "I intend to do much better by mine than that ancient trull my mother hooked me to."

"What changed your mind?"

She paces the room, hands clasped behind her back, as though assembling her thoughts for a speech. I wonder if she's rehearsing what she would have told her mother, if this is part of the elaborate defense that someday she'll be forced to launch into. "One, she is of an age where she can decide for herself whether or not she wishes to work and can say with some realism what she might decide to end up as."

I can't help it, this startles a laugh from me. "How old is she, thirty-five?"

She snorts. "I'm serious."

"So am I." I settle on the couch, leaning back to laugh at her. "People change all the time, and what we are apprenticed to is often not what we become. Look at me, for example. Jolietta would have shoved me into life as a Beast Trainer, and imagine how unhappy I would have been there."

"But you knew you didn't want to be a Beast Trainer," Adelina says.

"So your prodigy knows dead certain that she wishes to be a publisher?"

"Well." Adelina settles down onto the couch beside me, and I tuck my feet underneath myself to make room for her amid the leather cushions and discarded books, two of them, as though she'd been reading them both at once while lying here. Her eyes are thoughtful. "I don't know that she wants to be a publisher, I'll admit that, but it is a good profession. She wants to be independent and comes from a family that would have seen her apprenticed into some work that does not use her quick mind as publishing will. They had talked of apprenticing her to the leather tanner."

We both wrinkle our noses at the thought. Leather tanning is restricted to the southern side of town for a reason. It stinks. Both the butcher houses and the vats of pigeon shit in which the leather is soaked to soften it make the area around them redolent and the housing cheap.

"How did you come to encounter her?"

"I'd met her first because she's the sister of one of the writers I've been working with." I avoid raising an eyebrow as she blushes at some thought before continuing on. "I found her along Salt Way, crouched beneath Sparkfinger Jack's statue."

"That's ill-omened."

"There is no God for luck among the Trade Gods."

"Since when do you follow the Trade Gods?"

"Perhaps there is a thing or two still that you do not know about me, Bello Kanto." Her tone holds more tease than menace, but it makes a shiver run down my spine all the same.

Adelina insists on bringing the girl in to meet me. She's tongue-tied in my presence, a slip of a thing, dark-haired but pale-skinned as though she holds more than a trace of northern blood. Her eyes are violet and would be pretty were her face not so pinched and thin.

She watches Adelina intensely, dwells on her every motion, almost mirroring it in miniature, half echoing every word under her breath. She takes Adelina very seriously, and this reassures me a little. And surely Adelina deserves a little hero worship of the kind I bask in every day, that of the students who surround me. That is one of the great pleasures of teaching young things, to watch them listening, to see yourself through their eyes, so much more splendid than you know yourself to be.

It reminds me too much of Skye. When I feel tears burning at my eyes, ready to be shed, I excuse myself and leave.

Chapter Twenty-Seven

Teo's Struggle

The revelation that Miche and Murga were the same had shaken him to the bone. But it made sense. If a Beast could turn into a Human and back again, then couldn't magic do something similar—change a person until they were no longer recognizable?

But that meant sorcery. Teo stopped where he stood in a passageway between the tents. Was Murga Shifter or Sorcerer? Sorcerers were more to be feared than anything. Sorcerers had led to the establishment of Tabat, a refuge for those fleeing the Old Continent, whose lands were torn and tattered from countless magical battles waged over them, regardless of the devastation.

Was that worse than being a Shifter or not? If he went to Bella, told her what he knew, would she kill Murga or him? Or both?

He remembered her coldness, her eyes looking through him as though he didn't exist. He felt a quiver of anger. She had taken him in, and then thrown him out without a second thought. She'd sold him to Miche, for all he knew, or at least given him, like a trinket, to her lover. Like the discarded coat he still wore.

Perhaps she deserved whatever Miche/Murga intended to do.

Teo knew, deep in his heart, it was not anything good.

He went back to speak to Murga, pushing his way into the tent without looking to see who was there. The Sphinx towered over him as he entered, reacting to his presence by knocking him to the ground with a heavy paw.

"Let him up. The boy's no threat," Murga said.

Teo rose. The Sphinx snorted and Teo shrank back, embarrassed by the inadvertent gesture even as it occurred. He drew himself up a little, shoulders twisting towards the tent entrance. "I will go to the authorities."

"'Deed you can," Murga mocked. "Go up to the highest, boy. The Duke himself has a hand in all of this. He thinks to stir a false rebellion, to get the citizenry to set aside the elections for fear of rebellious Beasts. But little does he know, I'll slip the reality in for his counterfeit. I'll see this city burn before more Beasts die in its service. Do you know how many Dryads are burned alive each day in order to strip the magic from their bones? Three at least, and more when it's needed. That's what goes into keeping your friend Bella Champion of Tabat."

Dizziness shook Teo. "The Duke ..."

Murga took a step forward. His heat reminded Teo of Grave's fever, a fierce sunlight evaporating Teo, reducing his will. "Thwart me, ordinary boy, and I'll tip them off to a nest of Shifters up North. You know them well, as Ma and Da and little sister. You've seen by now what's done to such. If you won't behave for your own sake, then do it for your village's."

Fear froze Teo where he stood.

He'd never thought about the consequences for his village.

They'd send soldiers, burn them like the Dryads. He remembered them, crouched along the *Water Lily's* railing, stroking each other's hair and whispering. The look on the face of the one who'd helped him escape. What had happened to her? If Murga was correct, she would have been burned, burned to fuel the aetheric lights, the Great Tram, all the magicks and machineries that kept Tabat running.

Both the Sphinx and Murga were watching him. He realized they were seeing everything flashing through his mind, and that Murga had anticipated this moment.

"Get out, boy," Murga said. "We have business to discuss."

o o o

He rummaged underneath his cot. He didn't have much, but he had accumulated a few things: the clothes that Bella had given him along with a few other pieces that others had discarded and a fine leather jacket that someone had left behind one night and never come to claim.

"What are you doing?" Maisie asked from behind him.

His heart leaped into his throat. "You mustn't say anything!" he hissed. "I'm leaving!"

"Why?"

He thrust his clothing into a bag, adding a handful of souvenirs he'd gathered, like a brilliant red paper hat with a black feather cockade. "Murga's a bad man," he told her. "You should leave too."

"I don't have anywhere but here to go."

"I don't either," Teo said, "but I'm leaving anyway."

"Murga wants you."

"Tell him you couldn't find me."

But her eyes were adamant. She'd picked her side, and it wasn't Teo's.

Chapter Twenty-Eight

Bella's Last Day

I rise in the dark hours when false dawn tugs at the horizon, resolved to set everything right. I can't bring Skye back, but I can live as though I was the person she thought I was.

I will busy myself with important things. I'll talk to Leonoa, and we'll sort this out. I will pay Leonoa's bills and not leave them all to Adelina. I will say nothing more about Glyndia, who is surely just a fancy. If I continue to resist her, Leonoa will only grow more stubborn.

I can put up with Glyndia's hostility for the sake of the cousin I love.

And then I'll go to the circus, find Teo, and apologize. I'll tell Lucya that I will be there at the Brides of Steel more often.

She'll tell me why she felt she had to put Skye up. I'll forgive her.

At least, I hope I will.

When I get downstairs, Abernia says, "I have a package of spices coming on a ship that's just arrived. Will you pick it up for me?"

She looks tired. The fuss and furor have not been easy on her, and being known as Bella Kanto's landlady seems a double-edged sword now. On the night of the riots, all her front windows were smashed. I will give her extra this month, much extra, to cover them. And I'll run her errand first, then go to Leonoa.

By the time I get down to the docks, the day has worn on to a clear morning that retains a glacial edge.

I like this weather best, this ice-contained stillness. It suits me. I pass through preparations for two political rallies but keep my head down.

The planking of the old pier creaks in time with the clack of my boot heels. Overhead, gulls screech derisively, and slouch-bellied pelicans huddle on the pilings, one turning its head sideways to bite at the retreating water as a wave flows back past it.

At this time of day, many of the docks' denizens are setting off after breakfasting, usually on chal and bread, or pastries. A press of sailors moves past, their pace less leisurely than my own. They are tanned men and women. Most are pure Tabatians, their olive skin burned brown by weeks of sun. A few are Northerners or mixed blood, their skin ruddier, often showing red where the sun has overpowered it.

Their eyes are pale blue or green. I've never found Northerners very attractive. They seem unfinished, at odds with the world as it should be. The sailors move past in a cloud of tobacco, sour sweat, and subdued voices. They must be fresh off one of the ships that constantly pass in and out of Tabat's rock-clasped harbor. Situated on the southeastern corner of the New Continent, the city is a hub that served Verranzo's New City, the northeast coast, the Old Continent, the Southern Isles, and the even further, more exotic continents such as the jungle-states and the desert lands, like the Rose Kingdom.

A quick glance tells me what I want to know. No many-masted, fat-bellied *Saffron Bloom* rides at anchor in the pier used by the College of Mages ships. I go into the small docking office maintained there nonetheless. Leonoa will appreciate word of when her mother might be expected. Outside, a quartet of dock workers shifts bales of cotton onto waiting carts pulled by sad-faced mules.

A bell jingles welcome as I enter. The usual press of people crowds the dock office, and the air is close and warm. A few recognize me, and a ripple of talk spreads through the waiting Merchants and Captains. A dark-haired, narrow-faced Captain waves me in line in front of him, despite a few mutters from further back in the crowd.

"I saw you defeat Donati," he says. "Magnificent! And you haven't aged a day since then, it seems." I bow to him with a gracious smile.

The clerk sits taking advantage of the sunlight. He hunches over the counter making notes. Beside his elbow is a pamphlet entitled *A Basic Primer of Tabatian Politics* written by A Friend to the Common Folk. The light falls forward over his shoulders, onto the block-printed, thick pages.

"Any news?" I ask.

The clerk looks up. "The *Bloom* hasn't come in, still no word. They're not officially overdue yet, though. They were supposed to arrive sometime this week."

"Picked your party yet?" I ask, nodding at the pamphlet. Someone behind me shuffles their feet, clearing their throat.

"It's all so complicated," the clerk says. "Everything changes depending on who's saying it."

"It's easy enough for me," I tease. "The Gladiators are supporting the New Year Party."

"Ha, that's what I heard," he says. He is blonde-bearded, New Continent stock with more than a trace of northerner in him, and a wry smile. "Well, no one ever accused the Gladiators of spending too much time thinking." He winks. Cute but unschooled, and beyond the physical, I find northerners irritatingly naïve, full of emotion and half-baked beliefs.

"Look," I say. "Let me leave you enough money to pay for a messenger, and when my aunt's ship comes in, you can send me a runner?"

"Very well." He takes the silver skiff I pass over and gives me a piece of paper. I write my address on it, and he tucks it in a cubbyhole with similar slips. He turns and looks at me as though wanting to say something. His eyebrows are blond, twisted like a Hippogriff's.

"It's okay," I say as he hesitates. "Yes, I'm Bella Kanto, yes, I enjoy being a Gladiator, and my next fight will be a Midsummer Beast match."

"No," he says, forestalling me with a hand. "I just wanted to ask if you need change."

Someone snickers behind me, but I ignore it.

Outside, the gulls are still jeering. The *Saffron Bloom* is always early. I find the lack of word worrisome. Should I say something to Leonoa, who is undoubtedly as aware as I of the absence?

I've always felt as though Leonoa's mother Galia reluctantly shared herself but Leonoa's parents did well by me nonetheless.

Years later, I pay my landlady well to keep the sheets turned down, a warming pan in the bed, and I always associate the moment of sliding into the bed's comfort with my aunt and uncle's presence. The world felt more right, somehow, when I could go every week to their mansion and eat solid, well-cooked food in their comfortable, clean surroundings. Later, when Coro Kanto died, it was myself and Leonoa, bantering back and forth beside the preoccupied Galia, who usually ate while studying maritime charts. Leonoa, who would have come for a solid meal herself, and who would scold me yet again for one thing or another, like the way I treat Adelina.

Thinking of Adelina, I feel guilty, but thrust it aside. Leonoa is altogether too ready to meddle in my life, and she always has been. I scan the horizon, the familiar shapes of the harbor's rocky walls. Flakes of snow ride the wind, scudding along like ash in the crisp air and dimpling the sea's surface with the unseen kisses.

My aunt is past due, but it isn't time to worry yet. I'll run Abernia's errand. Then I'll go to the Brides of Steel and help drill the students. Lucya can't keep me away. I'll maintain a presence.

I move along the street at a swift, fluid walk, wondering what else I should do. Adelina sent word that one of the largest bills is a series of daguerreotypes that Leonoa had commissioned to paint from, and that my cousin is angry about the loss. That will make a suitable offering of apology.

I bound up the front steps of Three Coins Tailoring. It has been recently inspected and placarded—a handbill on official yellow-colored paper, as yet unsoftened by wind or rain, is pasted up on the door.

I swing it open, reading the Certification of Suitability for Trade. Merchant's Guild and Moon Temple approval skirt it, affixed in gloppy wheat glue. Seals cluster beneath that, testifying to the approval and patronage of several major political parties and an abundance of small ones.

Bolts of fabric line the shop's walls, charmeuse to gauze. A spill of yellow velvet, figured with many-petalled crimson flowers, is unrolled on the counter to catch the sunlight coming in through the freshly-washed window, flickering in the shadows cast by passersby, wagons, and other trade. Spices perfume the air; bales of cinnamon and sacks of cardamom seeds that have neighbored the fabrics while cargo on its way into Tabat.

The proprietor's twin sons, two or three years old, wear elaborations of the velvet on the counter. They sit stiffly as though admiring themselves in the long mirror opposite the door. Bess the tailor fusses over one, coaxing the intricate smocking of the aprons to best advantage, yellow cuffs bright against their dark skin. Each wears a floppy beret, one red banded in yellow, and its counterpart yellow banded in red.

"Is it a special occasion?" I ask.

Bess turned to face me with a smile.

"We're going to a Merchants' rally tonight!" she exclaims. Her voice is fluty and over-cultivated, and its cloying quality sets my teeth on edge. "It's good for them to see the future, to know what it's like as we step into a brand new age!" Her voice ascends in pitch and volume on the last words, as though declaiming from memory. She adds, "Plus, anyone seeing and admiring them can ask and know where to get the same for their own little 'uns." She nods at the door. "Politicking's good for business."

"Of course," I say. "I came to pick up my shirts. I had three black silk, full-cut, black glass beads at the cuff? Ah, perfect."

The efficient Bess takes the paper-wrapped packages from a shelf. I breathe out admiration as she unfolds one enough to let the beading, a pattern of leaping rabbits worked into the three inch cuffs, flash in the light.

Bess writes up the bill, brows crinkled in concentration as ink spatters through the curlicues of her name, on a long slip of white paper stamped with the shop's title.

The children and I contemplate each other in embarrassed silence as she does so.

"They're cheerful outfits," I say to the tailor, receiving a handful of Moon Bank skiffs in change. The mother beams effulgently despite the dour expressions on her children's faces.

"Enjoy your outing," I say to them and exit, package tucked under my arm. I feel a surge of gratitude that I'm no longer a child and now capable of choosing my own costume, thank you very much.

On the steps I pass a lanky figure, some sort of Mage by the cut of his clothing and the lack of golden chain around his neck, but with northern blood to him, judging by the blue eyes and the pale undercast to his skin. He nods to me as we pass each other. Is he familiar? I think he might be one of the Silvercloths. It irks me not to be able to place him, but some avoid the games, for one reason or another, a few of them good.

On Light and Lattice Street, I pause at the photographer's shop. Larger shops shoulder it on either side, looking as though they might squeeze it out of existence at any moment. An abandoned cage occupies the front window. In previous days, hasn't there been a Gryphon that used to be there, dozing in the sunlight?

Photographs line the walls inside, each an invariable four inches by six inches. One line features people photographed with the Gryphon. Below that, there's a procession of people photographed with a Sphinx outside the gates of the College of Mages, and a small Dragon, each time with a different toddler posed beside its toothy smile. I shiver at the last and look back to the Gryphon pictures. I'm amused to see Teo in one, looking thin, awkward, and newly arrived.

"I'm picking up a package for my cousin."

The photographer pauses, eying me. She's a square-faced, serious young woman with a beaky nose and glossy brown hair. "Who's that?" she says.

I shrug. "Leonoa Kanto. How much does she owe?"

Still eying me, the photographer does not reply, but pushes a thick envelope of daguerreotypes over the counter.

I flip through them with impatient fingers: Miche surrounded by Beasts; a herd of zebras posed with tigers on their backs; a vast coppery tank and its lurking denizen; a pair of Mermaids combing out each other's hair; a vacuously grinning man thrusting a broom at the camera; Miche again, all taken at the circus, presumably. No pictures of Glyndia, which I am just as glad of. My dislike for the swan-winged woman has not faded with more familiarity.

"Miche Courdeau," the photographer says, looking over my shoulder. Of course, she must have taken these. Something in her voice snags at me. I'm well acquainted with the signs of someone coveting one of my lovers.

I pay it little thought as I linger over the pictures of the Humans. The ones of the Beasts remind me too much of the pictures that Leonoa painted, the impossible, blasphemous pictures that seemed to ask: What if Beasts were Humans? I worry about the city's disruption when Alberic is ousted, but if the Beasts rise up in protest, it will be a thousand times worse.

I put it aside as she push the pictures back into the brown paper envelope and pay the bill, whistling in surprise at the charge. No wonder Leonoa couldn't pay it.

"Chemicals aren't cheap," the photographer says. "And we don't usually get slides brought in on their own like that, that we end up doing the developing on. It's the latest science, you know—you pay a price for this sort of thing." She shrugs, and I shrug back.

"Miche owes some as well," she says. "You recognized him, didn't you?"

There is a truculent hint to the way the young woman speaks. I allow myself a faint smile. A Gladiator's glamour is something no ordinary lover can compete with.

"I'm not responsible for his bills," I say, but she remains sullen as I count out my coins.

○ ○ ○

I buy irises from the flower shop. I'll keep them by my bed.

○ ○ ○

The ship Abernia mentioned, the *Jasmine*, is down a few docks. An area I'm more familiar with, where the buildings are a little more rundown, the shops shadier, where there are more pawn and dice shops, disreputable apothecaries, and taverns. The crisp air smells of salt, carried on the wind from the south.

Skye would have appreciated this day.

I make my way up the gangplank, admiring my reflection in the glittering water as Skye might have seen it. I'm still lithe and lean. I get better with age. No wonder people are drawn to me.

A sailor directs me aft to where the Captain stands.

"Captain?" I say, approaching.

He turns, a dark-haired, dark-skinned man, the purest of Old Continent blood. Next to him stands a Water Human wearing one of the elaborate canvas suits held up with a clockwork frame that allows him, or her, to survive in the open air. The machine is like a tank with legs. Plates of glass affixed in the sides allow glimpses of the Human inside, colored blue and scarlet like a singing bird, with stripes of turquoise, black, and mottled gold, a profusion of fins and frills like drowned fans. Not for the first time, I wonder how one water-based race has managed to define itself as Human while all the rest are considered Beasts. That must have taken some fine-grained negotiation.

"I have a package to pick up for Abernia Freeholder," I say.

He frowns but appears to recognize the name. "Very well, I see." He says something in rapid Southron to a passing sailor, who nods and speaks to a passing, younger sailor, who darts off to speak to a cabin boy. The boy disappears into a hatchway.

I stand in silence with the Captain and the Water Human. I unobtrusively look over the latter. It's been several years since I last interacted with one, but it doesn't look as though the basic equipment has changed. Spindly metal legs telescope in and out at need—currently half-slouched but still holding the six-sided tank upright.

This one's coloration speaks of the coral reefs around the Southern Isles, as does the cargo being bundled onto the dock: bales of cotton, kegs of rum, crates of muscovado sugar, and citrus fruits. I catch a flash of fins, long-spined and poisonous. They're hell to fight, fast and covered with deadly barbs.

Noticing my scrutiny, the Water Human speaks. Its voice emerges from the brass-and-jingle affixed at the top of the tank to intercept the words that bubble from its mouth before it pauses to suck air from the metal tube at its side.

"Do not look at us. You interrupt our business."

Even for a race noted for its pugnacity, that's abrupt and rude. I quirk an eyebrow even as the Captain rushes in with explanation and reassurance.

"She is running an errand for a friend. She will be gone once she has her package."

He turns to me. "You are Bella Kanto, the Gladiator, are you not?"

I nod. The cabin boy emerges. Rather than pass the package back by the same chain, he hands the canvas-wrapped parcel, about the size of a doubled lunch bucket, directly to the Captain, who takes the package and without glancing inside, hands it to me.

It's unexpectedly heavy for spices. I start to unwrap it, but we both glance around at the sound of a shout.

A hurdy-gurdy shrieks out a brassy song on the boardwalk, a crowd of sailors and dockworkers gathered around it. Two listeners have faced off—a slight boy in Temple robes and a crab-hunched dockworker, arms long and muscular. As we watch, the dockworker plants his palms in the middle of the youth's chest and pushes him backward. His arms windmill as he goes sprawling in the midst of several overturned barrels full of thumb-sized, silvery fish and a crescendo of gulls descends to gulp at the bounty.

A whistle blares and two Peacekeepers come stamping up. More people gather to watch. The youth lies on his elbow, shaking his head with a dazed and glazey look. Then a bell shrills. Odd. To have called a Sniffer, the Keepers must have sensed sorcery somewhere about. The Captain tenses at the sound.

"There may be some matter here and there of tariffs, as always occurs," he says, even as he glides towards the plank, towing me and leaving the slower moving Water Human far behind. He gives me a merciless, humorless, close-lipped smile. "Bye now."

Releasing my hand, he steps backward, disappearing among the crowd swarming along the pier.

"Cap'n!" comes a panicked shout as a sailor onboard the *Jasmine* witnesses the vanishing, but he does not reappear. The blue and buff Peacekeepers are moving through the crowd, rounding up anyone who looked out of place.

Something is wrong, I can feel it. The charms around my neck twinge, and one even sends out a spray of sparks as it fails against some working.

I swear and waver. Sorcery means all sorts of possible harm. The innocent bystanders need to be cleared.

"Get out of the way, you fool!" I shout at the youth. He sits by the side of the road now, cross-legged in a puddle of flapping minnows, rubbing his scruffy hair. Looking up, he scrambles out of the way of a steam wagon.

The Peacekeepers flank an elderly man, his face pale with fear of the Sniffer, a construction of wires and claws that walked as though it thought itself Human. How has it arrived so quickly? It must have been close by.

Blue sparks chase up and down its frame, and the air is scented with a sulfurous smell. As I watch, it turns, its long arms flexing, the cone of its face unblinkingly fixed on … me.

The package's solidity is fixed firmly under my arm. What has Abernia gotten me into?

I should surrender. I should just give it to them and explain.

But imagine the headlines in the penny-wides, the spoofs on plastered news bills. I cannot be associated with sorcery. They'll think that's how I've won so long.

If I run, I can ditch the package somewhere, get rid of it, and come out of this clean. I take the same swift, decisive action that has so often stood me in good stead in the arena, ignoring the charms, the magic all around me, somehow focused on me.

I run.

o o o

I've had nightmares like this before, chased up and down the streets of Tabat, trying to find succor, no harbor in sight. I run up Pin and Needle with the Sniffer at my heels, the slower Peacekeepers behind it. If I can get out of sight of them, I can hide the package and whatever contraband that I'm now sure it holds.

The Peacekeepers are quick and untiring, but I have the advantage of nimbleness of both foot and mind. I slip through cracks, make split second turns, take the stairs behind the Dizzy Theater, then scramble up some scaffolding to circumnavigate the police booth at the corner of Spray and Spume. At the top of the hill, I pause, panting. I start to unroll the canvas, but a Peacekeeper whistle shrills, and again I scramble out of the way.

At first I'm amused, rehearsing how I'll tell the story over drinks. But a growing certainty clutches at my heels, even as the thickening charms slow me, make me clumsy, and slip bad luck and stumbles in my path. They are relentless, inescapable.

Eventually I will be caught.

How can they know where I am most likely to run to ground, where I stop to catch my breath or bearings? It's as though the Peacekeeper corps has some mind reader at their disposal. Finally, I dart around the corner of an alleyway and find myself face to face with three scowling Peacekeepers.

I'm not too worried at the sight of them. After all, the Duke's Guard are here to keep the peace, and many of them are former Gladiators. They'll sort things out before the Sniffer can reach me with its claws.

They press forward, trusting in my respect for the uniforms they wear. They're right to do so. I do respect them, do stand down with impatient grace, knowing that they will take me before the law, which will act as it should, as it always has, to protect the innocent and punish the guilty.

And which, I wonder, am I?

The panic thickens my thoughts and makes me a creature of reaction and panic. I should have checked the parcel before I took it. That was basic common sense. My mistake was that of a silly third year student. I sigh, drop the package and the irises, and hold my hands before me so they may be manacled.

The Sniffer comes running, launches itself at my mid-back. I feel its approach even before I hear it and side-step, hands still out. It lands in a clatter of claws, flailing to round on me while avoiding the Humans. The closest man loops a collar over its neck and it goes abruptly still, although fiery coals still burn in its cog-lashed eyes.

I think surely they will open the package here and now, but they hand it, one to another, a careful chain that fills me with trepidation. They apparently have some idea regarding what is inside it, an idea that fills them with dread and horror, and makes them turn their faces away from me and speak in hushed whispers. I try to jolly up to my two guards, but they ignore all my attempts at pleasantries.

They leave the flowers lying in the street to be run over by steam wagons and trodden on by careless feet.

o o o

The jails are to the southeast of town, downwind of the Slumpers, where the air is thick with smoke and stink. They take me and the satchel into a room where an officious sergeant records my statement, and then the statements of the arresting officers.

"Very well," the sergeant says, and finally motions the officer with the satchel forward. He lays it on the desk with a flourish. Another whispers in the sergeant's ear. His bushy eyebrows ascend like caterpillars wiggling their way up in the hope of becoming butterflies.

"Wickedness!" he breathes. His hand trembles as he fumbles with the satchel's catches. He cracks it open, and a foul smell comes from its depths. I can barely make out a series of fist-sized lumps. The stench is dreadful; the officers and I gag. The sergeant retches and closes the case.

"Throw those windows open," he says, drooling bile. "Take her ladyship off to a holding cell and this—this to the evidence chamber, the one that locks. Send a messenger to Magister Rosen that there is a case to be heard, one that the Duke will take an interest in."

"But," I begin, incredulous, only to find myself hurried out of the room, elbows painfully clenched by guards on either side.

They throw me in a cell that is barely broom-closet sized. I can sit on the stone shelf built into the wall but cannot stretch out my legs or arms. An unused chamber pot crouches under the shelf.

The stone is cold and hard. After a while my back burns, so I constantly shift back and forth, standing, sitting, standing, sitting.

I contemplate a crack running along the stone. Is it an opening or an abyss? I become aware that I am shivering: deep, bone-rooted tremors that shake me to the core.

This cannot be happening to me.

I am Bella Kanto, after all.

Chapter Twenty-Nine

Teo's Last Chapter

Teo knew the Dryad standing in the antechamber of Murga's tent as soon as he went in. She was the one who'd been on the ship with him, who'd attacked the Mage so he could run free. He gaped at her. How had she come here?

If she recognized him, she made no sign. She stood slumped and weary, as though so tired she could barely draw breath.

Teo said, "You're the one, aren't you? From the *Lily*, I mean?"

She looked confused. "*Lily?*" she rasped.

"From the boat. We were on the boat together."

Her face cleared. "The boat. Yes."

"How did you get here?"

"I was in the menagerie," she said. "They helped me escape." A shudder racked her. "I saw the furnaces. I will see them gone now."

"Close the flap, boy," Murga said harshly. "You are going to see something new."

Magic. Murga was going to work magic. On him, or on the Dryad? But he shivered and did as he was told, closing out the evening air.

"You came back to the city to help overthrow it," Murga said to the Dryad. "I will help you find a way to avoid rooting, to escape your tree shape, and continue aiding me in that work."

Her voice was dull as old leather. "The urge to root is very strong. I am dry and ready to lay down."

"Sleep," Murga said, passing his hand over her eyes. He caught her as she fell. Teo stood back, uncertain what to do.

"Hand me that purple chalk on the table," Murga said. He cast a glance at Teo.

"I … this is wrong," Teo stammered.

"You're in too far now, boy. You've been taking Abolitionist tracts for me about the city." Murga's grin was the most ominous thing Teo had ever seen. "And you brought me what I needed for this spell earlier." He pointed at a mass of bright blue cloth on the desk. "Bring me that."

It was the cloak of one of the acrobats. What was inside was still warm, and the blood seeping through the cloth stained Teo's hands as he unwrapped it to show the two hearts it contained.

"Shifter blood is best, but Human blood will do," Murga said.

"They worked for you, but you killed them," Teo stammered.

"They were Human and not to be trusted, boy," Murga snarled. "Far more will die before I'm done."

Shaking, he helped Murga draw the line around the Dryad. "What are you going to do?"

"First she must become her tree," Murga said.

"You told her you were going to make it so that didn't happen."

"Not precisely." Murga glanced over at an axe and saw in the corner. "But I will make a form for her, of her own living wood— something like a golem. She will be a fearful warrior when her time comes."

He knelt beside the unconscious Dryad, muttering under his breath.

The body twitched and sprouted. Arms lifted, becoming branches, and as each limb sprouted, Murga hacked it away until only a stump stood there, as tall as Teo. Murga lifted a saw that glittered in the dim light and began to shape it into planks, passing each length to Teo to stack in the corner for the next step.

Hours went by. Hours of Teo passing Murga implements as directed and holding the wood so that he could work it. His bones ached with fear, but there was no escape, only the rasping of the saw, the whine of bending wood, and the smell of crushed greenery.

When he was done, the Dryad was a boxy thing of new-hewn wood still weeping with sap, pegged together with glittering spikes of crystal and bone. Tiny letters, in a script Teo could not read, ran across every plank, inscribed with painful care as Murga muttered, dipping his quill in a vial of ink mixed with sap and blood drawn from his own wrist.

Finally he stood. Teo didn't move from where he crouched near the desk. He wasn't sure his cramped muscles would be able to move.

"A fearful warrior," Murga said, looking down at her. "A fearful warrior indeed."

He rounded on Teo. "And what marvel will I make of you, boy? I'll steep you in magic—even now, having been drawn into this spell, you're closer to what I want you to be, what sharing my dreams will make you." He moved to the desk and extracted a glittering strand from a drawer. He held it up.

Teo's eyes fixed on it. His coin! Or his sister's really, but of those in the tent, surely Teo had better claim to it than Murga.

Murga smiled and tucked it in his pocket. "You're an unexpected gift, boy. The Gods must have sent you." He surveyed what the Dryad had become. "She will kill, and the Human Mages will be blamed for it. Soon there will be riots. And blood."

o o o

Teo's head pounded as he stumbled from the tent when Murga finally dismissed him to go fetch chal. Murga had his coin, and surely that, in the hands of a Sorcerer, meant the man had power over him.

And he meant to destroy the city and all the people going about their daily lives. It wasn't right.

Bella would know what to do.

Surely she would know what to do.

o o o

He raced through the streets, dodging slower moving, startled pedestrians, circumventing steam wagons and bakery carts, scrambling up the Tumbril Stair. The day was bright, so bright that everywhere around him sunlight gleamed on melting snow and ice.

Icy droplets flew as he splashed through an icy puddle on Bella's street. He drew up, looking at Abernia's house. Two Peacekeepers stood on the front porch while another two were carrying a chest out to the wagon that stood before the house. Abernia was on the porch as well, hands on hips, face unreadable. A second story window was open, the bard and a companion hanging halfway out to watch the proceedings. As Teo stared, another pair of Peacekeepers exited, carrying the suit of silver and crystal armor that had stood in Bella's quarters.

Teo hadn't thought his heart could beat any faster, but now it did. Soldiers! What did it mean? He ducked through an alleyway and circled back to the garden. The fence was tall, but he managed to scramble over it, collecting a few splinters in his palms. He brushed at them as he picked his way through the muddy ground with a cautious glance up at the Fairy nest in the tree far above him.

He eased the door open and crept inside, listening as hard as he could. Footsteps went up and down the front staircase. He wavered, uncertain what to do.

Abernia swept into the kitchen and pulled up at the sight of him. "You!" She cast a glance over her shoulder. "You need to get out of sight, boy. They know you're promised to the Moon Temple. You're one of the things they've been hunting for."

"How … how do they know?" he stammered.

Her lips turned downward. She hesitated, and then said, "I told them."

He took a shocked breath.

She stepped forward, but then stopped as he recoiled. Her hands twisted her apron.

"It was nothing against you. Someone paid me well to find anything Bella was doing which she might get in trouble for, and you were part and parcel of that. But there's no need for them to cart you off. You can't stay here, though."

She moved to the cupboard and began sorting through things, filling a basket, but then she stopped as a thought struck her. "Here. Pack it with the food you like. I'll be right back. I've something else to give you, you might as well take it. If someone starts coming back here, go down to the cellar." She vanished up the back stairs in a flurry.

Teo didn't waste time in packing up some of the fish biscuits and a small round of cheese. He remembered doing this at home before he left. It seemed a thousand years ago.

Abernia came back down. In his hand she carried a birdcage, which she thrust at him. He took it automatically, then almost dropped it when he realized a Fairy buzzed inside.

"It's Miss Bella's, but she wouldn't want it taken off to the Duke's menagerie," Abernia said. "It needs mending but you can set it loose once it's hale enough. Filthy thing."

"But what's happened to her? To Bella?"

Abernia glanced towards the front of the house as there was a shout and a crash. "She's been arrested for sorcery. It's some mistake, I'm sure, but they're finding every charge they can throw at her, and all her goods are being confiscated."

Another crash. She waved him at the door, then changed her mind and hugged him.

"I'm sorry, Teo," she said. "They'll be watching the house." She fumbled at her apron and then held a few coins out to him. "Good luck to you."

He left through the back, basket in one hand and cage in the other.

As he went through the side gate, a hand closed over his shoulder.

"There you are," Murga said.

He blurted, "She's been arrested! You caused this!"

"Oh, certainly," Murga said. "I could not work against the city till the heart of its magic was gone. Now I'll see this city overthrown. I've plenty of allies in that, even some unwitting ones." His fingers tightened on Teo's shoulder.

He leaned down to whisper in Teo's ear. "And when I'm done, Beasts will rule Tabat and be slaves no longer."

o o o

Murga dragged Teo back to *The Autumn Moon* and his tent.

"You are valuable, boy," Murga told him. "But whether or not you're alive has very little effect on the overall price. You're more convenient alive, but that could change if you were to pose sufficient trouble."

His shadow bobbed up and down on the canvas of the tent wall as he paced, turning at the end of every few strides to go back the other way, each time fixing Teo with a gaze that felt as though it skewered him to the floor. It was not a kindly examination, but rather a dispassionate one, as though Murga were looking at a stump or vine or some physical aspect of the landscape that might pose him some inconvenience if not handled correctly.

He stopped pacing and stroked his chin with long fingers, drawing them to a point as though shaping an invisible goatee.

"What to do with you to keep you safe until I'm ready to use you is the question. Do you like dogs, my boy? My fine Shadow Twin of a boy?" He didn't appear interested in Teo's answer, though, for he turned away to pace again back and forth, his shadow resuming the march along with him.

Teo didn't mind dogs, certainly, but he was not particularly fond of them either. Still, they seemed no more offensive than any other animal used to watch one's belongings. The only one he had truly interacted with was Scholar Reynard's dog, Cavall.

He wondered why Murga would be asking such a thing, but even as he was wondering that, Murga wheeled to point a finger at him. Orange fire flickered on his fingertip and leaped to crawl over Teo's form. He felt it sink into him, changing him, making some bones stretch and others contract, skin changing into fur. It was like shape-changing, but wrong, not like falling into another form but being forced into it. He looked down to regard his paws. Murga had asked if he liked dogs just before turning him into one.

Teo flung his head back and howled out his confusion, bewilderment, and sorrow. Who would save him now, with Bella Kanto gone?

Chapter Thirty

Bella in Jail

After several hours—I do not know how many—two guards came and hauled me along to a hearing chamber. The magister sits on the other side of a desk, dressed in buff and blue. I recognize him as Grey Rosen, a veteran of the Piskie Wars who frequently comes to arena matches. The satchel sits on the desk in front of him, its catches undone.

Rosen glares at me, white hair a frizzy corona around his balding head. He wears a simple, undyed tunic and trousers, a linen cloak over them. It occurs to me that these are his nightclothes, and I smile.

"What are you smirking at?" he shouts. The question goes off in the chamber, too loud and sudden, like a firecracker that he has lit moments ago and has been waiting to throw.

"I'm sorry," I say, "to have you brought out for this misunderstanding."

"Where did you obtain this package?"

"From the Captain of the ship I had just come from. I don't know his name."

"Captain and crew are all vanished," he says. "The ship's cargo had been off-loaded as well, aside from a few left-overs of cloth and rum. No one is anywhere to be found. Except you."

He points at the satchel. "Do you know what lies inside there?"

"No."

"You claim you don't know what you were carrying?"

I gape, speechless as a fish taken from water. How can he think me complicit in something like this? I am the Champion of Tabat.

He stares at me and then speaks, slowly and clearly as though to a child. His tone is not unkindly. "You claim you don't know what you carried?"

My mind seizes on the question, and I realize how ridiculous this all is, that I've been caught somehow through circumstance and cantrip. "I know it sounds absurd," I stammer. "But you know how these things happen in a disturbance. Someone shoves a package at you and you hold onto it, not realizing what you are doing."

"I find it hard to believe," he says. "That anyone could carry ... something like that and not sense its malignant nature."

"I had held it for but a handful of minutes, Magister."

"Do not presume on earlier acquaintance, Kanto!" he snarls. I fall back in the face of that nigh-lethal hostility.

The magistrate fumbles with the satchel. "You'll want to look away," he says to the guards.

They do, but I cannot. My stomach cramps with horror. Half a dozen baby heads, each preserved in a pint sized glass jar. They are still alive—their eyes move, their mouths work. Darkest sorcery, to be used in even darker spells. It's a wonder my soul hasn't been blighted in the exchange. The closest one catches my gaze, its mouth working. What is it trying to say? I can't begin to imagine. Dread encases my body like a cocoon.

"A character witness has come forth, but not one that will help you," the magistrate says. "She tells us you have hidden away a boy that belongs to the Moon Temples."

Marta stands there. She looks at me with a smile, a cruel, happy smile.

"Your title and all your holdings are forfeit to the Crown," the magister says with relish. "What you have on your back, you may keep. And you will wait for the Duke's pleasure in your cell. He is usually busy in the mornings, but perhaps he will have time for you in a day or two."

He shouts and waves despite my questions. They drag me out and put me back in the holding cell. They give me neither food nor water, and my spine is swiftly ablaze again, an odd multi-starred pain spreading out from the small of my back.

I think about the heads. I think about dead Skye. The heads and the girl become mixed in my mind, as though the heads had caused the murder. I imagine the heads committing the murder, somewhere creeping bodiless towards the oblivious girl. I think of the smell of Skye's flesh burning. I beat my forearms against the wall.

I sit there for hours, stretching when I remember, or when the pain grows too much. Arena pain is worse, but it is swift and masked at first by shock and adrenaline, then by the physician's medicines. This is as though I have been transported back to my days with Jolietta, icy hours of ache and desperation and unhappiness.

I hold myself until I can bear it no longer, then give in to tears of despair.

o o o

Everything hurts. Not a minor hurt or the hurt of overworked muscles, I'm used to the latter. When you're the foremost Gladiator in Tabat, when you spend your days laboring on the instrument of your profession, your body, you know it well.

Not even the heat of arena injuries, the set of bruises laddered down a leg or a swollen wrist or even the saw grate of a broken rib matched this.

No. Worse than that: pain inflicted after pain, hot layers of it till even the breeze on my cheek is painful. Pieces that have never hurt in all my years of life were now outraged and burning. I think the fingers of my left hand might not recover; the two smallest stick out at awkward, quarreling angles, and the nails are all gone, candle flames of agony, a stiff hand of glory, no matter where they rest.

One ear gone, too. The skin of a forearm. I won't think about her feet, or hair, or other places.

They'd wanted names—real names—names of people who would be dragged in for their own sessions with Pain. Pain, like an evil sister, beside me to wipe sweat from my shorn head with fingers that tug at me, won't let her sleep, won't let me escape. Pain with eyes like knife-glitter that precedes blazing white torment, or subtle graduations of existing hurt, amplification and elaborations building on themselves, until I was housed in an engine of agony, heavy armor plate spike-lined with radiant heat.

Across my forehead a band of agony still gathers, as palpable as a band of iron. I'd thought my skull would break; I'd heard the internal creak that presaged it.

My blood throbs against tender skin from the inside, filling my ears with its pulse.

I'm not Bella anymore.

Nothing like this would happen to Bella Kanto.

I'm a cardboard shape, Bella Kanto for some stage play, a prop. A thing made of meat, to be dragged here and there, from machine to machine, for amusement.

Blood and urine sting my inner thighs. Tabat's Torturers have the latest equipment, techniques, ichors and ingredients they are eager to test out on something other than animals and Beasts.

The last thing they tried, the main Torturer (surely Pain's younger brother) whispered in my ear, was a substance that came from the Southern Isles' shallowest waters, spiny fish found only in the warm, warm waters there. Long spines, each coated with something that consumed, ate away at me from the inside wherever the tip was inserted, creating hollow pockets inflated to the bursting point with fire.

Two of Pain's siblings stood taking notes. One recorded the endless murmur of the voice that directed them to note the reddening of skin, the twitch of particular muscles, the acceleration of the heartbeat.

The other wrote down my answers to the questions asked over and over by the second voice. Who told me to go to the ship? Who was to pick up the package? Who had been aboard the ship, and what did they look like? What had been the coloring of the Water Human? What had I been paid to betray the city? How many sorcerers were plotting to destroy it?

The story as I told it did not satisfy them. They went through it again and again. I gave them every detail I could scrape from the aching, cracked bowl of my skull, and it was not enough.

Names. Real names. I could have pulled them from her memory at random, but how could I bring someone else here? Betrayer Miche, to be certain, and the Captain and crew that had carried such cargo. But surely Abernia was no part of this treachery. I will implicate no innocents and especially not Leonoa, who the second voice returned to again and again. Was she not an Abolitionist, willing to treat with Sorcerers to raise Beasts to unnatural power over Humans? Perhaps she was a Sorceress herself and her body manifested the rigors of her magic?

My throat is a raw tube from screaming.

The door swings open with a crash that I am too weary to flinch from.

Alberic, smiling.

I cannot read what lies behind that smile.

Chapter Thirty-One

Coda

In the little nest, which is all that Berto managed to salvage from the remnants of his shop, the eggs begin to hatch.

Bella Kanto is defeated. Spring has come early to Tabat.

To be continued in HEARTS OF TABAT

About the Author

Cat Rambo lives, writes, and teaches by the shores of an eagle-haunted lake in the Pacific Northwest. Her fiction publications include stories in *Asimov's*, *Clarkesworld Magazine*, and Tor.com. Her short story, "Five Ways to Fall in Love on Planet Porcelain," from her story collection *Near + Far* (Hydra House Books), was a 2012 Nebula nominee. Her editorship of *Fantasy Magazine* earned her a World Fantasy Award nomination in 2012. She is the current Vice-President of the Science Fiction and Fantasy Writers of America. For more about her, as well as links to other stories set in the world of Tabat, see http://www.kittywumpus.net

Other WordFire Press Titles

Our list of other WordFire Press authors and titles is always growing. To find out more and to see our selection of titles, visit us at:

wordfirepress.com